High praise for

SCAVENGER

by Christopher Chambers

A NO-HOLDS-BARRED crime novel . . . a 21st-century twist on traditional hardboiled noir.

PUBLISHERS WEEKLY

IN SCAVENGER, CHRISTOPHER CHAMBERS shows us a Washington D.C. we've never seen through the eyes of a sleuth unlike any we've ever met. A harrowing noir odyssey through contemporary America.

VINCE KEENAN, editor-in-chief, *Noir City*

CHRIS CHAMBERS'S SCAVENGER is a clever mystery told with wry wit and a vivid second-person style that straps you in for its roller coaster ride. You open this book and that voice starts speaking to you and you want to hear what it has to say. Simply put: this is a damn good read.

MAT JOHNSON, author, *Incognegro, Pym* and *Loving Day*

CHAMBERS COMES OUT of the box swinging hard in this fast-moving, down-and-dirty crime novel that kicks up the tarp on the sleazy, duplicitous, double-dealing underbelly of our nation's capital. Into this shadowy knot of deceit walks unconventional detective, Dickie Cornish, a homeless, down on his luck survivor for whom the stakes couldn't be higher, or the risks greater. Two thumbs up for Chambers!

TRACY CLARK, author, *Borrowed Time*, winner of G.P. Putnam's Sons Sue Grafton Memorial Award

CHRIS CHAMBERS HAS created a wholly original character that exists in a world at once familiar but startlingly brutal.

S. A. COSBY, author, *Blacktop Wasteland*

SCAVENGER IS AS HARD and unflinching as noir gets—an immersive portrait of life on the streets in Trump's America. Yet, in the person of Dickie Cornish, Chambers has delivered a voice of idiomatic, hard-won radiance—and a truth-seeker equal to all the lies and all that lies ahead.

LOUIS BAYARD, author, *Roosevelt's Beast* and *Mr. Timothy*

LITERARY CINÉMA VÉRITÉ, Chambers delivers a sly, slick and twisty hardcore mystery well worth the read.

GARY PHILLIPS, author, *Matthew Henson and the Ice Temple of Harlem*

CHRISTOPHER CHAMBERS NEVER disappoints. The adrenaline hits the reader on page one and doesn't let up. SCAVENGER is witty, profane, propulsive, and gripping. It turns DC into a hardboiled wonderland.

VICTOR LA VALLE, *New York Times* bestselling author, *The Changeling*

SCAVENGER

SCAVENGER

a mystery

Christopher Chambers

THREE ROOMS PRESS
New York, NY

ISBN 978-1-941110-94-2 (trade paperback original)
ISBN 978-1-941110-95-9 (Epub)
Library of Congress Control Number: 2020935933

TRP-084

Publication Date: October 13, 2020

BISAC category code
FIC049050 FICTION / African American / Mystery & Detective
FIC049070 FICTION / African American / Urban
FIC022010 FICTION / Mystery & Detective / Hard-Boiled
FIC050000 FICTION / Crime

COVER AND INTERIOR DESIGN:
KG Design International: www.katgeorges.com

DISTRIBUTED BY:
PGW/Ingram: www.pgw.com

Three Rooms Press
New York, NY
www.threeroomspress.com
info@threeroomspress.com

To Dad

SCAVENGER

CHAPTER 1

Wake Up, Toad . . .

YOUR FINGERNAILS SCRATCH PATCHES OF SKIN on your chest where defibrillator pads burned the hair away. Fentanyl's the suicide-high of choice for dour whiteboys and dizzy pink-toes out in the Virginia and Maryland peckerwood burbs. Congratulations for being the Jackie Robinson of that shit in the District of Columbia, boy!

Oh . . . you *weren't* trying to kill yourself? That EMT was just merciless and sloppy, bringing you back with marks on your body and your dome scrambled. The shrinks and social workers up there with the rest of the bipolar dope fiends and diabetic schizos at Medstar *conspired* to keep your big ass up on the ward.

Hey, at least you're out of the restraints and down-dosing methadone.

The tremors ebb. You promise to stay away from Auntie Smack and Uncle Fennie forever. You promise to kick the Kush, washed down by that Goddamn Mickey's green grenade swill . . . and Mister Fred and Mizz Eva come to visit with home-cooking and their own promise that you can stay with them, hot bunkin' like voucher folk do until you find a roof. And you sigh . . . show fucking shame for what you've done to yourself . . .

. . . and they hold your big hands, bristling with IV tubes like you're a marionette on strings . . . they say your boy Kenyatta—"Sponge Bob" onaccount of the nigga's squared head—he's froze like a Butterball turkey in what the ole-timers call Malcolm X Park and the ofays gentrified to Meridian Hill. Eva's sobbing because her Godson, that fruit-cake named DaQuan, he's out of rehab from budget cuts, goes and puts out Whiteboy Bob Hope's eye with an oyster shucker and the cops got a BOLO on him . . . and five of your friends and a whole bunch of kids died from dirty spice . . . their corpses brittle and twisted on the pavement like so much kindling.

And yet none of that's why you're catching feelings, right? None of that's what you're dreaming *right now* . . . in the cold and dark . . . under these stinking wool blankets!

Five years since she ran away. Admit it, toad. Or what did she call you? *Sapo.*

"*Si . . . soy tu sapo*, Esme," you groan in that fold between sleep and waking.

And so it was yearning that summoned you, ass out of your blue hospital gown, nutsack swaying, bedsheet trailing behind you as if you're a zombified *yeti* toddler. Shuffling right past the hospital's toy cops who've pretty much seen it all in that zoo, huh? Despite the gray in your Frederick Douglass 'do and the layers of gristle there's still your bearish height and a tight end's frame to contend with, so *unh-unh* . . . no one's going to tackle you in the lobby.

And you're across Michigan Avenue where the hipsters who are walking their hounds or pushing their brats' prams costing twice more than Fred's SSI check put you on Instagram and call MPD. Bleeding hearts say you have the civil right to leave Medstar crazed and half-naked.

Wake up.

Or else the dream rewinds . . .

Little girl in her denim leggings and long braids clipped with goofy orange barrettes comes on a push scooter. Stares. Two more children run up on foot onaccount that's their school, they whisper, careful not to wake you. But it's a Saturday so it's okay for you to sleep.

"But he nekkid in a blue thing," the girl on the scooter muses.

"He a pervert, 'cause you can see his thing!" another shouts, and the others shush her so the sleeping ogre stays asleep.

Then an older child . . . a boy, in the purple Ravens jersey . . . rolls up on a bike.

"That a pervert," the smaller ones all direct in hushed little voices.

But the older boy sucks his teeth, scoffs, "That just Dickie. He don't belong here!"

He scoops up a small shard of busted sidewalk concrete, slings it like you're Goliath and the rest of the children scream and scatter when you rise, babbling, wincing, spinning like a wobbly top . . . and the boy pulls his mobile phone. You smile and beg him to call Eva and Fred . . . Verna Leggett . . . Esmeralda? Names his face shows you he doesn't know. He taps nine-one-one—you hear the tones, familiar music.

The cops are tuning up your ass, because you won't lie down . . .

. . . and dreams're all Disney compared to what's outside. *So wake up . . .*

"*Shut up* . . . shut the fuck up!" you cry into the frosty black air.

3

Don't get facety, boy. But you better wakey and get moving, onaccount the glow from the itty-bitty clock on that keychain dangling above your head says 5:21 a.m.

Steam should've been your usual wake-up call. Six or so hours after the midnight blast there's always that morning purge, blowing warmth into . . . what you got built in there?

"Air p-pocket, under the tarp," you mumble, hoarse. You pretty much always mumble. The offal in your blood and the amperes in your noggin make your affliction worse.

You know—your affliction your mother and her crew were so damn hot to share with shrinks and teachers. That big jigsaw puzzle brain of yours is missing a few pieces. It's just that when you were young and winning and handsome and wrote essays and didn't speak much—no one noticed.

Yeah, Number Eighty-eight. Pride of the Catholic League. Crushing Gonzaga and DeMatha and Good Counsel and St. John's. Catching that pigskin and blocking on sweeps! Worth turning you over to your mother's prune-faced nuns and queer priests to keep you away from those public school monkeys . . . no thanks to your motherfucker of a jenkty granddaddy who wouldn't part with a penny to send you to a for-real white private school once he paid your sister's bill, no matter how many whiny tugs his redbone daughter made on his fucking cardigan sleeve like he was a bigshot ofay . . . as if being a nigga dentist on Sixteenth Street back then was something rare . . .

. . . and then you're all Joe College in your letter jacket and the blue and white of the Howard Bison. *So?* Could've been Annapolis—all the brass said they'd get you in. *Annapolis*: every no-college-having master chief and gunny's *dream* for their child damn you! An officer . . . *Lord* . . . what happened?

"You know what h-happened," you whisper, grim.

And that's why you entomb yourself, rolling a skin of that three-g bag bearing the likeness of the loveable Great Dane, Scooby Doo himself. You were mad for that cartoon. Now you worship almighty Kush, the irresistible K2.

Hell, not everyone got to sit on their asses watching cartoon dogs. Some people, they had to wet-nurse faggot ofay lieutenants and chew blood in Quang Tri City while the ARVN shit their draws and rabbited.

"And some people prayed it'd be the North V-V-Vietnamese who'd shut you up. But Huntington's D-Disease, c-catheters, diapers—that's karma enough."

Ouch.

Did you say karma? You're groping in the blackness onaccount it's a bit chillier in your hooch than usual. Feel the tear? The seam between the tarpaulin floor, canvas walls . . .

"Lemme fix it in peace so's I can get outta here!"

Alright, boy, do your thing . . .

Digging in a filthy fold of canvas you find a chipped coffee mug, and it's wrapped by two metal clothes hangers you'd bent to form pincers. In the mug's a tube of chalky denture cleaner, plus antique mucilage and rubber bands. By your foot's the secret ingredient: screw top bottle of Manischewitz. Mister Fred used to chew that juice back in the day with ole Benedetto, when they taught you that the Tyrannosaurus Rex was a scavenger who no one fucked with it.

Something raw and clammy grazes your head. *Aim one of your little flashlights, fool!* You see? It's not just a tear to contend with, eh? The walls of this hobo mansion are moist and groaning inward. Didn't you pull the lines taut at the museum rainspout?

The canvas is already laden on the inside with what now's glinting, reflecting, refracting in component colors as if indeed in a cavern lit by glowworms. Layers of keys, photos, buttons, watches, federal ID badges and lanyards, driver's licenses, CDs, DVDs, pendants and chains, a brass doorknob, a baby's pacifier still crusted with breastmilk months later. These are spoils of dead things and dead places picked clean. They clink and jangle as you move about.

You fling off your stiff blanket, poke that frightful head from the dingy flaps of your hooch.

Sleet's encrusted the bare shrubs and naked trees in a sugarcoating of tiny silver beads, glowing eerily in the spotlights ringing the museum grounds. The ice is weighing down your fabric burrow as the hawk blows through the tear.

Back inside, you collect your lighter . . . Fred boasted it could blow-torch his old rock pipe like a jet's afterburner. You add your alchemist's recipe. Melt that shit, especially the rubberbands. With a make-up brush you spread the mixture on the joined ends of the gash. The sleet abates as you wait for the repair to dry.

Snug again, you aim the little flashlight at your toes. Not black, more of a coffee bean red. *Red good, black bad.* That's what Benedetto and Fred taught you. But those ramshorn nails, boy . . . how long can walk on those?

And now it's 6:02 a.m., and decent folk're rising, pouring joe with half and half, brushing their teeth, watching Al Roker and traffic updates, dressing their kids for school . . .

. . . yet maybe you should have read the Sunday *Washington Post* copies you shredded to insulate your billet from the steam grate's wet concrete and wrought iron, because now you're poking your head out once again, craning your neck to catch a view of the big oaks and ginkos in the sculpture garden. Usually a security guard over there . . . pre-sunrise joggers bundled against the cold . . . intrepid early-shift commuters taking short cuts across the National Mall.

Not a soul this morning. Just a blush of yellow and lavender over the Capitol dome to the east, signaling dawn.

See, back in the world, it's another day of petty cruelty. Uncle Sam's padlocked himself by order of the cracker Mafia and its Don yet again. First times it was over "mongrels" at the border, causing pillage and such. Then it was over how sick and broke to make folk, or whether too many Buicks and smokestacks caused the mutant weather. This one? Chaos for chaos's sake. But hey, you'll have your own commute to yourself without all these chumps who sardine themselves onto the Metro or sit on 395 for two hours arriving to mock you or lay on the mawkish pity.

Because you are a working man. You're out of that tent, swaying like a gorilla in hungry shoes as you walk . . . detached soles flopping on the icy sidewalk like a nag's hooves across a frozen country lake. Thread-bare baggy corduroys, old pajama bottoms under that.

That black Chinese knock-off of a Canada Goose parka is doing the job, though. Lucky you weren't comatose when rich folk gifted them to random hobos, bums, winos, crackheads. They didn't want you all perishing in the snow: frozen mummies in full view of hayseed red-hatted Make America Great Again tourists or the sheiks and Boris and Natasha oligarchs hitting the President's hotel down the street.

Now, you're wincing as you pass the iron-latticed window abutting your hooch. Through the pane, stacked around the reconstructed scavenger T-rex, are a bunch of signs ready to go out on the sidewalk. *All Smithsonian Museums are closed due to the Shutdown your President wanted to avoid at all costs, because learning is good. Merry Christmas & a New Year of Greatness . . .*

. . . no time to dawdle. Clean up, go make that money. The light dapples the drab olive-green snack bar across from dormant fountains the ofays were rushing to convert into the winter ice-skating rink in time for Christmas. Now the rink's closed, thanks to President Agent Orange, as is the snack bar. You cross into the garden and survey the building. The ladies' room is chained and padlocked. The men's shitter, wide open.

Kate and Princess sleep in the ladies' room after you deciphered the punch-lock combo. It's four walls and heat they otherwise wouldn't have, and they won't go near the shelters. Now you watch them bug out from that open men's room door; you can't watch them 24-7. Still, the ladies see you, wave at you like you are a superhero in the movies.

Kate's cheeks are ruddy from the cold; the rest of her is a piglet's pink. She's got this look of someone's drunk aunt, mixed with a middle school teacher. Ex-hubby took the house and her sanity, and so atop her graying maize colored hair is a red "Beware the Deep State"; her shopping cart brims with babydolls and dingy clothing, Red Bull cans.

Princess shuffles over . . . taut, brown pockmarked skin, wig askew on a head healing nicely from sores Kate tended. She's cradling one of Kate's dolls as if it's alive, and pantomimes breast feeding it through her open dirty trench coat. She's gloveless but you could stick a staple gun to those fingers and she likely wouldn't feel it. Oversized galoshes with no underlying shoes shod her feet. Better, maybe, than Kate, who wears those damn Birkenstock things year-round. She kisses your cheek, plops down on the cold wet pavement in front of Kate, cross-legged.

You watch Kate gently lift a smelly wig off Princess's bald pate, massage her scalp.

"How you doin', old girl?" you ask Princess.

Eyes closed, enjoying the sensation, Princess whispers, "My ministry-ation."

"She's on her monthly," Kate explains as she lights up a jack, takes a puff, "and hell if I know how she is because I'm sure menopaused as fuck, baby! Ponce de Leon must've shownt her that fountain!"

You chuckle then ask, "Y'all runnin' low of ibuprofen, ointments, t-tampons and stuff? Verna's gonna get wise to me housing that shit."

"Miss Verna's already wise to you, Dickie," Kate cackles, already butting the lit jack and fumbling for the pack in the vast folds of her dress. "She sweet on you, big man."

You kiss them both goodbye on their frigid cheeks and say, "All's I need is you two."

"No woman's worth hot-dosing and dying for, Dickie," Kate suddenly presses. Bless her booze-soaked soul. "You God's last good man. But if you don't get Esmeralda outcher head she and you both gonna be in a dark place, in the house of your enemies, and only one of you are gettin' out, sweetie."

She gets a shrug on that one.

"*But see here* . . . we bugged out 'cause of some noises in that bathroom, ya dig?"

"I'll check it out. Get somethin' to eat . . . "

About that noise, huh? No cleaning crews, no guards. They're all unemployed. Gotta be raccoons or rats. And there doesn't seem to be anyone else in the ugly box of a bathroom;

the meager sunrise is now throwing weird shadows, making it difficult to discern movement beyond the painted windows. You do your shuffle-skip to the door, slip in.

Smells of a loaded toilet the moment you enter, and you can't even make out the tile pattern on the wet floor: islands of frozen pink vomit surrounded by the blackened muck of spoiled Autumn leaves, toilet paper, candy wrappers and plastic cups, and an unknowable crust the consistency of coffee grounds. This your Ritz-Carlton, your Army-Navy Club. Look there, past the skittering cockroach and lumbering waterbug: a jimmie, still in its package. "Ribbed and Lubricated." And another . . . spent.

Indeed, there's one maybe five-foot square clean spot abutting the wall along the sinks and window. In the middle there's a baby doll with blue ribbons in its hair. What was it you built Kate and Princess to sleep in . . . keeps the muck, creepy crawlies off?

"Oiled . . . oiled t-tarpaulin like my tent, then a scrounged kids' tumbling mat, aluminum c-curtain rods . . . from a community center Dumpster."

You strip down, look at yourself in the grime-smudged mirrors. Good to see you wash that finger before scooping up a gob of the medicated toothpaste you keep in your pocket. That stuff you got from Verna, like they give teething babies. You dab it gingerly . . .

"Fuck!" you screech, jaw suffused with pain. Choppers, boy. First thing to go . . .

A stall door behind you suddenly jiggles, and you no longer are a diseased bear. You turn, erect, alert. There . . . another sound: a snort . . . a cough? A gathering of mucus becomes a harsh spit on the vile floor.

10

"Yo . . . " calls a voice with very little adult bass in it. "Smokes? Fo'-gee o' *Ivanka Crunk* . . . *Scooby Doo Snax*. Stamp, nigga . . . "

"Ain't got n-no smokes, man," you stammer. Stop the mush-mouth. No matter how swole and tall you are, these animals will always consider you a punk for the stammer.

"Nah," the voice intones as you turn to face it. "I-I *gots* smokes. Kush, nigga . . . *jhi*-like a deck a Xanny, yo . . . cash or trade. Trade means ass or blowjob . . . "

You aren't facing much. You're at least two feet taller than . . . okay more likely a he, right? So slight, skeletal. Long braid clipped to real hair draws your eyes to the flesh of his scalp and hairline: mottled with scars, bunched in small keloidal nodes. He's got on stained sports denim leggings. Black coat looks to be something your mother's gaudy sorority sisters would have worn in the Eighties. Leather, big shoulders.

"Okay, lis-sen," he re-adjusts. "I give you head, fi'teen. Give it me, ten. Or, it's *anything* y'all want, moe. I got jimmies . . . don't do no raw-dawgin'."

"Tape," you say in that monotone and with that sleepy stare. "Got some?"

He stares back at you, incredulous and quips, "What is y'all, moe—a retard?"

"You said 'anything' I want, moe. I need tape f-f-for my shoes. See? Duct tape."

"Fuck you an' yo' crazy ass, nigga! I'll fuck you up!"

"How old're you, young b?"

"Old enough to kick yo' big ass if y'all wanna tussle."

"Park Police gonna come through here, shutdown or no. You best g-get your ass out. And don't let me c-c-catch you ruckusin' with my girls Kate and Princess . . . "

11

He's all up in the crazy now.

"I ain't never messed wiff that fat white rolla and that ole sick bitch if thas wha they say!" he hollers as he paces before you. "So you jump, nigga! Got a twenny-five hid by my dick, full clip."

"Park Police'll shoot you dead."

He's dropping the mask and the armor now anyway. They always do.

"*Kill* . . . cops come soon, real live? They all crazy on a nigga, too, not like DC cops who just let you go wiff-out a case, right?"

You nod and huff, "Trump's world now, moe. B-Barack days're a dream." You survey him again. "Why you here, young-b?"

"Salvadorans up in the Mickey D's on F Street . . . they threw me out las' night an' . . . I ain't eat since Tuesday . . . and . . . "

His voice flattens, evaporates. These kids, out all summer and the previous winter— a legion of sentient corpses, splayed on the pavement, even behind the FBI's HQ and along the granite facing of the Supreme Court Building. Lucky ones died of the dirty K, eh?

"Sheriff Road niggas . . . that where my, um, jont used to be . . . they see me like this, and they call me names and want me like them niggas want sex in jail, moe. Nah, cause my foster brother's niggas, Fifty-second Place Nation . . . I mean, it ain't no 'nation' it's like five niggas . . . but they be Debo-in' er'yone who fuck wiff'em . . . they got my back so they goin' get kirkin' on Sheriff Road if they mess wiff me." He wets his cracked, painted lips. "Foster brother, he catchin' cases, so I be gone. Keep things peaceful . . . "

You smile. Not diss to this child, though. It's just your affliction.

"So . . . so you a s-sort of Helen of Troy . . . in reverse. Selfless?"

That kid's shell reconstitutes fast . . .

"Fuck you I ain't no 'Helen!' I ain't no faggot!"

"Calm down, young-b," you offer. The near whisper, the deadpan sucks the fury from him. Indeed, you see something brighten in his eyes, there in that dank, stink place.

"Hold up, I seent you befo'. You that nigga who help folk *figure* shit, right?"

Oops. You're a celebrity among the emaciated and the infected.

"Jhi-yeah . . . you Dickie!" he exclaims, all stalker and fanboy. "Gawd . . . muv-fukkas get jacked, get a nine-milli-meter beat-down . . . and you *figure it out* so's they peeps can put shit right, *right*? I hear fennie napped you but came back f'om the dead!"

The fawning hurts you more than the fury, doesn't it boy?

"Lis-sen, young-b . . . Pakistani dude . . . owns a place down from Fr-Franklin Park. Ever sleep in Franklin Park, summer-time?" He nods and you add, "Man's got a restaurant. Feeds any folk who c-come by in hard times."

"My auntie, she worked in the cafeteria, Agriculture build'n . . . white muvfukkas say she a contractor so she gone, no pay, no back pay . . . "

"Take her with you. Try the naan-bread. It's *halal.* Akin to . . . J-Jewish kosher. Means no bullshit in it. Fresh."

"I wants *meat* . . . a burger. Stamp, moe!"

"Nah, it's good. Butter chicken, lamb . . . veggies for your blood . . . then you get up to Central Mission . . . stay away fr-from the city's mens' spot. Only other place with room is up to Mitch Snyder's. Long time ago a white man n-named

Benedetto and ole gray-dick Fred taught me how to make things. How not to die. Anyways . . . safe beds . . . "

"*Kill*, moe . . . they prolly all hugged up on yo' big ass 'cause you a monster, gee." He's not as addled as he looks. "I wanna know where *you* go now. To eat."

"They full-up there, moe, at St. Jude's and So Families May Eat . . . S-F-M-E."

He meets those names with a derisive chuckle. Yeah, he's heard of them. He'd qualify for neither. He's the ghost, not you. By the Hi-Five-AIDS, a beating or a bullet. Another kid will take his place in the toilet stall. That much you *figure* . . .

And so you zip the parka and you are shoving him out of way as you make for the exit and *Lord have mercy,* he smells worse than you. He follows yet stops at the door as if he's a vampire and the dawn will burn him. And you bless him, because that's your affliction, right?

" . . . *ne nos inducas in tentationem . . . sed libera nos a malo.* Amen."

Not every urchin was an acolyte. "*S'up moe!*" he screeches after you. Showing him your back and mumbling that Papal drivel wasn't the best move. "You lay mojos on me? I-mo live *foreva,* nigga!"

You purge his face from your mind as his voice fades, and you're loping across the Mall with the Capitol dome's gray on your left, G-Dub's obelisk stabbing a still dark sky on your right. No noise but your big feet sloshing through patches of fallen sleet and hoarfrost.

That little encounter should tell you the real world's awake now, toad. And it's hungry.

CHAPTER 2

Little Black Santa Claus

You tug a wool watch cap tight over your furry head. Cowboys . . . *really*? All those years watching Sonny and Billy flang it to Charlie Taylor and Art Monk at RFK, oblivious to ticket prices . . . and you yank a *filthy* Dallas cap over your bowen-ass head? Okay, better run like Emmitt Thomas on account there's maybe twenty minutes before the trucks leave . . .

"I c-c-can run!" you huff to the air. "But it's so cold. It hurts . . . "

That *ain't* why you're dawdling, boy. Five years she's been gone and you *still* under her spell . . . tight skirts on those hips, no bra on those missiles, the high heels and painted toes . . . more Latinate than Latin with that porcelain skin and oh, the bone-straight ink black hair she'd flip at all those lil' sorority gals and she had a line long as train smoke of sisters wanting to kirk her good for hijacking you!

You rub your fingers together as if you got your mother's prayer beads. "After the scourging, m-my Son was led to the pr-pr-praetorium where the soldiers wanted to further amuse themselves . . . *Agnus Dei* . . . "

Please—that heathen rolla laughed that shit! Remember her hustle? *Balam Chi* . . . that's her familiar, like a Halloween witch's black cat. The jaguar . . . the number seven . . . and she calls herself *bruja* and sketches the Mayan hexes and trills the Mexican black magic. First time she got you high was the sherm, right? Why's someone so wealthy stealing embalming fluid from the mortuary sciences lab for the most ghetto high on earth? And even now as you trudge toward South Capitol Street you're tasting the bitter cherry bite of a joint she's rolled. Quite unremarkable Bobby Brown inside. But the formaldehyde cuvée renders such a satisfying finish to the palate for that vintage. Mind the lighter flame though . . . *sapo.*

Fake-ass conjure woman! All she did, all she's *doing*, is turn you out. That's not love.

You're sprinting now, huh? Tough love works. Just wipe those damn tears away!

Too bad your tribe can't cheer you on, or they'll betray their commandeered nooks in the Cannon and Longworth House of Representatives buildings. Ever since Agent Orange decreed that you bums'd be thrown in the frozen Potomac, more folks have been huddling at the hem of the Congress's skirt.

But damn, here comes the Captain, though: wide awake, beat-footin' and shimmy-spinnin' to some tune in his head and wearing nothing but sweatpants, ratty slippers and a droopy gray cotton polo shirt that was white when the donation van came around handed it to him! He's all scratchy because he was a pro at skin popping; plus ice and wind ain't a thing if your nerve endings are dead.

"S'up Richard?"

"Can't talk, moe. Gotta hit them trucks. Last cr-crews before holiday . . . "

He's just awake enough to hook your big arm, just delicate enough that if you pull away too hard, you'll jerk his shoulder out of the socket.

"Real live . . . watch y'self, moe. Ya know Peach up in Park View an' shit?"

"She a friend of Black Santa Claus . . . so?"

"She say your fatboy Santa Claus been spittin' mad life on you, cause there be *clear people* doin' the ghetto Google on you, moe, and he hears there a dollah in it. He gotta *big* mouf', homey . . . "

Little Black Santa Claus running his mouth? Hella every day. Little Black Santa Claus spittin' to white people? Ridiculous, if only because why would any ofay be bothering to pry into your foul shit, boy? *Exactly.*

"He's just old," you dodge. "Uses my name like a cr-credit card." When you see him dip in a dance pantomime you ask, "Whatchew rockin' out to, Cap'n?"

"*Chuck Brown*, nigga! All day! White man can shoot us and lock them spic chul'drin in cages . . . but fuck if he can stop the Go-Go, the D.C. swing! *Heeeeey* . . . needin' that money, that cash, that *moolah moolah moolah* . . . "

You give him fist-pounds just as a Capitol Police officer rounds the corner, bristling with an HK and gear all popping from his webbed belts and his vest, as if he's Special Forces and you two are al Qaida and ISIS. Old boy, he keeps beat-footin' Anacostia style and the whiteboy's getting pissed. Last thing you hear is another verse from *We Need Some Money* until a yelp and cry and you are peace-out because nothing can keep you from your appointed rounds, eh?

And that beat-down is well out of your mind as you cut across pock-marked lots and under crumbling highway ramps to Half Street, Southwest . . . lungs straining from the icy breeze. Your landmark is a huge, new-fangled digital billboard: "America: Great Again, Get Out if That Offends You!" Just below that message of love is ole St. Jude's Mission Chapel.

In warm weather St. Jude's is a pleasant sight. War of 1812 vintage stones all tickled in the clean white and bright orange of those climbing hydrangea and trumpet vines; elm trees shade the "new" 1950's brick and cinderblock residence hall. This winter, however, the stone is deader and dingier. The hall, just a barracks housing the hopeless, looks . . . *shit* . . . more hopeless. Still, no boys have been raped there. Papists're doing at least one thing right.

Connected to the church residence *via* a well-alarmed, surveillance-up-the-ass corridor, is So Families May Eat or "SFME." Independent of the Catholics but still "affiliated," it's for the females, the kids, rather than you raggedy-ass single men. SFME's all smoked glass and steel, and, ironically, it's uglier in spring and summer.

SFME's money came mostly from Uncle Sam until Trump's *capo-regimes* took over. Rumor is one of the big benefactors these days is some bastard running food services for private prisons full-up of niggas and ICE concentration camps full-up of Mexicans. If you are about bombs, spies or locking mugs up, D.C.'s the place to make some bank. Everyone else can just get in line for hot soup.

The trucks idle at the curb fronting the church and SFME, coughing out a cloud of exhaust that hangs pale pink from the vehicles' brake lights. They come twice a week, all year.

Okay, so you all call them "trucks." Most folks would say beat-up panel vans. This shivery morning it's two old windowless white Ford Econolines and a black Dodge.

There is a line of bodies for the trucks and one for grub, but the faces on folk in either spit the same song: terror mixed with confusion, anger welded to grim resignation.

The grub tribe's bigger, and not because folk are lazy. It's the children who swell that gathering there in the dawn murk. Amazing how quiet they always are. A lot of cats're huddling there, too, just to be close to babies and baby mamas and mamas and younger siblings. The real man labors for his bread and doesn't slink in with women for a hot meal. You're woven from a tougher skein than your mother and your sister . . .

"Don't . . . *don't* you mention their names, damn you."

Nah, *you* best better check yourself because the Fords are already packed; the white men in charge are kicking flailing limbs inside just to get the doors shut.

You survey the black Dodge. Maybe a third full. Another white man's in charge, but this one's a bit off. Silly-looking red ski cap—the fruity pompom on top. Red scarf. He's studying what looks to be those iPad things and he's clearly picky about who he allows on the crew. Couple of regulars turned away, like Bert and Mayfield. Mayfield's probably zooted but Bert's the best worker out here so what's up? The white man's checking his watch . . .

. . . and your dithering ass gets caught.

"Dickie? Dickie Cornish!" Verna calls to you. The glow of SFME's sign now cuts the morning gloom; folks are ambling inside. "Just your luck my dear. The nurse is coming at noon . . . dental assistant, too. I'm making you an appointment."

19

Your face is stitched with the shit-eating grin of bad choices, boy. Yeah, you owe her. But you got to make that paper. Yeah, she'll feed you. But you got to get high.

She's in a silver North Face bubble jacket, wool cap, those Ugg boot things. Got some surplus meat on her, but it seems to lay in the right places. Brown skinned yet good hair. It's not that barley curly auburn like your mother's . . . the kind that invites the damn freckles, like the ones spotting Alma's face. You had a few freckles like your sister before you got more pigment. Real men should have hue; light-skinned niggas are pantywaists. Guess any freckle on yourself now's prolly got six legs and is moving. Verna's so small you got to bend hard to hug her. That she embraces your filthy ass is angelic. Or desperate.

"I miss you V-Verna but I'm out . . . "

"Don't gimme that *bullshit*, Dickie. We can clean you up, list you as a volunteer at SFME while I get the friars at St. Jude's to reserve you a bed tonight. I got that dap."

The trucks are starting to pull away.

"It's Christmas. Give my sp-space to someone else."

Now get in the damn truck!

"Dickie listen—you're what . . . gonna be fifty in a couple of years, right? Your file says you've been on and off the street, shelters, VA, inpatient mental health and rehab . . . almost half your life. And you almost *died* . . . and this is *after* you promised to stop. Now I hear you're living . . . in a *tent*? Two vulnerable women, Kathleen McCarthy and Princess Goins, depending on you?"

"If it was a b-boat . . . it'd be seaworthy, I swear. And the ladies are okay."

"Oh Lord . . . honey I know you a whiz at scrounging like that 'McGuyver' when I was growing up. But that was TV bullshit. And the ladies need beds and meds." She sighs then whispers to you as you side-eye her. "K2 will kill you as dead as the smack and fentanyl, just slower, harder. You think you're made of iron. You're not."

That last van, the Dodge, is still idling. *Move!*

"They're vultures, Dickie! Snatch you all up like the slave-traders who ran this city before the Civil War!"

"I'm em-employed."

She's silent yet her eyes are raking you as you trundle away. *This bitch.* All she's tossing is the politesse these psycho-welfare types spit like the soft-bodied coral slugs building a reef. It's the hard shell that hides the disdain and disgust.

Oh shit . . . she's not done. Knows the right bait for that jigsaw brain . . .

"Hold-up . . . finished-up our new system . . . integrates HUD rental assistance, HHS and D.C. Human Services, the police and domestic violence databases . . . TANF, SNAP . . . Medicaid and CHIP. Brother Karl at St. Jude's says how much you like puzzles, labyrinths and getting on the computer . . . *I'll show how it works*, run dummy queries. Just today, hot meal first."

You bite that chapped, peeling lower lip to resist the temptation. Never let a female see regret. Besides, there's the fella with the cash.

He's much younger in person than the sloppy ofays who look like they did their thirty years in Corps. Well, this guy's not congruent with the sit-ref. In addition to the fruity pom-pom cap, he's got on a pricey leather bomber jacket; the red scarf's in fact a "Washington Capitals NHL Champs" thing. He cradles a clipboard as well that iPad.

Suddenly he calls to the driver of the van . . . sorry, *truck* . . . about getting going. He sounds more disappointed than you.

Yet out of the wet dark comes a familiar corpulent form and a welcome loud voice.

"*Lard bun an' cheez*, wha'hopnin' bred'rin! Yar sight fi mi cataract eyes, no!"

Sometimes, like now, you can't remember his real name. Fitz-something. The Christmasy-red balaclava he wears in the cold is oddly reassuring. He must have twenty of the damn things because you've never seen him without one in winter and they're never filthy.

"*Kill*, Black Santa Claus!" you call to him, showing the most excitement you've managed in a week of puffing Scooby in your hooch. "You out here to make money too?"

Damn if he doesn't looks like ole button-nosed Kris Kringle in blackface, and that gets him plenty green money when he hits City Center with its Tiffany's blue and Dior silver. Rich folk behold his old-time spectacles covering his squinty eyes, that beard and brushy eyebrows of white against his black skin! And then there's the old clay pipe like some shit slave would have smoked, clenched in those bright teeth. Crowns, compliments of the taxpayers . . .

Before hugging you up he takes a furtive chew on his juice—a half-pint of Southern Comfort because his favorite Caribbean rum doesn't come in a bottle that small, as it was meant to sipped on balmy evenings. He's sausage-ed that big belly into a khaki winter work jumpsuit some Department of Public Works or PEPCO clown likely left unattended.

"Mi get mi coffee at de good white peoples at de Potter's 'ouse ova Adams-Morgan . . . yar neva come so, Dick. Dey ev'm ride mi fat ass do-in 'ere, free. Yar must come, mon . . . "

"Nah . . . don't have nothin' to do with busy pl-places, man. You know me."

"Ya mon. More den yar know. Come so."

This is all real live because this white dude's not waving the jump crew "truck" on. He's standing there, waiting alright. For Black Santa, for you.

"Dick, dis Mr. Uss-ter-haus. Mr. Uss-ter-haus, dis 'im mi tole y'bout. Strong, 'im na got na sugar, na spells or fits, ten finga an' ten toes ev'm widde cold weatha . . . and 'im not 'ear na voices in 'im 'ead."

Well, nobody's perfect . . .

"Jay Oosterhaus," the white man says with a broad toothy smile like you're the ambassador from the Congo. He grips your hand hard.

"Um . . . Richard E. Cornish, Junior." Can't you look at him in the eyes, like a man?

He checks his iPad, not the clipboard, then looks you up and down. "Yeah . . . you got some gloves . . . but man, those shoes, wow . . . you okay, fella?"

"I-I-m f-fine, sir."

"I mean . . . cold as the legendary brass monkey's ass here, eh?" It's making your gut boil when he taps your arm with the clipboard and gushes, "Hear you've got institutional knowledge of what's out there on the street. Good man."

You nod.

"And good damn salvager, eye for value . . . *saaaaay*, what's the going rate for a discarded fridge over where the Hispanics live, Mt. Pleasant? Or, say auto parts . . . finding a master cylinder . . . perhaps some brake pads, all intact in an alley in Shaw?"

You throw a "what the fuck?" stare at Black Santa, who's chewing on the old slave pipe while grinning in bizarre jubilance.

True to your affliction, you answer. Deadpan, monotone and in cloying detail.

"Um . . . low of f-fifteen to high of sixty-eight for the r-refrigerator depending on model; Samsung ironically lower-end because the technology inside . . . typically busted or fried. Master cylinder? Clean, no damage, twenty . . . yeah twenty . . . never heard of finding unused brake pads in an alley . . . usually a whole assembly, c-c-calipers and all. Please—can you give more con-context, sir?"

"Welcome aboard."

Your weak smile turns to a grimace when you behold the driver.

"Ahhh, *big Dick!*" he calls to you as he hands each cat three green trash bags—the tools of your trade.

"Name's 'Dickie,' you know that."

He's pimping that expensive outdoor gear white folks love—Patagonia down vest, leather baseball cap, aviator shades like he's some bush pilot. You know him as an ugly black turtle named Diallou. From one of those French African spots but loves the good ole U.S.A. You've heard him boast his primary gig is selling dick to white women.

"*Mais non,* I call you 'McFlurry.'" He looks to his boss with a smirk and recounts, "*Alors,* dis one, I drive on crew dis pas' summah and boss stop wid dem ovah at McDonald near Howard University, where homeless dem sleep all day. Dis one get in beef wiff manager becaw you have four dollah, and McFlurry wiff extra nuts and chocolate be *five* dollah . . . and de day *so, so hot.* No McFlurry for Big Dick. Him holla at manager *et tout le monde,* po-po come, t'row you out on parking lot. *Les Américaines.* . . slave mentality . . . won't go work for extra dollah, want *négocier* a damn McFlurry . . . *ha!*"

Don't find feelings here, son. Indeed, Oosterhaus quickly intercedes.

"Now-now, Diallou. We're lucky to have Mr. Cornish on this crew. You fellas grab some floor, stow your gear . . . "

"Shimmy ova an' small yarself," Black Santa advises as you climb over legs and feet to find a spot on the floor. With the door sliding shut you're now cheek to jowl with maybe fifteen other men, like the Middle Passage or *Ben Hur* galley slaves. And then there's the timbre of body odor, farts, piss, stale breath and wet vinyl . . .

"Good t'ave yar 'ere buoy," Black Santa gushes. "We gwine nort' east . . . not nah cross de river . . . "

He's not talking coconuts and callaloo, Junior. Sure, there're juicy spots across the Anacostia River full of poor people. But that carrion got less meat to pick. And that's why you stick with the jump crews prowling east of the axis provided by Rock Creek Park.

"Black Santa advises. "Dis gwine be easy money, says dis white mon."

"So it's him you were running your mouth to . . . about me?"

"Buoy do-in be sa facety—why mi do dat? It Yuletide, mi yout'. And mi Santa Claus!"

Maybe he's right; you sniff and see bags of McDonald's sausage biscuit. Cardboard cartons of McCafé coffee . . . sugar . . . crème packets. This might not be so bad.

Through a crackling last-century-vintage loudspeaker hanging from wires up front, comes Oosterhaus's whitebread voice.

"*Hel-lo*! My name is Jay Oosterhaus . . . new coordinator, General Real Estate Recovery Systems, as it is under new ownership. Want to get a feel for what you gentlemen do so I came out myself. The food's our way of saying thanks for protecting our assets . . . "

"See," Black Santa assures you, beaming. "Na worry. Na evil come today."

CHAPTER 3

The Ticket

STILL, YOU DON'T ASK BLACK SANTA about what Captain blathered back there. But the cat can tell something's up as you're heavy-browed, staring.

"*Chut*, yout'. Na be sa facety wid Santa. Yar cross wid mi?"

You shake your head. He pats your knee; that and the greasy food and fragrant Joe quells your moping.

"Okay, here's the ticket for today, gentlemen," you hear over the speaker. "Foreclosure in Bloomingdale . . . debtor's items remain on-premises. Two restitution evictions, one for-cause eviction. Commercial trash-out." You swear he's swiped more than a few glances your way. "One possible residential trash-out . . . picked crew." He queer?

The rest of them shoved in there aren't paying Oosterhaus any mind anyway. These cats make quick work of the sausage biscuits. The coffee's slurped down so fast a couple dudes show burnt tongues!

Diallou jerks the truck from the curb and you jostle and sway as you wolf down your meal, scan faces.

Uh-huh, lots of regulars besides Black Santa. Misfits, too,

sadly, like Lil' Roach, his ski mask pulled half over his grill as if he's ready to wild-out a Seven-Eleven. He's been buggy from the time the Park Police kirked him. Found him face-up under a grating—over which traversed women and girls in their shorts and sundresses, protesting a certain Pussy-Grabber in the White House who would have envied the upskirt view. Nightstick time.

His nigga Big Roach is a different kind of loony. Got a couple inches on you so he's gotta be six-five, six-six? Looking cray in his muddy blue North Face bubble coat and same style ski mask as Lil's . . . and working his tongue around the mouth-hole as if "Lurch" in the old TV show was a pervert. Just did five at Rivers—a shit-box run by a prison corporation that warehouses D.C. inmates. Went in a big dullard, came out a soulless ape.

Your boy Stripe's been jockin' you since you climbed in. Reptilian glower, flaring nostrils, flared acne. He's flipped down the hood on his Miami Dolphins jacket and there's that blond-frosted mohawk fade he sports to prove how much younger and meaner than all of you he is. Still hasn't forgiven you for bestowing his nickname: the gremlin creature from the movie. When he's not extra zooted with that army of zombie spick bums laying on the fountain in Columbia Heights, he's running between the psycho MS-13 boys under some clown you know as "Blinky" Guzman, who Trump has named the new John Dillinger, and their nemesis, the Otis Place *Brigada*: Guardian Angel wannabees. Both tribes beat his druggie ass on general principle but hey, everybody's got to try to belong somewhere, right?

"*Oye, chico intelligente*," Stripe says, waving in your face like an annoying grade school prankster, "You 'figure' anything lately? Like you Batmon and shit? Guess you coul'n't figure how not to fok-up a hot-dose a fennie. *Ha!*"

Such pleasant conversation!

So, the first stops on the ticket carry more than the usual drama onaccount it's four days before Christmas. Crying, pleading, cigarette butts flicked at you, spittle landing on you. Epithets: crow, maggot, buzzard, hyena—not the king of the dinosaurs. Nah, ole T-rex doesn't pile a chest of drawers passed down three generations, racks of clothes all smart for church, baby toys and dolls, old pictures in gilded frames . . . all at the curb to wilt in the cold rain and sleet. Oh, but jewelry, prescription vials containing any shit, beer and Fanta left in the fridge, liquor left in a closet, AA and D batteries, Tide detergent, outdated phones and chargers, gators and Nikes, small flatscreens and PS4s—that's the tasty marrow. Motherfuckers like the Roaches and Stripe're adept at stashing the goodies like hamsters for a return trip to complete the pillage. Federal marshals and landlords don't care.

Now, the third stop fucks with you—three-bedroom apartment on C Street, Northeast, near old RFK. Young woman in a bathrobe, a black Nylon wavecap on her head because it's early as hell, weeping at her mother's bosom, little boy at both their knees. That's the for-cause. You're pulling out stacks of hair styling magazines and they give way to nursing textbooks, binders full of math problem sets. Younger girl in the wavecap's in evening college, and someone's been beating on her mom, so says Black Santa, stone-faced.

"Happened to my girl LaKeisha . . . my c-c-computer girl," you shared with anyone who'd listen. "Lives in Shaw Branch of the library, got all those computers in there but she got her own in her shopping carriage . . . thieves that wifi . . . *my girl.* Learned it in the Army . . . "

Of course nobody was listening. Just swathing box springs

and mattresses in shrink-wrap, green-bagging socks and sundries as if so much garbage.

"If she calls nine-one-one too many times . . . pr-protective order or not, that landlord catches hell from the city, from the cops . . . then the landlord can legally say you're a nuisance, in br-breach of a lease no one reads. Puts you on the street. If she *doesn't* call, lets some nigga in to eat her food, beat her mama and her and her kids, then she keeps a roof over her head. It's called a 'Catch Twenty-Two.' From a novel . . . 'bout war."

Lil' Roach finally responded with, "Fuck them rollas, Dickie. They got problems. Well, I got troubles!"

At least you scavenged another trophy for your tent. The older mom's Ballou High cheer squad baton, Class of Ninety. Fits right up your parka sleeve . . .

. . . and there's no more coffee in the truck. Just grim silence under Diallou's grinding gears, the occasional fart or belch.

Black Santa decides to assemble you haggard men for the campfire tale, as is his skill, and he chides those gossiping about Sponge Bob.

"Show de dead mon respek . . . like ya ragamuffins show mi Dick 'ere respek."

Years back, a black President of the United States, a black First Lady and two lovely daughters stood in aprons at SFME and prepared a plate of food for ole Sponge Bob and his Queen. Then embraced them. Whispered a solemn grace with them. Watched them eat. A current President of the United States whose slumlord inheritance was measured in the ones and fives poorfolk scraped together each month seems to have laughed when told of "human popsicles" in

Meridian Hill Park, caught unprepared by the freakish cold. Told the world it was proof the climate wasn't changing.

Well that shut down the murmur, real fast. But your pudgy sidekick wasn't done.

"And dis mon, Dick, he a old'ead, him take care a two sick womons, mind 'im bidness less dere street justice be done. 'im Batmon an' ya na laugh, Stripe!

"*Coño* Santa Claus, dis ole *baboso*? Shit . . . he *Rain Man*, not Batman." That's his dig at you, for his own nickname. Keep glowering at the lil' punkass. "So wha he fuck wid Ghenghis Kann? An' save dat faggo' DaQuan?"

Now the campfire tales begin, and you shrink down all bashful, eyes flicking side to side like you a paranoid toddler. And when you venture a goose-necked peek, you see Osterhaus staring at you again when not tapping on that iPad. And when he is tapping, it's as if he's following Black Santa's narration, noting Stripe's quips or the Roaches' tongue clicking. Oh, you hate being the center of attention, but this object of scrutiny thing's really chapping your butt so you try, try not to even look up . . .

. . . and Black Santa's getting to the part where not even MPD or DEA can nail D'eantre "Ghenghis" Kann for plugging poison . . . or more poison than usual K2 to eliminate the competition's customers up Maryland Avenue and Benning Road . . . and you use that jigsaw puzzle brain to *figure* out his sister's importing cheapass toys and tchotchke from China, including little foil bags. The real Scooby Snax comes in little clear bags, with foil labels. The Street, not the courts, take Ghenghis out, and you're a ghetto star. Free Scooby and re-ups from the competition!

You risk a turn toward the front. Uh-huh, the whiteboy's

nodding and you jerk your attention to the DaQuan and Bob Hope matter que'd up. Dark Columbo! Homeless Holmes, barely out of Medstar with your dick dangling out your hospital gown—remember how you solved this one? Miz Eva's friend's son, shacked up with that awful hillbilly Bob Hope, goes and puts out Bob Hope's eye with an' oyster shucker on account Bob Hope says DaQuan didn't like his sweet potato pie without Cool Whip after a meal of raw oysters. BOLO for assault with a deadly weapon and attempted murder; an FBI advisory because DaQuan rabbited to Virginia.

DaQuan'd be busted were it not for you having ole white-girl Kate make an anonymous call to MPD. No oystershells to be found; the shucker was something DaQuan picked up getting whiting from the Viet Cong at what's left of the old Waterfront Fishmarket now that the rest is condos and restaurants and yacht slips for Trump's foreign gangstas. What was found? An application to D.C. Housing to replace DaQuan on the apartment voucher with fat Marcia . . . LaKeisha found it, all damn public and unencrypted, and printed a hard copy in ten seconds. Bob Hope was bi—and loved heavy women. You plucked Marcia's curling iron from a Dumpster, crusty with what's likely DaQuan's blood. Stuff like that. They go and arrest Bob Hope in ICU, Marcia in the Shrimp Boat over in Southeast . . . DaQuan comes out of hiding (you found him anyway), gets the apartment to himself!

Bravo, Rain Man.

No one *untouched* and placid could have figured that shit, just as the kid in the nasty men's room lauded you.

Yet, you cock your ear a bit toward the front, and from under the chortles and shade you hear Oosterhaus mention to that bastard Diallou, "I'm satisfied. The beauty shop trash-out's

31

been cancelled anyway. Pull over into the gas station and we'll square the money for the day . . . see about volunteers for that special job . . . "

. . . and you knock your big head on the van's steel bulkhead and pray inwardly. Inward, though, as if you can keep a secret in that skull? Stripe's onto something, even though his addled spick mind can't fully get it. The brain that showers you with technicolor figurin' also drowns in pools of deceivers and betrayers, soul-thieves . . . all immune to the ultimate painkillers of fentanyl hot-dosing a syringe of citric acid and black tar flakes.

Surprise!

Oosterhouse decrees a ten-minute piss break, etc. in the Valero station there on Rhode Island Avenue up near the Home Depot. How convenient, in case he requires slaves from more sunny and exotic climes. Some of you are in the truck where it's indeed warmer, drier despite what you know to be Diallou's standing orders not to idle and waste gas during any stop. He's bundled up, sipping on some hot broth from the Motherland that smells like hot peppers and feet.

You've plopped down near a stand of bare forsythia camouflaging God knows what these mugs have ripped off and can't keep on-board. You're fingers throb. You can't feel your toes. Your numb nose is dripping copious snot, and—*Merry Christmas*—that itch, that twitch is starting. Fiending for the tasty K. Get your green and get away from prying eyes, forget this mess, these families . . . curate your baton into your canvas museum. Curse Esmeralda by lighting up, inhale, watch the world ooze . . .

. . . yet the Fates and Furies got an alternate plan it seems, as Stripe saunters straight for you after relieving himself on, not in, the gas station.

"*Oye*, Rain Man . . . " he calls to you.

"Not now, kid."

. . . and damn if he doesn't sit his narrow ass right down on the cold concrete next to you.

He pulls his vape pen, alternatively sucking and talking and it's annoying.

"Fok . . . what it like . . . to die and come bok, hospital?" Your deadpan doesn't work. He blows vape smoke and comes in with, "*Mira*, we need . . . *cómo dicen?* A truce. *Jefe, por ahí* . . . " he says, gesturing to Oosterhaus, " . . . modderfokker ask all kinda questions 'cause he want just *Mexicanos, Guatemaltecos, Hondoranos* . . . but no *Salvadoreños* on de crew. Him just show up, old *jefe* gone. But him around yesterday . . . week before. Him ask bout *las familias* who lose apartment for no money, Him ask about *Mexicanos, Guatemaltecos, Hondoranos* only. Me say first—dat modderfokker, he ICE . . . "

Stripe shoots a dual stream of picante smoke from his flared nostrils. Maybe he's hoping his youthful paranoia can mate with yours.

"He doesn't look like I-ICE under-c-cover," you acknowledge. "But the truck . . . him picking folk...*auditioning* . . . rather than just piling us in. Yeah, strange."

"*Sí*! Audition! Dat's de word. No usual *desamparados, imbéciles,* eh? *Sí*, bad men like Roach but bad men what know de street. Oosterhaus . . . like him draft a *futbol* team, *comprende?*"

"All-Star team."

He hunkers low and whispers, "Because him *also* ask . . . 'bout *you*, bro'."

No punch to the belly, but you still feel woozy. And yet you still back your boy with, "No . . . Black Santa, says he just c-came around . . . today."

33

"No, bro'." With that, Stripe gestures toward the jolly elf with his vape pen, over there near the truck sharing a flask, giggling. "Wha'—you think fat man only one whiteboy asking 'bout you? Him ask me if you speak *castellano, español* . . . " That got your attention. "Den Santa him come over an' say *'Oh, like tell before . . . Dick him speak good Spanish. From hanging wid crazy bitch long ago.'*"

Okay not a perfect transcript, or the kid's lying his gold fronts off, but you either got to punch or lunch, that's the code . . . aw, shit. You gonna *lunch*?

"Known this mug since before your n-nuts dropped. He wouldn't clown me . . . "

But your eyes don't lie. Stripe shoots you a lizard's leer.

"Ev'rythin all fokked, not'ing right,' Rain Man. Where you been?"

Easy. You been wrapped in a filthy canvas cocoon, high.

"ICE *deportaron a las niñas a la esclavitud, asesinato* . . . back to Guatemala, Honduras. Dey come here, *sexo*, for fat rich gringo foks, cops get tips from Otis Place Brigada where girls sleep, are slaves . . . *mi hermanos mara salvatrucha* doing dirt! Irving an' Georgia Avenue, bro'.

"That's where my fr-friends live . . . Eva and Fred . . . "

He shrugs, like he's expected to know two old blackfolk in assisted housing, then reveals, "Cops rescue dem, but like I say, ICE fokkers send dem right bok to death gang. Other girls, Brigada an' lawyers be hiding dem . . . safe houses *y las iglesias Santuario*. Some girl no' lucky. Dem find in Potomac rocks and waterfall, fake ID, shot in head. People getting *killed,* bro . . . from you hood. ICE no stop it. ICE more like 'referee,' huh . . . *en un partido de fútbol.* Cops figh' *mara salvatrucha,* but ICE no. You *figure,* say dat fat *mayate de Navidad.* So, figure dat."

"Not my business, kid."

"*Serio.* It will be. Me feel the *hechios.* Very bad. *Tía* Carolina— she help cops find girls. *Mujers* say she put spell on ev'rythin. Spells wha' bring even you bok from dead, Rain Man."

And he's up just when Oosterhaus is yelling for you all to gather. Black Santa doesn't look happy.

"Mi na licky-licky wid dis fuckery, dis lie, sar!"

"Sorry but that's it for the day," Oosterhaus says with a phony-ass grin. "So please get in line for your pay, gentlemen. It's been a very productive morning on our, um, maiden voyage, and I guess we'll see you after the New Year . . . "

More curses, mumbling, grumbling . . . but you are a-ok just fondling the baton up your sleeve. Seeing you, the others start to line up. Here comes that green *gwap*, straight from a locked little metal box Diallou produces; the bills are bound pimp-style with a rubber band . . .

Of course, Black Santa won't shut up as he extends a swollen, cut-up hand and gets eleven dollars. A five and six ones per man, for five hours work in cold.

"Jeezum Creema, mon!" Black Santa exclaims.

"Goin' rate is *ten*, Pops," Diallou says with a grin. "Dollah bonus cause a weadda."

"It two dollah busfare from 'ere a fi me get bock St. Jude, den two more where mi lay mi head! Give it 'ere ya pussy-clot guineamon!" and he snatches his king's ransom and grips it greedily.

"Senegal, no Guinea! *Merde!*" And now his jaundiced yellow eyes are staring at you. "Big Dick, *heh.*"

You take the money, fold it into your grimy pocket.

The rest of them are dipping out, with Lil' Roach snickering and Big Roach tossing "Imo choke you" looks. Yet as the coterie of dusty old men wanders away, Oosterhaus nudges forward, a five-dollar bill . . . a whole Happy Meal's or half a Subway Turkey's worth . . . in his pink little hand.

"Mr. Cornish, you are a natural leader, mature . . . diffused the situation with the debtors, your teammates."

"No . . . no sir . . . I-I'm not."

"The one's leaving . . . we don't need their ilk now. How'd you like to take a little detour . . . "

You swallow, very hard at that word.

"Sir . . . I got to just take this money and—"

"I think you are fit for *special* work. Starting today. You want to lead a crew? There's additional money in it, the other men, plus a bonus."

"I-I suppose," you reply, unmanly, still looking everywhere but his gaze, "But . . . "

"Easy-peazy trash-out only, swear to God. Vacant rowhouse owned directly by one of our affiliates with a HUD subsidy. Desirable part of town near the Convention Center."

He points to the truck. He's already got Black Santa, Stripe, Stevie, a couple of others gathered and it must be for real because you see Diallou climb in and idle the van motor, burning that gas that's more precious than you flesh and blood men. Black Santa looks sheepish at you . . . you'd think he'd be thrilled at the prospect of more cash and not paying Metro fare.

Stripe's gesturing with his head, mouthing a word in Spanish. *Hechizo* Magic . . .

"*Okay*," you mumble.

It's as if you bought him a new Saab or Audi, for he balls a fist in hipster delight and plants it on your shoulder despite no permission from you for a touch.

So, the Dodge is capacious, almost an alien vessel when there's only five of you in the back. And suddenly Black Santa's not selling wolf tickets about his money. He's shooting you a thumbs-up and grin with an eleven-dollar Bangladesh wage in his grease-stained pocket.

But that's not what has you mumbling random words to yourself under the alternate wheeze and growl of the engine. You hear Oosterhaus on his mobile phone, seemingly oblivious to both your eavesdropping pose and how his voice carries in a near empty van.

"The ticket's done. Yeah, asset's aboard. I'll keep you posted if he hits something . . . "

And now you wished you'd stayed with Lil' and Big Roach.

CHAPTER 4

Lightning

DIALLOU'S WHISTLING SOME MOTHERLAND TUNE AS he steers down L Street Northwest and turns on 12th . . . and there, among the rentals converted to condos, are the last high-rise apartments the city subsidizes for people like you, so close to glittery downtown.

You remember the halfway house, after the Air Force freak-out . . . that building right there? Half deck of Xanax and a pint bottle of vodka was your version of the evening's martini in the courtyard. And yes, you see the corner store where you terrorized normal folk back when addicts, geriatric winos and hookers were the average customers.

But the bulletproof glass came down and single beers in paper bags were replaced by rosé from Aix de Provence for the Beckies and pale ale for their bro-meister boyfriends. Goodbye salad days! The yuppies got all but a few corners on lock, daring the working gals to come back. Then again, son—they weren't exactly gals, were they? You had friends on the stroll, didn't you? More than a few had Adam's apples and twigs, more than few are in Potter's Field from the deadliest catch . . . the Hi-Five. You tested?

"Once. Nothing."

Hmmm . . . well, Diallou's doing a shitty job parallel parking. You all finally push by him to mill about on the sidewalk. Above, the sky's dim with occasional sunlight clawing through, but the wind's kicked up like frozen razor blades.

"No like dis shit, bro'." Stripe shudders to you. He was pensive at the gas station. He's all-out spooked now. "Me got peoples that was up round dese place. Friend of *mi tio* . . . him get snatched, find him in pieces by *l'aeropuerto. Y mujer* . . . dey say she walk in front of Metrobus. Some say pushed."

Black Santa hears this and editorializes, "Dem MS-t'irteen ragga. Murderers, na propa shottaz . . . "

"Hey fok you ole man. No one talkin' to you . . . "

"Stop," you caution. "It's a trash-out. More . . . more money." Yeah, enough for a four-g of Scooby, maybe Ivanka Crunk; leftover coin'll buy peanut butter for Kate and Princess.

Oosterhaus is trying to get the attention of this tall, jumpy codger with gray peppercorn hair, broad shovel nose, ill-fitting paint-stained black sweatshirt and green work trousers. The man's yelling this into his phone.

"Yo Dez, that you man? Dez, hey man, the General Real Estate folks is here but wiff this shutdown nona HUD folk are at work and I can't get the auth'rization."

"Mr. McFadden?" Oosterhaus is saying to him. "You unlocked the unit . . . owned by our realty affiliate?"

"*Dez*? Nigga call me back . . . um, yeah, yes sir . . . buildin' open but the unit's still locked because Dez—that's Mr. Samara—he supposed to get y'all the okay from HUD, but there ain't HUD paperwork onaccounta the shutdown and no paperwork onaccounta Dez's stupid." He's jingling a huge old-school key ring clipped to the belt loop of trousers curled under by his belly overhang. "Say, y'all don't scare easy do ya?"

Oosterhaus is now feeling the heat of all you all's glower. He gives a nervous chuckle, titters, "Um, well . . . anyone know how to use a crowbar without damaging a door?"

"Lord a mercy," Black Santa scoffs. "Dis fuckery."

Stripe's still hasn't made step toward that place as you whip around to see him gaping up at the second floor . . .

"*Los Muertos,*" he pants, chest pumping. "*No limpiar los hechizos.*" He looks at you now, squinting, shaking his technicolor-coiffed head.

"Sure there's nothing else you w-w-want tell us, Mr. Oosterhaus."

Cracker's showing his true colors, son. Blows out one of those supercilious white man sighs and muses, "Thought you were a leader, Mr. Cornish?" Of course, his eyes are bugging out as if you slapped his mother. "Do you want this money or not? I mean . . . I thought you had the self-control or intelligence to handle instructions and be discrete?"

"These guys are . . . r-reticent . . . "

Mr. Charlie-incarnate huffs, "They, like you, volunteered."

Stripe shouts from the sidewalk. "*Vine aquí porque vivo en la calle . . . no tengo nada!*"

"Okay . . . sorry I was terse, Mr. Cornish . . . *Dickie.* See, you are doing a great service to my company . . . and we will remember this help, fella. We need this apartment . . . *filtered.*"

You hoist an eyebrow like some hobo Vulcan, from your "Star Trek" days in front of the TV. Well you're giving Oosterhaus that same frosty stare from your smudged and hairy face. Illogical.

He's got no choice but to plead, "I swear. Extra *ten bucks* for each of you on top of what you're getting . . . how's that sound? It's Christmas!"

Black Santa looks to you and shrugs, "Money be money."

"Hand me the crowbar," you tell Oosterhaus, and then, "Stripe, *no seas niña . . . vamos!*"

The first-floor landing smells like cooked pork and onions and Lysol; the stairway to the second floor is narrower, winds in a bizarre curve so all of you are ascending single file, slow and deliberate like pith helmeted bwanas in some ancient tomb, with a lumbering McFadden, having some conversation with himself, native pathfinder. He even holds his flashlight like a torch. Oosterhaus brings up the rear.

"PEPCO turnt off the power," McFadden tells him. "I brought this here flashlight and stuff up there cause the tenants, they nailed plywood to the winda frames . . . "

"Why dey do so?" Black Santa whispers.

McFadden chuckles nervously and adds, "I know—thas' fucked up, right?"

"*Dios mio,*" says Steve. And abruptly he and Stripe are pointing at something smeared on the doorjamb, the casings, even the transom above.

"Oh, that's dried-over chicken grease," McFadden reassures you all. "These folk has grease rubbed e'ry dang where. Goin' be a bitch ta scrape off, put some primer down and a lick o'basecoat . . . "

"*K'iche'* . . . " Stripe's suddenly babbling, " . . . *uchben* . . . " And it isn't Spanish.

Takes a few seconds for his words to register, and when they do it's like an ice pick to your nuts. You ask McFadden to sweep the door again with his flashlight beam.

"Fuck . . . *n-no* . . . " you say, eyes darting.

"What's going on?" Oosterhaus calls from the rear.

Black Santa's in on it too, having yanked off his wool cap to expose the Dr. Seuss "Whoville" white tuft of hair on his dome, and he's squinting at these pictograms and circles and dots and outlines of stylized birds and monkeys and jungle cats like he's a pro . . .

"*Obeah* . . . or dem Santería, dem rum-drinking *babalorisha* an' dem *iyalorisha* witches call de *orishas* . . . dem lay curses on who fi come 'ere ta do wrong."

Oh, he's not far off, eh Junior?

"*Stop,*" you hiss, eyelids clenched then open.

Lucky for you Oosterhaus didn't hear. He's on his iPad again, and clearly, he's not buying what you primitives from warm, dark and barbarous climes are selling.

"Let's pop the door please," he exhorts with another breathy sigh as he tap-tap-taps.

A little shaky there at first, but you get that crowbar right in the crease between the case and frame. *Crunch!* The door opens with slow squeal as if in human pain.

"Massi mi Gawd," Black Santa shudders as McFadden aims the Maglite beam into the dusty, rancid void. Then you see his own eyes widen as the flashlight's glow hits the walls.

Like the doorway, the walls are festooned in brown, as if by the finger of a ghost up another ghost's ass. More K'iche words, but now they're more complex than the mess above the door and it's too much for Stripe. He airs out. All you hear are his footsteps on the stairs but not before he cries. "*Tia!*" Auntie . . . ?

Yet the broad, mighty beam illuminates nothing on the floor but ordinary reassuring trash. Reassuring to the others, yeah. Not you and Black Santa.

"Yar t'ink *she* be 'ere onc't? Yar gal? But . . . naw, Dick."

Your girl. Esmeralda. You are caught in a gape so wide the flies in that apartment, buzzing in the dark, could land on your tongue.

"You can read this stuff?" you suddenly hear from Oosterhaus, in the rear with the gear. "Come on, you're the *smart one* . . . like these guys told me . . . "

Time to air, like that punk Stripe. No place for you in there, and yet, maybe it's your affliction answering. Or maybe you pray it's her, calling . . .

"It . . . it's Mayan," you whisper as you enter the darkness, the stench . . .

"*Bruja*," Stevie mumbles in Spanish.

"*Sí . . . bruja . . .* " you mutter.

And with that scary, alien exchange, Oosterhaus punts.

"Okay, uh, gentlemen," he calls, almost cheerily. "Gonna check on Diallou . . . "

He's Audi. One of your crew asks, "D'fuck's all that, then?"

McFadden jumps in with, "These folk cray as bedbugs— here the paperwork wiff the tenant names." Why he's handing this to you, hey—maybe you exude HNIC.

"*Contreras*, Nestor," you read, " . . . *Soloronzano*, Sabine. Man's deported? Woman's deceased?"

"Look, here the real tip: these Spanishes, Dez say they got all kinda conjurer women boilin' and burnin' bushes and shit to keep bad mojo away, sickness away, keep that MS-Thirteen away . . . keep Immigration away . . . keep HUD away. I dunno."

But you do now. You crush the paper into your pocket as bile rises from your gut and into your mouth. And it's not from the rot in the air. You need a wall to prop yourself on, as you're shivering now. Underfoot in the dark, there's only the pushing and shuffling of what sounds like empty cups and half full cereal boxes and spent tissues, broken glass . . . the squish and pop of mouse carcasses in various degrees of decomposition . . .

McFadden catches you in the light. "You aw-right bruh?"
You jerk a nod.

"I'm out. This place sucks."

He escapes, belly and keys jiggling. Yet he leaves you that big bitch of a Maglite.

You're the new torchkeeper, boy. Do your job and maybe the maledictions chewing at your ear, speaking the unspeakable, will go away, right? You illuminate the windows there in the living room. Yes, they are boarded up, nailed from the inside.

The rest of the guys fan out into the shadows with their flimsy green trash bags.

You call to Black Santa, "These . . . are w-words, numbers, letters, phrases . . . the *Popul Vuh*, the creation m-myth. Mixed with modern . . . modern Mayan." He sees your pained face in the meager light now. "These tenants what got bounced . . . they're Central American . . . n-not Mexican . . . "

"'ow so?" Black Santa presses.

"Mayans in Honduras too, Guatemala . . . I can tell. I just . . . can tell."

"You right *hermano*," Stevie adds as he opens his trash bag. "Afraid."

"Ya mon. 'fraid of ICE," Black Santa quips. "An' centipedes an' roaches, dem!"

You grope for a broom with your free hand as the other aims the Maglite. "Over here . . . the myth of the Hero Twins, who challenged evil ones in *Xilbalba* . . . Mayan Hell . . . to a s-s-sacred ball game . . . those symbols, those are the b-b-ball courts at Chichen Itza, Palenque. These are protection hexes."

She taught you well when you weren't fucking and fucking up.

A blaze of light cuts into your eyes. Two of the fellas have ripped a sheet of plywood from the window; they attack one another and the plank crashes to the floor. For an instant the cold is bearable . . . until the hawk claws its way in through the broken panes of glass and you all are choking on frigid particles of lint and dust.

"See mon," Black Santa observes with a chuckle, "jus' garbage. Na witchcraft. N' Esmeralda."

Hearing her name sends you to the kitchen. You spit into the sink and lean there to regroup. Stevie's heading down the hall to rake out the bathroom spoil; the others bag the garbage.

Stevie wakes you from the day-stupor. Your first thought is of a backed-up toilet given the overall timbre of the place.

"No, check it, *hermano* . . . " he mumbles. And he's pointing to one of the two bedrooms.

Metal cots stacked as ersatz bunkbeds and climbing almost to the ceiling. They are so rusty, flimsy that you'd need a tetanus shot just to lay your head. The mattresses are gone, inexplicably, but the lingering smell's enough to make the stretched canvas beds at St. Jude's seem sumptuous, inviting.

On the floor are empty feminine napkin boxes, spent cartons of powdered baby formula. A pink pacifier. Another binky, this one caked with dust and a stained cloth elephant doll affixed to its base. You hear a fly buzzing.

Then, a squadron of them, and Stevie's screaming in Spanish and the stench hobbles you. Black Santa waddles in just as you aim the beam and there is a living writhing, wriggling, buzzing mound of generations of flies and maggots, each feasting on what looked to be a loaded disposable diaper, then dying, then in turn supplying meat for the next generation.

But as Black Santa gasps and snorts, the cheer baton, freshly scavenged this morning, slides from your sleeve. With it, you poke at the mound, and out of the syrupy, crusty filth comes whats look like hospital-grade bandages and tape gauze dressings . . . and a set of little wrist bones, a tiny radius, and an ulna. Nothing you hard and ragged men haven't seen before in a basement of a vacant rowhouse, in the dregs of a Dumpster, wrapped in rags against a rusty chain-link fence in a fetid alley. It's not a thing unless you make it a thing, so you don't make it a thing.

"Lard, 'ow many gals, babies, yar t'ink be hidin'?"

"Dozens," you whisper. Guess one or more didn't make it.

"Hey . . . *mira, hay más* . . . " Stevie adds as you and the elf file out. "Lotta shit for *niños* . . . kid vitamins . . . coughing shit, pills expired years ago so maybe they take from old people . . . all up in the bathroom . . . bathroom all tore up for demo, maybe?"

"So?"

"Yeah but this thing was on the floor, bro . . . "

Even in the refuge of the natural light you still can't believe what he's handing you.

Card stock. Ecru, stiff. A watermark and utterly alien to this mess.

Oh, so you remember your mother's fancy-ass stationery; this stuff is even more fine, right? Come on, Junior, you'd spy on her, and steal her first and second drafts from the rubbish to guess what was between the lines of the neat boring nothings she'd write, then cross-out. Say it: she wished she'd married one of the high yella ROTC or Annapolis niggas, or a dentist, or lawyer. Not your *toad* of a dad . . .

Richard, I am sorry I disappoint you as a wife and have been backsliding. I anticipate this evening you are at the Sergeants' Mess for "chow" but you might still be hungry for a meal so there is meat-loaf and fries, carrots in the fridge. I will comport myself better. I will make sure the children do not back-talk you nor eye-ball you, as is proper . . .

Black Santa nudges you awake. "Wot's dat?"

Stevie shrugs and muses, "Trippy, huh? All in the bathroom. And check this out."

Yeah, the callused ridges of your thumb can sense the embossed letters: *Casa de la moneda de la República de México, Banco Nacional . . .*

. . . but he's popping something just as alien in your free hand: the most jenkty nasal spray injector you've ever seen . . . got the shape of everything nurses or EMTs have shot up your beak to clear the snot or save your life. And this gadget's got a metal body, like a cannister . . . looks like the CO_2 tubes powering your BB air pistol as a kid, back when boys played with manly toys. There's a bar code sticker on it. A final hiss and the thing's spent, though there's something familiar about the taste and smell of the residue on your fingertip.

The big brain, no matter how addled, is kicking in for sure.

"Esteban, give this shit to LaKeisha . . . got on sc-scarf and cornrow braids and always at the computers, Shaw Library on Rhode Island and Seventh . . . every day, ev-every damn day till they kick her out. Say Dickie Cornish needs her. Say 'Jon Snow from the North, he put it in the TARDIS.' I know it s-sounds *loco* but she likes that crazy shit."

"Dick, *jeezum creema* . . . " Black Santa scoffs and he tries to tug you away.

Your fierce look backs him off and you finish with, "Jon Snow. TARDIS, *comprende?* Tell her I need to know what this thing is. It d-don't fit here. Don't forget, man. *Por favor . . .* "

Stevie's nodding and pocketing the device, and he watches as intently as Black Santa is fidgety and clowning when you flip that fine piece of card stock over.

On the reverse side you all see someone's gentle, almost fastidious curlicues of ink, with a message more succinct than your dithering mother could ever produce: "*No más. No mi sigas.*"

And the hairs on your neck rise like before a lightning strike.

CHAPTER 5

From Grandpappa

"*THIRD STREET TUNNEL AT I-395 CLOGGED due to police activity
. . .* " comes over commercial radio station's traffic and
weather. The unit's two-way, however, is crackling with, "*Copy
that, T456, just drop him at Howard U. Hospital or Medstar cause
GWU and Sibley say please no more . . . or from your twenty you're
closer to St. Jude's shelter, L and Half Street, Southwest.*"

"Ten-four." The black lady cop signs off and turns to look at
you. "See what y'all did?"

The traffic breaks and the white female driving hits the
siren to get the rest of the chumps out of the way.

The white cop declares, "You injured, you need methadone? What's today's date? Tell us and my partner will take
off the cuffs."

"Esmeralda Rubio. She's . . . *here*. Apartment . . .
bathroom . . . "

You're lucky you got MPD finding you wandering like a big
black wraith, and two women gendarmes at that. Trump's
crew would've put you down like a whimpering stray.

"Never mind . . . I wanna go home."

"Was' yo' name, baby?" the black cop asks.

49

"R-Richard Elias C-Cornish, Junior, ma'am."

"I *know* you, sweets," she says to you after some quick glances in the broad rearview mirror. "I seen you at Smithsonian Metro Station this past summer, though . . . *uh-huh*, acting a fool, then you passed out. The tech gives you a whiff of Narcan and you was right as rain, singin' Catholic choirboy songs . . . "

"Wasn't me."

"Right." She and the whitegirl cop exchange glances, then she follows with, "We think you're better off at St. Jude's rather than the hospital."

Last thing you need is Father Phil, Brother Karl-Maria, Sister Maria-Karl . . . and Verna. Maybe Verna, but—that would be a sin.

"Con . . . Constitution and Ninth . . . please . . . please."

The Explorer halts in front the museum. They pull your big ass out, uncuff you just as wind-lashed battalions of snow flurries descend. The flakes sting your face like delicate white gnats, then die on the filthy wet pavement. They climb back in, laughing.

The black cop jokes, "Shoot him full of anti-psychotics but not so much that he can't get it up . . . fumigate him . . . a shower and shave and trip to Men's Warehouse and cologne and some root canal and he's at the Park on Fourteenth . . . *girl*, you know me!"

They get a call, the blue and red lights of the cherry tops flash and off they go.

No way they'd blue-Uber you to where you really want to be . . . for escape, for refuge. You got real cash in your pocket so the first thing you do is hail a red cab. By law they got to stop. This one sees the green and does so, and you tell the dude darker than you with all his Coptic trinkets hanging like the stuff in your tent "Southwest." He's cool because it's all tighty-whitey down there these days and you have ten buck fare plus one.

Not like before, eh, *sapo*? Like when civilization ended at a McDonald's parking lot, and the cops'd rather pick up dates there than bug you while you based and sniffed. Nothing around but underground dance-clubs for queers and dykes, titty bars, gloomy brick or faux-stucco housing projects . . . you used to call the pioneer yuppies and EPA workers down there "volunteer victims."

Now it's Oz's Emerald City . . . a frontier to cross from St. Jude's to your boy Croc . . .

Marion Barry may have been reigning sovereign back in the day, but Croc was the hereditary young prince of everything discreditable down there, from the pee-wees pickpocketing the leathernecks on liberty to the jezebels selling nickel bags and punanny in the ladies room at Hogates and the Channel Inn . . . and not too many folk on the Anacostia Flats knew that Croc was the pulling guard in Catholic school when you all would run the fake power sweep . . . the white boy QB would take the snap . . . student body left . . . he'd rear up as you monster by a linebacker then pop out in the flat. Croc'd mow the sucker down; the QB would let the ball fly and you'd catch it wide open . . . poetry!

Bet your ass the nuns and priests in the bleachers knew who Croc's daddy was, though. Yet Croc still got expelled for beating down kids who ran their mouths. Mother moved back down south; his dad the King died in prison, put away by scum who suck Trump's kneecaps and claim his own crimes ain't crimes. The Prince's empire is now down to one half of a ramshackle duplex. The other half's being gutted for a celebrity chef's new spot in the Nation's Capital.

Croc's still quite a sight, though: black leather pants barely containing his big ass, black tee shirt with his belly peeking through. Black faux gator-skin version of an Aussie slouch hat, ringed with more teeth. Walking stick inlaid with even *more* teeth. *Real* gator-skin ankle-high boots, tipped in chrome.

His sister brushes by you on her way to work and you recall her hot little self when she was a ghetto debutante. Today she's five feet tall, five feet wide, mottled skin . . . taking care of a grandchild who by all clues is asleep in a crib upstairs with only great-uncle Croc as sitter.

But Trouble Funk's popping that Go-Go on his now ancient stereo. It rescues you from your inner terror and outer fiending just enough to get you that beat-feet like it was 1986, and the sight of you doing so coaxes laughs from Croc so hard he wheezes and coughs his mirth into your face as you embrace . . . which is a struggle thanks to that belly of his. With a laugh, you both collapse on the sofa where Croc watches *The Price is Right.*

You hear the baby cry and Croc grunts himself off the sofa, labors up the stairs. You're next hearing Croc making cutesy baby sounds to calm the child; he's back down, cradling the infant, and you gape. Not over the irony that he makes baby sounds but that he's able to carry the child, his walking stick and a plastic container of product without tumbling down the steps.

"*Kill,* man . . . ya look bad, like you seent a ghost, so Imogiveya ten-g, *gratis.* Need skins? And I got a nice lighter that lights even in wind, rain."

"Got one myself. I'm good."

"Ain't none of us good, moe. Was' upwidchew?"

"She's callin' me."

"Aw Dickie shit . . . stop that."

"Real live . . . *today*."

He sways the restive infant as you begin to weep. And then his own tears fall like he knows you can't wait such is the pain. He's pointing to a door, ajar, leading to the cellar.

"Cot down there, moe. Handle your business. Let yourself out."

And you sing "*Scooby Dooby Doo*" upon that first draw. Only takes one puff to glass your eyes. You whisper another name, "M-Marguerite."

Oh, you want to pick a fight, huh, with that picture congealing in your dome . . . the black catsuit you saw her wear like the pinktoe in the old British spy show . . . her prancing around to her stacks of Fifth Dimension 45s . . . *Stoned Soul Picnic . . . Working on a Groovy Thing* . . . doin' that ole fruge and watusi with you and your pale sister in your pajamas! More fun, born higher than your liver-lipped, dark-skinned, no-college-having daddy, eh?

But guess what? *Esme's still calling,* and even the K isn't exorcising her. So you pray to Benedetto and Mister Fred, who showed how scrounge and lash discarded curtain rods and a broken old folding deck chair and other useless shit, Junior! Nah, she's got you, and Croc's Kush is weak, only tick above ground basil sprayed with Glade Air-freshener. *No más . . .*

. . . and you're back to sucking Tina out of Esme's glass pipe, and she'd have her feet in the air with you on top. You'd nut and the chemicals'd take over, keeping you grinding and when she came, she'd turn into the *Vucub-Caquix*, bird demon of the Maya Hell. Make a conventional niggas's dick shrink, eh? But not you. You were about the show. *Apres*-sex, when most couples are sipping wine, or plain sleeping, she'd trade a deck. The Xanny'd take effect and she'd babble in Spanglish about her crazy boho little sister Marta who crushed on you, right? Marta was *Ixtap,* goddess of suicide, with the noose charm around her throat . . .

. . . but the frost stabs your lungs, coughs split your sternum . . . your toes no longer ache because they are numb.

Whoa.

This is no hallucination or ruined high. This *ain't* Croc's cellar.

You've just been tossed off the Number Seventy by a fearful driver . . . Convention Center and Seventh Street and you don't remember how you got there. It's only four blocks to that building and mumbling, staggering, you home in on it like a pigeon.

Not a human soul is present. Your eyes acclimate to the dim ambient light from the street, and you discern one practical reason why security's so lax. Glossy posters . . . plastered after you ran, no doubt. The place is to be gutted down to its oak beams . . . soon to be smoked glass and steel and hammered tin and brushed chrome, with any surviving Mayan glyphs buried under coats of matte *ecru.* The lofts are to be christened, "The Marvin," for native son Marvin Gaye.

Even that hellish room smells of primer, scrubbed of the remnants of the child, as if it had never been born.

You shine your little light down the hallway to the bathroom. No stench, just a thick chemical odor that chews your nostrils.

As you enter the bathroom there's a rustling sound beyond the reach of your light. Then high-pitch noises, like the colicky gripes and nasally squeals of homeless toddlers and babies once huddled there.

Another step, more rustling, squealing, another step, they stop . . . as if something is listening for you. With your foot you push the door wider. The mildewed sliding shower door is off the tracks, shattered into forbidding daggers of glass . . .

. . . and a sooty gray and white cat appears, carrying a squirming, near naked kitten in its mouth by the nape. You pivot and aim the flashlight toward the tub, from where it appeared. Wriggling in the filth and rust are a handful of other kittens, newly born from the smears of blood and withered umbilici.

"What'd you c-c-call it, Esme?" you mull aloud. "All these families hide papers, cash. 'Auntie stash.' *Aja de Tía . . . fuerta . . .* "

You look at the medicine cabinet as the mama cat transports the last of her children, keeping an eye on you. The medicine cabinet's the *first* place your fellow scavengers search when raiding an evicted tenant's home. Yet no one looks behind it.

You're Number Eighty-Eight again, sinew straining as you tear the cabinet out, and mama cat's staring at you with glowing eyes from the darkness as if to say, "*Bingo.*"

A small metal box sits on the joist, covered in drywall dust and ancient plaster. With a *click-clack* your thumb trips the latch.

A heavy, smaller case falls out. Sumptuous red leather.

"M-Miss Kitty," you whisper to your audience, "I'm not a bad person, I'm no loser."

You flip the small catch and raise the lid.

Embedded in a red felt mold are gold coins . . . eight of them. *Estados Unidos Méxicanos—República de México, Banco Nacional* . . . an eagle with the serpent on one side, "heads." "Tails" . . . a soccer player? What? Or a soccer ball and Mayan and Aztec glyphs . . . *Copa Mundial de Futbol,* 1986 . . .

The paper, *Rain Man*—read the printed leaf inside. "Nineteen Eighty-Six *monedas de oro* . . . World Cup . . . "

And out falls a piece of card stock identical to the one crumpled in your pocket. Same texture, same watermark. Different handwriting in faded ink.

"*Mi pequeño hombre, Jaime . . . una vida dorada está por delante de ti . . .* Happy tenth birthday, Jaime . . . *y oda mi amor . . .* Grandpappa."

You remove the other card and read it again . . . in English. "*No more. Leave me be. I can't take it*"

And then you run. You run gasping in that dogshit language of shame, "*Ave Maria, gratía p-plena, Dominus te-tecum. Benedicta tu in mulieribus . . .* " Your legs and feet are on fire with pain. There's only one safe place to hide this, to hide yourself.

CHAPTER 6

Fool's Gold

REMEMBER THE LAST TIME SHE WAS here with you, at Miz Eva's and Mister Fred's? Their housewarming, basically. Approved for assisted housing in this spanking new hi-rise above the rowhouse hovels along Georgia Avenue. The ofays despised it as it reminded them of the projects in every old Seventies movie about the Bronx or Cabrini Green, but it was nice, with good people, working people, even hipsters, and Esmeralda bought the *Rioja*, from her Mexico, not the usual peach Alizé Eva once swilled, chasing the pills and weed, or the Manischewitz for Fred that the Taliban peddled up before these white goo-goos made them take down the Plexiglass, stop single-servings to go.

Only you and Esme drank that night, recall? Couldn't even respect the old folk's sobriety. But you looked good, first time since they booted you from the Air Force, after you ruined college. Decent clothing from Marshall's. A bath and shave . . .

. . . you're clutching the red case of coins from Grandpappa to Jaime at your breast as you skulk past the guard, jump on an elevator and up three floors. Maybe the guard remembers you from when you stayed there on the sofa, the same sofa you and your Esme sat on together, celebrating. Maybe Eva's vacuuming it, as no one answered the buzzer.

Maybe Eva's in the john, as no one's answering the knock. Maybe Fred is coming back from the trash chute, as you realize the door is open . . .

Poor Miz Eva. She couldn't truly scream. Throat polyps. Impossible for her to wail for help. Not much over five feet tall, less than a buck dripping wet . . . hard to see someone that puny facing down the Devil, putting up a fight. And the Devil went and bashed in Miz Eva's skull with the kitchen fire extinguisher . . . and you are wheezing rather than screaming as the blood is still warm, metallic . . . her eyes are shut, yet her nostrils are red and raw and you skitter away . . . only to find Fred . . . his face a shade of purple, his tongue and eyes, magenta.

The Devil'd wrapped an extension cord around his neck.

You cover your mouth with both blood-steeped hands, not just to warrior-down the puke but to stifle your scream. And if your fingers are on your face they aren't laying your prints everywhere. But they've been everywhere. These ole motherfuckers are your heart. The heart that's about to bust your sternum . . . the heart that's pumping the Kush molecules to your brain, and telling that brain you came to rob these old people, and killed them onaccount they'd righted their own lives and had enough of saving yours.

That's what the cops will say.

And you don't bother to see if their Social Security and SSI stash behind the microwave is intact.

No, you save your howling for the night and get the fuck out and keep your face twisted away from the hallway cameras and keep your bloody hands inside your coat . . . along with that blood-red leather box of gold.

You are stumbling through the garage, yes, spilling out onto Kenyon Street . . . and you fall smack into the yard of a darkened row house, windows boarded up just like the one that gifted you a baby's bones and coins and Esme's words. Tattered police tape flutters in the frigid, wet night wind around the gate; a memorial of dead flowers under fresh ones piles up at the fence. *For the girls trafficked*, a wet, faded poster says in Spanish, *and held as slaves, then dumped as garbage by these men* . . . and there are glued pictures of Trump and officious white faces. Finally you vomit, as no one would look for your DNA there.

Keep yourself in the alleys and on Sherman Avenue, boy. Cut over to Georgia only at the last moment. After the cab all that's left of Oosterhaus' cash is enough for a Metro card, one way. You need an angel to fight the Devil . . . and yet each face on the subway looks like a hobgoblin's. The Metro cops prance on cloven hooves . . .

. . . and yet you collapse not to St. Jude's vestibule, but SFME and you shout for the guard to find Verna. Of course, Verna. Appearing under an umbrella against the alternating raindrops and snow flurries. A seraph in a simple gray knit dress, leggings, gumshoes.

Sobbing, on your knees, you crumple onto her and she doesn't even gasp when she sees the blood.

"*Shush* . . . I'll call Father Phil . . . your friend Mr. Cockburn . . . Fitz Cockburn . . . *Santa*? He's got a bed there for the night. The nun's'll get him . . . "

"Don't wanna talk to him!" you cry.

Verna shakes her umbrella dry as you enter sets of sliding doors buzzed open by the guards. You immediately catch the aroma of butter and garlic, heard the clink of cutlery on plates and murmur of people made safe. That's not for you, boy. Not anymore.

Rather she steers you to her office, but not before you pass the larder they call "Ft. Knox." The vault-like door is ajar as staff is retrieving supplies for the babies and baby-mommas and slackers under Verna's care.

Again, it's something as simple and lovely as dinner for the hungry. You're damned: it's not for you. Your treasure's in a cursed box in the folds of your ratty parka. That stuff in there's for the meek and innocent, from bins of barrettes, cartons of toothpaste, pallets of baby formula, to drawers of lice killer. Verna's got to know your jigsaw brain had cracked the code and you'd been raiding the place for Princess and Kate. You'd be back in an MPD unit now, in chains, if she didn't . . .

. . . and so you sit under a blanket, shivering until your molars chatter as you watch Verna kick off her gumshoes and slip into some summer-looking canvas kicks. You catch a flash of bare feet, bright painted toes.

"Um . . . that c-c-color polish . . . Brits call it v-v-varnish . . . that's vermillion, not scarlet."

She shoots you cocked head and replies, "'Bright Cinnabar.'"

"Th-They used to make it from c-cinnabar nineteenth century. The pigment."

She sits at her desk and says with razor earnest, "Just stop. The blood . . . it wasn't yours. But the nurse tells me your BP and pulse are going to stroke you out."

You eye the electric carafe on her credenza and meekly beg for hot coffee.

She fires back, "You look like you dug yourself out of a buried coffin so this can't be plain ole withdrawal . . . "

"*N-No . . .* "

"Then what the hell have you gotten yourself into?"

Don't faggot out now, Junior. Maybe you did kill them. Maybe the coins are imaginary. You're having a conversation with the thin air now, aren't you? *Ha*! If you turn on the spigot of snot and tears, even the cops might buy a hey I blacked-out dodge!

"Mr. Lahiere next door, who works for Father Phil, Brother Karl-Maria and Sister Maria-Karl . . . and those names are a trip might I say . . . he emailed me. Says Fitz, who y'all call 'Santa Claus,' watched you freak out, tear out of an apartment screaming about an 'Esme.' I called this company who exploits you all and they couldn't locate any 'Jay Oosterhaus,' nor would they confirm you were working this morning."

"C-C-Can you keep a *secret*?" you heave up.

She produces a red box on her desk. Your eyelids splay and she whispers. "Is this the secret? Gold coins. Gold, Dickie. Did you steal it? Did you hurt someone . . . the blood?"

"I-I need your help."

That's why normal folk don't trust bums or addicts, boy. Reality shifts: you all lie or omit. She hits a button on her desk phone, sighs and says, "My parents, school friends and such always drill me: why do you do it? Why do you care? It's not even about Trump declaring war on us, us who are different, or on the fringe. See, *you* are society's canary in the mine. The survivors, the scavengers . . . and if you perish, the rest of aren't far behind. That is why I do this, honey. Self-preservation."

You are wracked with chills and yet still won't tell her about Eva and Fred. How long before that backfires?

There's a male voice on the speaker and Verna acknowledges with, "Frank, buzz Mr. Lahiere over at St. Jude's," then she adds, "We need a form B-four-A for a referral to Father Rufini or Brother Karl or Sister Karl whatever . . . yeah we can do the paperwork if they authorize the bed, a locker and supplies for Mr. Cornish. Then come in here . . . "

"The . . . the coins, were in that apartment," you admit. "D-Didn't house them. But they mean something. Something scary and all's I-I wanted to do was st-stash 'em for a bit."

"Where—here?"

Your big moment? "Nah, with my friends." And? "Uh . . . m-maybe you can find out more . . . what they are, who they m-might belong to . . . "

"And who's 'Esme?'"

"You got my 'file.' Gotta mention it in there somewhere."

Your voice winds down like an ancient clock as Frank, a big Latino with nerd glasses, knocks and comes into the office.

"Mr. Lahiere'll find some clothes that fit. Let's go."

"I'll take of this," Verna says, pointing to the box. "You can't do a damn thing until you are clean and clear-headed. Don't worry . . . "

Ha!

Frank gives you a small premixed cup of fruit and yogurt and a paper cup of hot tea. Mr. Lahiere, as short and squat as Frank is tall and lean, arrives from St. Jude's and takes you after Frank assures him you've been checked for wounds, creepy-crawlies . . . your mouth and keister inspected for whatever will fit.

On the St. Jude's side, there in the spartan barracks, you're on a bench and beside you there's a pair of draws, hopefully your size. A towel, washcloth, powder for your prurient skin, a bar of glycerin soap and disposable flipflops . . . though you don't want anyone repulsed by the sight of your battered toes.

Lahiere hands you a tube from SFME's larder—same unguent you steal for Princess, to salve your scalp after washing out the shampoo . . .

. . . yes, the locker room and showers haven't changed. Burnt orange tile walls and floors . . . rusty fixtures leftover from the Fifties. The place seems clean, though—smells of Clorox and Lysol and Lestoil.

In the shower, the almost scalding water has an iron taste to it, like Eva and Fred's blood, yet for a few minutes you let it wash the sight of their bodies into the gurgling drain.

Lahiere comes in with the sharps as you stand naked and cleansed. He hooks up the electric trimmer. No black barber is he, but your head feels lighter! He sweeps that matted hair on the floor into a whisk scoop, then leads you to a sink of steaming water, hands you scissors, loads an old school safety razor. Single double-edged blade. Plastic razors just gave prurient bumps to men unaccustomed to hygiene. A nick or two later, a douse of cold water and splash of cheap medicine-scent aftershave and you search the mirror.

It's you. It isn't you.

There's a female voice outside the door, penetrating the wet funk being sucked away by a laboring exhaust fan. It's a nun . . . one of the little novices the men leer at not so much because they are young, but because they are all Brazilians. In her accent, she reminds Lahiere to take written inventory of the sharps.

She also tells him to give you the correct wristband and soon he's snapping a red one with white trim on you. Not to celebrate Christmas. It means homeless substance abuser. Green trim: psychosis or defect that would have nominated you for a hospital ward back when there were adequate hospital wards. Need both? Red, no stripe, means garden variety hobo derelict. Black Santa always gets red, no stripe.

Lahiere hands you some high-water khakis and a wrinkled button-up shirt, looks you up and down, as does Frank when he peeks in. The only things you note are their gaping mouths. You are human again. For at least a few hours . . .

. . . and the nun's a pretty little thing with bronze skin, bright eyes and white teeth, an upturned nose. Like the friars in there, she's wearing sandals in wintertime. In broken English she says your cot is in C-row, number nine.

"*Muito obrigado*," you answer. Yes, you know Portuguese. Yet you can't tie your own shoes.

The common room is a cavernous spot that was once the undercroft of the original church's nave, with low ceiling beams and plenty of tables, chairs, two beat-up sofas and a large flatscreen TV. Like a frat's club room for hobos.

Black Santa's playing checkers with Stevie.

"*Qué tienes?*" you call.

Stevie rises, big smiles, but it's Black Santa who rushes you, tears running down his mole-dotted cheeks. He strokes your clean face, fingers your cropped and combed hair.

"Lard Jesus be t'anked . . . mi worry, bredrin!"

And then you shove him away. "We gotta talk. You and me have a *pr-problem* . . . "

The elf's shoulders sink, he skulks away just as Stevie and a couple of cats mob you, pat your back.

As the robed turnkeys watch like prison hacks Stevie quips, "*Tu chica LaKeisha—esta muy loca. Orale.*" He hands you a scrap of notebook paper. "She say she got some friend who do drug testing. She says call her soon."

LaKeisha's scrawl's almost indecipherable but you pick out the main points, reading aloud. "*Intra-nasal actuator . . . Israeli d-design but no FDA.*" Cannister pressurized . . . no pump-mech needed . . . actuator feed. How would something like this be with refugees, illegals?

Stevie muses, "Yeah it ain't *chafa* it hi-tech . . . but you have to hol' my ass down if you gonna stick this up my nose."

Yeah.

You see Frank waving. Verna wants you back on the SFME side. You nod, yet move to Black Santa, who's buried his head in his veiny blue-black hands at the checkers table.

"Yar 'ate mi so . . . " comes his muffled, weepy voice.

"I-I just want the truth." Ah, good boy! You demand in others what you can't show yourself. You'd have made a good officer! "She was there, man. Esme. No doubt, no c-c-coincidence. I got high, I went back. *Found* something . . . " He raises his head, locks his wet pinkish eyes with yours. Now your eyes water, your mouth gums up more than usual. You want to scream and embrace this fat silly motherfucker yet still you don't trust him.

"Mi neva 'urt yar, Dick."

You lean close to his ear. "But . . . you got me put on that truck . . . they were looking for me, right? Just say it."

He won't. He averts his eyes quickly, yet gropes your forearm, squeezes tight.

That's how he wants it? That's how you're going have to leave it because Frank's pressing you. As Frank leads you away, Black Santa stands and repeats, "Mi na 'urt yar, Dick . . . promise. Mi show yar, mi prove mi'self."

You follow Frank back to Verna's office, pulse throbbing in your temples.

Odd. She's a bit more at ease—no interrogation face, no dire vibe. Indeed, she shoos Frank out and tells him to close the door, pauses so there's no eavesdropping.

"*My God.* Dickie Cornish . . . your feet are busted but you look . . . like life can begin again. If I was *that kinda bitch* I'd take a pic and post it."

"I-I have something to tell you. I want to talk to . . . the police."

"Hold up. These coins . . . "

"Not about the coins. Verna, listen . . . "

"Dickie calm down. It's not bad. It's *good.*" She removes her reading glasses and smiles at you. "I did some Google searches . . . and you're lucky people are working late, answering their own phones. On the *real* . . . this gentleman from the Mexican Cultural Institute, Mr. Diaz-Soames, answered my email like I was his guardian angel . . . and he wants to see you, immediately. The series numbers on those coins make them among the first struck, purest gold content! Probably in the initial batch offered to oligarchs and *junta* types."

You shut your eyes.

"Meaning, honey, this batch is worth . . . ready? Ten grand, if not more." She rocks in her chair. "Talk about urban legends! He wants to thank you. He's talking about rewards and such from the person, some bigshot, who actually lost these things. That's how critical, how valuable they are . . . "

And Esme cursed them. *No más.*

"We'll drive over in the morning. He said there's a garage in the building"

"W-We?

She nods. "You've been in this thing called an automobile before, huh? We drive residents to appointments, usually medical and psychiatric or legal, all the time. Besides, I'm the boss-lady. I'll let Brother Karl-Maria know right now. I'm sure Rufino will okay it."

You swallow hard.

"Dickie, with a reward . . . money . . . you can fix yourself up. Refer Miss McCarthy and Miss Goins to some real treatment and housing. Do what your friends, Eva and Fred did—make it out. Live productively. You found, literally, *a gold mine . . .* "

You shrink in that office chair to the size of a crumb, though she's looking right at you. Hey, you bee-lined straight here for sanctuary. You could have wandered back to Croc's, for absolution. Smoke till you die and it'd all be done.

You're a fool for forgetting option three. Run, again. Might be too late.

CHAPTER 7

Reward

IT'S BRIGHT AND SUNNY, FOR A change. Not warm enough for Verna to drop the ragtop on her Cooper Mini, but the yellow beams coax many penned-up folk to the street for last-minute Christmas shopping despite the shutdown, the purges. The friars gave you a scarf and a threadbare corduroy blazer, a gray scarf, gym socks, cheap prison kicks. You look like a zooted professor, but you are clean. Yet the comfort is discomfiting.

Then the all-Christmas all-the-time station on the car stereo breaks for news and weather.

. . . the Wizards beat the Pistons, in NBA pre-season, One-oh-four to ninety-nine . . . and, moving to the homicide of an elderly couple in the Park View neighborhood of Columbia Heights of D.C., a Metropolitan Police Department spokesperson announced this evening that they have received numerous anonymous tips yet will not confirm that they've collected other evidence at the scene. Eva Boudreaux, age sixty-nine, and Fredrick Cross, age seventy-four, were found dead in their apartment by their caseworker. Police say there was no forced entry, but a small television and some cash were missing from the premises . . . now the weather for National Capital Region, brought to you by Subaru . . .

You were wild eyed and terrified, but damned if the TV and cash were "missing."

And you are glad she's out of the car, dashing in for coffee and pastries at her toney spot on toney Fourteenth Street. You remember that block for the strip clubs, and tales of epic brawls between swabbies and leathernecks, or when the two joined forces against the local spooks. Verna edges through the packs of babbling young white shoppers and climbs in.

Immediately you insist, "I wanna get out . . . "

"Here's your coffee. Let me see your eyes? Cravings . . . withdrawal?"

She's almost like your mother or Alma busy-bodying you and throw up your hands.

"What's your problem?"

"Take me back."

"Listen . . . I thought that went well. Are you nervous we're on some date, though you're going to be a wealthy man, soon? I'm glad you and *Senor* Diaz-Soames had the military in common . . . his air force and yours?"

"*Huh?*" you snap. "I-I got into the Air Force after I lost my football and academic sc-scholarships."

"Wild blue yonder!" she gushes. "And your dad . . . he's a Marine . . . gunnery sergeant? Became sergeant-major? That's a great achievement."

Thank you, sweet thing . . . .

"Whatever. I wasn't an officer. Ten years and barely got to E-Four. I-I was good at . . . puzzles, pr-problems, categorizing, though. They'd put me in a r-room with satellite and aerial recon stuff . . . first Somalia, Sudan . . . then Iraq, Afghanistan.

I'd tell them what it is. If friendly, they'd leave it be. If not . . . they'd fuck it up. All on my word. Like God."

Why don't you tell her the rest? After you tell her the best . . .

"Well, Diaz-Soames didn't even get mad when you kept badgering about K'iche Maya and this Nester Contreras who got deported, and Sabine Soloranzano . . . killed by a freakin' bus? I mean, yeah they looked the other way 'cause these two were running some sanctuary city hostel . . . "

"It was filthy . . . it was a cattle-car . . . "

" . . . but how could he have known they were both working for the Consulate as janitors?"

"Because *he* works for the Consulate. Please let's *go* . . . "

The Cooper peels away from the curb and you aren't touching the coffee. She can tell your mind's going in a dozen directions and shit, it's only a matter of time before the news re-loops.

"I like the way he shut you down about the stuff you said was scrawled on the apartment," Verna quips at you. "How the folk magic's stronger than the *narco trafficante* power and the smuggling *coyotes*, because 'hope is stronger.' You ought to listen to that . . . "

Now you're lunching. *"El Patron,"* you mumble.

She's headed over to Sixteenth then downtown. "That was the grandfather. The guy who bought the gold coins as a birthday present. Love the way he said the name: 'Don Porfirio Max Bracht-Hernandez' Banker, timber interests from the Yucatan to Guatemala, to Honduras. He was their Ambassador to Guatemala for three years in the Seventies, Ambassador to Honduras for one in the Eighties. And I had no clue how many of these mugs were German. 'Argentine-German,' but I like how Diaz-Soames says, the 'good' kind, pre-Second World War, and how he loved the 'natives' and *mestizos* alike, ha!"

It's ticking, boy. Feel it? The roadside mine, the booby trap bomb, that is you. And she's running her mouth, all gooey, that you look and smell like a proper man. You're sweating now, fiend. Feel it?

"But look at you, man. I was taken back when he said who the little boy was but damn . . . Jaime Bracht? Or . . . " she's exhaling slowly, " . . . *Jaime Max Bracht-Reyes Gonzalez*," using the "H" sound for the "J" in Jaime. "Had to Google him right there and I felt like such a ditzy girl, too. Just recalled his pic in *Capital Style* and *Washingtonian* in the beauty shop . . . giant house on the river in McLean, ranch at his hometown in Texas . . . hunting cabin, up in Pennsylvania."

You break from your creepy trance to add, as if a computer yourself, "Secretary of Homeland S-Security. Resigned three years ago . . . to run a pr-private equity fund. Import-Export Bank of the Unites States and Trade Representative under Obama but Trump referred to him as 'my Pitbull.'"

She giggles and says, "How do you go from the President's boy and token Latino racking and stacking his own people . . . to, Lord, what did he Tweet? 'The Frito Bandito' and good riddance? What on earth's that?"

"Cartoon pitch-man for Frito-Lay . . . p-potato and corn chips," answers the jigsaw puzzle brain. "Verna . . . I'm scared."

Even a quick glance at the stoplight at L shows you sweating. Glistening.

"A woman I knew. Got me turnt, derailed m-my life . . . she must've known Jaime Bracht. It wasn't these Soloranzano people who stole the coins. It was her. Her handwriting. And she's Ixchel's jaguar . . . "

"What the *fuck*, Dickie . . . "

"'Protector.' Witchcraft . . . "

"Dickie, this foolishness is not helping."

"She's back. Five years and she's back and I know she knew I could find her . . . "

"Shit!"

Verna takes a hard left onto L, the little car skids to a halt at a fire hydrant after a chorus of angry horns and curses.

"You have to take me to the p-police."

"Why?"

"Because Mizz Eva and Mister Fred are dead. I saw . . . bodies. Fresh. Was gonna stash the coins there. Bracht's coins. That blood . . . was their's." You cup your hands to your face and shout into them, startling her, *"Wasn't a robbery . . . news lies . . . and now everything's sucking together all at once, Verna . . . "*

Verna hits the blinkers. Touches your shoulder. "What happened to you, Dickie?"

"Maybe this is what I'm sus-supposed to be."

"You have an education . . . family and—"

"And all that put me on the street. Alone. If it wasn't Esme who turnt me it'd be someone else . . . "

"File says your father is still alive. Soldiers and Sailors Home?"

"It's 'Armed F-Forces Retirement Home and Hospital.' And he's a vegetable."

"Um . . . siblings?"

"Alma. She committed suicide. Years before my m-mother died."

"Um . . . oh, oh Dickie . . . I'm . . . so sorry . . . "

"Wanna hear the story? It's better than Eva and Fred. Better than these cursed coins! Yeah, Alma went to the girls' school af-affiliated with my boys' Catholic school. So smart, so pretty. Looked like Mom . . . you shoulda seen Mom and her. I mean, Halle Berry and 'Olivia Pope' and Beyoncé and so many all rolled into . . . two. But . . . see, 'cause Dad, he was like some big cruel . . . *toad* . . . and Mom she was like the n-nymph of a dragonfly . . . "

Maybe you should shut up, Junior . . .

"*No*! See, Alma got like Ivy League sc-scores on her PSATs, but all she wanted to do was ski. We'd play those white schools in football . . . Georgetown Prep, Landon, St. Albans and she knew these white chicks at Holton and Sidwell, and out of the damn bl-blue, she's gets invited to their big ski trip, Pennsylvania. Mom called them 'fast white girls' . . . "

You built the alabaster statue to her in your head. Reality's *dirtier.*

"She came back . . . her grades, every one, tanked. She told me the white girls, they tortured her—laughed, badgered her . . . wanted her to be ghetto, jungle love and all that shit still in her even though she was proper, prayed the rosary like my m-mother."

Verna's eyes are wet. She touches your hand. "Go on . . . "

"They dosed her, then told the b-boy to come get her. We clear, Verna? These same p-p-people, I bet you see them on Google now, on TV, and right fucking here, in the Capital. But Dad, he *shamed* her and shamed my mother into shaming her. Called her Jezebel . . . put her in some dogshit 'therapy' with his old Marine pastor, not a real shrink. My sister took pills, chased it with Dad's rye."

Don't blame sweet saintly Alma. You're tougher, boy.

You grow a wolfish grin and say, "There's a preppy whiteboy in his varsity letter jacket, pr-profiling in his whip, talking about picking up some 'candy' before they hit Ocean City . . . and a blonde cackling to her girls about how Beach Week's gonna be more lit than the ski trip . . . and I go to my boy Croc who's just got expelled from my school, whose daddy rules the city from the Waterfront to Benning Road . . . and I say 'Croc . . . they hurt Alma,' and Croc loved himself some Alma . . . lil' nerdy, pretty Alma . . . and Croc says 'These preppies and their girls come down to the jont near Club Fifty-Five for weed, pills, blow all the time. Whatchew want me to do?'"

You should see Verna's face now. But you can't. Magically, you're in front of that Magnivox console TV . . . long, time ago, down at the Sergeant-Major's quarters at Eighth and E Street. "*D.C. drug violence touches Bethesda teens with tragedy today* . . . "

Good work, *Rain Man.*

"Now're you gonna fucking *let me out?*"

You're over, son. Done.

You get to laying down the borrowed shoe leather; your nose is numb and runny, your face twitching. That's not the weather, though, Junior. It's the ache. The fiend.

And your monkey is at its screeching, paranoid, zombie zenith in the hour it takes you to near-stumble twenty blocks to the granite and limestone and marble of Constitution Avenue. That canvas *cabin in de sky* awaits, huh? Then what? At least in your cocoon you can say fuck the world for caring about you, fuck the world for hurting you . . .

But as you approach Constitution you spy Park Police units, a paddy wagon, an ambulance gathered at the museum employee lot, just around the corner from your homestead. You trudge closer, up the drive into the grove, and clear as day there is poor Princess clutching one of Kate's babydolls

. . . as a ring of blue surrounds her, corrales her. The sound as they close in, *God* . . . that shriek, as if the cops are ghouls. To her, they are . . .

. . . and there are news cameras on the Mall. Just the select outlets, not the traitors like CNN. Folks are laughing; the cronies are about to come out for the press conference you hear from bystanders and witnesses fascinated by the toss, the hunt, the round-up, droving, running game. One crows, "It's like that old movie 'Planet of Apes' just these are the friggin' apes. POTUS beats these activists and bums once and for all!"

You clock the motherfucker and he's out, twitching.

A Park cop—white chick, swole with cropped hair like some of these pushy lesbians on the force—well she goes and rips the dolly from Princess. Princess wails. Grabs for it. The cop shoves her to the ground, yells, fingers a Taser holster. Princess is a bag of bones, of no threat to anyone. But she does not "comply." She "resists." So she's a threat. She's tazed. Princess, barely conscious, mouths a guttural, mournful cry from the ground; you hear Kate shrieking and pleading along with others already locked inside the vehicle. Not a soul watching says anything, protests . . . until they see you bum-rushing the paddy wagon like some kid's video game hero with a battle-axe. Yeah, son. You're done. Over.

You Mike Tyson the female cop who tazed Princess, slam another into the van's wheel-well.

"*They're my people!*" you cry as the first Taser darts fire but fall wide. Bullets next time, boy. But the miffed, juiced crackers who populate the new-school Parkies want to dominate with skin. Four rugby-scrum you . . . and as they drag you down, verything goes TV *slo-mo* . . . and a golf cart's inching along, towing a small open trailer. Shoved in the trailer, folded upon itself in a heap are aluminum rods and canvas and wood and oiled tarp . . . and objects and items and shiny or reflective things, whimsical and solemn things, scavenged over the months, spilling or falling from the mass of fabric and frame, pinging on the black top. Glinting in the occasional slats of sun . . .

. . . and your thrashing wanes, your howls and moans grow silent under fists and knees.

. . . and you're in some white empty place . . . as if your muscles, viscera, bones have atomized. You reassemble in a cop unit and you're bleeding, and the pain returns. *Exquisitely.*

CHAPTER 8

"Let's go for a little ride"

THEY SAID THEY TOOK YOU TO the hospital overnight. In your fugue it could've been Mars. You just hear that the doc certified that the knots on your hard head, bruises on your body and blood on your face were "preexisting," from years on the street.

You rise from the padded steel "bunk" and realize from the banter, the uniforms, the bright white paint that you are a guest of the Metropolitan Police Department . . . in the cage at the First District. Check out the irony. You could spit and hit St. Jude's and Verna from here.

The Park Police decided to hand you over to the locals. Less hassle for them because they still record the collar and enjoy the fellowship of beating you and hog-tying you; their bosses can boast how they've cleared the human refuse from the Mall . . . even though the monuments and museums of the republic are shuttered . . . .

No bail anymore in D.C. But for assaulting cops, do you really think you are going to get an ankle monitor? Ponder that as they slide you a brick-colored jumpsuit and slippers, and you and the rest of the grim, silent cats in the cage strip and don their togs. One dude is wearing a red and white Santa cap. Another wasn't wearing much at all other than dirty draws and a pair of flip-flops. You claim a space at the end of a bolted bench to put on the papery slippers.

Finally, an older black cop rolls up to the white-lacquered steel mesh, and he's glowering right at you. The Park Police blithely did the dump and run on this supervisory shift, and of course he's hot . . .

"Big man. Yeah, I'm talking to you, nigga. I know you. Yeah . . . you are rash for me this whole dang year. And now, *today* . . . hour to go in my shift and I was out the door for Christmas leave, then I gotta take the call and get custody and do paperwork from the Park Police fo' yo' crazy ass? *Listen* . . . lemme tell you what's about to happen. Would be C-ten, and the judge'd have your ass rockin' 'round the Hanukkah Bush at the CDT with the other elves."

You know the lingo. C-10's the courtroom at Superior Court where they present felony arrests . . . and have the option of shoving you over to federal court . . . as you did assault federal Park Police. Yes, Junior. Federal time, with Latino tots and Muslim terrorists.

He's smiling now, letting you stew, head throbbing, before adding, "But my man, they got something *extra* planned for you. *Look at me when I'm talkin' at you mutha-fuckah!* You goin' into residence substance abuse cold turkey, in the CTF annex. They gonna bolt your dick to a hard bed and sweat the bad outcha'. *Have a holly jolly Christmas . . .* "

Yet his glee's ending because of voices from the service desk. A white female cop with a blonde pony-tail whispers to your tormentor and he in turn winces, curses.

"*Get his damn clothes!*" He looks you up and down. "What—you *Ivanka's* chauffeur? You'll be back. You know it. Y'all kind always fucks up!"

Your heart's sunk down all the way to your stomach and you can't even begin to fathom why he's bitching. He's the one who gets to go home. But quickly you spy two figures marching down the sterile corridor toward the cage. Both in suits, swathed in charcoal, dapper topcoats, silk scarves of various shining hues wrapping their necks.

Both wear visitor's tags. One sports a thick brown briefcase.

"Mr. Cornish? I'm Oleksander Nimchuk . . . "

"P-Pardon?"

The bland Mr. Charlie accent doesn't go with the alphabet soup name. They must be filming a documentary. He's got blond hair ending just below the ears with a speckling of gray, like some middle-aged surfer but for the close shave and smooth skin, the starched white collar and patterned silk necktie.

"You can call me Sandy if that's easier."

"Y-You don't look like a 'Sandy,'" you croak. "You . . . you . . . look like . . . a lawyer. And no PD, either."

"Poetic and prophetic. I'm a partner at Burke, Huddleston. Here's my card. You're being released. Superior Court Judge Linda Trask signed this order here . . . see at the bottom . . . here is a copy of the concurrence from the federal magistrate.

The other white man's stepping into view. Check out the thick Windsor-knotted tie and white spread collar. And you can smell him from the cell. *Bay Rhum.* Nice bit of bronze to his skin, and not even a hint of gray in his precision-scissored, walnut-colored mane; not a wrinkle on his brow or the corners of his blue eyes under his tortoise-shell frames.

"Y-You . . . hired by Verna? You . . . expensive?"

"Oh my no," the other man with the blue eyes responds with a chuckle, and you curse him inwardly for thinking your pain is funny. Indeed, his voice is all cool tonics to crisp dominants like a Frank Sinatra tune. He's now crouching to eye level with you as you squat inside the mesh cage.

"You are a mess, Mr. Cornish." He hands you his pocket square through the steel and not one cop around protests. You wipe your face, spit into the soft cloth. Keep it balled up. First time you scavenged a trophy in plain view as he follows with, "But we are happy to meet you. We tracked you down not an hour ago and I had to drop everything when Sandy called."

"Who the f-f-fuck are you all? I'm serious, dude . . . "

"So am I, Mr. Cornish. My name is Jaime Bracht. Let's go for a little ride."

And thus, you're sprung. Mr. Charlie can work his voodoo, huh? You got your Tylenol and PeptoBismol for what the cops did to you, Saratoga Water to wash it down . . . all in the limo. Indeed, Bracht tells you this is a custom Hyundai Equus limo, compliments of his South Korean clients . . . and he takes a dig at his former boss, Agent Orange, over his cupidity for their neighbor to the north.

"I'm sure the little twat tells Donnie that if you're worshipped as a deity, your cock actually will grow!"

"Y-Yes . . . and um, pardon my . . . smell," you cheese.

The lawyer, still going by Sandy, is sitting next to you and nods.

"Birth to age twelve I grew up in a boys' home in Kyiv. Smells don't bother me."

Bracht sighs, adds his two cents.

"I'm afraid my nose is untrained but for the locker room after football practice!"

"Y-You don't have an accent . . . "

"Scrubbed long ago when I came here on a student visa," the lawyer says.

"No . . . I meant . . . *you*, Mr. Bracht." Careful boy. You aren't on steam grate anymore, and this ain't Black Santa. *"Estabas emocionado de recibir las monedas de tu abuelo?"*

A smart, circus-trick you are . . . because he's grinning, then he parries, *"Excelente. Pero tenía doce años, un Apple Two GS que podía jugar Zelda y Donkey Kong.* Grew up in Plano, Texas. That's my heritage." Bracht's eyes narrow as he studies you. "Wow, you are a big dude. Bet you spit-roast these chickheads out here, huh?"

Lord. "Um . . . spit-roast?" Deflect, boy. "Um . . . *Sandy* . . . you're Ukrainian then, not Russian? But Mr. Bracht's a Tr-Trump guy, right? No conflict for you?"

"Fair question . . . " Sandy replies, and Bracht smiles approvingly, " . . . buried in a dig . . . or was that a 'burn?' But this ride isn't about me, Mr. Cornish. It's about you."

Bracht fixes his blue eyes on your bloodshot ones.

"Richard E. Cornish, Junior. Jay highly recommends you, sir."

An ugly, intimate sensation washes over you.

"Jay . . . *Oosterhaus*?"

"He's a Harvard MBA, man . . . he couldn't've looked the usual redneck who supervises a crew of guys trashing the belongings of evicted losers."

"Sir, uh . . . are you, cross with me, for any reason?"

"'Cross?' *See, Sandy!* He's erudite . . . and yet he thinks I'm some sort of *Kaiser Soze*! No, Mr. Cornish. It's the frickin' opposite. *You* are a unicorn among unicorns. You are like some homeless Superman, and we are John and Martha Kent. We've been looking for someone with a combination of your experiences, skills, as it were. But . . . " he smacks his knee and it startles you: " . . . *you!* You fell into our lap and blew the punchlist to hell. If I were inclined to kowtow to the clown Mike Pence, I'd say God himself sent you."

You're fixing on his cuff links as he speaks, because in his bizarre exuberance, he's monkeying with them. Bald eagles, not Mexican gold eagles, eating a snake. Strange mix.

He claps his hands to get your wandering eye.

"Indulge me . . . I just want to say I've never *met* a homeless person before. I mean sat and talked. Swear to God."

You're listening, smiling, occasionally sneaking a look out the tinted glass. And who is this cracker driving? An old-school Marine Corps flattop cut into his dome? Close to a Hitler mustache when you see him turn. Boxy gray suit as if JFK was still president.

Bracht prompts, "Earth to . . . *Richard*. Mind if I call you Richard? Dick? Rich, Rick?"

"Dickie."

"Mr. Sugars up there's been with me since I was a lad working for Dubya and Condi Rice. Great, great lady B-T-W. I wish Michelle Obama would have embraced her more. Think of that combo . . . *Chocolate Empresses*. They'd run up Donnie's wrinkled ass!"

He's raising his right hand, palm-up. You stare. He's frowning.

"Dick . . . Dickie! Give it up for your *queens*, man! Your black queens!"

You slap his palm; he grips your fingers into a shake. And you give him a little something extra.

"What was that, with the thumb and stuff? Interesting."

"My frat . . . frat shake."

"*I love it.* Glad you kept your wits. Sandy says you're in quite a rumpus."

"They . . . they destroyed my . . . home. My stuff. L-Locked up my friends."

"Ha! Every April Fifteenth that happens to me . . . "

"You pay quarterly, Jaime," Sandy the lawyer quips. "And not terribly much."

"*Ha*! So now you're spreading client confidences? No, Dickie . . . Sandy and I aren't talking about the melee at the museum. Did you know you are a murder suspect?"

You're a cockroach in there, shrunk down on the upholstery. "P-Pardon?"

"Yes, we have information from the Metropolitan Police Department based on evidence adduced at the cozy little flat of . . . who're these old farts again?"

"Eva Boudreaux and Fred Cross," the lawyer says.

This magnificent bastard. *Keep your head up*!

"I didn't . . . didn't kill them. I found them . . . I *loved* them." They're just lolling, as if you're talking about the weather. "Mr. Bracht . . . I-I know I owe you. I stole from you . . . "

"Come on Dickie, you aren't wasted and I know you're an intelligent man, so don't insult me. Those coins, Mexico, my grandpappa . . . even my father—fuck 'em all. I see you as an investment opportunity, potentially high yield . . . and this is merely due diligence. I mean, look at the city . . . who'd have thunk there'd be a Tiffany's on New York Avenue. Say—how'd you turn a Commie feminist dyke into a cock-hungry dollar-bill chasing hottie? Give her one of those blue and silver boxes, *ha*!"

"Mr. Bracht . . . please . . . "

"Call me Jaime. I want us to be friends. Hey . . . help me settle this with Sandy. Eons ago when I was working as an intern in the Senate, I always had to take New York Avenue into work when we were slumming in Maryland. Rain or shine, there was this black dude always naked from the waist-up. Scars zig-zagging on his chest . . . no left arm, a frickin' mess . . . "

The limo stops and from the front, the crew cut ofay grunts over an intercom, "Valet or garage, sir?"

Bracht commands, "No, take us over to F Street so Dickie can eat . . . then drop Sandy off at the firm. *Thank you, Mr. Sugars.* Okay . . . anyhow this fucker was a mess. Always at the Bladensburg Road light where traffic gummed up."

"Outboard." The suits are crisscrossing squints and grins at that. You repeat. "His n-name. 'Out-board.'"

"Hold it," Bracht stops you. "As in a *motor?* Oh, this is going to be a show!"

"Family's black watermen on the Ch-Chesapeake B-Bay. Oyster barges, crabbing, for generations. But Albert, he was schizophrenic . . . family couldn't handle stress, shame . . . money. One day he fell off a dock. Boat propeller . . . fucked him up bad."

Bracht's blue eyes are wide as dinner plates as he claps his hands.

"*I knew it . . .* a propeller!"

"Well he p-passed four years ago . . . "

"Sad. Uh . . . you hungry?" He hits the intercom. "Mr. Sugars, stop at the corner at Thirteenth and grab our guest some lunch. Anything on the board of fare will do . . . "

"I-I'll pay you back . . . I got money . . . "

"I doubt that. I mean . . . evictions—that can't make you more money than panhandling even with these yuppie bleeding hearts and millennial little girls away from daddy."

"Been doing jump crew three years . . . with one . . . interruption."

"I'd call fentanyl an interruption, true."

"How'd you know . . . ?"

"Amazing how times are good for some and suck for others." He winks at you. "Between us men of 'color,' it's pretty racial. We have properties in counties where Donnie's a god and half the people are sitting on their asses collecting some form of government largess . . . yet evictions aren't an issue. White people let white people slide, right? Easy to keep 'em in the net rather than churn and burn." He leans in and whispers, "*Mobile home loans and rentals.*"

"Sir?"

"Not a fan of *The Graduate*, I guess? 'Plastics.' It's a joke . . . "

"Directed by Mike Nichols . . . the late Buck Henry wrote it . . . Paul Simon wrote *Mrs. Robinson* just in time for soundtrack . . . "

Bracht grins. There goes your jigsaw puzzle brain again but . . . nah . . . his is a different sort of grin, like he's impressed.

"My counsel here, Mr. Buzzkill, thinks your brain's cluttered with that kind of stuff because you get high. I think it's the other way around. I think you get high to quiet that mind, and *that* is the hallmark of out-of-the-box thinking, eh?" The grin evaporates. "But, uh . . . given the drug abuse, living on street, blah blah . . . we still gotta ask you serious due diligence questions. Ready? Sandy, he's yours . . . "

Play along.

"You are a 'spice' addict, smoked crack cocaine and meth, a.k.a. 'Tina,' true?"

"I'm . . . trying . . . okay."

"Yes or no's fine. Do you hallucinate, have violent episodes, catatonic states?"

You close your eyes and whisper, "Yes."

"Abuse alcohol, Xanax to even-out your withdrawals and episodes?"

"Yes."

"You are homeless, a.k.a. a vagrant?"

"Um . . . Mr. Nimchuk . . . "

He holds up his index finger like the old friars at your grade school to stop you.

"Let me finish. You attempted suicide earlier this year?"

"It was a hot dose . . . "

"Yes or no."

"*N-No* . . . "

The lawyer shrugs, continues with, "Fair to say you are alive now because you are resourceful, a scrounger . . . *a scavenger*? Using what no one else will use. Seeing what others can't see. I believe Jay characterized your street rep as one who 'figures,' examines?"

"Okay . . . y-yes." That almost a whisper, boy.

"Don't be embarrassed, Bracht jumps in. "Most humans are either prey or predator. But that third category . . . the *scavenger*, is unique. Can't have predator and prey without it."

"Um . . . yes . . . yes, sir."

"You good, Sandy? I'm stoked."

"Let's start phase two," the lawyer says with a nod. He starts fingering his mobile and Bracht is just staring at you. No more levity. Just a quiet, sterile stare . . .

. . . as Mr. Sugars jumps back in the limo with the Micky Dee's bag and cup, lowers the partition to hand them to you.

Bracht and the lawyer giggle like girls when you mumble a Catholic prayer and then tear into the cheeseburgers, the fries.

Nimchuk asks, "Have you ever been diagnosed or adjudicated mentally ill? Brain injury? Autism spectrum?"

Where to start, huh?

"Asking because per your Air Force service record . . . "

You almost cough up your Coke. Yeah, how'd they get that, too?

"You were lucky to get a general discharge. Was that your father's influence? You attacked your commanding officer . . . "

"May . . . May I . . . just not talk about that?"

When Bracht nods, studying you, the lawyer relents.

Bracht says, "We should have this guy up to the hunting lodge . . . with his survival skills and eating habits he'd us teach a thing or two. Know how to use a shotgun?"

"Um . . . sir, that'd be in Pennsylvania?" They are slack-jawed, then almost panicked you have intelligence on them. "Um . . . a friend, she looked you up on G-Google . . . about the coins. Only need to hear or see something once. I retain it. It's . . . an affliction . . . "

"Well, I have a beautiful place near the Buchanan State Forest. Sadly too close to a fast food hell called Breezewood."

"We'd drive through Br-Breezewood to get to my grand-mother's in Ohio."

The limo barrels up to K Street, turns on the access street and halts.

"Um . . . Mr. Nimchuk . . . Sandy . . . could you m-maybe check on my friends, Kate McCarthy, Princess Goins . . . they were arrested at the museum, wh-when I caught my case. Please . . . they'll go to the city women's shelter if the court dumps them. Can't go there . . . "

He looks to Bracht, Bracht shrugs. He answers, "Women—are they pregnant, in reasonable health . . . kids?"

Yeah that's a weird reply. "*N-No* . . . they're old. Why?"

Bracht sighs, then says to him, "Sandy do your best for the ladies, okay? Um, Dickie where d'you want them sent—that mission by the ballpark where you scrub up?"

"No, So Families May Eat, there in Southwest."

"Sounds good." He winks at Nimchuk. "See to it, *Bastardo.*"

The lawyer gives a mock chuckle and replies as he slides out of the vehicle under Mr. Sugar's escort, "Will do, *Syrota.*"

When Mr. Sugars is back at the wheel he pulls the limo from the curb, and quickly, you see landmarks on K Street and realize you are headed toward the Kennedy Center and the river. Bracht leans toward you. His small talk silliness is gone, his giggling schoolboy face has hardened. He is now vulpine, almost scary.

"Alone at last. I have a job for you."

"I . . . *figured.*"

"Mr. Sugars and his associates have been unsuccessful in this task. Usually he is the gold standard, but this city . . . the homeless, the drug users . . . bog him down . . . "

The limo crosses the Potomac at Rosslyn, then swings south on the George Washington Parkway past Arlington Cemetery. Takes that long for you to come up with something clever.

"It's more about you being bl-blind, than us being invisible . . . Jaime."

"I like that. So . . . *you* will be my eyes. You will liaise with Mr. Sugars and his team."

"No cops?"

"If it can be avoided. I prefer contractors: former federal agents. Now, I'm prepared to help you out with rehab, provide cash and provisions. If you are successful, I will deposit funds in an escrow account, perhaps even a cashier's check."

"Successful at what?"

"Mr. Sugars will take over the briefing . . . *cool*?"

"But . . . what if I fail at what you want me to do?"

"Retrench from my investments . . . and I suppose you'd need a public defender. Badly."

You are now *way* past the airport, coming out of the woods into Alexandria's Old Town . . . and you're as a pale as you can get, nauseous . . .

. . . and the limo pulls up to a cluster of buildings that at first glance fit the age and brick, frame and stone architecture of this part of Alexandria, this part tailored for the likes of George Washington and Robert E. Lee. But you squint and realize this is just the ancient façade; multiple levels of glass and metal behind it evince cubicles and lit flat screen monitors and well-dressed bodies scurrying . . .

"'The StoneTower Group . . . StoneTower Capital,'" you recite from the flags and logo.

"Home sweet home. And where we part company. Any last questions for me?"

Lord, you cannot help yourself, can you?

"Um . . . Mr. Nimchuk . . . this actually . . . is Ukrainian of a G-German derivation. And you, sir . . . you're um, Germanic-Latino? The German thing . . . binds you?"

"You *are* good, Dickie. Yes, we did bind, just not in college. I was a rich boy at Princeton. He was a poor boy at UT Austin. We met at Baylor Law, in Texas, the Tory Legal Society . . . ever hear of it?"

"No. But you all are still *mixed*. Two worlds."

Brachts puzzles for a second on your puzzle, then nods and offers, "I suppose we got the *worst* of both, hopefully made the best?"

"Why is a man as *powerful* as you . . . self-effacing? I mean . . . newspapers say you didn't want immigrant children separated fr-from grown-ups, put in cages?"

His thin lips purse, then part with, "Why is a man as . . . *gifted* . . . as you, a homeless loser?" And now he's pointing a blade-like finger at you. "You talk about 'mixed.' I do not like that term. I do not like *metizo,* or *hablas castellanos* versus *hablas espanol* or Portuguese versus Spanish. I am an *American.* A *winner.* I am no sick, pathetic wreck."

"Like me . . . "

He composes himself, drops his finger. "Did I say that? Good luck, Dickie Cornish."

And the second he disappears into the lobby, you are thrown to the vehicle's right side when Mr. Sugars jerks the wheel and guns the engine. The tires scream and you're diving into a garage. Mr. Sugars punches the brakes . . .

. . . and he's getting out of the front seat, opens the door. Slides in across from you.

"Okay, asshole, pay attention. This is a hard copy print-out of the account in which Mr. Bracht's attorney will deposit funds, or from which he'll issue a blank draft for you and your rehab upon completion. *Check?*"

"Um . . . yeah, check . . . "

"This is one hunnert dollars cash. Check two?"

"Ch-Check."

"Notebook, a pen . . . slide off the top and it's a pretty nifty digital voice recorder . . . small memory so not good for dictating *War and Peace.* Short memos, given your memory lapses . . . or recording some dickhead confessing something to you. Check three?"

He slides a mobile phone—something black and big—from a coil of bubble wrap.

"Before you think you're James Bond, just know that the average fourteen-year-old in the suburbs is hooked-up with more stuff on his phone than you. This is your burn. We'll switch it out in a few days. Camera, hi-def video, my number preset, very limited ability to call out . . . we've blocked Internet except for Google and a few apps; kidlock in on Youtube. So no porn or Lebron or Kanye, whatever. Goes with this transceiver. You can clip it to a piece of clothing, use the magnet here to stick it on a car. Move this rim and it's activated, limited battery life, though. Track it with an app. Ten-click range, so it's for emergencies only . . . someone gets away from you, or someone's stuffed a hoopdy's trunk. Okay, now check five: our insurance."

"Thought it was jail."

"No time for proper rehab. Got any pop left in the cup? Take this pill."

More accurately . . . a gelcap. And you refuse to put it in your mouth. You're fully expecting to be tossed onto the concrete, but he's snickering. Yes, Mr. Sugars, who's face thus far has only registered disgust or menace, is snickering.

"Don't be a pussy . . . really think we'd poison you? This will address cravings, withdrawal etcetera. Broad spectrum: spice, opioids, alcohol." When you take the pill with a swallow of soda he puts a second gelcap in your shirt pocket, then reveals, "Experimental, derived from a new anti-epilepsy formula, and buprenorphine. Congrats for testing it."

Don't punch him, Junior. "You're welcome, Mr. Sugars . . . "

"The next generation will have an anti-psychotic. Do you hear voices?"

"No."

Good to get that out of the way.

"You'll be feeling like a teenager again in no time, so enjoy! Second dose in six-to-eight hours." He now holds up a blue plastic nasal inhaler. "Know what this other stuff is?"

You nod. "Narcan. This . . . looks different . . . "

"Only available now in few trial ER's and paramedic crews. Grab a snort pretty much every twenty-four or so hours or else what you just popped might put you in a coma."

You hold out your hand palms up for it, but he shakes his head.

"Insurance for the insurance. Forces you to check in with me face to face at least once a day to share intel and get your whiff. Think of it your *leash*." He hands you a brown paper bag. "Check six . . . for loosening tongues . . . "

It's six three-g hits of Scooby Snax, Rio, Trumpocalypse.

"*Nah . . . nah . . . nah . . .* "

"What, not your brand?"

"If I sell this, I'm slangin', a plug . . . a competitor."

"If we have to put down any mad dogs, I doubt anyone will care. Listen, Cornish," he follows up, "you do this detective job for us, clean yourself up . . . there'll be more work. There's always more work."

Here's your final prize. He hands you a folder containing hard copies of two digital mug shots. Your eyes, ruled by that magnificent and addled brain, fix on the data imprinted at the top, rather than the faces. *United States Customs, Dulles Airport, 7 April 1998 . . . Policía Federal Ministerial 30 December 2015.*

"One's older . . . the other's as current as we could get from

MPD. We want this person found; the location fixed so we can move in."

Mr. Sugars watches your reaction. Still that deadpan . . . and then, it contorts, melts. *Oh, son . . . that gelcap should've dissolve quicker onaccount it's bubbling right back up . . .*

"Her name is Esmeralda Rubio, age fifty. Sheet lists no aliases. Only relative in the states is a sister who's in violation of the Immigration Act . . . overstayed a student visa for American University. Marta Rubio."

Everything he's saying is garbled as if you popped a mollie and the jigsaw pieces of your brain scatter, reconstitute, fracture a thousand times faster than when you saw Eva and Fred's bodies.

"Cornish . . . *Cornish*? What, the DTs coming?"

Get out of the car and run. Roll the dice with the po-po.

"Our intel is you graduated from the same college as this cooze, correct?"

"*Yes.*" No dice, then. So much for the devil you know.

"The boss wants this wrapped up soon. Anything profound you wanna tell me?"

"She . . . she stole the coins," you mumble, chin to your chest. "Not S-Soloranzano and Contreras. She's connected to Sabine and Nestor . . . they stashed the coins?"

Cracker's laughing. "See, Killer—now you're thinking like a real detective!"

"Why . . . why you calling me 'Killer?'"

He chortles back, "Do you prefer 'Shithead?' You got money in your pocket and here's a Metro card . . . King Street Station's thataway. Hit me if something pops right away."

You want to tear out of there, jump in a hole, pull the asphalt and bare trees and light poles over you. Yet as you stumble up the ramp he calls, "Your old man's a Marine, correct?"

"Was a Marine"

"*Always* a Marine. *Semper fi.* I mean, you had custom quarters down there at the Barracks on Eighth, right?"

"Only r-recall the shit-boxes on Okinawa, Quantico," you mumble, head bent.

"Christ on a cracker—show some respect! He'd be proud to see you cleaned up, do real work." He climbs in the limo, shouts through an open window. "No biggie."

"Why?" you croak like the forlorn toad you are.

"'Cause I, Burt Sugars—I'm your daddy until this operation's complete."

CHAPTER 9

Devil and the Deep Blue Sea

THE ESCALATOR DUMPS YOU OUT OF the Navy Yard Metro station; the winter sun's low over your shoulder so you've already lost most of the day captive with Bracht. And this moment, Father Phil Rufini's ceremonially washing a bum's dirty feet at St. Jude's to show the hopeless men there is hope, direction, purpose. At SFME, the staff is preparing for Santa Claus's arrival this coming Christmas Eve by begging whitefolk in the suburbs for castoff toys. You? Well you're a gumshoe now, eh? All geeked to do your dirty work for a dirty ofay.

Tell yourself it's self-preservation all you want . . . you really believe that smirking bastard when he says you got a double murder rap hanging over your head? Besides, you're taking a big risk, fucking with the Queen. At worst, she'll call a bunch of cats come to beat your ass if the snooping doesn't sit well. At best, she'll toy with you, send you on your way.

"Between the devil and the deep blue sea . . . " you whisper.

A Salvation Army couple greets you. Sure enough, they're in their archaic red uniforms, including a damn bonnet and cape on the woman. His brass trumpet accompanies her voice and adept ringing of a small hand bell.

"Come adore on bended knee . . . Gloria . . . in excelsis Deo."

Maybe that pill's working, onaccount your dome's clearer. Still, under the music, you're talking to yourself. Nothing new. But what is new—you're being very conspicuous about it . . .

"It's not 'between a rock and a hard place,' or 'the monster or the whirlpool.'" Hear that? You aren't stuttering. "It's about sending one bastard over the side in a bos'un's chair to make the repairs, dangling, by the thinnest cordage . . . between the Devil and the deep blue sea. He was expendable . . . but he'd *survive* if he found that niche . . . "

Of course, the fellow carolers—most of them posh because they either live down there or are on their way to the twenty buck a head holiday wonderland inside the National's stadium—have you pegged as either rude or a nut. Maybe you aren't conspicuous enough, or, you look at your togs, feel your face, you look too much like one of them.

When *Angels We Have Heard On High* ends, the maroon-clad players ask for requests and donations. Your hand is the first up and pleasantly you ask after a ten in the kettle shuts down the onlooker shade, "How about a real D.C. Christmas song? Donny Hathaway!" You look to the crowd and when you hum and do your best to sing, the Salvation Army folks, to the either dismay or utter joy of the disgorged subway travelers start accompanying you on Donny's iconic song. A few of the whitefolks even try to sing along.

And then the bait's taken.

A fair-skinned elderly black woman crowned in gray knots of hair peeking from a scarf parts two Missy Anns pushing baby strollers and herding well-bundled tots. She's swathed in a long dingy white skirt, under layers of rags like the gypsy mama in the classic *Wolfman* movie. She butchers the song as badly as you . . .

"Fire is singin 'bri, we carolin' dru da night . . . an' dis Chrid-mas, will be . . . "

You call to Thunder, her chihuahua, tied up to a bench beyond the crowd. Thunder scents the old you and confirms your identity with ears-back yelps and rapid tail wags.

"Oh my Gawd . . . Dickie," Jenn trills, breaking from the song. She's the Queen. Queen Jenn. Ole Sponge Bob was her consort. She's outlived the most tenacious among you on the streets . . . been chased from every monument and edifice, from Union Station to the Jefferson Memorial and there are fools who believe that the inane club music song *Gypsy Woman* big back in the day was written about her. "Gib me some suga. Den gib T'under some suga."

You do so. She inspects you, though, drawn-on eyebrow raised.

"Ya straight, ya clean, boy?"

"Sort of." You take her had. It's crisscrossed with veins, boney. "Jenn, not gonna bullshit you. Do you know about Eva and Fred?"

She nods and whispers, "B'ess dere souls." But her eyes suddenly flash at you, and she jerks her hand away. "Weren't no *robbery*. Lotta deat' on dat street. De Spanishes girls. Den dis."

Relieved the response wasn't aimed at you, you cheese, "You and me must be the onliest peeps thinking it's all together, part of the same evil." She nods again, sits to stroke the little dog as you add, "And Jenn, they got no living kin here no more. In Potter's Field they go after being burnt up. And I can't visit to pay respects."

"Why y'all catchin' me all up'n mah feelin', boy?" Uh-oh. "Let Gawd dis'pence wrat'. Dat's how all y'all mens git kilt. Wrat' then guns and mo' folk die ova bu'shit."

"No looking to settle with who killed them. More like . . . you remember that Mexican girl I used to run with? Esmeralda Rubio?"

Her eyes narrow and she comes back with, "Ya 'member T'under's mama, dat lil' bitch 'Lightening?'"

"Come on, Jenn."

"Why y'all ax-ing me dat, lest y'all t'ink dat bitch deaded dem, huh?"

Too slick, Junior, *Ha*!

"Didn't say that, Jenn. Just peace of mind."

"*Ahhh*, onaccount she no ghost? Onaccount y'all t'ink dat trick be runnin' de streets a'gin, same time de Spanishes die, den Eva an' Fred die?" You're licking your lips, hungry for her next words. Now Jenn's looking at you all coquettishly and squinty-cute like a gray grande-dame, as if savoring memories of her old paramour. "One ain't got nuffin ta do wiff de odder . . . "

Best be clever. "But you agreed when I said them getting dead was related to Esme."

"Ya know Eba, she was a conjure woman jus' like dat Spanish huzzy wha' ruint y'alls life, Dickie. She tole dat girl dat layin' roots and writin' devil words fo' fun or fuck wiff people is gonna put you, Dickie, in he grave. Bet ya'll di'n't know dat conversation. Mah Kenyatta, wha y'all call Sponge Bob, Fred, alla we wan' see you alive, boy."

"Sorry I bothered you, Jenn. Sorry I wasn't here for Kenyatta . . . "

You bend to buss her gaunt cheek, but she pulls you down to the bench.

"Dat gurl . . . she back."

Pick up your mouth from the ground, son, and stay mute, onaccount the Queen's corroboration is law and you aren't allowed to say jack-shit . . .

"Maybe a year? Eba seent her."

"Eva?"

"Yeah. Ta tell de bitch ta stay away f'om you boy." You acting, or is this twisting and gasping real? She thinks it's real, as she adds, "Baby . . . *baby*. Y'all was run amok, in de horspittel den out, den in. Fred say de nigga outta control—y'all bein' de nigga in ques-tion."

"I don't owe that chick a thing." Don't jump the gun.

"Word is yo' gurl, she settin' up cards like I set up cards. Like Eba set up cards: de *Tarot*. Fortunes fo' dem Spanishes. Mexican voodoo an' roots, scarin' her peoples inta doin' what she please. But now, it please her ta help her folk, not hurddem."

She abruptly starts humming along to some other golden oldie—this one in her head. You take her forearm. Gently. But the grip's enough to push out a wince; the rat-dog barks. You release her, as now eyes are on you from passers-by on M Street.

"Ain't got cause ta grab me, Dickie. Na cause nor right. She leans forward, eyes cold, "I bet if I read yo' Tarot I see's nothin' but chaos. Word on da vine be someone sprung ya f'om Central Deten'n. You ain't clean up *dat* quick. Wha' dey want f'om you . . . and don't lie and say it 'bout Eba an' Fred."

"That's between me and who sprung me. So now we come around in a circle, Jenn. Esme's back, Esme's seen Eva. So maybe Esme know who killed her. So now you can tell me where Esme hangs."

Thunder's barking at you. Yeah, you're different now.

"Okay, Dickie . . . I hear on de vine she wuz in Mt. Pleasant wid her Spanishes, furst. Den she gone fo' mont, maybe two, den she come back 'round Georgia Ab'nue. Cards, roots, spells, like I say. Near time po-lices fount dem gurls down Kenyon Stree', gub'ment sent 'em back ta die. Y'all can *avoid* her dere. *Not* speak ta her dere, catch m'drift?"

You nod. "Thank you, Jenn."

She yawns, shoos you away. "Ya got whutcha wanted. Watch ya'selb, dough."

"Cause nothing's what it seems to be . . . "

Her face hardens into a scowl.

"No! *Onaccount everyt'in' wha it seem ta be. Prolly worse! Now git!*"

The Queen commands it so you step. Yet there's a weird yelp from the little dog and you swear it sounds human, so you turn.

"She don't go by her name when she was yo' ho', cov'd in Maybelline an' White Rain hair-spray. Now she called 'Carolina.'" You scribble that in your new hi-tech notepad with your hi-tech felt tip pen. "*Tía* Carolina." You almost drop the pen.

"Auntie . . . " Like Stripe said before he lost it in front of that apartment . . .

Queen's singing again as you tear away from her, full trot, to St. Jude's.

Tía Carolina . . .

. . . and you walk into the vestibule at St. Jude's, right past the astonished security guard, to Brother Karl-Maria's conference room, chattering friars and fretting nuns and a couple of residents hobbling on frostbitten nubs that once were toes. You're putting on that kind of show, son.

Among the ragged men in the group counseling session therapy are Black Santa and Stevie. Stevie rushes to you, yet the elf stay seated, turns away.

"Yo, Santa . . . Fitzroy," you call, knowing his real name. "I don't care about Oosterhaus, moe. I need you. Dead ass." And he's looking back you, intently and not in fear, onaccount you are different. Your speech, your eyes.

You squeeze Stevie's fat hand and ask, "I need to find Stripe, *hermano*. Fast. He knows something I need to know."

Before Stevie answers, the honcho monk clears his throat, steps to you. In a second the head penguin, Maria-Karl, is at you back. Knives ready?

Not at all . . .

"Dickie . . . good to have you back and thank you on behalf of Father Phil."

"No matter how small the voice, it echoes in Heaven," the nun adds, and you are grimacing as if she spit on you. "The gift will bring joy here and at SFME."

"Gift?"

"Verna Leggett is on a conference call now with her and the Diocese's counsel . . . and Mr. Bracht's attorney. The appraisal for the coins has already been emailed. Twenty-one thousand dollars, and we've already had a buy offer at Thirty. Advice is to hold on."

Yeah, you're different.

Still, Karl-Maria steps in, "But you still need to apologize for breaking up our session."

"S-Sorry?" And the stammer's from pure shock.

"Verna's got some other news, but well, you and your cohorts have confirmed beds through the Twenty-sixth . . . it isn't a miracle, but it warms us nonetheless."

"Um . . . yeah . . . thanks."

Stevie peels you from them with a smile, leads you downstairs. The hall smells of more Lestoil and bleach, Vending machines line the wall . . . junk you wouldn't see on Verna's side.

"Bravo, man," he says, then tells you Stripe's gone missing. "Don't know where you been with that rich man, but out here it's lit . . . Brigada's underground because of ICE raids . . . my cousin say he wife's family, they sick in them camps now. The flu, hepatitis, all them itis's. Some them girls ICE sent back had babies, man. Babies gone, bro', girls dead or deported."

"What's this got to do with Stripe?"

"Him runnin' his mouth, bro', saying *mara salvatrucha* be snitch, be making deals, man, wid ICE. Trump on TV yell about MS Thirteen . . . while somebody wid him laying serious money laying down on them, running more bodies. *Sexo,* here . . . "

You rub your eyes and ask, "So no cops been around here, looking for me?"

"Bro' just this merde wid rich man who say you beg him to help."

"But I was arrested, by the Park Police."

"Ain't nobody hear that, man."

Interesting. You are about to ask him if LaKeisha had any new bits on that damn nasal thing when you hear footsteps on the stairs.

"Wha'yar wan', eh? Mi de debbil so, but now yar come fi wan' Black Santa love?"

"I'm in a spot."

Yeah, his talking, and people's ease at talking to him, is an asset you can harness. You know that from your new dandy mobile phone, an article on being a detective. "How to Work Sources and Create New Leads." Easy reading on the Metro.

"We need to find Stripe, talk to your old friends up there on Georgia Avenue. Stuff like that."

"Wha'hopnin'yout'?"

"It's what you said was impossible, coincidence. I'm looking for Esme, Santa. *She's here.* A year or so. Yeah, pick up your mouth . . . "

"Lard . . . okay . . . "

"'Okay?' That's it?" You pull the surveillance pic and mug shot of Esmeralda from your tweedy jacket. "I am official now, Black Santa. Am I not crazy now?"

He nods sheepishly yet presses, "Yar know 'bout Eva an' Fred dem?"

"We're gonna dip our toes in that too."

"Why, Dick?"

It's as if he's about to cry, such is the cracking in his voice. But he's always been wrapped tight under that Kris Kringle bullshit, huh?

You dismiss his manner and snap, "Why? Because ain't a thing in this city that's hurting and stinking and stifling that's not hitched to something else bad. House right across from Eva and Fred's place, marked up just like that apartment." You face Steve. "And there's this—what'd you know about a *Tía* Carolina?"

Black Santa slides his jelly ass to the floor by one of the vending machines as Stevie reveals he's Colombian; the Pacific coast, at that. The Maya crap in that apartment might as well have been Greek to him. He adds he never visited hoes because they were all young girls like his daughter back home. Besides, the ones he knew of were mostly Salvadoran,

Honduran, Guatemalan. But there was a woman who helped in a *picadura* . . . a cop sting on flesh traffickers, then tried to find homes for the females swept up in the mess. And this meshes nicely with what Stripe was babbling out that street. Good thing your brain's bent, Junior, sucks up everything in your ears, from your eyes.

But then Stevie growls, folds his arms. "Maybe . . . *Vi a una mujer y una niña que se parecen a las dos* . . . photos"

"Nah . . . these are two shots of the same person, not two different *chicas* . . . "

"*Si, dos!*" He insists. "Young girl, older woman, maybe she *advino . . . profeta . . . bruja.*"

"They say she does Tarot cards—that help? Listen, I need this before we find Stripe."

"*Borrachera*, all time," he says. "Tarot, yes."

Your brow furrows like plowed bottomland and you pull out your pad. Black Santa perks up as this whole thing is alien to him.

"So, you've seen two women," you say, scribbling." One old like the one pic, young like the other . . . and what, the older one's doing Tarot?"

"No, I seen two woman . . . Columbia Heights . . . like that. I *hear* of 'Tía.' *Bueno?*"

"Her and another. *Joven.*"

It's as if Black Santa was summoning the stones to speak.

"Dickie . . . lissen, buoy . . . Lil' Roach an' Big Roach dem, durin' de work, dem talk all mawnin 'ow one see yar ole *mujer* 'anging. Him say *mujer Mexicana . . . muy tentador* . . . " He pauses then says, "Up dat way, Columbia 'eights, Petwort', nearby-to . . . Eva an' Fred."

You pull him from the floor and you don't let him go.

"Stevie," you say as you lock eyes. "*Nos da unos minutos a solas, por favor?*"

He whistles and bounds up the stair.

"This is not why I'm in a fuckin' spot, Black Santa," you whisper, searching your feet. "I've been . . . hired . . . to do something." Now he's searching the marred, scuffed floor. "I got some drugs to clear my head. Can you tell? I got a phone . . . no one else knows about it; I may have fucked things up by telling you."

"Bun an' cheese . . . *argh* . . . "

"It's Bracht.

"Oh Lard . . . why 'im wan' dis gal, Dick? Mexican trollop . . . "

"It's not about coins."

"I don't find her, I might be goin' away. Nuff said. Now you see why I need you. I don't care about you spreading my name around. I'm stuck. Devil and the deep blue sea."

"Nah mon. Jus' de Debbil, 'im . . . "

CHAPTER 10

"Propa Shotta"

"HIS NAME WAS ALEXANDER NIMCHUK, ESQUIRE," Verna relates.

"Never met him," you say.

Must be in the script because she nods. There's something up her ass. You disappear for days, she hears you're an ass hair from catching a federal case, monstering Park Police officers . . . and yet here you are, Yuletide fresh and bright-eyed wearing the same clothes she last saw you wearing . . . when you jumped out of her car!

"Imagine our surprise when our advocacy office finds out you were actually in MPD lock up, and you left custody signed out to . . . I love this . . . *your private attorney*. Charges have been dismissed."

"Correct."

She turns to Black Santa. Both of you are in her office on the SFME side.

"Mr. Fitzroy—"

"Marm . . . mi Chri'tian name be Fitzroy. Mi give'm name's 'Cockburn' but de 'c-k' silent when mi not 'round far yar yankees. Mi share it wid 'er Majesty's Royal Navy adm'ril

106

Cockburn, wha' burnt dis infernal city to de groun' in Eighteen an' Fourteen."

"I see. Don't you usually have a placement at Mitch Snyder's downtown? Didn't lure Dickie onto that jump crew?"

"Mi go where de breeze it take me, an' Dick, 'im a grown-ass mon."

"Dickie . . . I suppose you want to see Kathleen McCarthy and Princess Goins now? That's another Christmas miracle, dropped like a bomb on my doorstep . . . "

"Yeah but first, I wanted to ask you . . . remember the the new network you said you could share had Black Santa not 'lured' me. Food stamps, private and government benefits, health tracking?

"*First*, its SNAP . . . EBT card. Not stamps. You know that."

She's folding her arms across her chest, dipping back in her chair. Yeah, she's not happy.

"Well? I have a dummy query I could run. Made up name . . . "

"No. Let's go."

The Christmas tree in the dining hall must be fifteen feet high. Scotch pine. You had Frasiers growing up because your mother loved fuzzy-wuzzy longer needles. Couldn't hold those glass ornaments for shit, though.

A staffer brings food; you and Black Santa attack like predators, not scavengers, digging in your spoons until the bowls screech clean, and leaving not a morsel behind.

Verna watches you two feasting as Kate, Princess giggle, fiddle with their tissue paper holly and ivy diadems. They say, "You hung out with *the* Jaime Bracht."

"Jaime Bracht," Verna begins. "StoneTower Group . . . private equity, ha! Real state slumlording, financing arms sales, toxic chemicals . . . our benefactor. All because of Grandad's coins. Ya know I did some digging. He's been estranged from his late grandfather and his dad down in Mexico City for years."

"I'm walking a new path here, between bad things, for the first time in years. And now I'm vindicated, I have a job . . . these two women are cared for."

"Calm down . . . I meant no offense."

Two bright-eyed young fellows—one slight, with cornrows, the other squat with a mop of back curls—are standing to your right, in the lane between the long bench-like seats. Both have big dark eyes, almost girlish lashes atop them. Standing, they aren't even as tall as you are seated.

"What'd y'all want?" At least the rudeness isn't in your Rain Man monotone.

"Dickie!" Verna gasps. "They stay here, *you* are the guest."

One of the boys declares, "We think you look like a football player."

"I'm not."

"This is Malachi," Verna says, interceding. "Malachi Johnson."

"And I'm Vinny Padilla."

You see the Latin boy's gripping a well-dog-earred Walmart holiday catalogue . . . from last Christmas.

"I'm Dickie."

"*Sooooo*, you a football player, then?" Malachi presses.

"Was. In high school. Then quit, in college . . . "

"Cool," Vinny acknowledges.

They turn to leave, and you finally grow a personality.

"Um . . . you lookin' at *bikes* in the catalog?" As they nod in unison, you shine with, "Well . . . Merry Christmas, Verna's gonna hook it up. She's about to get a lot more money in her budget. Know what that means?" Black Santa does his best to stay straight-faced. "Y'all stay away from the knucklehead beefs, cool?"

They shake your hand, move away.

"I cannot believe you, using those kids as a foil against me," scoffs Verna. "*Especially* them. Vinny's here with his sisters; only hot meal they got was in school until they came here after his father died . . . no medical insurance. Malachi's here with his mother until he's placed in foster care. His father's in prison."

Now you see why detectives—especially old school gunsels like Mr. Sugars—aren't popular. They hurt people. Never any good news. Always in the garbage. That's why Bracht picked you, right?

"Dickie, while you were 'out of custody,' did Bracht or anyone pay for treatment for you? I'm guessing it's suboxone, tiagabine . . . but they don't work overnight . . . and you'd be sick."

"My baby's holistic and natural!" Kate bellows. Princess, ever mute, smiles and nods.

Verna smiles back but keeps the laser beam on your ass.

"You are an educated man. You've heard of Faust, then? Making a deal with the devil, because he couldn't handle the demon within him?"

"That's pretty messed up, considering I came to you. I'm sick, yes. I must work, stay clean, keep the freedom this man— this *wealthy, famous man*—got for me. Can you have the same faith in me he has?"

As Black Santa nervously eyeballs you, Verna snaps, "That doesn't even come close, to giving me comfort, Dickie."

Verna rises, takes your bowls and silverware to the busing station. Black Santa nudges you and is about to speak, yet quickly Verna returns with two mugs of coffee.

"You didn't answer my question, Dickie so I'm going to guess you are indeed on something experimental. Fine. That's between you and your new friend. But nothing will work, until you work a program, truly chart a new course. Going after the person who by all accounts made you an addict is neither. And I will recommend to St. Jude's you not hustle them into giving you a base of operations for whatever you are planning to do . . . until you take independent counseling and rehab, life training, all that stuff, Dickie."

"I have to check-in tonight, okay? With a . . . counselor."

"You know we and St. Jude's have curfews?"

"Yes." And you cluck your tongue because you know damn well St. Jude's will let you slide.

She crisscrosses looks with Black Santa, who puffs himself up, proud and responsible.

"What'll it take, Verna? Seriously?" You punctuate the question with this big galoot smile. Might soften Verna's incredulity but it sure as hell isn't melted until an older black woman, one of the volunteers, commandeers an old upright piano in the corner from some tots who were banging the keys. The lady begins to play.

Instantly, you can tell that the high notes are tinny, the low range hollow thus the piano is sore in need of tuning. Still, Malachi and Vinny are the first to sing along.

You rise, look to Verna and assess, "Damper heads . . . striking wide . . . felt's worn." That brain starts clicking. "Can you get me some foam . . . maybe old slippers or pillow linings from sofas you all might toss. Sharp scissors or a knife. Elmer's glue . . . any white stuff kids use."

"*Ain't this* . . . " Verna whispers to herself. "Uh . . . okay . . . "

"And if you got a steel rod . . . some sort of hook . . . that would bend the damper wire. Then the long pliers . . . "

"*Daaaa-yum*," Malachi intones. Hopefully he wasn't eavesdropping the addict shit. "You like some kinda fixer-man?" Vinny's nodding along.

Soon you have folk feeding you materials, as if you are a surgeon; the rest, including Verna and several kids, watch intently like they in a vintage operating theatre. Black Santa's retreated to the St. Jude's side, claiming fatigue.

Piano fixed, thirty-six hours till Christmas morning, and the music begins anew: *Jingle Bells*. The kids are singing. Verna's smiling, clapping . . .

. . . then she touches your arm.

"I'm sorry for being so extra, Dickie, really. Thanks . . . "

"I could have done this before I met Bracht. But no one wanted to give me a chance, they saw, they smelled, an animal."

"Listen . . . I'll think about what you asked. The network . . . maybe I can do a dummy query but anything else is . . . illegal."

And the buzzer sounds off and you are back in the St. Jude's east vestibule, flashing your wristband to the young guard as is the protocol there between the facilities.

"Seen the old fat man, name of Black Santa?" you ask him. He's wearing a Howard Bison jacket not unlike your old varsity togs. Must be a student, part-time.

"This ain't daycare, dude. If he ain't in the common room, he's in the dorm." The brother's reading *Washingtonian* magazine. Cover's ablaze with "The Death of Chocolate City."

"Good riddance, Chocolate City. Go-Go, the Waterfront, crabs . . . "

"Man, go pee-pee somewhere else."

"Crying, fiending, cowering, o.d.-ing, freezing, broiling, starving—dying. AIDS, bullets. Wasn't any nigga Camelot for them."

"Man, you need to g'won now. Folk cared about poor people back then, for the record."

"Fuck 'poor.' I'm talkin' zero. You bitch less about change if you haven't got shit."

Damn, boy! Those pills really rocked your inner Colin Powell. You get a salute.

"Yeah you, Dickie—I heard about you. You work them jump crews. What—can't base your own by just stumbling around, smelly, zooted, mumblin'? Nah you gotta help these rich folk pick people that had jobs, homes, real shit clean, toss their shit on the curb like they were garbage? Oh so you can say, 'see I don't beg for quarters.'"

"Don't have to listen, moe . . . y'all don't know me."

"Yeah, we know you. You ain't no unicorn."

He chucks the magazine at your feet. It opens on the floor right on a piece, "City under Siege: The Eighties." You reach down and flip a page. *Ah, good.* Pic of Oscar "Slice" Williams, III, confidante to politicians and athletes . . . and the only kingpin the other kingpins like Rayful Edmunds feared more than the feds. His arms embrace two strapping teens in muddy pads and jerseys. The caption discloses, *Son, Oscar "Crocodile" Williams, IV, 1989, teammate Richard Cornish. Source: Estate of Adelaide Cornish.* So Bracht's money is going to make you well, huh?

So thank the Lord your little fat safety valve Black Santa finally arrives, pushing through the lounging men with a jumble of clothing in his arms. Looks like he raided the Goodwill bin;

a cute little Girl from Ipanema novice brings the imprimatur—
a handwritten note on Father Phil Rufini's stationery:

> *Richard, perhaps you would consider attending Holy Mass with
> us Christmas Eve, as we take some of you gentlemen who wish to
> partake to the Basilica of the Assumption and you are a Catholic,
> of course. RSVP verbally.*

Jesus, money talks. Even to folks who wear robes and sandals
year-round. Bracht has the world figured out.

The novice says in her luscious mother tongue, *"As roupas
são para você, senhor Cornish . . .* he wan' zhou to look like good
man with job, eh?"

"Na yar bride o' Christ. Mi say dis mon need look like a
propa shotta. A rude buoy!" He drops the peels on a small
side table.

"*Shotta?*" you say. "I'm no damn gangsta, Black Santa! I'm
on the clock! This is real shit, moe. *Wake up!*"

The elf retreats, fretfully.

"I'm sorry . . . I'm so sorry. Yeah, I mean . . . you're right.
Peels I'm wearing now . . . like a clown . . . "

Your tone and words bring Black Santa back, though he
says nothing.

Let's see what he has, then. Long black coat, material's more
like a trench coat because it has an attached belt . . . big collar,
and yeah it'll shed the ice and rain well. Black trousers . . .
matte black like the coat but you want jeans. Better in the cold.

"Trouser is trouser, yout'." Black Santa replies.

He's got a white Oxford button-up shirt for you, oddly on a
hanger and in a dry cleaner's plastic. A black wool cap with a
red and green brim dangles on the end of one of his sausage
fingers. You could say it's a Muslim's skull cap or an African's
kufi. But hell, just say "beanie."

"I'm not wearing these peels, moe. All black up in this jont like I'm undercover Five-Oh . . . and this cap? That thing's not going to cover my ears in the cold."

"*Chut* . . . mi can't 'ave yar stride dese street dem like some rasclot ragamuffin. Naw mi see yar a monnish mon, stridin' tall!"

And looking like a ghetto Johnny Cash? Chocolate Kris Kringle directs the nun-ling to empty the prize out of a paper bag onto the table.

For men who'd pretty much been near murdered by assholes for these, she might as well have spilled Bracht's granddad's coins. In shock, you whisper, "Tims. Oh shit . . . for me?"

He nods. "Merry Christmas, mi yout'. De brides o' Christ went t'rift store an mi claim dese. Mi way a say t'anks . . . far yar puttin' up widme foolishness."

Black leather, black as the whole outfit . . . lace-up, waffle soles . . . he lays them by your feet and they look only a tick too large, even for your big feet. Nothing gym socks can't equalize. Though in the tongue's scrawled *Romeo* in what looks like permanent marker ink.

"Prev'us owna. Ain't na t'ing. Lemme see yar, mon!"

You slip into the small washroom in the corridor connecting the common room with the kitchen. There's no mirror in there so you're safe from your doubt.

And yet when you emerge . . . ooo's and ahhhs of approval make you want to retreat, as if you're truly wearing a freak's costume.

Finally, you can catch yourself in the small hall mirror.

"I'm in the Gestapo," you muse.

Black Santa places the wool beanie on your big head like he's a squire and that thing's your helmet. He got to stand on a hassock to do it, given how erect your spine's gotten in the last twelve hours thanks to a little gelcap . . .

"Belt de coat, mon. Dere," he says to you. "Na frass. *Dick 'im a bad, bad mon!*"

The derelicts, even the nuns, cheer. You laugh, embarrassed, but you laugh.

"Get your hat, pull on something warm," you tell Black Santa, and he grows a smile you can fit a dozen mangoes into.

"Mi sleut' widchew . . . yar weren't lyin'?"

No, you weren't. You and he march out into the setting sun and cold.

You text Mr. Sugars as you walk. First night out, on the clock.

You head across Eye Street SE . . . toward the silver, green and red bursts of light adorning the new buildings and steel skeletons of the ones yet to be born.

He starts a random rant about gays. You let him chew his pint to calm himself.

"Sa wha'now bred'rin," he gasps after a long swallow.

"Here's how I want to quarterback this so pay attention. You get off at Columbia Heights, where Esme would have been in closest . . . proximity . . . to Miz Eva. Sniff around your old haunts. Hit the *muchachos*. You're the only *mayate* they trust 'cause they see your drunk ass a lot in Adams Morgan." He frowns but you meant him no offense. It's just time to work. "Then meet me in front of the Target by dark, like five, five-thirty. I'm getting off at Petworth, I'll search east, then go west."

"Why Petwort'?"

"Because Lil' Roach was itching to tell everyone he saw Esme. East of the station is his and Big Roach's prime thieving territory. West of the station's where Stripe hangs sometime. Or we can catch him right there on Fourteenth."

You all hit M Street SE and the music hits you just before a gust of icy wind. Different location, same Salvation Army brass, the same voices and clang of the hand bell from this afternoon.

"Silver bells . . . it's Christmas time, in the city . . . "

The songs that enervated you when you emerged earlier today from the station now get you more cised than when you were a boy: out of school for the holiday, watching your mother drink cocktails with the non-com's wives, light cigarettes for their husbands with them staring at her all fine in her new dress. Her hair and face, perfect. Only time of year that bitch bothered to doll up when asked . . .

"Shut up," you whisper to the air.

The subway workers in the booth are checking you out. Not disgust this time, *oh no . . .*

. . . now they're perked up, and your ego's close to prompting a hard-on for the first time in a long time. Maybe you'll be able to pee and shit correctly, too, for you are drawing even more eyeballs as you and Black Santa roam the platform like a ghetto Mutt and Jeff.

Silver Bells still sticks in your ear; you shoot a verse to your newly- minted sidekick.

"This is Santa's big day . . . "

He shakes his head and replies, "Mi luv yar betta as the ole Dick."

"What you see now was the *old* Dick. The 'propa' Dick. *Before her . . . "*

CHAPTER 11

The Ant Farm

YOUR TRAIN WHINES INTO THE PETWORTH station, and you figure Black Santa's already been belched from the deep gullet of the Columbia Heights stop down the line.

Easy to imagine what he's seeing now: IHOP, Bed-Bath-Beyond, Target, Marshalls . . . various other such shit you find in the average barren suburban strip mall . . . and what the fuck is a "Wawa?" The Petco and Best Buy, *yep*, still there, with MPD officers posted like comic mall cops . . . playing games on their phones rather than walking beats outdoors.

Recall what was up there before? Your grandfather's dental office, where you all and hoodlums alike got your teeth cleaned. Or rather you and Alma did. They got gold grills and that old bastard billed Medicaid for it. Every hand was out, yet there was plenty to go around; the "Spanishes" were pretty much hemmed into Mt. Pleasant and nowhere else sucking up the oxygen, right Junior? You respect these folk after seeing all this? Say it—they're worse than these spooks who want the yuppies and hipsters to vacate, just the black dentists, lawyers, accountants are gone, the fries and gravy and hand-patted crab cakes and half smokes they ate for lunch are gone . . . the dives and open mic night are gone, the beads and cowrie shells and exotic fruit and custom-cut meat and fragrant bouquets their clients all offered, are gone. Same liquor stores, though. Owned by the damn Viet Cong.

Still . . . how do these ofays keep falling for the same grift run by landlords, by Bracht? Three-grand a month? For the privilege of dodging half of El Salvador each morning on the way to work, then sharing a sidewalk with scary, mumbling bastards like you every night after spin class? *Ha!*

"Stop! I'm on the clock!"

Not finished yet, Junior . . . . .so your gin-soused, half-wit uncle'd buy a Goddamn plastic ant farm for you every Easter. By Memorial Day, the roiling mass of ants, industrious yet aimless, would be dead no matter how much table sugar and water droplets you'd shove in there. You've plucked a Little Debbie Swiss Roll out of a garbage can, and yet you are too proud to forage in Columbia Heights for the same reason those ants worked and died: too much, not enough, all plastic.

So now you're praying Bad Santa's stepping gingerly through that sprawling nest of legs, mandibles and stingers toward the creatures on this heap's fringe. Those *muchachos* . . . Stripe's tribe. Boy, they are a sight that'd get Trump's dick hard without pills or flattery: huddled in clumps at the plazas and fountains . . . tangled amidst the *al fresco* eatery seating disassembled for the winter . . . sprawled, prostrate, on the colorful brick pavement . . . waking to hoot at any female within range. Mumble in Spanish to other passers-by.

Get them to talk about "*Tía* Carolina." You got this, moe. Hard to fuck it up. Did she tell their fortunes, lift spells, scribble hexes? You laid some bucks on your sidekick for loosening tongues, but hey, he's Santa. Rather than give them the cash he'll probably buy a burger and fries, a fifth of rum . . .

. . . and you're mulling this as you climb from your destination, where Georgia Avenue meets New Hampshire Avenue. Though the bus traffic and bustle are palpable, there is little of the ant heap quality tainting what's one stop down the line. No packaged cheesy diversity. Everyone sticks to their tribal grounds—beer gardens, curated cocktails . . . the beauty shops and bullet-proof carry-outs . . . the botanicas and laundromats.

Metro cops, in their unfriendly blue BDUs, web belts and black body armor make you the second you step off the escalator into the waning sunlight. Those black Johnny Cash peels, son, flowing coat, Tims—now you are someone to be feared, challenged . . . and one is tailing you as you amble up New Hampshire. You hear her gear clacking but pay her no mind.

You stop, abruptly, staring dead east toward the hill that marks the neighborhood's eastern border and the northern line with adjoining Park View.

And to the cop's surprise, you turn and ask with the most Caucasian vanilla earnest accent, "Excuse me ma'am . . . the Old Soldier's and Sailor's Home is up there, correct?"

"Uh . . . yes . . . " she fumbles, " . . . Armed Forces Retirement Home, go over to Upshur . . . "

"Thanks."

You put her off her game. Nice work, gelcap. But she's re-upping her cop bearing as you move away.

"How are things today? Everything okay?"

You keep walking, stride fluid, no pained shuffle.

"Sir, I'm talking to you . . . "

You don't stop. Instead you reply, courteously, hands where she can see them, "I'm good, officer. Happy Holidays."

And you leave her nonplussed and shrugging . . . watching you disappear into the checkerboard of century-old row-houses. Two days ago you'd be stinking and mumbling and abusive, and she'd have you in zip-ties.

You stick to broad oaks, parked cars as cover. Don't want to be mistaken for your quarry, right? Indeed, with the shut-down, and school letting out today for the holiday, more folks will be on the street.

Doesn't take long for the bait to appear.

A blue and orange FedEx truck cuts across your path at the corner; a UPS truck swings past you up the block. They are like the Spanish galleons of old, and the booty's about to be laid down on porches and stoops in plain view of the cor-sairs chasing them. Which to track? You figure the FedEx truck's carrying something someone needs today, fast. You go with that instinct, though keeping the brown truck in your line of sight.

Sure enough, the driver's out a few houses down to the right. Four juicy parcels: two Amazon boxes, one soft mailer with "Anthropologie" emblazoned on it, one from Chewy. Hell, you've heard of folks lifting insulin and injectables, auc-tioning them to folks with sugar or lupus for cash, or bartering for weed or unbricked phones. There's even a market for stolen dog food. Some people are desperate, yeah but most of these niggas are just trifling and larcenous. Neither are that crafty. Don't have to be, as the cops don't give a shit. Indeed, here comes your proof . . .

. . . the MPD unit rolls right past you and the idling delivery truck, turns at the stop sign. You crouch near a light pole for a few minutes . . . the truck leaves . . . the po-po never come back.

Trap baited . . . still no quarry for the gumshoe in second-hand Tims, huh?

Wait . . . your less-filmy eyes spy movement . . . a door, vibrating as if activated by a bored ghost, there on the ground floor of what once a stately corner rowhouse. The structure's now a bland showpiece for yet another suburban developer and its border-jumping carpenters and masons. Popped-up two stories and out thirty feet, like a giant shoe box with windows. And what used to be the coal chute's dug out and turned into a utility door servicing four condos. That's what you're seeing doing the shimmy in a flat cold calm, no wind . . .

"Line's dancing," you whisper, like the skippers on the Chesapeake used to say when the sergeants'd take their sons out for bluefish. Dumbass house flippers make everything pretty but there's always access to a crawl space . . . plywood 'cause they're cheap. Of course you know that. Because you watched, you listened. And *voilà*, out of the door slides Big Roach.

His ski mask is yanked up; no shame even in burglary. And he's styling with his newly purloined Fendi tote bag under his arm and looks so feminine executive-on-the-go with a laptop and iPhone in his other hand. Some whitefolks are going to come home from skiing in Vermont and get a big surprise.

You creep closer, ducking onto stoops whenever he checks his nine and six o'clocks. He's not looking for you, anyway, nor the cops. He's wary of nosey hipsters. He stuffs the electronics in the Fendi, carries it now as if he owns it. It's such a ridiculous sight it just may work, and now he's picked up the scent of his next meat, naked on a porch.

There's some bare forsythia right next to the steps of the house. No good for cover but at least you'll be obscured long enough to get in striking range. Brave *and* focused, Lord you want Esme worse than Bracht right!

Most of these spots have digital security cameras. There's a warning sign right on the house—no deterrent to Big Roach sticking his ugly grill right in the doorway. his greedy ass scoops up the parcels and ambles down the steps . . .

. . . yet to his left all he sees is a big black blur.

Linebackers used to launch like that at you back in the day, that CTE mess.

The boxes and the Fendi tote bag fly up as you smash him down to the cold sidewalk and yeah, you hear something pop in his hip and shoulder. He sees your face long enough to recognize you without the dirt and hair, but before he can scream your name you've twisted just enough of his huge bulk off the concrete to get your right arm around his neck.

And now you squeeze.

He's thrashing, bucking . . . yet you constrict like a boa until he's making a noise halfway between high notes on a harmonica and toddler's whine; snot, spit, blood fly from nostrils and lips.

"Ain't . . . scared a you . . . n-nigga," black Lurch strains. "M-My daddy was . . . a Bl-Black Panther . . . bitch . . . "

"He didn't teach you . . . it's a bad idea to run your mouth . . . in choke-hold?" you growl. "Learned this move . . . in the Air Force. Ain't nobody . . . coming to help you . . . " You see a pudgy white man on an expensive bike roll to stop, eyes wide. "*P-Package thief*," you groan to him.

"Oh . . . um . . . okay . . . I'm gonna call nine-one-one."

"Nah . . . I . . . got this . . . "

He peddles on, fast.

"Where Lil' Roach at? Don't you lie . . . I'll let go just enough so you can answer without passing out."

"Up . . . up on Upshur . . . "

"He strapped? He got a blade?"

"F-Fuck you . . . "

He didn't get the message. You see a piss stain widen on the crotch of his droopy, beat-up jeans and Lord if that doesn't make you feel alive more than surviving the fennie and smack. You've arrived, son. But give him a break . . .

"I'm gonna loosen up again . . . and you are gonna tell me where you and Lil' Roach saw Esmerelda Rubio . . . yeah . . . *my girl* . . . if the truth's in you I'll let you go without lullabying you . . . and I promise not . . . to tell . . . the next white motherfucker coming down this block to call the po-po on you. The street . . . will never know . . . I beat you down till you pissed yourself . . . "

He's seeing stars. Helicoptering arms're trying to reach your face, legs pump—the body's last hurrah, nothing more. You loosen up a smidge.

Some little kids in backpacks and maroon uniforms, hoodies, earmuffs come by; they stare. You tell them this is a bad man. All but one nod and that outlier, a small boy with a frosted faux-mohawk not unlike Stripe's chastens them, *"Aw, y'all're snitch muvfukkas!"*

"No!" you shout at him. "He steals, he hurts people. *Y'all hear?* If any one of you . . . want to be like him . . . I'll come back here and choke you out, too!"

Nice work. They scatter, fast.

Talk about snitching, well, Lurch isn't the dullard you thought he was . . .

"*Aw'ight, aw'ight* . . . I di'n't see the bitch. Lil' Roach say he did . . . we was up Georgia . . . all them pigs, amba-lance . . . was swarmin' 'round that building, bringin' bodies out the elevator."

It'd be easy to lunch, allow him to bust loose and drop fists on you until you're glassed or dead. It takes all your newfound will to hold him and fire questions in the face of the words *apartment house* and *bodies.*

"*What* apartment house? Was it the new Park View tower? Talk!"

He coughs and clarifies, "Yeah . . . shit . . . some senior cit'zens got deaded in there . . . only big buildin' on the muv-fuckin' corner, moe. Damn Dickie—we're you been?"

Oh yeah. *Where you been.* That hurts worse than what you kirked on this fool.

"They . . . they . . . say that's Dickie's bitch, she back in the jont, moe . . . they say she . . . in the crowd and run away and housing po-po went after her . . . try to question her."

She was there hours after you. Now you're wrapping your long legs around his lower torso like you're the mixed martial arts king of Petworth to sate your own fury.

"*Arrrrgghhhh* . . . .n-no . . . Lil' Roach tell me straight . . . he say she damn fine, still. He don't know why she wit' a touched, caveman nigga like you. He say shit just ta fuck witchew!"

"That ain't a fact, moe . . . he never met her, never knew her!"

You got to end this fast because cars are coming by, more pedestrians and this nigga gladiator contest is attracting attention.

"H-Hold up!" he relents. "Real live . . . all he doin' was saying what them folk be sayin'. Ask that fat lil' Santa Claus nigga. He know them mugs . . . by Eddie Leonard's . . . on the block all day an' night!"

No, Black Santa never told you. But the Captain warned you, days that now seem like weeks ago. You loosen the grip on Big Roach's neck, diaphragm and kidneys just for a second, yet not for mercy's sake.

"They say she ate all up in the feelins'—like she knew what happened to the senior cit'zens."

"They . . . who's *they*?"

"Yeah nigga, *they* . . . them niggas . . . always up by Eddie Leonard's . . . and that boy be slingin' the Xanny, the her-on . . . he say to Lil' Roach 'Damn, that Dickie's bitch an' she back wit' the Spanish mugs cros't Fo'teenth Street.' His name be Stoli . . . "

Stoli, like the vodka. Stoli . . . same mug who plugged you the hot dose that put you under the defibrillator leads . . .

"Yeah Lil' Roach say Stoli, he sell your bitch some Xanny . . . that's how come we know it really was her. Stoli say the Otis Place *chicos* be watchin' her. *Brigada.* Stoli the only nigga they do the biz wit . . . he hang at Park Morton where he baby mama lives . . . "

Taking advantage of the fugue his revelations cause, he manages to wheel a fist around to the side of your head. That'll raise a welt for sure. You extract more piss in reprisal until you realize it's time to get the hell out of there. Cops don't care about thousands of dollars in parcel larceny but spooks wrestling on the sidewalk brings them in legions. You release him like that Seminole alligator wrestler did a fifteen-footer—remember when you and your sister were in Orlando for summer vacation? Yeah, fast and with distance. Still, a kick to the nuts keeps him down and writhing. Mean streak, boy . . . real mean.

"I'm going to put these packages back. By the time I get off the porch your ass better be gone. You come at me an' mine in retaliation, I'll have something for all y'all. *Look at me.* I'm a new man . . . "

And sure enough, he's limping north up Fifth Street as you return the packages. Just in time, as you see an MPD unit peeling off from Grant Circle, lights flashing. Guess you two were spotted, dancing. Yes, they will find Big Roach first. Yes, they will roust him and maybe his ass will be sent back to Rivers.

Sad story. Not your story, though. You roll into the alley, cut through the clapboard fences delineating backyard lots until you emerge on Rock Creek Church Road.

By now it's dark and it's getting colder. You make for the subway to rendezvous with Black Santa, who's fixing to have some explaining to do, trust.

On the ride down your mind's stuck on the Otis Place *Brigada.* Esme was never a pillar of their community so why do they have her back? She despised peasant immigrants. Plus, she's Mexican; these cats are Salvadoran and from most other banana republics, even some black as coal Dominicans and Panamanians! Never as hardcore as the MS-13 boys; as far as you know, the worst is some of them plugging the *mafafa* and even meth to pay for housing and immigration lawyers for their folk. Thye band together, unlike your people, to set up laundromats and the *cambios*, where Pedro can send his Yankee bucks back home. Lord knows they've glassed many a nigga who's tried to roll construction workers on payday.

Shit. And your girl was hanging with them, close to Eva and Fred.

126

Above ground, the ants of Columbia Heights buffet you, just as the headlights, the streetlights, the Christmas decorations pop on, in scary synchronization. The whitefolks are tugging rollaway bags now and either meeting Ubers and Lyfts or charging straight for the subway for the airport or Amtrak. The happier ones are doubtless headed to balmier climes and sugar-white ski mountains; the grim ones are in for round two from Thanksgiving—enduring peckerwood relatives in red MAGA hats.

The spick contingent, fresh off their minimum wage gigs and late paydays, are only now hitting the jont in waves for Christmas shopping. Easy, therefore, to miss a gathering up from the Chik-fil-a of some youngins around Black Santa. Their North Face or Columbia bubble jackets obscure all but the top of the elf's red balaclava. No way he could cry for help over the blare of horns, sirens, bus engines and banter.

You push past the ants to get across Irving Street. *Damn*, his pudgy ass's blocked from escape by benign street vendors hawking LED light-up toys and *mujers* offering yucca fries and *elote* smeared with mayo and cheese. Not so benign are four kids looking barely thirteen or fourteen, maybe? All like little girls in those damn skinny jeans these kids like.

Neighborhood knuckleheads. Yeah, it's a doggerel that blackfolk shouldn't fear other blackfolk, but the I-don't-give-a-fuck in their eyes is terrifying. Indeed, last time you saw Fred alive, he was complaining how these toy criminals deciphered the security on the scooters and dockless rental bikes on which they lean.

They see you coming . . . in your big black coat and black beanie . . . the ruddy swelling on your face. They give a collective gulp as if you're half bogeyman, half baller.

"Yo, you loopin' fo' Stoli?" one child queries you. "He ain't call us, moe."

"Kill, moe . . . I ain't hit the corner yet . . . " another offers. "I know you?"

Another's eyes widen and he gasps, "No nigga, *he Five-O* . . . I seent him bustin' Tariq yessarday in fronta the CVS!"

Without a further curse or threat, they mount their networked scooters and bikes, peel off and scatter to make their rounds for whatever older scumbags were paying them to be the Pony Express for weed, Tina, meth, pills.

Black Santa's palpably relieved.

"Likkel 'oodlums, dem . . . folla mi cause mi ask questions."

"You get any answers?"

He inspects your wound.

"Look like someone did, bred'rin. Big Roach?"

You shrug and reply, "The info's more painful than what he did. Esme was there when Eva and Fred's bodies were found . . . and Jenn left that out."

"Ya talk ta Jenn, Lard?"

You nod, then survey skittering ants. "She may be walking ten feet from us, for all we'd know."

"Mi *Espanol* not sa good but 'ere's wha'apinin'. Keep counta yarself, buoy . . . "

He tells you first what you already knew. That Esme disappeared, five years ago but then snuck back, left more than you hanging. ICE is looking for her sister Marta. Marta . . . lil' sexy, weird boho Marta—she's been hiding in plain sight here, all these years, but no one cared until now. It's got Hell to do with Trump. It's because of Esme's return.

"Dem 'ave same story wha' Stripe tell you. Esme, 'er 'elp cops dem bus' up gang traffickin' dem Spanish gals. Whole houses ova Mt. Pleasant an' ev'm ova on Kenyon Street, near where Eva get dat apartment. She call 'erself 'Auntie Carolina,' use Obeah ta scare dese pussyclot gangtas."

"*Ixchel . . .* " you mumble under the din of the boulevard. "Sanctuary. Trafficked girls, their kids probably . . . born of rapes and unprotected sex from the tricks. Shit. Any mention of the Otis Place *Brigada*?"

"Dem *Brigada* buoys, dem see me talk up dem campers, but dey na say where Stripe at. Ya find 'im up Petworth."

"No. And that's interesting . . . given that they're tryna protect Esme."

"Dem just as soon beat me bloody, like dese 'ooligans."

"But they didn't, right? Because the natural order's all . . . tw-twisted, Black Santa."

That stammer stings you and widens his eyes as well. What Mr. Sugars giveth, eh? How much time before you revert to Bruce Banner . . . or Mr. Hyde?

"Yar al-right, Dick?"

"F-Fine," you say with a gulp. "Let's walk."

"Okay . . . de Spanish boys say she come bock, den disappear again . . . dis time fa couple days . . . den, come bock only—"

"When Eva and Fred died," you interrupt.

"Not just, mon."

"Wait . . . what?"

"Some odder fuckery. Dey say sudd'nly 'er payin' grocery an' shit fi some gal, 'igh school, uppa Bell on de cornah."

He means Bell Multicultural High School, just around the corner on Sixteenth Street. Indeed, you noticed two of those kids menacing Black Santa wore the blue polos and skinny khakis of Bell under their unzipped North Face, and one was young enough to have on the middle school maroon of

Lincoln, which shares the campus. Damn shame, especially when most of the student body counts parents from Central and South America.

"A high school girl? Maybe one of the girls trafficked . . . she was helping her get a new identity, maybe . . . "

He shrugs as his little legs struggle to keep up with you but reminds you, "Esteban . . . Stevie . . . 'im say 'e see young an' old version in yar photos, eh? Yar t'ink . . . well?"

This is the same old goat who told you Esme, this Soloranzano woman's apartment, the hexes . . . even Oosterhaus setting up the crew . . . was all coincidence. You toss him a jaundiced glare yet move on . . .

"They mention anything about . . . about Eddie Leonard's and a mug named Stoli?"

He shrugs again but then whispers, "Peach. 'er might know shit."

"Captain told me Peach told him you were running you mouth about me. That same Peach?"

Oh take umbrage, alright. "Ain't na fuckery. Mi take yar ta Peach an' dem now."

"Good. Cause that's my next stop, corroborated by . . . *damn* . . . " Another twinge. "Big Roach."

It's a new hood once you and he escape the ants. Tall naked trees break up the street lighting, and no one sane would be walking up Irving Street alone. But there they are: pink-toes and junior Mr. Charlie's yapping on their hands-free, roaming right by you two, an odd if not menacing pair in the dark.

You hit the hill past Sherman and the vibe's still all nicey-nice and Ubers and GrubHub deliveries to homes you know damn well used to shelter bent trapping and tweaking and skin popping back in the day, as Croc's daddy knew who his customers were on Georgia Avenue. Now the closets that once hid AKs, dirty mattresses hiding dime and nickel bags and triple beam balances are now storage for kayaking and rock wall climbing gear . . .

. . . there're reminders of the old grit, however. Cheetos and Hostess wrappers, broken bottles of Heineken and Dos Equis, cups from as far as the Mickey Dees down by your school. Summons and even eviction writs, how about that? Condom wrappers looking like Kush 3-g pouches, Kush 3-g pouches looking like baseball card wrappers. Baggies, hypodermics. Sloughed wound bandages, blood and pus still wet. Loaded disposable diapers. Tumble-weaves from someone's tracks getting tore-out in a fight.

You give a deep sigh, tell the fat elf, "Part of me wishes to go back two days. When things were simple . . . ya feel me?"

"Simpler? Nut'ing simple about being on de streets, dem. Only t'ing simple is 'ow yar take bin rubbish an' duct tape an' make a dee-yam Range Rova wid it!"

Now that makes you laugh. But not feel better.

Black Santa quips, "Gwine be long night if we na makes curfew."

"We'll be okay. Listen . . . you think . . . you think Verna will do this data search for me?"

"Blouse an' skirt, Dick, if'em she can't, den yar gotta trust dat ragga gal LaKeisha. Yar won' dat? Accept wha Verna do, and do-in push."

It's now that you both peer at the high rise at the crest of the hill: spot-lit to give the appearance of full occupancy. Not enough moms on welfare and old folk like Eva and Fred to cram in there? How about the teachers, clerks, cops, firemen who must push cookware at Macy's part time just to afford a jont in the city that isn't a shithole?

Indeed, horns and the whoosh and groan and exhaust of city traffic renew, as Georgia Avenue beckons. The old row-house and storefront façades witness to street revolts and sidewalk grudge shootings remain, though now occupied with coffee bistros and day spas, art spaces and doggy daycare. It's the remnant, appendix Georgia Avenue where you two are headed, heralded by a plasma donation center and a wig shop.

One kid's already dumped a scooter at the corner and swapped a small brown paper bag for a wad of ones and fives held by another boy. The one with the cash also hands over a palm-sized object, both dark and silvery.

You and your Sancho Panza exchange looks, for years of avoiding such objects breeds familiarity, huh? It's .25 or .32, maybe even Croc's old sock gun, the .380. The transaction's all within the glow of the streetlamps, in plain view at din-nertime rather than the wee hours.

To your right, a man you think is named Maurice lays on the sidewalk babbling. Squatting next to him, a girl you know as Shirley shouts at two blonde women holding hands as they lead an energetic, full-size schnauzer trotting ahead on a leash.

"Ima cut you dyke bitches! Ima come in yo' lobby like yes-surday and cut you! Y'all worse than faggots!"

The dog barks, lunges. She yells how the po-po'll shoot the dog before they put her back in jail. Thanks to the bleeding hearts running this city, she might be right. *Unh-unh*, this is no ant farm . . . even the ant hill, up here. This is a hornets' nest, gilded in glitter paper. Act accordingly, Junior.

CHAPTER 12

Eddie Leonard's

BEFORE THERE WAS MCDONALD'S OR BURGER King, or this D.C. *haute* cuisine serving *foie gras* sliders, there was Eddie Leonard's and Hot Shoppes. A dozen at least, right? When you were little your mother would order your tuna melt at Eddie Leonard's. Crinkle-cut fries with gravy on them. A Rock Creek cream soda . . .

. . . and now there's only one Eddie left; Lord knows how. Beyond its bulletproof glass there's a cold sidewalk made fetid from years of heroin and rock stepped-down to grocery store products . . . spit, pee, blood and other offal. The bus stop shelter smells of the cheap yardbird fried up by these Viet Cong . . .

. . . and there begins the nightly opera, even in the cold. Bipolar addicts—sound familiar? Hypertensive old grizzled drunks, nigga tweekers, pill poppers, diabetics smoking your Kush . . . and of course the occasional heroin and fentanyl jockey, a bit more adept than you at carrying their baggie and works to alley.

It's all in the open, under the stars peeking through creamy clouds, and made that much more tragic by the presence of hipster condos and gastropubs. They all have plate glass windows that are better than that Netflix thing—petty shoving matches over jacks and single beers . . . somnambulistic wanderings into on-coming traffic, occasional fist fights, rare stabbings . . . the once in a couple weeks fatal shooting. That this lil' tableau has continued despite the shrinking habitat is a testament to the crushing weight of the hurt out there, but you can't dwell on that. You're on the clock and it's ticking as your stutters and tremors come faster.

Black Santa's now doing a pretty good census of the denizens this night. Peach, you tell him. Do not forget Peach . . .

. . . and yet your vehemence regarding that homeless old rolla gets a bit back-seated when you zoom in on Stoli, a dreadlock-topped fool with the scraggily goatee still on his chin, thinking he's Superfly in a glistening black leather peacoat. This plugger's raised the tactic of using the campers and addicts as human camouflage to high art. You recall that shit from the Air Force, when those Talibans'd dig in among the markets, the schools, just like the VC did back in the day? Easier to hide among the bums and freaks to dispense product and get paid, than do it across the street at the Park Morton projects and risk some surly single mother egged on by white goody-goodies snitching you out to the Housing cops.

"Small yarself, Dick," Black Santa advises. "Some dese peoples na warm ta yar."

You hang back. An exterior brick wall provides a good shadow; it's all that's left of the old structure, razed for a new apartment building. In the Eighties it was a flophouse where inhabitants traded sex for rock. Way before that, it was your pediatrician's office.

Unfortunately, your post abuts the main door to a dance studio, and you're finding it difficult to not look menacing to the airy folk leaving their final before Christmas, as they chatter. Still, you keep your eyes stapled on the action . . .

. . . and that must be Peach right there in the motorized wheelchair . . . doing wheelies and spins in the damn thing while Black Santa's prancing around her. Peach is puffing on her jack, blue-ish gray "pixie" cut wig askew from the wheelchair acrobatics, cat's eye glasses dangling from shoelaces at her chest. That old bat is one of the few like Eva and Fred to survive the Reagan's crack rock, W's recession, Obama's promises and—so far—Trump's sickle.

There's a camper you recognize, wearing an Orioles baseball cap over a black wavecap, and a weird braided ponytail swaying from underneath. Ole James isn't six feet under? That mug's got so much lead in him he could write his name with his finger on a piece of paper. Good thing the liquor dulls the pain.

Back in the day, Georgia Avenue folk called him "Scorpio." Not for any street malice. It's just that he used to twist a steel arrowhead into the end of that ponytail—thus a scorpion's stinger. Like Black Santa, he's one of a few Eighties survivors you know, HIV-free supposedly . . . losing only his ability to walk upright. He's stumbling around, crook-backed like a letter "C" and propped up by a metal cane of cheap drug store quality. Lord, the scene's like some twisted college reunion.

And none of them pay Stoli any mind.

You, however, catch the nervous eye of a white girl toting a pair of strappy dance heels.

Look at you, being all proactive! "Excuse me, Miss?" Your polite mien is the only thing convincing her not to scream.

"Anyone ever try to figure out what's going on out here?" Yes, you are being legit.

She sighs in relief, thinking you less likely to smack her and take her shit.

"I try to stay out of it," she says. "If they don't bother me why would I bother them?"

This skinny guy following close behind injects himself, huffing, "I mean, you guys used to pop out of unmarked cars and arrest these dudes, clear the corners. Now I guess we must wait until more condos come up before all this crap fossilizes? Now that I'm furloughed, I get to see the dysfunctional crap going on in the daylight, too, and, like, if you guys have a sub-station around the corner why it's so hard to keep order?"

You guys? Keep order? He thinks you're an undercover porker. *Ha!*

"Thank you for your . . . candor," you reply with your deadpan and flat voice. "But ignoring them . . . or more accurately . . . *buying product from them,* isn't helping . . . "

You hear this fool gasp and grumble *"How dare you"* as you peel yourself from the wall and lope across Lamont Street to launch yourself. You aren't trying to be discreet or small tonight, though the Youtube videos teaching elementary sleuthing advise both. Shit, you have no time, and there's Stoli . . . .

Upon seeing your approach, a wide-eyed Black Santa cries, *"Jeezum creama!"*

The violence against Big Roach in the waning daylight energized you. Now you're keyed on the bastard who sold you the fentanyl. And poor Stoli looks up from counting his green a bit too late. You're on him like a mama fly on a steamy turd, and he's pinned up against the bus stop's smudged glass wall, and he's whining how the glass is going to break soon if you don't let him go . . .

"Izz-dat muh-fukkin Dickie Cornish?" the Peach drawls as she wheels closer, as if you do *not* have a dope-trapping dreadlock fool smashed onto the bus stop glass? "Lawd it *is* you. Baby, why you monsterin'?"

You look to Stoli, who's neck's locked under your forearm.

"Business . . . and personal, Peach. I'll get to you in a sec . . . "

"I ain't no *Ghenghis Kann,* nigga," Stoli hisses from under your grasp. "Imo'goin' let you hang yo'self."

You take that to mean he's not strapped or carrying a blade to fight you off. He's too smart for that—so close to the police station around the corner. They probably tolerate his monopoly presence anyway—you know, it's Cop 101. Best to let one somewhat civilized plugger plug, then ten niggas cowboying with the potential of a white mommy with a designer papoose strapped to her walk in front of a stray round.

And Stoli knows the cops don't know *your* big ass anymore. Cops hate wild cards, so you better speed this reunion up . . .

"Woman calls herself '*Tía* Carolina,'" you holler at Stoli, then the old woman. "Where?"

Peach spins her chair to Black Santa and shouts, "Fitzy, y'all best collar this dawg . . . we ain't fittin' ta move onaccount Dickie's bullshit!"

"Dick, come so," Black Santa meekly implores you.

"Ain't nobody here wanted see ole Fred, Miz Eva die," Peach declares in her dry rasp. "But yo' girl, she come back! Yeah . . . she here an' Lawd if she ain't got sump'in ta do wiff it . . . "

You nod to her, but you keep Stoli pinned though his minions have already scattered across the street to either hide or bring reinforcements. Black Santa sees this and nervously confirms, "Like mi say . . . dem Spanishes wha know Stripe tell Esme all ova dat build'n when po-po Eva an' Fred murda'd bodies. Year befo' dat, down de street, Esme dere when po-po find young gals' bodies. M'suppose she say enough is enough. She snitches on gang brothel. She try fi speak hex and witchly shit on other houses, protect odda gals..."

"Facts, Santa," you cut in. *"Need facts!"* Now you're an inch from Stoli's nose, so close you can smell the fried fish on his breath. "And you, my nigga . . . with your H, dosed with F, got anything to add?"

Oh, he does.

"Been eatin' yo' Wheaties, moe? All swole and tough from rehab?"

"Just got a hard-on for you. Keeps my head clear."

"Dickie, your smelly ass came to *me* . . . miserable and callin' the planets for a one-way ticket to Pluto. Don't you blame me, motherfucker, for shootin' that shit in your arm!"

Though prone and pinned, Stoli's staring right back at you in defiance until Peach breaks the silence.

"Dem Brigade Spanish boys come down yessirday after Fred an' Eva bodies be fount," Peach chronicles, " . . . tell us ta leave *Tía* Carolina be or they rackin'niggas up."

"So?" you grunt back at her.

"So . . . de hood peaceable until she come back! Fed-lookin' white men comin' 'round den. Say dey goin' lock-up Brigade boys like they MS-13 killas, and dey goin' lock us up, too, for 'obstructin' justice' onaccount we don't know where dis bitch *Tía* Carolina be at?"

Son, when you ever hear of the Feds sweeping into this neighborhood, rounding up black and brown alike—to find one woman who actually broke up the pimping and trafficking?

"Mr. Sugars and his crew . . . " Goddamn right. Now your impatience and their riddles are getting the best of you, so you offer, "Got the K, some jipjacks, *better* than what this fool Stoli slingin'. Cash for anyone who gives me the real live."

Stoli's wriggling free of your grip but he's keeping his distance.

"Slingin' dope now?" he huffs, sweat glistening on his face in the cold night air. "I got friends comin' who have my back . . . " But he dials the wolfing back when sees Black Santa plucking a fan of bills *from your coat pocket* to offer the crowd. Mr. Sugars is sure as hell an able quartermaster, because suddenly you have instant allies. Stoli adjusts his attitude accordingly. "Okay . . . I dunno why Peach is shit-talkin' your ole bitch, Dickie."

"Y'all shut yo' hole, Stoli!" the old woman shrieks as a Metrobus whooshes by, avoiding the bus stop and shelter given what's transpiring there. "Dickie's bitch be dime-in' Eva and Fred fo' money or shit so they let her stay in Murica! Truff ta power, nig-gaaaaaaaah!"

She hits forward then reverse on the chair as if revving engine and burning tires. Silly as the sight is, it's got Stoli agitated.

"This ole hag lies!" he shoots back. Odd how this motherfucker who almost o.d.'d you is now pleading for you to listen to his side. "Here yo' fact, Dickie: Tía ain't murderous. She like drugs, dick, and money in that order . . . but she don't kill old folks." Now he's moved in the streetlight's glare as if on a stage, about to deliver a speech. "But on the real, I hear she loved them old folks what got killt. *Cause she tole me so, this mornin'.* If folk dead because of her, it's by accident, not her hands. I just gave her what she wanted . . . 'cause she say she a 'new person' . . . 'Tía' and clean. Only take weed and the Xanny. A Mollie to wake up."

That's quite a diet, Junior, for someone smoking sherm in college and graduating to crack and Tina. You buying the "reformed" Esme? Didn't work for you, did it?

"Only other time was for a shitload of codeine, Vicodin," Stoli concludes. "She *swore* it weren't for her." With an exaggerated shrug, he reveals, "The C's for her sis, she ain't sick. Bad off."

"Wait . . . Marta?"

"The Vikes is for some other girl. Somethin' bout 'complications' and pain. Maybe it's one last lil' ho she's shepherdin' I dunno. All I say is now your grace period's up, nigga. I'm out, and if you fuck wid me again, you gettin' dead and I ain't leavin' it up to the fennie . . . "

"*Marta's with her?*" you whisper, your mouth suddenly dry.

"I said grace period's up."

Peach jumps in, with her jack perched on her lower lip and not an ash spilled.

"Ease up, Dickie! If yo' girl *Tía* Carolina got a sustah, den dem Otis Place muv-fukkahs prolly got her stashed, like they stash yo' girl. Nah, *Tía* Carolina, she got some *shortie* who be runnin' wiff her. Maybe they dykes . . . maybe dykes need Vike like I used ta git cramps?"

Black Santa skulks around then lays his fat ass on the grimy curb, whispers, "Dem buoys mi speak to, say she travel wid a girl, maybe kids . . . sometime dey need 'ospital . . . "

"You choose now to tell me this?" Indeed, you're jolted by a spell of jelly-knees, and your dome feels like a sinus headache's coming on . . .

. . . and yet Peach blows out nostrils full of cancer smoke at your big mutt self and says, calmly, "Dickie y'all jus' don't know wha' yo' ass's gotten itself into, huh? *Fitzy do.* Ain't no one outchere wanna get kilt for dis bitch, don't matter how sad it is she helpin' lil' girls, dead girls, pregnant girls . . . "

It's crook-backed James, a.ka. Scorpio, who hobbles forward and points a finger down the block.

"Stoli would tole you if you hadn't scur-red him away, Dickie. Sometimes, he and this Tía lady, they go in there." He's pointing to a botanica, still open, just a few feet down the block. You crane your neck and see the lights still on behind the plate glass of a small shop with the words *Flores y Velas* painted on the pane.

Peach scoffs, "Don'tchew get involved, Scorps!"

"It's the right thing ta do, Peach," James hits back. "And them girls who was held as hoes, then what got freed in the bust after Tía snitched—I seent lotta them in there too, like this past summer and then Fall, when they dressed for school. Safe place, remind'em of home?"

"Which school?"

"Bell. On Sixteenth . . . "

"*Shit.*"

By now, the police are coming around to see what all the fuss is about. First there are looks from their units rolling by, and now you hear radio chatter and discern the spin and clicking of their bike gears.

"See wha y'all gone and done?" Peach whispers, not wanting to arouse the curious law, approaching on their bikes. "Y'all worser dan her wiff her Satan cards and spells . . . "

"I'm going to check the botanica. You stay here, Santa . . . " Your fingers twitch. "Listen . . . I need you man, c-can't have you lyin'. What's done with Oosterhaus is done . . . we're here, now. Just don't blind side me, okay?"

"Of course, bred'rin, but . . . " he taps an imaginary watch on his wrist. Curfew beckons.

You search the faces of these streetfolk, and whatever Mr. Sugars gave you to sharpen your mien has sure enough dulled. "I-I didn't mean to scare you all."

"Them's already scared, Dickie," James laments. "Thas why we gettin' mo' fucked up . . . got my hit already."

"We ain't like you, baby," Peach adds. "You jus' broken. Us? We tore-up in pieces . . . " And she gives that raspy belly-laugh and spins that chair in a three-sixty as you walk way from her universe of a few square feet at Eddie Leonard's.

CHAPTER 13

Revelaciones Especiales

THE AROMA OVERWHELMS YOU AS YOU enter the botanica. Sickly sweet overtones; woodsy, pungent thereunder. The merchandise is behind the Plexiglass. The only thing outside the glass is a display case of generic votive candles and a cooler stocked with Fanta, Arizona Ice Teas and Sixteen ounce Sprites, small Red Bull cans. At the register behind the glass is a young Latin girl with pale skin, long black hair, wearing a polo shirt. She's taller than most of their midget chicks. Pestering her on her phone's earbuds is someone named Paco, judging from rapid number of "*Fuck you, Pacos*" she's been declaring since you entered, even though she's eyeing you and getting a smidge agitated.

You turn toward the beeping door because the famous Paco himself strolls in to do the quarrel face to face.

Paco's wearing a light blue North Face bubble coat . . . quite the change from the ubiquitous black. His hair's in a burst mohawk and fade, sort of like Stripe's without the dye.

"Excuse me," you inquire.

She sees you, she wants to help, but Paco's not having it.

"Excuse *you* . . . yo' *Bigfoot* . . . " Such is the bluff and bravado of youth.

"Um . . . miss . . . I want to buy a candle."

Paco's pissed you're dirkin' him. And you repeat, "I want to buy a candle."

"Thank . . . thank you sir. Um, like, um, what kind? For scent or . . . "

"*Hechizos.*"

"Oh . . . okay . . . um . . . "

"Gray for deep thought. And a black one . . . "

Suddenly the store landline rings. She picks up and her face contorts.

"Stop playing on the phone, eh! *Fuck* . . . " She slams it down. "*Mierda*, it's like, one thing or another!" She's quickly apologizing however and saying, "black candles, those are, like, powerful and stuff . . . "

"Actually, I-I wanna talk to whoever owns this place."

Paco's now agitated.

"Hey dude . . . yeah, ignore me again and see what happens. I ain't afraid of you, big *coño.* You don't get to say shit to her or me."

"What if I'm the police . . . or ICE, undercover."

"You ain't ICE . . . ICE is fucked because Trump ain't payin' no one to work."

"Nah, fella. ICE is getting paid."

"Lemme see your badge, *oso.* And who be your back-up . . . those old *moletto-mayates* drunk and homeless out there?"

"No."

"My uncle owns it!" the girl intercedes. "But he's only had it for like, since summer. It was vacant."

"Do you . . . have you . . . uh . . . met or know of a woman. *La mujer es una . . . bruja*, needs *velas . . . Tía Carolina?*"

She's shrugging her shoulders, shaking her head a bit. Either this child's already great at poker or she knows nothing. You played a hunch and did your best, eh?

Yet quickly she cocks her head to the side, gives a strange giggle . . . and then dumptrucks the world on you . . .

"That's like, rando, eh? You know Lourdes and her *mami?*"

"Pardon?"

"You deaf, bro'?" Paco joins in. "Rando . . . *random*, bro'! See now you ain't a cop, bro' you *loco*." He sucks his teeth and calls, "Luz you ain't got to say nuthin', eh? Close your mouth and let's go home . . . *pinche mierda . . .* "

It's like he wasn't even there. She's still going . . .

"Yeah, *ah-hah*, Lourdes say her mami come here all the time before *mi tio* bought this store and then after. Power Ball jackpot tickets . . . before *mi tio* have it she always lost, right, but after, because of the energy in here, she came, like, within two numbers of winning, twice, eh? And Lourdes say it was a woman was like dressed like a ole *telenovelas* slut, eh? But her mami say a couple times she a *bruja* . . . bring bright magic against the bad *hechizos* so she read *las cartas*. Almost win a jackpot, eh?"

"Tarot."

"*Ah-hah*, that's why it's so rando you come in here . . . "

"Hey, hey man . . . " Paco says, trying to stay tough and relevant. "The fuck you want?"

"You know a lowlife named Stripe, lives in the Saint Stephen's church community center basement on Sixteenth?"

"Paco see!" Luz screeches, "like . . . is so *random*, eh?"

"The white church? He my cousin's stepson," Paco shares freely . . . dejectedly. "Why? He owe you money?"

"No. He believes in the *hechizos*, and the Maya *K'iche'* language for the very old Maya symbols that still hold power. That's no bullshit, kids. He's scared of this *Tía Carolina* and maybe you should be, too."

"He's *cavernícola* . . . live under there, tunnel . . . man," he moans, as if your black isn't in the secret.

"Tunnel?"

The teen sucks his teeth and huffs, "Luz, it's fuckin' late, eh . . . and you need to close out and lemme walk you home."

"Paco I'm fine, eh? Stop playin' . . . you aren't my papi, jeez. No school till like, January, *day-um*. Lourdes, her mami say this *bruja* is no, like, *fake-ass* because *La Brigada* say she help them and police mess up those boys, you know like . . . " she's whispering now, " . . . *mara salvatrucha* . . . and these Jewish guys who speak Russian who help them . . . was all up in the neighborhood, eh? Up Park Road and Mt. Pleasant, like, where my grandmother live, right . . . who gets them fake IDs . . . "

"Luz!"

The whispers end. "Shut *up*, eh? He's no cop, yo'!" She's back to teenager-ing at you. "Like, they bring these girls in from El Salvador, Guatemala, Honduras . . . not so much from Mexico anymore, right? They're like fourteen like my sister Valentina, and they are like prostitutes, and they was in our school and even in Lourdes' geometry class but they didn't know shit about geometry or anything . . . and the *bruja* rescue them . . . but then that fokker Trump go and deport them to Mexico when they were the victims, right? *And they ain't Mexican right?*" The whisper comes back. You hunch closer to humor her. "But this *bruja* who look like a prostitute save them . . . from gangs, right. See, gangs they use the evil *hechizos* to scare these girls and families . . . poor and don't know shit. But

Lourdes' mami, she say *Tía* Carolina she use the good *hechizos* to fight it. Old spooky shit like the Maya—understand?"

You nod. This child should have been the first person you interviewed. You get a C- on your sleuthing exam, son . . .

. . . and Paco's ready to spill.

"I know Lourdes' *mami*. Her mami like all these old peeps in this neighborhood, yo'. They talk too much. *Revelaciones especiales*! Lourdes say shit, her *mami* say shit . . . cray, bro.' Shit like the *bruja*, the witch Tía—get this: she tryna find some *chica* a job, a bed, enroll at school . . . "

Another girl, *again* . . .

"This *chica*, this fancy-ass *puta* who think she better than anyone in school. And she a prostitute, huh? Dead ass."

"But . . . I'm guessing she wasn't one of the girls *Tía* Carolina saved . . . maybe hid . . . like in apartments all over town. Maybe off Twelfth and N Streets, even? Maybe she rescued her from ICE?"

"Twelfth and N, eh?" Luz chirps. "Hey, my uncle lives down there."

Paco rolls his eyes at his girl and huffs, "Who the fuck gets rescued from ICE, bro?'" White mother-fokkers everywhere say even *we* who was born here ain't even shit."

You grab a stool, look him in the eye and it makes him feel important. "Hold up a sec . . . " You pull out that phone. No messages from Mr. Sugars. There's just one app to find shit and you do. Trafficking. Latinas. Girls as young as twelve coming here . . . and they aren't hiking across the desert like migrants seeking asylum for their toddlers or shoved into trucks by the *coyotes*. They're imported like wine and cheese.

"Tell me what you know," you whisper staring into his eyes. "You know more than the older folks. Notice I didn't . . . didn't say 'adults,' 'cause you are an adult, right? A man."

"*Sí serío*, I'm a man, dude," he swelling. "Look I know this *chica* too. She was different. Different look, no *metizo*, act all superior *como* like we are mice. But she dirty, bro'. Then soon she gone, out. And *la mujer* reading the cards, she gone too. Now you show up. Ain't no *rando* nuthin' . . . "

"Was this *Tía* Carolina?" you ask, showing them Esmeralda's pics.

Luz hedges and says maybe. Best to show Lourdes' mami. Paco's only good for a shrug and says Lourdes and her *mami* live up over Spring and Sixteenth in the Woodner apartments—an old Howard U. haunt of yours after the coach bounced you. Roach motel back then; now full of both hipsters and voucher tenants. That could be the next stop and you are thinking of cutting Black Santa loose so at least he can make curfew.

But it looks like Paco's had a come to *Hay-sus* moment in his head, because he's motioning to you.

"Don't mess with Lourdes, bro'. She dumb as fuck."

"Hey Paco day-um," Luz complains, "why you say that mess, eh?"

"Dead ass, bro'—the only friend . . . if you want her that cause she *loco*, too—this *chica* had while this *bruja* had her stashed, her name Pashmina. They was in home room together. *Especiale* . . . "

Pashmina? What kind of name is that? And now your gut's bubbling and it's not from a K2 ulcer . . .

"Special ed? Doesn't fit."

You were in those programs as a kid for a spell, eh? So why doesn't it fit?

"Come *on*, bro. Special program, 'cause they was *both pregnant* . . . Pashmina dropped out, too. They say Feds after her, like ICE, but . . . in whiteman suits, no style . . . "

Your brain's cooking, despite the pain. Full burners now.

"Hook me up with this Pashmina?"

Luz gives a great big smile and for the first time you see she's wearing braces on her teeth.

"I'm FaceTiming Lourdes, okay. She, like, can ask her *mami* anything. Maybe find Pashmina's address. What'd you say your name is?"

"I didn't. I was never here. I scared away a drug dealer outside . . . ask any of those old folks down the block. I want to help *Tía* Carolina . . . get from the Feds . . . so I need to talk to Pashmina, okay?"

With childish exuberance and naivete Luz shows you Lourdes' chubby face, too much lipstick . . . and Lourdes freely shares an address on Fourteenth, a couple of blocks north of you. Not the one given to D.C. Public Schools, she says. These are the actual safe places, likely overheard from fraught friends and family when it comes to shielding loved ones from criminals here or down there . . . or from Uncle Sam.

"One thing," you say in your low voice to a nervous, restive Paco. "What's this girl's name—the ho who acts like a spoiled brat and who was in Pashmina's class?"

You pull out pad and pen as he grunts, as if in on a joke, "Piedade."

You write it anyway and reply, "'*Piety*?' A teen prostitute with that name?"

You take out the burn to check the time as no one's given you a proper watch. Two hours till curfew. And suddenly Black Santa's in front of the door that Paco has locked, waving.

Luz adds, wincing as she watches your cohort, "These *chicas* the gangs bring, like, they keep them in darkness, you know? Like, they say train tunnels in Mexico. Keep always in dark until their skin, like, lightens like they white girls. Piedade, in Pashmina's homeroom, like, Lourdes say one day she laugh and say she no in some tunnel, dark and scary. She say she come in the bright light, in, like an air-conditioned bus with wifi . . . hello, *wifi?*"

"You got her last name?"

Lourdes's broad face answers from Luz's screen, "*Pashmina? Something funny: Manzana . . .* "

"No. 'Piety' . . . Piedade's last name."

"*Uh-huh, Guatemalan, no Mexicano,*" Lourdes prattles. "*Shit I can't remember . . .* "

Luz has an epiphany. "From when she got out of gym . . . oh, shit . . . yeah . . . like it's Soloranzano. Piedade Soloranzano."

You slump back onto the stool, and the phone almost falls to the floor.

"*Soloranzano . . .* you're sure?" and your voice is almost a whisper.

"Dude . . . bro'?" Paco presses. He doesn't know why your face has gone blank.

"Um . . . yeah . . . let that fat man in the store, Paco." You point at Luz. "Tell Lourdes to tell her *mami* not to talk to anyone about this. Not . . . a soul! You both got a safe way home?"

Paco speaks up. "Yeah dude—my scooter, the alley."

You take out a twenty and tell him to bring the scooter inside. "Lock it up in the store. Here's fare for a cab."

"You're like, scaring me, eh?" Luz complains, clicking off with her friend.

But she's not half as scared as you are now . . .

CHAPTER 14

"She's still my blood"

"WHA'GWAN, DICK?" BLACK SANTA PRESSES YOU as you stroll west along Monroe Street to Fourteenth, "Yar cross wit' me, eh? Well fire fi yar, cause mi don't—"

"I don't wanna hear it," you warn, your tone and extra height cowing him.

James is your new recruit, to keep an eye on your old one. He's keeping pace despite a diabetic foot and bent walk.

"Spanishes ain't gonna like us rollin' up there asking questions," he says. "Whedder she 'Tía' or Esmeralda—she sure was a purdy mess. Workin' roots and shit." He catches your big arm. "Dickie, Peach di'nt mean no harm 'bout y'girl or disrespek. Peach just talk shit and she get scared and talk shit s'more. All them muvfukkas on edge, can't you see? Even Stoli di'n't come back ta shoot yo' ass after you kirked on him."

Piedade Soloranzano . . . Sabine Soloranzano: your mind's flipping and rolling those names and so you don't even hear half of what this old nigga said.

Finally you wake up, "My employer says he wants this wrapped up by Christmas if possible." And you don't care if

Black Santa and James are crossing fretful looks. "If you wanna air out. Go. I got cash to add on your Metrocard, can get a cab for you, James . . . "

"Yar daft," Black Santa says with a jolly, belly shaking Santa laugh. First you'd seen in two days. "We yar back-up."

Yeah, check them out. Bet you feel better already, huh?

Pashmina's usually at the Colonial Laundromat on Fourteenth doing loads for elderly neighbors, and lives, per the address Luz and Lourdes quoted, over a taqueria. And there's like a hundred taqueria's on the block . . .

. . . and worse, while you all are invisible to the hipsters rushing home, the Latins on who's turf you three have marched like a busted Spirit of '76 are definitely staring, reporting. You guys roll up into Colonial and not only is she not there, none of the *mujers* and *abuelas* yanking underpants out of the dryers know who the hell she is.

The Otis Place *Brigada* still considers itself a neighborhood watch despite the less savory shit these spicks do to pay the bills, so watch it.

You see a taqueria built into a stand-alone frame house. Its small neon "Carryout" sign's on yet there're no diners evident through the plate glass. There are, however, wooden steps, like a fire escape, up to an apartment portion and it can be approached without anyone in the eatery or the sidewalk fronting Fourteenth seeing you. Shadows cast by a giant walnut tree's trunk and branches obscuring the streetlights and headlights are a bonus.

"Often you must make a judgment call," you say, reciting one of the amateur gumshoe videos on the Youtube, on your new toy. "James, you stay as lookout 'cause you don't do stairs well. Black Santa you come up with me . . . "

Black Santa cautions as you reach the door, "Mi 'ope yar know wha yar doin', mon . . . "

Yep. You draw a breath and ring the ancient buzzer. There are lights on, the faint smell of something sweet being rendered, like sautéed fruit, maybe for a pie? You hear voices—female possibly—yet no one answers until you hit the buzzer again . . .

. . . and the person cracking the door with the steel chain taut is a mere teen like Luz, but chubby, pooch extended over her pajama bottoms, black hair in a bun, D.C. United tee shirt stretched by ample breasts. Glasses, a tinge of acne on her chin and forehead . . .

"How much?" she says, seeing only you.

"Pardon?" The ill-at-ease mutter seems to make her less inclined to think you are a robber.

"Postmates? Johnny's Dragon Carry-out?"

"No." You position your foot for a quick thrust onto the jamb and you pray your charity cast-off Tims are legit enough to take the blow. "I'm . . . a friend . . . I spoke to Luz, Lourdes and her mother . . . "

"*Wait,*" she says, eyes narrowing. And then she panics. "Good-bye," she says with a gasp and she slams the door . . . on your foot.

The pain's bearable.

"I-I'm a friend . . . look . . . a friend of *Tía* Carolina. Come to help. My name's—"

"*Fuck!*"

A shoulder into the door seems extreme yet suddenly your foot is throbbing and you dislodge it; she shuts and locks the door as Bad Santa muses, "*Brigada* come shoot us!"

You shout through the small pane of smoked orange glass, "I'm Richard . . . *Dickie* . . . please I need to find her, Pashmina . . . I am no damn cop!"

You hear shouts, cries . . . a pause and a curse likely from Pashmina's mouth. The door lock trips . . . and the chain slides . . .

"Come in," you hear the teen say, sternly. "Slowly. This is trippy shit."

"No, Dickie, no . . . " Black Santa warns, and there's not much space on that landing to avoid the spray from a shotgun blast or semi-automatic's full clip coming through the door.

You open it anyway.

Sure enough . . . there's the betty. That jigsaw brain pulls from the bizarre catalogue and you know instantly it's an autoload, Remington . . . factory camouflage so someone managed to house this from a sporting goods store . . . and as Black Santa whimpers and cowers, you note the length of barrel missing, plus the stock, the duct tape at the grip. No way this girl prepped a betty, the way it's shaking her hands. That doesn't mean you won't get killed, son.

"P-Pashmina . . . " you call to her, hands empty. "Is that your name?"

"Shut *up*! Anyone else with you? You, out there, *viejo gordo* . . . get in here and you better call anyone who helping *I swear*!"

Despite James' long slow climb your whole hobo troika is in the modest living room, old boxy TV on, playing some music video station; strange how the sound's turned off.

"Nobody moves," the girl orders, undertone of fear in her voice despite leveling a sawed-off shotgun.

"You have a pr-pretty name. Different, but pretty."

"*Mami!*" she calls, and she seems distraught, puzzled, as if you had the gun and were aiming at a goblin only you could see. "He . . . he knows my name! This *him?*"

There's no noise until, from the kitchen comes a metallic scraping and knocking on the floor, dulled at times by area rugs. A woman, weathered and withered appears, bracing herself with a walker. Her skin is sallow, she has very little hair under a Nationals baseball cap. She's wearing a nightgown under a fleece zippered top, slippers. Then you see the IV bag and the line, dangling from a slender metal stick, clamped to the walker.

She adjusts her glasses, gasps at you . . .

. . . and you are fixed on her face. That face . . . deflated . . . as limp, wrinkled as a spent, dry balloon.

That face so full and plump and ruddy that she was called *Manzanita* . . . Lil'Apple . . .

. . . by her older sister.

"*Ricardo? Mierda en un palo* . . . " And she almost yanks the shunt from the top of the boney hand, trying to cover her trembling lips.

"Marta?"

This was the girl who chattered about becoming a famous girl artist like someone named Frida. Traipsing in her sister's dorm . . . or cramped apartment, ratty sandals but perfect toes, that short embroidered homespun shirt of blue, red and yellow, her heavy breasts hanging free and enticing underneath a gauzy peasant blouse. Jamaican spliff tamped with *chiba* in one hand, a plastic cup full of cheap tequila and cheaper lemonade from Giant in the other. No ice.

What did that cracker Elvis Presley sing about lil' sister? Trippy—that's what Pashmina said. And only Marta would give a girl a crazy name like that. Here you are, boy. Sleuth-away, if you got the nerve . . .

"*Pashmina*," Marta calls, voice breaking. "S-Stop . . . put it down."

You brace yourself on a chair and all James and Black Santa can do is gape. Especially Black Santa, who never knew Marta but heard her name. And now he's as transfixed and floored as you.

"Ricardo, I don't know who brought you here, but I can guess *what* brought you here. She thinks only of herself, like always, and fucked me over and my child . . . and my grandson. Now we are targets, hiding." She smiles and eases in the chair keeping you from falling. Pashmina lowers the boom-stick yet tosses you, James and Black Santa a panoramic ugly stare as her moter explains, "Her name is *Pashmina* Manzana-Landa," Marta explains. "I am Alicia Landa. The last name is—"

"Apple. And the Landa is ambiguously Hispanic . . . could even be Austrian."

She nods.

"So the aliases work?"

She nods again and after a heavy cough says, "So far. We have a little Alpine blood in us—didn't Esme ever tell you?"

"No, or maybe I was fucked up and didn't hear . . . "

"I was trying to be clever but never as clever as *mi hermana mayor*. Esmerelda's like Trump. So much noise it drains you. Surrender's easier than fighting or picking up the pieces."

"The quiet was my tomb. So I loved the noise." You share a moment when she nods, knowingly. But then you ruin it by asking, "Why didn't you ever look for me?"

As Pashmina rolls her eyes Marta chuckles and says, "Where, Ricardo? And the last time I saw you on the street

you didn't look like you do now. You looked like a wild animal
. . . and you couldn't even recognize me!"

"Is that why your sister abandoned me?"

"You don't want know the answer to that. Because it has
nothing to do with you."

"Bullshit."

"Get him out of here, Mami," Pashmina scoffs. "*Brigada* can
deal with him."

"No!" she snaps, and the act of yelling seems to take a year
off her life . . . a year she doesn't have. "I was messing around
with my visa for years, Ricardo . . . yet always under the radar
even when I had my daughter. Now they want to say even she's
a criminal, and the baby here isn't American."

"Esme . . . and I . . . have done fucked-up things . . . "

"No. *No*! You both were broken people who found each
other. And she's been broken by shit you cannot imagine,
Ricardo."

"*Soy negro*! That scared your family back home!"

She shakes her head and says, softly, "If only it was that
simple. My family is . . . *complicated*. Esmeralda was *bruja* long
before she met you. It was her armor and her weapon. Not her
beauty, her body. *Those were curses*. And now here we are. You,
a casualty. I and my girl, prisoners."

"Yeah," Pashmina sneers, "so now you got the Christmas
family cheer, what the fuck do you want?"

"Not to hurt you or your mother."

"Oh, so you and these two homeless old farts are like the
Avengers or Justice League, eh? Those babies Trump got in
cages at the border—maybe y'all should go rescue them, huh?
Before they all get took by barren white bitches who've already
bought them from the Feds, top dollar?"

James mugs and Black Santa, being Santa, just shakes his head and says, "Gossip, gal. White mon na do dat . . . "

"Shut up, granddad. Oh and how'd your ancestors get here from Africa? Swim?"

"*Pashmina!*" The shout's loud and stings, but it's Marta's last measure of lungpower.

"No, Mami, they should ask those girls who got set free by my Wonder Woman *bruja* auntie, the ex-junkie . . . crammed into those safehouses already overflowing with shit and garbage . . . and then *deported* before they live as people, not filth, and now they are dead! Their little brothers and sisters, caged like puppies, waiting for rich white bitches reading Bibles and driving Benzes to turn them into little brown white kids, eh? Fuck, *everyone* here knows." She's picked up the betty again and staring down Black Santa who wants no damn part of a shotgun barrel waved in his direction; he's shaking like Jenn's chihuahua. "I'm not stupid . . . heard someone was tryna get drunkass *pendejos* down in Cohi to snitch. Was it you, old man?"

"*Pashmina . . . collate . . . y soltar la escopeta,*" Marta wheezes, until a wince shears her face. Pashmina now rushes to her side . . . without the shotgun. You see James eyeballing the weapon as it rests on a side table near the door. You shake your head; he shrugs.

"I'm ok," Marta says, catching her breath. "See, Ricardo—she's a lot like her auntie. The strong part. Not the fake 'Tía.' So say your piece, then you must leave . . . for good."

"Someone . . . someone is paying me to find her." You watch her wince again and it doesn't seem to be from physical pain this time. "She stole gold coins . . . she stashed them. I found it. They want me to locate her. Then they will likely deport her."

"'They,' eh?"

"Yes. 'They.'"

"You're *that* mad at her?" Marta then turns her head and tells Pashmina to tend the fruit jam cooking on the stove. "Reduce the heat and strain, okay *mi encantadora* . . . " When her daughter balks she curses in Spanish. Pashmina skulks away . . . whisking away the shotgun before James can hobble over to it.

You sigh and ask, *"Para la bébé?"*

"Sí how'd you know?"

"My . . . source told me Pashmina was in a pregnant girls' homeroom with another girl. Plus . . . I saw a stroller over there. Big box of Huggies. How old?"

"He'll be a year in January." Marta then pulls a cigarette from her gown pocket and a lighter, sparks the jack, takes a satisfying draw. "I do it away from the baby. It's not like I'm getting better so fuck it, huh? Now, where were we. You are that furious with my sister that you would turn her over to men would hurt her . . . because she stole?"

"I don't . . . *shit* . . . I don't know if that's all she did. As for what she did to me, we can debate, but . . . she may have, well, hurt my friends, Eva and Fred. Remember them?"

She puffs and nods, without any emotion, then says, "My sister stole money from them once, when they got clean. Bet you didn't know. Not to get high but to get me a security deposit on a spot up in Silver Spring. I even had a job as an art teacher and paid her back so she could pay Eva back. She told me she fessed up to thieving and Eva hit her but then she said Eva said it will be our secret. All this happened when you were in one of those deep holes we dig. But yours, Ricardo. *Dios mio.* Yours go down to China."

Don't go all jelly, boy! You hate her. Bracht knows you hate her so don't listen to this!

"She tried to make good when she came back. Stayed away from you. Even helped this advocacy group that worked with the cops, FBI. Use her potions and *K'iche* hexes to keep away perverts, and gangstas . . . *los camaradas.*"

"Away from who?"

Pashmina chimes in, shrilly, "*Chicas . . . joven . . .* even little girls they fuckin' smuggle here. Part of immigration the government doesn't mind, dead ass! Almost as much as they love the little girls and boys in cages down on the border for *las blancas* to pick at for pets . . . or to *rape*! Selfish siddity *puta*! Leaves all diamonds and pearls and extra like she's better than us, comes back *loco*, talking like a for-real *bruja* . . . and yet she still can't help us, her own blood!"

"*Silencio!*" Marta rebukes. She coughs then says, "She's right, I hate to admit, Ricardo. And she kept saying, 'Perverts are in our blood.' Something else she had to run from. And then the heat comes . . . " She shrugs, butts her jack on a coaster exhibiting similar burn holes, sucks her teeth because she can't find another cigarette in her gown. "Government . . . more like a *Men In Black* movie, just not funny. Hounded my job, Pashmina's school." She looks up at you smiles, like the tempting lil' sister of old. "They couldn't find us. But you did. Perhaps meant to be?" And you are really hating yourself— nothing new—when she beseeches, "You must tell these men who pay you . . . that Esme is gone, that 'Tía' is a myth. That her sister is dying. That there is no niece."

"Marta—"

She reaches up to touch your lips and whispers, "When we are young, we know we are going to be old one day and die.

What we don't count on is being middle-aged, falling toward being old. In that time the Goddess sends you clues, and if you ignore them, the Goddess sends sickness. I ignored the Goddess, for Pashmina's safety, and now my granddaughter's. Promise me they will be safe."

Feel the gnawing on your nutsack, Junior? You sure about this next move?

"I'll . . . do what I can, with my employer. But . . . who is 'Piedade?'"

Her chin sinks to her chest and she whispers back another question.

"Who's paying you, Ricardo?"

Abruptly, Pashmina bursts from the kitchen, indeed carrying a squirming, alert baby wrapped in a yellow blanket. The baby's got fine shiny waves of black hair and a noticeable tint.

"*Piedade*? That's why you came? For that skinny *puta*? Like her baby is better than my Andre? Like her baby's what . . . from some white boy, eh? *Mami! Estoy harto de la mierda*! Fuck Auntie . . . I want a life with my Andre and DeVonte!"

And that's when your burn starts to buzz. Wonderful timing. You look to Black Santa and a wide-eyed, nonplussed James. "We . . . we gotta get out of here," and then to Marta, "I'll be back as soon as I can. I promise nothing's gonna happen to you all . . . *or Esme*."

Pashmina isn't having it.

"Hey . . . yo', *mister* . . . . she was telling kids at school in our class that her baby-daddy, he's white and when it mixes with the white in her, the baby won't be like us . . . he'll be the boss of our kids. So *fuck* Piedade." She's waggling her finger at you now, and you are mesmerized because it could be Esme, twenty years ago, reconstituted. "I hate Auntie Esme, or whatever that bitch is calling herself."

"Pashmina, please . . . " Marta pleads.

"No, Mami . . . her jumping 'round with that *puta* makes everything else hurt worse."

"Can anyone tell me," you say to Pashmina in a near whisper, "If Piedade is related to a woman named Sabine Soloranzano? Sabine's *dead* . . . yeah little girl. Dead as my friends Eva and Fred. I'm starting to think the coins, the hocus-pocus . . . all wasn't meant for Sabine. It was to shield Piedade."

"*Mami? Dile que deje de hablar loco!*" Pashmina cries over the now agitated baby, "Come *oooon* . . . tell him to get the fuck out!"

"Ricardo, you better go. We'll be fine."

A jittery Black Santa cosigns with, "*Brigada* ruffians soon come!"

"No, you won't be fine. I'll come back, maybe Christmas Day."

"And we'll be gone. Don't follow us—*find her.* You already know how because my sister told you a long time ago, eh?"

"I don't know what you mean."

Mr. Sugars is blowing up the burn.

"You will. She's still my blood . . . don't let anyone hurt her."

162

CHAPTER 15

"Roger that . . . "

THE BURN'S DISPLAY SAYS TEN THIRTY-SIX p.m., and you are still on Fourteenth Street closing in on the bright lights of the Columbia Heights ant heap. And yet two old black bums have moved well ahead of your long legs, in sight of the small municipal Tannenbaum in the square off Park Road.

Snap the fuck out of it, son. Nothing to *figure* now but *figure out* what you are going to tell Mr. Sugars. Put both these two in a cab, send 'em down to St. Jude's for some chocolate and a warm cot.

You catch up with them and mumble, "In . . . geometry . . . when you have a lot of circles . . . you can prove not only existence . . . of a common tangent . . . you can use the tangent, to prove that some extraneous point in the same plane . . . is there, related, understand?"

"Uh . . . y'awight, fella?" James inquires.

You wriggle your head like a dog resetting its common sense and say, "I'm sorry man . . . take this." You take out some green. "Stick it in your draws, safe."

James tries to do a little Michael Jackson shimmy and turn, crooked back, cane and all. It annoys you that he'd act a fool at the sight of greenbacks when you're pressing him about shelter.

"Ya know even wiff-out cash in my pocket I'm yo' man cause this sho enough the mos' fun I had in a mess of time like we on a TV show."

You spy an umbrella in a corner waste bin. Multicolored like on the golf courses. You fish it out. The two extenders are bent, as is a rib; the two old men watch you re-set the joints, fuse a plastic flange on the runner with your lighter. Twenty seconds of work after a quick scavenge. You hand it to James.

"This is Nylon fabric . . . tube is composite. It'll keep sleet, freezing rain off you but watch it in the wind . . . "

He nods, almost in shock. He proceeds to use it as cane for his left hand and now he resembles some geriatric ghetto cross-country skier and he's happy as a lark . . .

"So Black Santa . . . what can I make for you? My head's all messed up and scrounging helps."

He grins and shrugs.

"Okay then, how much did Oosterhaus pay you to look for me . . . or some man, maybe older, flattop haircut, gray . . . maybe named Sugars . . . was he with him?"

Black Santa shakes his head, mutters, "Yar said yar waran't cross wid mi?"

"Do I look mad? Mad's all drained out of me, moe."

James cuts in, pointing with his spiffy new umbrella to a boarded up rowhouse lousy with green vacant property stickers. Uncle Sam won't help the city hire more housing inspectors. No inspections means projects rehabbing these rachet brick barracks into hipster palaces or chain-store anchors lay dormant, boarded up till some bargain basement crew buys things, re-ghettofies the place.

"White man love the hood, contrary to the news," James jokes. "It like a sponge, sucking up what he gives it. A wall too, 'tween what he cherishes and us. Too much mixin' make him nervous—that why he hates the subway."

"There a point here, Scorpio?"

"Nah . . . just don't mess wid ole Fitzy. He absorbs for folk. Keep shit stable. An' he was tough as steel when I met him. I said it. Want this um-berella back, then?"

"Ain't a thing, James." You look to Black Santa. You pat his doughy shoulder and say, "I want you to come back with me. Please." You motion toward the ant farm's bustle and neon. "You, too James. Got money for cabfare. Enough for all of us. I can get you in, get you fed . . . "

But James is using his new dandy umbrella to pry off a piece of particleboard so he can enter a wrecked building.

"Got my bunk rightchere, Dickie. Hey Fitzy . . . show Dickie what you got for him."

And with that he disappears into this brick haunted house.

At that moment the call you've been avoiding all evening returns. This time you answer, staring at Black Santa, who's still like a statue on the dark sidewalk.

"I-I'm sorry . . . Mr. Sugars . . . yeah . . . Nat's Stadium before midnight . . . yeah I can update you. Good stuff . . . wrap it up if not on Christmas then soonafter . . . yes, again, I should have checked-in, but I was questioning witnesses . . . yeah, I'm needing the Narcan . . . "

The fat brown elf's shaking his head, awed or frightened by the change in you. You click off. "What?"

Black Santa puts something in your hand. A photo in a small jade-green plastic frame . . .

"You *stole* this?"

"Na mon. Mi fig yar can't be propa detective if yar in love . . . wid Esme an' sistah . . . "

"Yeah," you mutter, stroking the image with your thumb. "Y'all a bunch of Dr. Watsons . . . "

It's her, yet not her . . . no more than you looked like your-self before Verna cleaned you up. Her skin is sallow, her eyes hooped. Those tits you ached for are veiny and trussed upward in that dress too tight for a woman of her age, even a Latin, given what those chicks wear on those crazy TV shows of theirs. Hair's kissed with gray . . .

. . . those lips, though. *Damn.* Still ruby and full.

But that's not what's important—how you both aged one another. What's hitting you like a metal dart between the eyes is the other person in the photo.

Esme's embracing a pretty little thing . . . slight build, yes, but curves evident in that sundress, heels almost as high as Esme's . . . bone-straight black hair with big eyes like Marta's . . . upturned nose, lips matching Esme's. Flawless olive-toned skin.

Pashmina's right about her mother and Esme. Both have that castellan, white-bread thing, with only a passel of *mestizo.* And this girl matches that.

"Piedade . . . " you whisper.

They're posing at party . . . a children's party, and the kids at these booths and tables in the background are mostly girls, a smattering of boys, all of them "tweens" of maybe eleven or twelve. Look closely. Not very Latin. Pretty damn pilgrim WASP in fact. Indeed, this place is some sort of arcade. In Mexico? Hell, maybe . . .

. . . and this other girl who you call Piedade is a few years older than the others. Fifteen, sweet sixteen maybe, judging from the womanhood forcing itself through the baby fat. A girly-girl bearing, yet something smoky and knowing in those eyes, like those of the teenage models you see in discarded magazines.

You're staring the whole way down to Navy Yard on the near-empty train . . . and finally, hiding in the corner of the pic in plain sight are two huge mounted flat screen TVs. You reach for Black Santa, seated across from you in the otherwise empty subway car.

"Hey man . . . look closely at this. Something weird, even to your cricket-playin' ass?"

An NFL game . . . Atlanta Falcons hammering the Packers. On another there's Trump, with the split screen of some fanatical cracker getting sworn into the Supreme Court. No, not Mexico. And not recent . . .

"The girl . . . they say she was pregnant in school . . . and had a baby . . . "

Black Santa passes you back the pic and frame. He turns his fat cheek to the window and in an instant he's snoring.

"How's she shoved in a brothel then rescued by Esme? *Mi amore*, who did you steal that man's grandad's coins for, exactly?"

You wake Black Santa as the train pulls into Navy Yard Station, and the two of you look like a telephone pole in a black cape followed by a Hershey's Kiss with legs as you amble to the escalators.

Once in the open air your burn rattles with a text message.

No more surprises, no "sub-contracting" help from other homeless bastards unless we vet them first. Be on time! -S.

"Wha mi miss?" Black Santa queries after a yawn and snorting his nostrils clear. "Makin' curfew wid time ta spare!"

You shake your head and announce, "Not tonight. I'll see you soon."

"*Chut* . . . mon yar miss de curfew! Dem fi lock y'ass out again, gold donation or no."

Already two waves of dizziness have washed over you; your tongue's thickening. As much as you dread it, Mr. Sugars could not come sooner . . .

. . . and you shove Black Santa through the doors to St Jude's as incredulous security staff looks on. Now you are loping along the east side South Capitol Street as the cars whoosh below in the concrete chasm that constitutes the express lanes.

But for that traffic you're alone until the massive, shadowy shell of the baseball stadium unfolds on your side of the street.

And you're chewing on the minutes till curfew when finally, a boxy blue Crown Victoria u-turns on South Capitol at P Street Southwest cutting off an on-coming SUV. Not so unobtrusive a move, like he doesn't care if any motorcycle cops are prowling. And a Crown Vic? Well, this man looks to be a bit of a vicious dinosaur himself, so why be surprised at his choice of car? It slows at the curb; he hits the blinkers. He motions you to the window.

"You better pick up when I call next time!" Mr. Sugars barks.

"Canvassing . . . witnesses, s-sources. And I don't trust smartphones . . . "

"We just might make a human being . . . hell, an investigator . . . outta you yet, Cornish. So give me the skinny before some D.C. Barney Fife comes along thinking I'm buying drugs or I'm a homo picking up a black stud."

You make your report. Lucky for you, deadpan is your default expression.

"I have her pinned in the Mount Pleasant, Columbia Heights and Park View neighborhoods, to specific persons, witnesses. Pretty narrow territory. Corroboration on the alias *Tía* Carolina. Spooky card reader, homespun witchcraft and fortunes."

"Outstanding! My guys were out in the field for a month and couldn't even draw a bead on her—and that's with cyber-support and friggin' drones."

"Drones?"

"Wake up, Killer. What else you got?"

"Was . . . was last in the company of . . . a Piedade Soloronzano."

He purses his lips and you aren't sure if that's a tell or if he craves hot coco.

He slowly removes a pad and pen from his overcoat and says, "Spell that for me, chief," as if it's a banality rather than a real clue. "Thought I'd heard every manor of spick names. Not alla them can be called 'Maria' I guess."

"Means 'piety.' That's almost how you pronounce it . . . "

He's scribbling and grunts, "Keep going."

"She is likely related to a S-S-Sabine . . . who was on the lease of that apartment where I found the coins . . . " You pause.

"Spit it out, Cornish," he pushes.

"Sabine . . . *Soloronzano* who was evicted from her apartment by the management company which contracts with the D-Department of Housing and Urban Development . . . and that company is one Mr. Bracht owns, invests in, and such . . . right?"

You're waiting for an explanation or admission and all you get is "Hmmm . . . interesting. And you first heard that about this Sabine where?"

"Mexican cultural center . . . part of the Consulate. Guy n-n-named Diaz-Soames. Mr. Bracht was in touch over the coins. But you know this already so why're you asking?"

"Closing loops, Cornish." And he's really going to town with his pen on his old school pad.

"This young woman . . . Piedade . . . g-g-gave birth to a baby. She was enrolled at Bell Multicultural High School."

"Ah . . . tell me more!"

"I'm going to hit some records tomorrow." Be cleverer, son, be slick. "Um . . . Mr. Sugars, would it be possible to check rental records . . . immigration, even Mr. Diaz-Soames at the Consulate . . . to see if Piedade and Sabine and a guy named Nestor Contreras were indeed related. Hometowns, anything. Might . . . flesh things out—so I can flush Esmerelda out."

Oh, this peckerwood loved that last flourish, son! But now he's noticing your tremors after the mush-mouth.

"Say, maybe you better take a snort of this Jekyl-Hyde juice now, huh, chief?" He hands you two tiny squares of Narcan-Plus applicators. You tear them open, shoot one in a nostril. "Shoot the second applicator in your nose-hole in an hour if you need to, but go ahead and pop that second gelcap, okay? These are half-dose in case you decide to try to jack me and go rabbit. *Though I'm pretty sure I can pull my Sig and put you down before you get a block away.*" He's glaring at you and for an instant you stare back as if he's damn serious. Suddenly he lets out a howl. "You're too tense, Killer. Look, you said at the last sit-ref you tracked down sources . . . "

You swallow the drip from your sinuses in the back for your throat and instantly the tremors cease, as does the pain in your skull. You swallow that second pill, as it'd been safe in the pocket of your new peels . . . an outfit on which this moth-erfucker had no observation or comment.

"I'll get you a list because most of them are of no known address, eh?"

"Touché. Any on Rubio's relatives—sister 'Marta Rubio?'"

Junior . . .

"No. There's a friend of hers, Magdelena, who we found and will surveil, plus a dozen safehouses . . . an underground, Otis Place Brigade, runs them like in Occupied Europe in World War Two."

"Watch your analogies, fella. They're lawbreakers and POTUS and such aren't Nazis. Now what's this Magdelena's last name?"

"That's why I'm curious, Mr. Sugars . . . I mean, you don't want cops, but there's ICE help . . . or DHS . . . yet everyone's telling me ICE . . . Feds . . . are all around, harassing folk . . . even tipping off MS-13. Doing it while the cops and FBI are breaking up trafficking brothels." You stare right at him and it's probably the first time you've had the sack to do it. "Kidnapping babies, too. Of the girls who get pregnant . . . "

"Roger that," is all he says to you. "Decent work. Okay, tomorrow's Christmas Eve . . . " he's handing you an envelope. A quick glance shows five twenties and then ten-dollar bills. "Now gimme the burn."

You hand over the mobile phone. He pops the back cover with some strange little tool, like a shrunk-down spatula.

"Actually, you don't need this tool," he comments. "See this seam? Just push that and slide your fingernail in."

He removes that chip-card whatever thing. Gingerly replaces it with another and gives you back the phone.

"What do I do with this?"

"It's better this way, now that I can trust you with the hardware. But if you want the skullduggery, hey, you'll get a whole new phone in day or so . . . then chuck this one. The river."

"All of this, over a woman stealing his grandfather's soccer coins."

"You are a smart enough boy to hear of F. Scott Fitzgerald, right? He said, 'the rich different than you and I.'"

You're getting ansty . . . just a couple of minutes to sprint back to St. Jude's remain.

"I'll work the baby angle," you relay. "Now may I go, Mr. Sugars?"

He's flipping through his pad and you look like a little child straining to keep pee in.

"Good idea . . . babies help leave a digital and paper trail . . . you people with your welfare and such. In the meantime, I'll search the eviction-tenant records on that spot." Finally, he checks his watch, puts away his notebook. You're about to ask him for a ride but then he smiles and adds, "Ya done good, kid," he says, sounding like an old movie. "One thing—was refreshing my recollection of your service jacket. Despite your old man's leatherneck pedigree, you went into the Air Force? You were in Afghanistan barely a week then you cracked-up, went after your C.O.? Great gourds, man—you give the *snowiest snowflake* a bad name. Oh well, lotta clowns were using over there. Home of the heroin poppy, Killer . . . "

"I wasn't using. Just booze."

He's dropping that big engine in gear when you tap the door. Annoyed, he hits the brake and slams the hoopdy into "park" and the whole chassis shudders.

"Mr. Sugars . . . you gonna tell me now why I'm 'Killer?'"

"The Air Force, Cornish. *Think . . . .*"

With scowl he pops the old Crown Vic into "drive" again and leaves you in a cloud of exhaust. He'll probably barbeque the car before jumping in his real car, heading to a family with a yule log blazing in a fireplace, cardigan and slippers waiting . . .

. . . and you've only got five minutes till curfew, Junior . . .

. . . and it's been a bastard of a day, and only rich whitefolks your age are in shape: golf and two thousand dollar stationary bikes and spa days and stuff . . .

. . . and the door's shut. The bolt's thrown, the alarm activated. Sorry.

You're sliding to the curb . . . pulse thumping in your throat and at your temples. Back where you started. Out in the cold.

The herald angels must've been singing your name, because a seraph arrives in the form of some dude the other security guards call "Vito." Nothing Italian about him but for his jewelry. You raise your arm, presenting your wristband to his flashlight beam . . .

CHAPTER 16

The Mother of Dragons

VITO PULLS HIS TWO-WAY. HIS VOICE is flat, mundane. "Perimeter check okay. Got a resident. Think it's that Dickie Cornish dude. No hypothermia alert tonight so should I make him go to one of the city shelters?"

They open-up immediately. Guess Vito didn't get the memo that you're a VIP.

Lahiere's on shift tonight. He, Vito, and one of the young friars—again in those damn sandals in the wintertime—pat you down, VIP status be damned when it comes to contraband.

"Went on a cake and bologna run for us?" Lahiere offers, though his look is all stink-eye. Places like St. Jude's send out folk like army ants on sortie to supermarkets for stuff in the throw-away pile. Cake and bologna seem to always be in abundance in the throw-away pile, so that's what ends up as snacktime fare. "Hot tea or cocoa in the common room, but be quiet, it's lights-out . . . "

Lahiere meets you at the locker room with a set of towels, soap kit.

"Too many men who can follow the rules are dying on the street, rummaging through garbage," he reminds you as he passes you off to Vito. Vito, ear buds in and head bopping to the mumble rapper *du jour,* leads you to most piss-smelling, tore-up and rickety cot in the jont. Penance, for breaking curfew. At least he can't confiscate your new detective toys like the phone . . .

. . . and somehow you've managed to fall asleep, despite the snoring, the mumbling, snorting, farting . . . the jacking-off. Thusly into the Land of Nod, east of Eden, you don't sense Esme, or Fred or Eva.

Rather, you dream of that girl. The sylph, sweet in her sundress. She has Esme's voice, that husky voice, heavy with the accent . . .

I am Piedade. I am yours, Ricardo.

"But Esme is mine. I can't have you both . . . "

But we are the same. See? Look at my baby. We, mi amor, are fruit of el tilo.

"The lime tree. The family. But did your family kill Miz Eva and Mister Fred?"

They were sacrificed so I may be a gift to you, Ricardo.

Black Santa wakes you as the sunlight cuts through the shades, but the coughs and complaints and farts would've been an adequate alarm clock. He hands you a paper cup of joe and a cookie. Without his gnomish ski cap he still looks like Santa Claus . . . perhaps even more. He's wearing a white tee shirt with suspenders bracing his trousers. He says he added a little extra cheer to the cup. Rum or Southern Comfort. That will get you tossed from St. Jude's faster than *chiba* or some pills.

As if it's reveille the bums and miscreants rush to get washed, dressed, up and out of the rows of cots and into the common room. Sister Maria-Karl, escorted by two smiling Brazilian novices with flawless twenty-year-old skin roll in for inspection.

She is stone-faced, as usual. They are giggling at you, as usual.

"Mr. Cornish . . . feeling better?"

You toast her with your coffee cup full of good cheer as your stomach growls.

"Well Mr. Cockburn's agreed to do St. Nicholas for the children at SFME today."

The two junior nuns chatter in Portuguese then giggle harder at the name, "Cockburn." You toast them, too. They do a slight curtsey and in unison bless you with "*Feliz Natal.*"

"He pronounces it 'Co-burn,' as the Brits do," you correct her.

"Um, of course. Anyway, as you missed the tree trimming here and at SFME, perhaps you'd like to assist with the children. Give out snacks, prizes . . . the toys?"

Try to be gracious. They have real prizes and toys thanks to Jaime Bracht.

"Rather not."

"You would make an ironic elf, Mr. Cornish. Please reconsider."

One of the Brazilian novices burns you, deservedly.

"*Pinte-o de verde para que ele seja o Grinch!*"

No translation needed there, and even Black Santa prods you.

"Get yar min' offa, well . . . *de job* . . . "

"Besides," Maria-Karl adds, "Verna Leggett's insisting."

"Oh?"

"Mr. Cornish, we do, as you, persevere. We do, as you, make much out of little. But we are all hoping you will have another audience with our surprise benefactor Mr. Bracht to see if his support can be on-going, post-holidays . . . he's a Catholic after all and—"

"He's not. He's a kraut with a tan and who speaks Spanish. Lutheran I'm betting."

"Oh . . . oh my . . . "

Yep. You are shading her. Because you can. What'd Mr. Sugars say about those pills—*you'll be feeling like a teenager again.*

"If his family originated in Bavaria, better chance. But it didn't. I read that his wife's Catholic, though. *Mea culpa, mea culpa, mea culpa maxima culpa . . .* amen."

She should have smacked you like the nuns of your youth. That's the sin of pride, snide bullshit coming out your mouth. But she just bids a *Frohe Weihnachten* and gets out your way . . .

. . . and yet it's hard to say what suddenly un-fucks you. Maybe it's Black Santa in the background, talking about some scuttlebutt on Kate and Princess doing so well in the food and meds department but they are clashing with staff. Maybe it's thinking about Marta, dying in hiding . . .

"Sister," you call after the head penguin, groggily. "I'll do it. Tell Verna . . . please."

Black Santa taps your shoulder. "De pay phone, of all t'ings. Someone from de lib-berry."

"Huh?"

"Shaw branch."

Yeah—you forgot?

You rush through the musty corridors to probably the last public phones in the Capital.

"Um, hello?"

The male voice on the other sounds young, effeminate and annoyed. Justifiably so for the last one. They close in twenty minutes for the holiday . . . but that's not the issue.

"LaKeisha for you. Make this fast, please!"

"Hell-lo, this is the Daenerys Stormborn . . . Khaleesi, Unburnt, Mother of Dragons . . . breaker of muv-fucken chains. Who this?"

"Don't play. Poor dude'll get fired for letting you use the phone."

"Jon Snow, reborn, yeah! Don't worry about him."

"What's up?"

"I am all up in the face of a enchantress . . . an alchemist. My sosh-worker. Emma Sharfstein. They hold court in the library 'cause we all up in here. Our cathedral of knowledge . . . like Samwise, nothing to do but read and watch DVDs of anything and everything George R.R. Martin, son! You feelin' him? Nah, you more C.S. Lewis man . . . "

"Come on Keesh . . . "

"Catch up your draws. See, Emma Sharfstein handles all our drug testing shit. Her alchemists favor I, the Mother of Dragons, with indulgences because I help them with their champ-ass lowest bidder networks. That stuff in that applicator . . . see, the shrinks are putting special K . . . ketamine . . . in nasal spray now for the down-times for manic bitches like me. Well, multiply this by a hun-nad. Mivacurium with some other alkaloid, son, derived from tropical curare . . . a deadly neuro-blocker."

Jesus Lord. Your world's just tilted onto another axis . . . again.

"You still there, Jon Snow?"

"Yes . . . um . . . keep going and stop calling me that, alright?"

"Dayum. Okay. Well, one auto-shot to the nostril and the mucous membranes suck it in. Five seconds, you are tingly and disoriented and your legs are like sticks. Two minutes and your diaphragm's not working. Almost like an OD. I can send you a pdf of the molecules . . . "

"Curare . . . mucous membranes," you repeat as you're cradling the handset between your neck and clavicle to write invisible letters on the wall.

"Not to be confused with succinylcholine. That's better suited for a needle rather than tartrate and propellant. Curare and the pufferfish

poison . . . the Haitian zombie-maker . . . yeah they can be dispensed in an aerosol...perfect way to incapacitate someone and leave no artificial trace for autopsy. Real black bag shit."

"Huh?"

"Black bag! Merc shit! James Bond! Fits . . . like counter-intelligence stuff. State of the art poison darts, sprays, coatings. Yet your boy Esteban said this thing was in a rachet apartment . . . "

"Yeah . . . " you whisper, your big brain on boiling. "If I monstered on you, shot that up your nose . . . then I shoved you outside . . . "

"Folk would freak the fuck out because I'd be looking crazy, like I was high, but that'd be terror because I couldn't scream or at least not loud . . . couple of seconds later I'd starting asphyxiating, my arms and legs'd seize up . . . "

Go ahead, boy. Indulge yourself . . .

"If you couldn't scream in the first place . . . you'd suffer horror, quietly."

"Uh-huh. Before I passed out and died."

"Or before you fell in front of a bus . . . "

There's a pause, and it's not from library staff trying get her off the phone. *"Is, um, Mexican Cersei Lannister come to vex you?"*

"Keesh?"

"I know the sitch. I saw Queen Jenn. Jenn still feeds me, loves me, finds me a place to lay my head where I don't cry for my babies . . . because men are mean, and cruel . . . and they chained us . . . and kicked us on the street like we were stray dogs!"

"Stay with me. Can you post up in Peets Coffee down at Metro Center, like you used to with Jenn after those terrible men hurt you all? I'll *pay* you."

"Just like in Peshawar Province . . . that kinda dangerous? Crackin' cellphones, hackin' codes, grind down the enemy's electronics?"

"Uh-huh. I'm so sorry."

"There are good bad people, and bad bad people, right, Dickie? Like you say? If I'm good bad, then if somebody gives a laptop they monster offa some fool, and it's all tricked out, and I let them touch me in return for it. Don't touch no one's Medicaid and bennie checks. Don't steal or be somebody else. That's good bad, affirmative?"

"Just good bad stuff. Stamp. Nothing where good people get hurt . . . "

"Then I am the Mother of Dragons—Drogon, Rhaegal, and Viserion are Mac, Dell and Surface. They spit dragonfire in code. Name your pleasure."

"City . . . the Coroner's files. D.C. meat wagon? Need anything on a Soloranzano, Sabine, a Honduran or Guatemalan national. And then . . . " You cough, to keep from tearing up, "Boudreaux, Eva, and Cross, Frederick. Don't think you ever met them. Died in that burglary and murder, Park View Tower, two days ago. Then a name Burton Sugars. Former Fed."

"If I can't get in the front door, I can find what outfit cleans the toilets, fixes the lights . . . does the labwork, yep, like with our piss-tests. Shitty security with contractors, Jon Snow. Spear-phish works every time . . . "

The line goes dead and you sink to the floor and your eardrums hiss like they are being sucked inward to your brain. *Black bag. Merc shit.* Eyes open, boy!

A joyful noise mercifully dispels the hiss and doubt . . . and now your head's filled with the chirp and screech and stomp of children across the way on the SFME side, and the guard lifts you up, asking with healthy suspicion if you've been using, or if you've been blowing off a trip to the overworked nurse.

Sooner or later you'll have to answer the question, son. State-of-the-art and black bag . . .

. . . though your unction and diversion's waiting for you in the men's room, with his costume in a big paper shopping bag.

"Ya see, bred'rin, bir't of owa saviour compel awl men ta take stock, be in repose."

"Let's just get this over with."

He perches on his toes to plop a ridiculous, cone-like green and red cap, with a jingling charm at its pointed top, right on your head. You want to curse but then you check yourself out in the smudge mirror and quickly all the badness settles back in a deep pool, hidden for now.

The clamor's louder. A bit throatier is the banter of older kids, perhaps twelve to sixteen, and you have gifts for them, too. Lots, as Sister Maria-Karl told you. Homeless addicts aren't the best with Dollar Store gift-wrapping, cheap tape and dull little scissors, but hey, it's better than many kids will get tomorrow morning.

Yes, tomorrow. Christmas day.

One of the little nuns knocks on the men's room door, announcing, "*Senhor, Senhorita Verna está aqui* . . . she wan' see zhou please . . . ."

You reply, "Santa's almost ready . . . problem with the boots . . . "

And when you come out, there's Verna. Like you've never seen her.

She's much taller in those red heels. A red wrap-dress that flatters her ample curves. Instead of the usual Afro-bangles and shells, a single gold bracelet hangs from her wrist, and she wears a small candy-cane and green holly leaf clip in her hair . . . hair that's relaxed and blown-out, white-woman style, then coiffed—upswept. *Damn* . . .

"Um . . . Merry . . . Merry Christmas," you mumble. Even little nun's backed up, either smitten as well or jealous.

"Merry Christmas to you, Mr. Cornish," she says with a giggle, noting your elf cap more than your gape. "Going to a party after this with my sister and brother-in-law."

"House party? Rum . . . egg nog, dancing?"

"Actually, it's a birthday thing for one of my brother-in-law's frat brothers, coming back to town. Imagine being born on Christmas Eve? Prolly worse than Christmas Day . . . everyone's thinking about tomorrow, not you. It's at the Park on Fourteenth."

You know the place well. Fancy niggas in clown suits, hooker dresses, all lined up across from Franklin Square Park, where your kind camped, were robbed, abused.

"Then it's home *by myself* . . . get up, start cooking . . . get over to my older sister's and her hellions with my specialties in Tupperware."

Her lips are moving, and all you heard was "by myself."

"Could I talk to you, before you leave?"

"Is it this drama with the coins donation?"

"No."

"Not happy about the context, *but* . . . you did good, Dickie."

"I . . . I need a favor. One we talked about before."

She touches her tongue to her ruddy upper lip as she smiles and says, "You're funny."

"I'm serious. I'm always serious, Verna."

"Not talking about him. It's about databases . . . "

All that holiday sweetness evaporates.

"I'll see you in there with the kids, Dickie."

She turns and walks away, heels snapping on the floor.

Besides, Black Santa's now trussed up and ready, adjusting the white wig and red cap.

"'ow me look? Me wan' Kamala 'arris as mi Missus Claus. Fine lookin' woman . . . "

The dining hall erupts with frenzied delight as you shake a wooden frame holding sleigh bells, and Black Santa enters with a bellyful of *ho-ho-ho*. Following up the rear are two volunteers pushing a cart with the gifts, then the little nun wielding a cheap video camera . . . and then Verna, beaming, aiming her own phone to capture the event. She's even got a few of you in that hat, and for a little while, you're tamping thoughts of Esme and Bracht way, way down.

You see two tots, maybe three or four years —a boy with broken glasses taped at the frame, and a girl with her plaited hair clipped in pink barrettes—shoot up from their cross-legged anticipation on the floor. Their eyes are wide as hen's eggs, little pouty mouths open in absolute wonderment . . . then come tears of bewilderment, as someone, at least, thinks they are worthy of a Christmas. They turn to their mothers, standing behind them and weeping themselves now.

The mothers look at you, and in seeming unison mouth, "*Thank you*."

Chickenheads, professional baby machines, dick-boppin' landlord-dodging tricks . . . okay . . . maybe today, they are just grateful parents . . .

. . . so the carols follow, and you're looking at Verna. You smile and try to carry the notes she's hitting. And Verna takes to the mic stand the staffers set up to the left of Santa's "throne:" her own desk chair taped with foil and construction paper decorations made by the children. She thanks the men of St. Jude's for wrapping a record number of gifts, putting names on two dozen, yet leaving many blank in anticipation of the night's ebb and flow of new faces, departures of old ones.

"You are men, *our* men," Verna acclaims. "Not numbers, not failures. You are loved."

Black Santa now whips the kids into a riotous lather, and the orgy of gifts and torn paper begins . . .

. . . and a boy of maybe thirteen or fourteen judging from the youngster's chin stubble and breaking voice walks up to you, not Black Santa. You hand him his present, matching his nametag to the gift label. "LeShawn." He tears the paper gingerly. Opens the box warily.

Neon orange over-the-ear headphones, certainly a cheaper knock-off of the prime brands under the trees of wealthier folk, and a book. An old-fashioned printed book.

He embraces you, says nothing. Sits down. Drinks his punch, eats a cookie. That's it.

Verna watches, eyes a little wet.

"LeShawn's father was killed in a drug beef two years ago," she explains to you, "out on Sheriff Road. His mom died of pneumonia . . . complications from HIV, yes—still killing because she was poor and black. Now he's here with his sister and grandmother, whose apartment building was condemned by the city when the landlord couldn't be bothered to fix it up. Hear they have a spin studio and gym, a French mussels and *frites*-theme bar already wanting leases. LeShawn, well, I'm not sure if he has an appetite for mussels. See, he only talks a few words a week, and when he does, he asks about his dad."

"I still need that favor . . . "

Oh, that sucks those admiring tears back into her head for sure!

"What's gotten into you."

"Clock's ticking. I wish I could tell you more. I-I respect you."

"Come with me," she whispers harshly, and you follow her, and all of the adult eyes in that room are following the both of you, trust!

She unlocks her office and cuts on the lights and maybe there's a part of you that hoped the lights would stay off and she'd close the door and let you hold her in that dress . . .

"What the fuck is wrong with you, huh? There? In front of those children—you sweat me?"

"Your network . . . connects to private charities and stuff, too, not just the government, right? You said you'd teach me and yet you dissed me the first time I asked to see it . . . "

"God you're like an automaton. Okay—no! I could lose my job . . . *be prosecuted.* They could trace me straight through to our sign-in codes."

"Cops . . . FBI, Homeland . . . Homeland Security . . . NSA spies. Can they access it?"

"*Arrgh* . . . black Jesus gimme strength . . . Dickie, come back to the dining hall with me, forget this drama. It's *Christmas* . . . "

"Christmas was a warm, clean place to sleep . . . until December twenty-sixth . . . and people went back to being bad. So, hey . . . *fuck* Christmas and just do this for me, *please.* Didn't I make it so Mr. Bracht would give you all a gift?"

She's all quiet now, lips pursed, high heels tapping. It's like a mask came off your face and fell to the floor and she wants to see if you got the temerity to pick it up, put it back on. Too much love in that dining hall. Too little out there. Mr. Sugars is out there. Esme is out there.

"Verna . . . do whatever you can . . . camouflage the search, anything . . . anything. If you do this I'll do whatever you want . . . I'll even leave tonight so somebody can have a cot. I swear."

"I don't want you to run away. Why would you think that?"

"Look at me. Why would you want a mess like *me* around?"

She cocks her head—an epiphany.

"Dickie . . . *Dickie* . . . *did you think* . . . oh my . . . " She inhales sharply, releases it very slowly . . . moves around to her desk. Her arms are folded across her chest now, and she's almost in a shrunken pose, as if needing cover. Her voice flattens to the almost officious tone you've heard her use on the phone. With strangers. Oh, something's leached out of someone, alright! "Okay—hunting for a profile on who? *Who?* Go on?"

Look her in the eye!

"Rubio, Esmeralda . . . "

"Oh Lord . . . get the fuck out of my office!"

"I can't explain now. But it . . . involves Mr. Bracht . . . " You move right up on her, looking down into her eyes and maybe what she sees in yours makes her shudder. " . . . birthdate the Twenty-fifth of June, Nineteen-seventy. a.k.a. *Tía* Carolina . . . Madame Carolina. Expired visa from Mexico, also citizen of Guatemala, I dunno. Possibly . . . um . . . trying to get benefits . . . for a minor, pregnant then . . . a baby . . . "

"*Wonderful*," she scoffs. "Possibly non-qualified immigrant status. Baby . . . born here?"

You nod.

"Is it yours?"

You shake your head.

She pulls her chair around and sits almost side-saddle, her red dress is so tight.

"Now get out. It'll take a while. I will hand you a hard copy. I will purge this query as a failed application. And we let the chips fall."

"*Verna . . .*"

"Please leave my office. You have children to entertain."

You are wandering the corridor, mouth open like a dullard and you hear the kids laughing and carrying on and yet you can't bear to face them again.

Before you enter the dining hall there's a buzzing deep in your trouser pocket. A bizarre and alien sensation, as you have barely owned a mobile phone in your life. You swing into another corridor and open the phone. There's a security guard watching but he just waves, because you are Dickie, Santa's helper. Reformed, redeemed. You brought the gold . . .

"H-Hello? Mr. Sugars?"

"*No . . . ha! Mr. Cornish it's me, Jaime . . . Jaime Bracht.*"

"Um . . . uh . . . yes, sir."

"*Mr. Sugars says you are doing a great job despite your handicaps. I just wanted to say thanks —in addition to giving me the heart to donate my grandfather's coins—*Feliz Navidad."

"Merry Christmas to you, too, sir."

"*I suppose where you are is better on a Christmas Eve than that fetid tent. Then again, Jesus only had hay and a stable, right?*" There's a weird pause on the line . . . as if he's listening, breathing while you listen and breathe . . .

"*So . . . I'm actually calling from our company's Dassault . . . and even for me such calls are expensive. Left Reagan about twenty minutes ago . . . bound for Burlington . . . that's Vermont. We switch off Christmases between skiing east and skiing west, though I love the Rockies and frankly the hunting's more challenging than at my Pennsylvania place . . . but my kids want maple syrup, the gentler slopes. Be silly to ask, but have you ever skied?*"

"No. My big sister. Her name's Alma . . . *was* Alma, she

passed away. She skied. Once."

"*Sorry about your sister. By the way, I hear children . . .*"

"Lotta kids here. Was helping with gifts. Hope your kids have a good time."

"*Meh . . . they're girls. Three of them, the oldest is sixteen and barely looks up from Instagram. The middle one's daddy's girl and the youngest, she's four, is my baby. Still, what can ya do? If only I had a boy who loves Cowboys games on Thanksgiving, a Remington, and a taut hunting bow. Any-who . . . good hunting to you, Mr. Cornish. Hope Christmas and the New Year bring you everything you deserve.*"

Click.

Look at you . . . you're shaking. Yet no way your dose's worn off.

Back to the workshop, elf. But you halt, seeing the teens Malachi and Vinny craning their necks, seeking you out. Not for bikes but for counsel and comfort. Not the first time some trifling bastard made a promise then was audi, eh? Now they'll go out and shoot some fool or rob somebody on the subway and it'll be your fault, right?

God co-signs with Frank hunting you down. Probably Verna wanting to choke you out in her office.

"Hey man—you got another call over on the side. I'm not your private secretary, and stuff like that can get you kicked out if you were over here with Miss Verna!"

Somebody must have a thing for Miss Verna and you are muddying it. You run back to the St. Jude's side, still antsy from Bracht's bizarre call.

It's the pay phone again.

"*Jon Snow. It's your lucky or unlucky day. My dragons have burnt a digital swath.*"

"How're you able to call out?"

"Actually, King of the North, my sexy beast of a Targaryen nephew, I'm on a burrowed line . . ."

"Borrowed, not burrowed . . ."

"No. Burrowed. Look son, you want this info or doncha?"

"Where are you?"

You know when you hear a ding-ding tone. Yeah, she's burrowed—into someone's car. "Put your seatbelt on. Get fewer looks. Did you boost it, or house the fob?"

"Neither, Jon Snow. Be shocked how many hipsters just leave'em unlocked. And get this—they're in Florida for the holiday. Been peeping them for a week."

The wifi's even easier for her. Again, too many volunteer victims with no code on their signals. Still, the sun's still out and some neighbor might make her. LaKeisha's got balls. When you've already lost everything and everyone, fear of getting caught is relative.

"Medical examiner doesn't got the pdf of this Soloranzano's report on the system yet but I have title-head notes. Likewise for Frederick Cross, but I got full toxicology for Eva Boudreaux. You sittin' down, Bobby Brown?"

"Just hit me."

"Sabine's say trauma consistent with vehicle collision but there's a parenthetical: 'intoxicant unknown' and they chalk it up to drug abuse . . . because her right nostril was severely inflamed. Fred's don't say shit but Eva's full report says 'presence of exotic molecules which could inhibit function of axon and muscle fibre, likely part of 'cocktail of abused substances' blah blah. Circumstantial but I'd say somebody dosed them. Same shit. Some people are allergic to tartrates, hence Sabine's nose but it's typically untraceable . . . Jon Snow, you there?"

Barely. "Keesh . . . don't linger in that car any more than you have to."

"I'll pee and book."

She gone and now you slide to floor, there between St. Jude's and SFME . . . cup your head in your hands. Someone's been busier than Santa's elves before midnight. And the unthinkable's been trickling out of the jigsaw pieces as they re-align.

"Esme . . . what have you done . . . that someone would do *this?* I could have hidden you a thousand years on the street, baby. A thousand Christmases. He'd never find you. He'd never find *us.*"

CHAPTER 17

Midnight Mass

YOU'RE DOZING, EYELIDS AFLUTTER, PRONE IN a comfortable chair in the TV room. The place was once called the "reflection room" by the staff. Now it's best to pacify your brother bums with a flat screen . . . news and PG-13 fare only. No sports.

You should be erect, eyes wide. Yet you are spent.

There's the attractive female anchor reading the prompter during the news break from the delightful Tim McGraw and Faith Hill holiday special the nuns and friars and staff are enjoying with you "residents" . . .

Suddenly, murmurs and movement that rouse you to attention.

It's Verna, hovering over you, still resplendent in that red dress, lips still ruby, glistening. And a face as bleak and cold as the December air outside.

Did you feel it drop on your lap? You are too startled to threaten the men making wolf-whistles as she saunters away. But you swing your legs off the ratty ottoman and call to her.

"Verna . . . please . . . thank you . . . "

She stops as if you ran your nails across an old chalk board.

"Don't talk to me again, Dickie. Dead ass, as the folks say." Yet before you can parse the treasure of paper she's dumped on your body, she winces a bit and reveals, "I got an email . . . Kathleen McCarthy and Princess Goins checked themselves out about an hour ago. They're likely back where you were *keeping* them . . . around the Mall. Proud of yourself—thinking of only yourself?"

"I don't keep anyone, Verna. Listen . . . it's hard, maybe dangerous . . . "

"Dickie, that's *it* . . . "

Lahiere jumps up from his chair, escorts her out. Your Dumbo-like ears hear him ask if you had caused a problem, maybe frightened some children earlier.

She assuages Lahiere, but then adds, "If he breaks curfew again, or treats this as a commuter stop, you should ask Father Phil to consider an expulsion conference. There're beds at the city men's shelter, if leaving him nowhere bothers you . . . "

Hearing that rends your heart from your ribs. She doesn't want you anyway, son. And you want Esme more than *not* hurting Verna, red dress or no, huh? So cut the bullshit.

You shuffle back to your chair before one of the other bums commandeers it. You read the print-out aloud, and your glare dares anyone to complain. Who wants to hear the inane shit on the TV anyway?

"'Denial of benefits . . . Temporary Assistance for Needy Families . . . TANF . . . D.C. DHS . . . '" you recite. "'Address Fourteen hundred Rittenhouse Street Northwest, unit unknown, mail returned . . . applicant not qualified legal resident . . . applicant not bona fide family member . . . Catholic Relief Services grant . . . supplement aid for pregnant battered women and for newborn under . . . Children's Health Insurance Program . . . Six-twenty Peabody Street Northwest."

You flip through more. Addresses climb out of the page. "'Ten-ten, Rock Creek Ford Road . . . CarePrime Recovery Center . . . subject age fifty . . . female address, Rockview Apartments' . . . *wait*." You flip through more pages. "'pre-scription approved, Catholic Relief Services and C-H-I-P prophylactic injectable generic . . . RSV . . . *palivizumab* . . . infant age six weeks, severe nasal and chest congestion . . . Walmart Pharmacy.' That's on Georgia Avenue. *Wait . . .* "

That's welfare largesse requested, denied, fraudulently obtained . . . drug rehab compliments of a charity and the taxpayers . . . shit for some anchor babies or whatever the ofays call the kids? It's what these Latins do when they border-jump, otherwise why border-jump?

"Because they're poor, and unprotected, like everyone else who came here on a boat except for us," you sputter to the air, "*so shut up* . . . and check the addresses, not the denials. Last two years . . . *till three weeks ago.* Walmart . . . "

Only landmark you have in that neighborhood is that Walmart. *Walmart . . .* seems alien to a city residential block. You'd only seen them when you were in the Air Force, where they were adept at destroying some peckerwood's quaint main street; you paid a visit to that one after Esme left you, remember? First stab at unaided cold turkey and your body revolted and you sprayed vile diarrhea all over the toilet stall . . . and yes, the one thing uniting yuppies and Latins and niggas that day was the laughter and scorn and eye-rolls flipped at you as the cops and security guards kept their dis-tance and their lunches in their stomachs by prodding you with mop and broom handles . . .

"*Dominus meus pastor est . . . I non vis . . .* "

He hasn't exactly *maketh* you lie down in green pastures or still waters, eh? *No?* Well, here comes your boy, Black Santa, and he's changed into the only pair of clean sweatpants he owns, and a tee shirt provided by the shelter. His beady eyes light up when he sees you.

"Verna come? Wha she wan'?"

You show him the heavy print-out.

"Bun an' cheese!"

You then notice he's carrying large sheets of drawing paper, screaming with kids' crayon and marker colors.

"What's this?"

"Ah, dis me as Santa drawn by likkle chil'ren . . . dis mi sleigh an' reindeer, dem look ike groun' squirrel cause when any dese chil'ren seen even a deer? De volunteers dem ran out of paper and give de chil'ren pages f'om ole tear-out maps won' draw on . . . "

"Lemme see."

Clever boy . . .

"Any more of these old map sheets? Gimme here."

Grumbling, Black Santa waddles off then returns with another stack of kids' renderings. He hands them over and you scatter on floor, much to the annoyance of your compatriots trying to enjoy holiday programs before lights out, and sugar plums and turkey and mistletoe and malt liquor percolate through their dreams.

The map scale's down to city blocks—a pre-mapping app way means of locating any of you passed out on the street . . . or kids in need of rescue and a temporary foster home for the night.

"Anyone want to find a neighborhood for me?" you announce. "Cash and my toothpaste if you help."

With Stevie gone the only taker is an old guy named Isaac, who's on a metal cane yet squats down to the floor on his aching knees, and it doesn't seem to shame the rest of your hobo-addict coterie until he groans a little from the movement. Black Santa joins in, dropping to the dingy carpet with two more fellas . . .

. . . and soon there are ten of you marking locations in pencil, marker and kid's crayon. A giant puzzle. Something you do well.

But here comes Sister Maria-Karl and Brother Karl-Maria, then Lahiere. You look up and they are caucusing. Then they leave. You bums are engaged, happy. It's like making children tired before bed so the anticipation of candy canes and full stockings doesn't keep them astir.

"Right here!" Isaac exclaims as if he discovered Bracht's gold coins. "Yessir."

On the floor the bums mark "X" on the addresses pinpointed. With the sheets spread out thusly, something ordered, rational strikes you. The sheets form something like the photo-mosaic images they forced you to devour in the Air Force . . .

"Gimme a marker," you bark. Then you draw. First, straight lines tangent to the plane of the map . . . same why your mind sucks in info when not addled by that damn spice. And the lines comingle to take on a form . . . curved and organic. Feline. An oval eye . . . nostrils, a whisker . . . a fang . . . spots. Now, an ear, tapered . . .

"*Shit . . . ,*" you mutter, almost in awe. "Right on top of the cops . . . "

You open your burn's map and then find a street view. There, a blurry image opens . . . two low-rise brick barrack-like apartments tucked in a hillside beneath the soaring Hughes radio tower off Georgia Avenue and Missouri, with the Fourth District MPD station but yards away.

Black Santa scratches his bald pate and asks, delicately, "'Ow yar be sure it right dere?'"

"*Jaguar Seven*," you whisper. You look up at him. "Just like lil' Marta hinted. *She once told you how to find her.* Her 'familiar,' and when you are in peril, you align yourself with your familiar's attribute. Maya say the jaguar doesn't smell its prey and enemies. It hears them. Uh-uh . . . witch bullshit to scare people, pump herself up. But sometimes I think she believed it."

"*Chut*, g'won widde rassclot nonsense."

"Nah." You tap the spot on the map with your marker, then show him the phone's street image. "*Esme's here.*"

Suddenly, inexplicably, he's rubbing his chin . . . somehow convinced.

"Den yar mus' go. But if yar do, dey lock you out, dey not gwine let yar'n again."

Isaac overhears you and lends his expertise.

"If you gonna go this the best night. These lil' senoritas be packin' the van . . . they drive to the Cat'lic big-ass choich wiff the dome in Brookland for the midnight service."

"The Basilica?"

"Yeah . . . see . . . they fittin' ta roll out now. Security ain't watchin' nuthin'cause they wanna go home."

You look to Black Santa and whisper, "*Fitz* . . . I put us all at risk by taking this damn job because if it worked I could take Kate and Princess and you, *away* from this slit-throat place. We'd have a roof, food, medicine, sunshine, music. I'll even get those bikes, for those boys over there at SFME. Now . . .

aw, man . . . I don't want to find her. And if I do, I don't want Bracht to have her."

"Yar t'ink 'im kill 'er?"

You nod, eyes wet. "I think his people have already done it . . . ."

"G'won who?"

You embrace him, as Isaac and the others watch. "People we love. Because they're leads until they are loose ends."

Before he releases you he muses, "Dat in yar detective schoolin' on yar phone?"

"No, that's all me. I'll see ya. Merry Christmas, man."

"Merry Christmas, Dick," he whispers in your ear, "An' forgive Esme. We can' stop we nature. Wasn't her fault."

A peculiar send-off. Still, the other broken men pocket your meager bribes; others bring your coat, that black beanie, wool gloves, your shoes. And their final gift, led by Black Santa, is a throaty rendition of *Silent Night* . . . further distracting staffers from their security monitors as the ecclesiastical bunch indeed start filing out for the pilgrimage to the Basilica of the Assumption for midnight Mass.

And you walk your big ass, dressed in black, straight out into the night, under everyone's nose.

Hugging the shadows while the van loads with nuns and brothers and priests, whisper a midnight mass prayer for your mother, Alma. For Esme.

" . . . *sicut erat in principio, et nunc, et semper, et in saecula saeculorum. Amen . . .* "

Despite your size and color, a taxi stops for you near Half Street. The hack, a pleasant African man from medallion pic and name, even asks you if you are surprising a sweetheart or family on Christmas Eve. Clearly, he's not a cohort of Diallou's.

"No . . . no . . . I'm . . . I'm headed for work . . . "

"God bless you sar. Gold bless all those keeping things running when rest of us sleep this holy night. Are you a religious man, sar?"

"No."

"I ask because I go off-shift soon but I cannot be home in time to read the Gospel to my babies. I don't mean harm, sar."

"If you say so."

"So . . . I will recite to you, and you do not have to listen." You aren't anyway. You want her to be there and see her face when you burst in . . . or you want it to be a mistake, a goose-chase, a red herring. You want to run away with her and keep her safe . . . you want to feed her to the police . . . to Mr. Sugars . . . ah so many things bouncing around, cracking the jigsaw up there, huh?

" . . . *And the angel said unto them, Fear not: for, behold, I bring you good tidings of great joy, which shall be to all people. For unto you is born this day in the city of David a Saviour, which is Christ the Lord* . . . " He pauses. "Thank you, sar, for this."

"Turn right up past Missouri, then on the left. Cut off your headlights, turn off the dome light."

"Sar? *Sar?*"

"I'm not here to kill you or rob you. I'm going to pay you then I'm getting out. In the dark . . . "

"Please, humbly I ask you on Christmas . . . think about what . . . what you plan to do."

"I have. And your recitation was . . . beautiful."

He takes $15 . . . follows your instructions as he's now backing up blind and in the dark before he turns on his headlights and peels away. And in that instant, you curse him. Random, silly and nonsensical. Because he left you alone, and alone, you realize that all Black Santa's "Batman" and

"Sherlock Holmes" jawing was vapor. You got lucky with Bob Hope's artifice; you were mad at wanting to punish Ghenghis Kann. And you have no idea what you're doing now, though, no matter the spring those pills've put in your step or your new peels and Tims. You cleaned up with soap and water, so? You're no gumshoe, Junior. You're still a bum, cleaning up the money man's mess. For a buck . . .

"*Stop* . . . "

Okay. For now.

But hey, at least it isn't late, barely scratching quarter to eleven. Yet as it's Christmas Eve, the only source of ambient light is what glows from the Fourth District Police Station just over the hillside, and the few lit rooms in each of two squat, square apartment buildings you're targeting.

Looming above in the night sky is the immense police radio tower anchored into the hill's slopes. From that angle, its darkened trusses and curved beams give it the look of a giant insectoid robot standing watch yet ignoring your mite-sized presence. You pray the cops, like their tower, are distracted by the headier, more profane lapses in humanity this night.

There's a Dumpster in the small parking lot between the two square buildings. Only a few cars are parked near it. Memorizing the plate numbers would have been easier even a few years ago. Tonight, you need the assistance of phone camera pics.

The cars aren't the honeypot, though. Anyone can survey parked cars for later reference. You have a special skill suitable to your hunches. And the object of your intrepidness is indeed green and rusted and ringed by white garbage bags— some intact, some torn by rats who are, in turn, stalked by feral cats who jump out of the way as you creep closer.

By the entrance to one of the buildings there are rows of brown paper shopping bags containing recyclables. Were you your old self, those would be fair game to pilfer and sell. But you're flush, you're important, eh? Zero clues to be found there. Neither are the garbage bags strewn about the periphery worth checking. Esme was many things. Trifling, not one of them.

You have your old little flashlight, recharged compliments of St. Jude's supply of AA batteries. Of course, in your previous life a Dumpster was a cornucopia; searching it in stygian blackness is okay if, like any intrepid hyaena, you follow your nose and stay alert. So, with the aid of a light you are confident you'll mine gold, quickly.

You flip up one of the Dumpster lids and, with the light clamped in your mouth, you descend into the strata of milk cartons, coffee grounds, chicken bones and banana peels . . . Kleenexes and catalogs . . . tampons and Target circulars . . . down, adeptly, like one of those sperm whales, sounding . . .

. . . and yet what is this sensation you feel . . . yeah, as you literally swim through what was once your medium?

Uh-huh. Revulsion.

It's like getting your virginity back. About as long as your self-respect's been AWOL. Clean clothes, a bathroom, a cot, hot food, a clear head—though that's compliments of Mr. Sugars. Still, it's good, huh? Yet here you are, in a cold, rusty steel box, tasting the filth on the end of your tongue, in your nostrils . . .

. . . and now the fear floods you. Recall the old rubric: *Don't get cut—Don't get caught?* Anything sharp, piercing flesh, will kill at worst, take finger or leg at best. But Esme's going to be careful about account statements, cancelled checks, explanations of health benefits, discarded prescription vials, hospital discharge forms, bills, traffic or court summonses, requests for immunization confirmations, school notices. A thing, an item, will give her away, not a document. Yet you can't afford to overlook anything, be it paper or prurient as you squish and slosh . . . and you freeze with each rustle or hiss or squeak from whatever is there scavenging with you. In the dark . . .

. . . and so many Latin names on torn pieces of paper and documents . . . yet nothing with *Solonzorano* or *Rubio.*

"*Aw shit,*" you hiss, for the burn falls from your coat pocket into the eggshells and spent paper towels to clang on the metal skin. You see the bluish glow and dig.

And then you realize that's someone else's mobile, chucked, about to wink out from no power. The names are in Spanish . . . you say fuck it and punch up the burn's number . . . because you can memorize that from one glance as well, and how such a skill serves you crawling in garbage well, here is the foul payoff, for now you hear a tone, to the left . . .

. . . and there it is, screen cracked, yet light glimmering, winking. Pray it still works or it's your ass.

You climb out of the Dumpster after a quick prairie dog pop-up and look around. Again, no one's coming, no one cares. Even the police station's dead, as if everyone went home but someone left a light on.

And in that dim light you see the stains polluting your coat and trousers.

The wind's kicking up, signaling another cold front. The breeze cools abundant moisture on your face, meaning something besides sweat oozes there.

Caked or dripping with urban offal, you skulk to the wall of one of the buildings, . . . halting under a window lit only by pulsing Christmas lights. You hear faint adult laughter, the high-pitched bark of a young or small dog, likely catching wind or noise of you. Where to now? And looking like you do . . . for that timid, lonesome realization sinks you to the ground, and the big man, the new man, the renewed man and redeemed man—he weeps like a helpless child. A failure. Steeped in garbage. A real gumshoe . . . *a real man* . . . would admit his tactical error and move on.

Hell, it's like the first night you spent on the street, with Esme who'd locked you out for sharing a score.

And so you rise after a siren blasts up Georgia, and the blue and magenta lights halt just over the hill in Fourth District's parking lot. Hide in plain sight, boy. That's it. Move when there's activity, not stillness. It distracts, diffuses. Just another lowlife with a broke-ass cellphone, nothing to see here, officer.

And yet at the foot of the hill, past a black and empty Walmart, there's at least one welcoming light. The neon sputters "Subs-Chicken-Chinese Food" and two young men vape at the entrance while an older woman pushes past them, moves to the bullet-proof shield to claim her goodies.

"Yo, check this mug out . . . " one young man chortles, blowing a cloud of sativa mist from his nostrils like a cartoon bull.

The other, wincing against the frigid wind, replies with a snicker . . . making sure you hear, "He look like cat shit so the cat meat in there prolly gonna taste like steak to his big ass, huh?"

Careful not to touch them as you edge past, you remark, "I just strangled some nigga and tossed him in a Dumpster, so cat meat's fine by me. Problem?"

Lord knows where that came from. But hey, it worked. The two young men exchange nervous glance and leave you the fuck be, air out.

The woman in there will not even look at you as she grabs her take-out bag and runs out. No way to ID you; no camera in that place except what you spy at the front door and you've got your skullcap covering your mouth.

The one Viet Cong who's not now throwing off an apron and shutting down tells you, in a plain vanilla suburban accent, that the kitchen is closing.

"Here's twenty," you expound, waving the crisp bill but fidgeting. "Can you unlock that bathroom, let me wipe this offa me. Some men . . . jumped me . . . and it's Christmas. Keep the change after you just give me . . . a small French fries and small Sprite and I'm gone. *Please* . . . "

"Look, uh . . . "

An older woman roams behind the Plexglass barrier, jabbers in their Viet Cong jabber. The man's perhaps a neophyte to the hood, eh? Someone's cousin, tapped to help on a holiday when he'd rather be home with his kids tonight?

But whatever mama-san says has moved him. Likely: *we stay open and have no trouble with these animals because of little perks like using the bathroom, so stop trying to the kill the goose that laid the golden egg that hatched and sent you to college and allowed us all to buy houses in Virginia.*

"Uh, it's unlocked anyway . . . we just tell people it's locked. Fries and Sprite are on the house, by the way, how's that?"

You nod, and it only takes you a few minutes to douse your clothes and there's even an industrial squirt bottle of Purel in there, and boy you have changed if Purel brings a sigh of relief to that face. Your fries, a paper tub of ketchup and your drink are waiting.

"Uh . . . we *are* closing, that part's true", the man says with a shrug . . . and still behind the glass. "Need a bag?" And yet before you can answer he chuckles and adds, "You know, even when you came in, really messed up, I thought maybe you were from the Fourth District Station up the hill. Those two guys out front avoided you . . . they were loitering all night."

"You should use paper straws," you mutter. "Plastic messes up the ocean. That's the law."

"So, uh . . . are you undercover?"

Mama-san exclaims, "He no police! Ha!"

"I-I'm just hungry on Christmas Eve."

Now it's mama-san's turn to show true colors.

"He lie," she scoffs, all sing-songey. "He bum he druggie like all . . . good ni'!"

You don't say a thing, you hit the street with your fries and plastic bottle. There is a dead hush out there, like one of those neutron bombs wiped out all life and indeed you turn to see that the Subs-Chicken-Chinese Food lights are off.

One last look, you say. Because you are a detective. Munching on fries, licking salt and extra ketchup from your hand, is the perfect cover. Having no home is the perfect predicate for a stake-out . . .

. . . and now you're lingering at the corner of Peabody and Georgia, blankly pondering the quiet, the flickering Christmas lights on the darkened storefronts.

A car suddenly guns past the Walmart and turns the corner into the glow cast by the Fourth District's floodlight. It's a safe place to stop—if deviltry's not your thing . . .

. . . or you want to hide in plain sight.

It's a Nissan Altima, and to your obsessive eye it's at least ten years old, white, and thus dingy, splattered by street muck. It pulls up the block, slowly, then stops. Engine's running but the dome lights remain off. Something's going on, you hear the voices under the *poom-pa-pa-poom* bass and horns . . . Spanish drivel masquerading as hip-hop drivel, polluting whatever speakers are in there.

You turn up Peabody—still nonchalant, still munching, sucking on your Sprite straw yet keeping to the shadows just in case someone does pile out of the car and hassles you for stalking. With the cops ten feet away . . .

As you dunk your last fry, the door swings open and strangely the car speakers go dead. You crane your neck and you catch someone get out then scamper around to open the right rear passenger seat.

You toss the bag and the Sprite in an already brimming corner can when you see it's a young woman with a long black ponytail, looking willowy even in her black hooded bubble coat, jeans, white kicks . . . and she's pulling a child from a car seat. A baby—who immediately bursts into a wail. You pull that pic liberated from Marta's wall from your coat pocket . . .

. . . and the shadows played by the Walmart's un-Walmart weird architectures obscure you. Still, you need to jump into a sliver of light to check the image before you back-up into the darkness . . . a little deeper this time . . . hitting the rail keeping you from falling six feet onto the loading dock ramp.

Your Dumbo ears rotate to the sound of sobbing and baby's cry.

"Sí . . . lo entiendo...pero no me gusta. Eres cruel!"

She moves away from the curb to calm the child and you hear from the driver, "Go inside! Sleep! Todo está bien, okay?"

And it's a woman's syrupy contralto.

Your adrenal glands gush into every muscle in your being, tensing you like a cat.

Esme's voice. It had to be hers. It had better be hers . . .

. . . and there are now two cops joking with each other as they leave the station . . . as the young woman and the baby head toward the Dumpster in which you swam . . . as the

Altima peels off in a hurried three-point turn and hits the intersection. Maryland plates. G-B-something. You take a step out of the shadows . . .

. . . and jump back into them, fighting down a throat full of acid . . . quietly. For now, these damn cops and the young woman, distraught yet comforting the baby, are both but a few yards from your sweaty face.

She's getting closer to the squat, bunker-like apartments. You can see the po-po following her with their eyes. They exchange nods when she enters the dull yet protective glow of the sole streetlight near the building's entrance. Then they go on their way.

Quickly they are out of sight and you leap to the grass . . . on the balls of your feet to minimize the sound. Once on the pavement you repeat the tactic, just in shorter steps, pausing only as the young woman jingles her keys while she balances the sniffling baby in the crook of her arm . . .

. . . and the unlocked door, slightly ajar, signals your chance to strike. *Yeah someone's killing people but God help you . . . God fucking help you, boy!*

"*Piedade . . .*"

She turns, mouth open as if she's practiced *not* responding to her name . . . and failed each time.

You slap your big, dirty hand across her mouth and shove her inside the dark apartment doorway . . . *damn you* . . . she's heaving mournful, guttural screams through your fingers as she clutches the baby close with one arm, flails the other, wildly to protect her child . . .

. . . from you, son. No *Ave Marias* or beads're going to save you now.

CHAPTER 18

El Jefe

You jerk your foot loose and shut the door.

Your hand is still clamped on her mouth and you pin her small body against the far wall with just your left forearm. Easy to crush them both with your bulk as she squirms, her shrieks muffled . . .

. . . but the baby's mewling isn't, and the noise escalates to the child's shrill cries as you alternately press your right index finger to your lips you shush her . . . lean in . . . whisper, coarsely, *"No lastimaré a tu bebé. No te lastimaré . . . "* Then repeat.

She stops flailing. And when her eyes, at once wide in terror start narrowing, wetly, you whisper, *"Te voy a dejar ir pero debes estar tranquilo . . . parpadea dos veces . . . si me entiende."*

Indeed she blinks twice, so hard and rapidly that you're sprayed with her tears.

"Do you speak English?"

Again, two fast tight blinks.

Yet as you begin to ease off, a familiar odor and its sticky, oily medium spices the air . . . and grazes your left shoulder in a glancing shot.

The spatter is enough to send you reeling, gasping, as the capsaicin bites into the corner of your mouth, menaces your eyes.

You aren't totally blind; she won't risk another stream because the child might inhale it as such proximity. You twist out of your coat sleeve and by evil luck manage to hook her with your right arm before she makes it to the door. Both of you spin back into the wall.

"*Don't . . . do that . . . again,*" you growl, with all the menace you dare hurl at this little girl, holding a smaller being.

You move off.

"You have any weapons in here?" you press as you scan the tiny, dank apartment as far as the light through the rust-stained blinds will reach. "*Dime, joven!*"

"N-No."

"Where's the light?"

"T-Table . . . *por ahí* . . . "

She's now shushing and soothing the baby with coos, murmurs, sways. You grope for a rickety table lamp beside what feels like a padded lounge chair, ragged upholstery. You switch it on.

The place is like a cell. Your eyes scan it: small fold-out sofa—open and covered in a heap of bedsheets. A TV—ancient and boxy—on a bureau, tiny kitchen with attachments for a stove and yet none installed . . . just a hotplate and dingy microwave. Old fridge that was once white, now a grubby yellow . . . a hallway leading to what looks to the bathroom. And everywhere there are old newspapers, magazines, bundled with bailing wire. *Aw*, you love bailing wire. In places the shit's stacked so high you'd think you were in one of those World War One trenches, lined with sandbags.

"Magazines, papers . . . *por qué están aquí?*"

She shrugs, mumbles, "No . . . no mine. They here already. This place . . . knock down soon. New, for rich people . . . "

Perfect place to hide. No way anyone legit would have found them . . .

"I only got you . . . because I got lucky . . . because I'm sloppy, I'm no professional. I don't know what I am . . . " Your afflicted rambling prompts only a mute stare. You snap out of it and bark, "Mover over here!"

That's more like it. She complies, still rocking the baby.

"My name is Richard . . . *Ricardo.*" She looks you up and down and you kick your coat, reeking with pepper spray, into the corner after you remove your gear from the pockets. "I just want to ask . . . questions . . . "

"You no *el Jefe?*"

"No . . . *no* . . . I mean, is that your pimp, your coyote . . . brought you to the U.S.A.?"

Her face instantly morphs from fear and defiance, to incredulity.

"*Qué* . . . no . . . *nooooo.* Him . . . *el Jefe.* No gang, no coyote! I am *no* girl like that!"

"Okay listen . . . sit over there. Take your coat off. I'll hold the baby and—"

"*I do!* Stay away!"

She lays the baby on the bed, sloughs her coat. She's wearing a pink pullover, skinny jeans with the pre-ripped look, cheap white knock off Vans kicks that can't possibly keep her small feet warm and dry. She scoops up the baby and the fold-out mattress sags and squeaks as she settles on the end of it.

"Okay," you say to her, trying to small-up your big self so as not to terrify her any more than you have, "I am *Ricardo* . . . I'm only looking for *Tía. Tía Carolina . . .* " And now the fear rushes back, as she weeps, shakes her head, squeezes her calmed baby. "Please can you let me stay . . . until she comes back? This is where she hides, right? From the people . . . from ICE?"

"*No,*" she cries. "*El Jefe . . .* you don't see?"

You study her as she tries to insert something into that jigsaw inside your skull. Indeed, she's more a sylph in the flesh than any photo could convey. Slender, a swan's nape, huge brown eyes. And yes, more European than *mestizo.* Odd for Guatemala.

"How . . . how old are you, Piedade?"

She's shivering now. "Me . . . *diecisiete . . .* seven-teen."

The child's too hefty and alert for a newborn. Based on Verna's search, you are going guess three months, at least.

"*M'hijo . . .* born . . . October," she whispers.

Bingo. Right around the time you were in the booby hatch for your hot dose of fennie. A lot was going on while you were in the hospital, son . . .

"When will *Tía* be back . . . I must speak to her."

"This place . . . for me and mi *bebé . . .* Tía, she go . . . own place, sleep, no one look."

"She hides *you*? Not the other way around?"

Your brain's cooking, *figurin',* son. So much so there're visible veins swelling in your forehead and that shit's creeping her out from that gaping stare . . .

"She go, me and Maximiliano sleep here. Bring food and diaper and med'cine . . . "

"So it's not like the other girls she saved . . . slaves . . . sex slaves *Sexo?*"

She shakes her head. The jigsaw pieces in yours are moving again. Fitting this time. And that hurts more.

"*El Jefe* bring me . . . say El Estor was garbage for me. Say I *bonita* and can work here, America. Get big university. Work for television maybe model like Khloe Kardashian, eh? Tía, her there. *La senora, su espousa* . . . her no like Tía . . . " She's frowning because you are saying nothing, just motioning her to continue. This is what you wanted, boy. Don't blame her . . . or Esme. Indeed, she smiles oddly and muses with such terrible innocence, "But *el Jefe, la senora*, they love me. Love me so much that I take care of *las niñas* . . . "

Your eyelids clench for an instant and say, "*Las niñas.* All daughters . . . "

"Yes," she answers, almost sheepishly. "I-I have *bebé* in belly once when *el Jefe* him come to me. I no . . . no pure. He put in me when I no pure."

She's sobbing now.

"Before Maximiliano?"

"Yes. I want pray to priest becau' I no pure. *La senora*, her say no pray to priest, her take me to doctor. Him see on screen, *bebé* she is *la niña* . . . *mi niña linda* . . . *muy linda* . . . " She strokes her son's fine chestnut hair. "*Mi niña linda* . . . " The tears stop, as if a spigot twisted. You finally lock glances with her and all you see is a blank, dead stare. Your usual look, eh? Right back at you. "But *la senora.* She angry on me. She want boy but she want any *bebé* for herself, not me. *El Jefe* him say take Piedade to new doctor. Him say *kill*! Kill *mi niña linda.* Kill her and *la senora* say she hate that and she on the TV, march against *el juzgado* 'Roe and Wade,' *comprende*? And *el Jefe*, him laugh. Him laugh so much I hear in my room. Abort like *mi niña* – it *pecado* . . . a sin . . . only for poor womens. Him call them *las vacas.*"

You've heard that before . . . the word, used just like this. "Cows?"

"Sí," she whispered, mournfully. "*Vacas negro* or wild animal . . . *loco y imbéciles. Vacas metiza, Indio* . . . *putas. Vacas* . . . 'hill-billy?'"

She lets out a moan, so low and deep it would come from a woman many times her age. It is so raw you dare not touch her.

"How many abortions have you had?"

Shuddering, she holds up a finger. Just the girl. You cup your hands to your face and now it's she, the terrorized one, who asks if your big ass is okay.

No. You're not . . .

"*Tía*, she cry with me . . . *Jefe*, him make me no pure again. Him put it in, it hurt . . . but no pregnant when man put it in bad part of me . . . like that when him *loco*, him do *Tía* . . . and me *together* . . . ." You sink your chin to your chest. You finally know what she's describing. "But him want son so very, very much, and him be so sweet to me and beg me to love him, and him do it inside me again in place for babies. I have baby in belly again. But Tía, she get more 'fraid . . . very 'fraid, find out . . . things . . . *niños*, when ICE say mama, papa no allowed . . . "

That stabs you to attention, eh?

"Hold it . . . you mean babies, small kids, like on the TV news?"

She nods and says, "ICE . . . *niños* take from mamas, give to *gringa* women . . . like *la senora*, if they barren. They make *niños* good Americans, good Christians. So nice clothes, shoes, birthday parties . . . new names *como* 'Mary,' y 'Connor' y 'Emma.' Not names like they born with . . . "

So you have to ask, "What if you are older children, teenagers like you?"

Her expression hardens, her eyes narrow.

"Then give to man like *el Jefe* who like *joven*. If big boy, to *los maricónes*."

"And *Tía* . . . she hated that."

"*Sí. Tía*, she take me . . . from nurse who come to house, rub belly. See screen again, and *Tía* see screen. This time, see *el niño, m'hijo dulce* on screen. She say it a boy and she won't let *el Jefe* take him, so *Tía* . . . *Dios* . . . *Tía hurt* nurse. And we go. Leave everything behind . . . "

"She stole something . . . worth more than gold . . . " you mutter.

"*Qué?*"

"Maximiliano . . . that's a family name, right? Jaime Bracht's . . . "

You stand, walk to her. Tell her what's chewing on you. You— the perfect sleuth for this job. The perfect patsy, when it's done. She gives a snorting, gasping sort of noise as she pushes her raven black hair off those regal high cheeks, now swollen, apple red.

"*Y mas . . . .*" she whimpers.

Oh, that's not the worst.

"*Mi familia . . . tambien. El Jefe* . . . him and *mi madre* . . . cousins? *Mi madre*, her *abuelo* . . . people . . . *Mexicanos . . . y . . .* "

"German?" you whisper, squatting down to her eye level to recite the whole family tree, but strangely she is shaking her head.

Guess the Devil's still out on Baby Jesus' night because it's also then that your phone—the one you thought you'd busted—rattles and buzzes on the table by the one lamp lighting this dusty cave.

"Keep your son quiet. Understand?"

You click on.

"*What in the ever-loving Christmas crackers is your malfunction, Cornish?*" rips a familiar voice. "*Now what's your situation . . . your device broken?*"

"No, Mr. Sugars. I'm . . . I'm talking to you now, aren't I?"

He pauses . . . oddly, without scolding you for the smart-ass quip. "*Okay . . . yeah . . .* " And now he asks, ever more oddly, "*Where are you?*"

"Working, like you warned I'd be, Christmas or not."

"*You said you were heading up Georgia Avenue this evening, south of old Walter Reed Army Hospital. Then you off broke off contact.*"

You never told him that. And Piedade's grabbing her son . . . cringing, shaking her head. Because Mr. Sugars' voice is very, very loud. And familiar . . .

. . . and you're taking the phone from your ear. Staring at it. Hitting speaker. His voice sends her into a panic, off the bed, down the hall to the bathroom. You engage him . . . and you are damn lucky he didn't hear the girl shriek. But now you know Mr. Sugars has a history with this girl.

The military, like law enforcement, doesn't prep a mug like Mr. Sugars to lie or gamble the way someone with nothing to lose does. *Show him.*

"I'll have this wrapped up . . . by tomorrow night. On schedule. See, I confirmed she's traveling with the teenager, and baby. I'll have them all in one place in twenty-four hours . . . please tell Mr. Bracht . . . "

"*Baby again? You're certain?*" He intones in lame surprise. "*We need to check the mother's ID, see if she was trafficked, get her and the child away from Rubio.*"

"Roger that," you spit back. He loves the fake-ass jargon.

"*Copy. Don't stay out of communication from now on. Hit me every hour on the hour. Don't make me have to come shake up the little old fat nigger you recruited, or that black activist at that soup kitchen shelter, okay? I'm out!*"

You shout to her, "He's gone! Come back. *Now.*" Hardly tender.

You're still staring at the phone as she returns, tip-toeing and barefoot.

At first you want to peel the burn open as if his Idaho potato head's inside and easy to grab and crush in your fingers. You kept your cool long enough—even during his punk-ass backhanded threat on Black Santa and Verna—to mix a theory. Test it!

With both mother and child watching intently you pry open the phone's back panel, inspect the new tiny card he'd inserted. Looks like someone spilled a dab of solder on it . . . a fleck . . . a splotch. But solder's silver, not gold . . . and this "splotch" has symmetrical edges except where a piece of the cracked cover must have scraped it.

"Señor Ricardo . . . ?" she calls, shyly. "You fine?"

"Anything but. He's been tracking me. Yeah, the 'lost phone' app's been removed. But he just reactivated it with whatever damn thing is on the chip. It's damaged though. Still, he's prolly be on my ass one way or another since last night . . . "

She doesn't believe a mere broken screen or cracked case disabled Mr. Sugars' all-seeing eye. But if it hadn't, why did he call? Why aren't you both in the trunk of his car?

"This man . . . others. They came after you, didn't they? *Joven* . . . be brave . . . tell me."

She sinks her head. Not clear with this girl whether she's distraught or in fairy land, lunching, but the pauses and wetness in her voice is real enough.

"They act like *federales, policia*. But they no. Real policia— they no like *el Jefe's* men. Good for us, say *Tía*. She find place for us so I can have Maximiliano, but then I sick, him sick . . . stay . . . one night then a week . . . with Sabine, Nestor. *Tía*, she *bruja*. She chant and draw, she say, so Nestor, him

215

and other people no tell. Nestor scare of Maya. But him more scare of ICE . . . *policia. Hechizos* keep him loyal. Protect us."

"So they turned them over to ICE, or killed them . . . and their children," you croak, as if speaking to yourself, "to leave no witnesses?"

"*El Jefe* . . . him no scare of *hechizos*, as much as *mafioso* . . . gang. Him have special men. They go hurt Sabine. Send Nestor away. Back home, he dead from *mafioso* gangs . . . "

"Go on," you grunt, checking the windows.

"*Tía*, her say she make her sister move and go away. No safe for us, no safe with *putas* in school who say me a *puta. Tía* come to friends . . . to ask for money, for hide. Men come, *Tía* say . . . men come to . . . to friends."

That quickens a pulse it took a while to calm.

"*My* friends? Their names were Eva and Fred. You recognize those names?"

She nods. She watches you clench you fists, trigger every muscle fibre in your being to bury the pain of what's coming. "*Tía*, her say men who work for *el Jefe* no hurt them . . . they be safe . . . if they just say where *Tía* is."

"That's not quite right, is it *joven*?" She tosses you a quizzical teenager look again. And you can't hold it in any longer. "They knew about *me* . . . because . . . she led them right to Miz Eva and Mister Fred. She didn't mean for them to die, right? But she knows that baby boy's daddy is a cold-blooded animal." When she shrugs, face blank from your menace, you shout. "And when they hurt Eva . . . hurt Fred . . . because they didn't find Esmeralda Rubio, the motherfuckers shoved that shit in their noses . . . two old people, helpless anyway, so they couldn't fight back . . . and killed them . . . "

"I-I dun-know . . . *Señor Ricardo* . . . "

" . . . because of her and me!"

"No . . . *Tía* love *los ancianos* . . . and you no bad man!"

"I *am*." Oh your eyes are burning and God damn you for it. "They killed them . . . to flush me out and hold something over my head . . . so I could find her . . . to find *you*."

Now you're groaning as you roll your mind's eye to Black Santa's fat, mole-stippled face, beaming at you when you showed up for the truck that morning . . . *yassa-bossing* to Oosterhaus. Why not add to her terror?

"Did . . . did *Tía laugh* and show her naked ass to Bracht when he wanted to get hard, huh? Look at me, *joven!*"

"*No se* . . . *Señor Ricardo*," she cries, "*Please* . . . "

"Yeah . . . yeah . . . did he get hard hearing about her time on the filthy streets with her nigger? Big nigger lowlife, drunk junkie bum . . . a waste of everything anyone taught him, gave him! *Dime, joven!*"

"*No se!*"

"Eva and Fred are slaughtered, I'm a ghost, but you, Esme saves you. Fucking *you* . . . "

Oh, she's shaking, mouth agape—but there're no more tears, no more outward terror. She merely holds her son— awake and squirming, fussing once more—to her chest. She raises her pullover, slides down the left cup of her bra . . . offers the boy a quince-colored nipple as if you aren't there. But you are, and she doesn't break her look at your face, even as the child feeds. A teenage girl, stronger than you . . . you with your happy pills and Dumpster-swimming.

"You say you come . . . for *Tía*. But now, you come hurt me, *mi Maximiliano*. Tell him . . . tell *mi bébé* why he is to blame! Hurt *mi niño . . . m'hijo dulce . . .* becau' *you* hurt! You want . . . *blood . . .* becau' you only man who bleed, eh?" Then the poise disintegrates, and the tears flow again. *"What about I, Piedade? I bleed! I hate! I hate all you!"*

Now you see the child's face. Eyes wide and scanning, lips bubbly despite his mom's cry. Yeah, and yours. The noise that will bring a knock on the door for sure . . .

Slowly, you reach out to her. "I'm sorry . . . so sorry . . . "

She looks down, turns away to complete the feeding.

"Piedade . . . look at me. I will protect you. I will protect him. But we need to talk to her. We need your *Tía.* My . . . my Esmerelda . . . "

At first, she ignores you, maybe to calm her own hammer and anvil heartbeats, but then she mumbles something about a pay phone, probably one of only a few in a stretch of Georgia Avenue leading up to Maryland. And it's right by the Fourth District station.

"I call there . . . she call back on telephone, old telephone, in room where she stay . . . "

Landlines all. No mobile or internet. Again, smart.

"Listen c-c-carefully. Call her in the morning. We will make our move then. Do not . . . tell her I'm here. But tell her you don't feel safe. When she dropped you off you saw a bald white man . . . an Anglo in a s-s-suit, driving by and it made you nervous. Because you've seen . . . seen him before. That's important. You saw him with Bracht, you saw him in front of the Walmart a few days ago."

"But I no see Anglo . . . dress like *federale. Tía* say no go Walmart. I only see *you.*"

"Doesn't matter. Get her here, just not now. *Status quo,* for tonight."

She nods and you pray she gets it. She's sprouting a bent smile, like she doesn't know what to say, what to think. She wipes the baby's milk-sopped lips with a tissue . . .

"*Señor* . . . "

"Richard."

"*Ricardo* . . . there *en la cocina* . . . *cerveza.* You want?"

Oh yeah you want, but . . . "Nah, nah. Can't have . . . alcohol. Not good . . . "

"You stay, with us. Nothing else I can offer. Please?"

You nod, force a smile when there's nothing but that baby's sweet yet snotty face to smile about.

And then, frighteningly out of the blue, devastatingly juvenile . . .

"Soon, you go kill *el Jefe*, for *Tía*?"

"No . . . *no.* Tomorrow is when I do *figuring*, so you and *Tía* will be safe. Tonight we rest."

You're playing with your phone, flicking that little defect on the chip with your thumbnail.

Guess she's mad you didn't take her seriously because she's standing in front of you in that tee shirt, moist and transparent where her milk-wet nipples poke, with an ugly, almost bratty expression on her face.

"*Tía*, she run-way when they kill you Fred, a *mujer. Brigada* come, save her, hide her again with I, Piedade . . . you let that happen? You no wan' revenge? You kill *el Jefe*, for *Tía*, or *Tía*, she die."

Oh, yeah, the thought of choking-out Esme again is always ripe, never withered. Not now. But why the sudden bloodlust from this little thing?

"No. No more compound sins . . . more sin. *Mucho más.*"

You mutter the mumbo-jumbo memorized for your first taste

of communion wine, all dressed in white. *"Firmiter propono, adiuvante gratia tua, de cetero me non peccatorum, paenitentiam agam et vitam meam emendem. Amen."*

And she seems to know that incantation, fair to say she's Catholic. She's smiling, almost admiringly, at you when ten seconds ago she was hissing about murder. You toy with showing her the photo purloined from Marta's wall. No, not yet. In the morning. Fresh.

"Ahora . . . you are not bad man. Jesu will watch you."

"Thank you," you mutter.

"But . . . if you try kill *el Jefe.* Just you will be a fool."

You cock back your head, as if this seventeen-year-old girl suddenly punched you after bussing your cheek.

"I said no more killing."

"Becau' he is power, and bad men will kill you. Then, he will drink wine with *Presidente* Trump, go back Texas. Sleep in big bed . . . *la nueva chica* . . . *puta* . . . on him. Not think of you in grave. I don' wan' you dead, Ricardo."

The bent smile comes back and you are sad at what abuse and rape and PTSD and being on the run has done to this poor girl. For yes, she slides off the bed, saunters to you on bare toes and hands you the squirming and cooing object of so much pain . . .

"I get *cerveza* for you, Ricardo. You get wha' *you* wan'. *Como un jefe.*"

CHAPTER 19

I, Piedade . . .

PIEDADE'S IN THE SHOWER. YOU CAN hear her singing and it's some juvenile shit, warbled in Spanish. The baby's keying in on her voice; you can see it in his darting eyes. He's wriggling in this cheap foldable bassinet with a J.C. Penny tag still on it. At least his breathing is less wet, less labored.

If she's trusting you with the boy then you can trust her, alone in the bathroom. Indeed, you're in that ragged easy chair, feet up, shoes off and the child is decent company. Piedade hung your coat up to dry after scrubbing out the pepper spray and lingering Dumpster stains with dish soap. You can hear the drip-drip-drip on the bundled newspapers stacked thereunder in between the girl's pauses for the chorus of whatever song she's completed in broken English.

"Piety?" you call, swigging your third beer as medicine. "You know, Esme's . . . I mean, *Tía*'s niece, Pashmina—her baby's pretty animated, like little Max, here. You all were in that school together . . . I mean, I guess Esme's more in touch with Marta than Marta lets on?"

No reply, just more singing. Hey, she did what she was supposed to do. She's called Esme on that payphone, as you ordered. You watched from the shadows so as not to rouse the MPD officers grumbling about Christmas Eve. You were close enough to hear some of the brief conversation, perhaps coded for your presence. You strained to her that voluptuous voice again. Even slight and grainy, it made you swoon, don't lie . . .

. . . and she's coming at dawn. You aren't going to sleep a wink.

Maximiliano coos and squeaks like a happy little piglet when Piedade saunters into the living room, big garish beach towel around her up to her chest. A smaller white towel is turbaned on her head. The *twap* of her flipflops around the scuffed parquet floor is hurting your dome, though. The baby doesn't mind.

She sits on the fold-out . . . and unwraps the turban, ruffles and fluffs it through her wet black hair. That hair takes on a redbone black girl's shag when it's drying like that, eh? Makes you wonder.

"You say something, Ricardo . . . Rich-ard?" she asks. "I hear. More *cerveza*?"

"Oh, um . . . no more beer. So yeah—you were you friends with Pashmina Manzana-Landa at that school? You were both in the pregnant girls' class?"

"*Qué?* I no have friends, Richard."

Red flag, son. But perhaps you're a little buzzed, certainly weary, and that chair is very cozy and the place, while a dump, is toasty. You let that dodge ooze out of your ears . . .

"Piedade," you then ask, gently. "How'd . . . *el Jefe* . . . come to you in El Estor? Why did he treat his *familia*, so bad. So . . . not pure?"

"You ask Tía, when you see in morning . . . "

"*Sarcástica?*"

"Why you not say once . . . tha' *el Jefe* pay. Pay *you* find *Tía*?"

Touché, girl.

"It would have . . . have hurt, confused you."

She's still wearing the towel and is hardly demure. After a quick wink at her son she looks at you: the hulking kidnapper now Christmas guest in this weird manger scene.

"El Estor, eh Richard? Okay, *sí* . . . *tenemos alemán* . . . German. Like *castellan*, they look . . . down at *los mestizos*, Maya . . . ugly . . . *las vacas*. Like girls they bring across border. Peasant only good for bed. *Los niños* only good in cages at the border. *Mi Maximiliano* . . . no! Him *primo*!"

The sudden coldness, the bratty callousness . . . red flag *numero duo*, Junior. But look, she's a fucking teenager. Even if she wasn't glassed she'd be saying messed up stuff . . .

"*Tía* Carolina hated Bracht for putting kids in cages, *metizo* or no."

She shrugs, side-eyes you as she slathers on a layer of baby oil. No bruises on that skin. No blemishes or scars from a serf's life, no rashes from worry that a bunch of pistol waving hooligans'll pull a train on you, shoot your father, beat your little brother into their gang. No gangster's put his cigarette out into that flesh because she couldn't keep up across the Sonoran Desert to the border.

"Piedade," you follow, tone a bit more hushed, "pay me no mind. I'm . . . I'm just tired."

She nods. Maybe she can tell you are sizing her up, though too immature, too sex-used to see it's not in the usual way. Or maybe she got that survival skill: reading you. Every predator, prey, or scavenger out there must master it. Yes, she senses her new knight in rusted armor is going to drown from the weight. And when she speaks, *fuck yes* it's disquieting . . .

"*Tía*, she sing *Acto de Contrición* becau' she sorry. Becau' sometime she jealous of me."

Hmmm?

"Couple hours ago, Esme was your savior . . . and you acted like you wanted Bracht dead."

"*Qué?* I not sorry. You sorry, Richard? *El Jefe*, say if you strong, you *never* sorry. So you weak, Richard? *El Jefe*, him say *el Patron*, Don Porfirio Maximiliano Bracht-Hernandez, very strong but weak when old man. *Jefe's* papa, Don Maximiliano José—him *weak* all the time."

Her eyes flash at you.

"I'll bite. Why is the woman who saved you and your baby jealous of you? Because I don't care about why people are weak. Everyone is weak most of the time."

She's not answering you. She's ignoring the baby even though he's suddenly fussing. She's peeling away the towel, showing all of herself, from head to full lips to fine black hairs on her pubis to her long, painted toes. And with a smile she wriggles into what looks like a man's cotton boxers, slips a tee shirt over her head. Still stapling her eyes to yours, she floats to the bassinette, plucks the baby from it. Takes him into the sheets and dingy comforter topping the fold-out.

You compose yourself because she's damaged. She giggles inaptly.

"*Tía* no speak nothing to you? Ha! *El Patron*, him big . . . Mexico *y* Guatemala, Honduras . . . *bigger* than *el Jefe* in Texas. *El Patron*, him build big things on beach . . . hotel, railroad, trucks. Him laugh at *los mestizos y* Maya. But then . . . him see, him love . . . *mujer mestiza*. Sabine . . . *mi* Sabine, come from Soloranzano *familia* . . . many Maya in her."

"So Grandpa had a side family is El Estor."

She nods and declares, "I, Piedade, only one girl, with my brothers . . . but I show no Maya, no *mestiza*. *Mi madre* is *el Patron* gran-daughter. *El Patron* . . . soon him say *acto de contrición* . . . him sorry for what he do, him give away much, much money to El Estor. Don Maximiliano José . . . him give *el Jefe* cars, big schools in Texas, but give away much, too, to *mestizos*, Maya . . . "

"That makes him weak to his son?"

She frowns as if you're a dullard and insists, "*Escúchame* Richard . . . him give money to blacks in Texas, Mexico, not just Maya. Dirty blacks like *Tía* make me go school with . . . dirty blacks *como* Pashmina boyfrien'!"

Uh-oh . . .

"Am I a dirty black?"

"No."

Somehow, your urge to defend this child is on the wane . . .

"*El Jefe papa*, Don Maxilimiano José, him different from *el Patron* . . . him have black friends in America. Him give money to blacks, *Tejanos* who want Bill Clinton, Obama, Hillary, Bloomberg . . . not Bushes and Trump in Texas. *Esto es un pecado* . . . a sin. *El Jefe*, him hate *Mexicanos*, only love Texas, America. Oil. Him marry *gringa*. Blonde, big American. Him say him save me from El Estor, from be *bastarda* . . . *como* Sabine . . . but *mi* Sabine, her love *familia metiza* more than *el Jefe* money . . . no want be saved."

This might be silk-spun bullshit, even for a teenager. So you take it back to reality.

"How did Esme know Bracht's dad? Tell me now."

"Ask her."

"Don't be sassy. Esme . . . she's had a tough life, her parents, her dad . . . went broke a few times that's all know. Broke trying to fix her."

Piedade rubs her belly. "*Tía*, broke here."

"That's not what it means but . . . " Oh, yes—again this little so-and-so can counterpunch. "Esme . . . can't get pregnant, can she?"

"No."

"I mean . . . that's prolly my fault . . . but why couldn't she give Bracht a son? Why you?"

She doesn't answer. You eye her backpack full of baby accoutrements like wipes, disposable diapers and such and you pray she doesn't find what you put in it while she showered.

"The light," she says, pointing to the lamp. "Better to sleep if dark."

"I prefer it on."

"Why you take *las drogas*, Richard? I no take, 'cep when *Tía* bring for pain, when Maximiliano come, and after. Girls take becau' they poor. *Jefe* take to party and dance, make him strong. Tía take to laugh, make her do things. But why you take? You want *las drogas* now, don't you? I see in you eyes . . . "

"People get high because of hurt, *joven*. Because to get up every morning and breathe and walk and piss . . . have a job or try to love someone . . . *hurts*. So bad it's like death. So bad . . . you need medicine . . . and the medicine comes from a bottle in the liquor store, or pills, or a needle, from a glass tube, or rolled up with herb. It's fiendishly easy. And ironic, cause you end dead anyway . . . and on that note—we sleep. Biggest day of our lives tomorrow. Merry Christmas, Piedade."

"No *posadas* for me this *Nochebueno*, Richard," she trills. "But I sing *posada* song for you—you sleep . . . no *hurt* tonight, no hurt for *Tía*. When *Tía* and you see each other in morning, we all sing, for Merry Christmas . . . "

Her voice, so impertinent and crass as any teenage girl's, is a tonic, when put to son and not drowned out by shower noise.

"*Mi esposa es María . . . es Reina del Cielo . . . y madre va a ser . . . del Divino Verbo . . .*"

Another few verses and your eyelids quiver, then fall . . .

. . . you're thumbing away Esme's tears. Yeah, she'll weep. She'll be contrite. She'll love you. And when she bears witness to Eva and Fred's suffering, she'll pray for forgiveness. You'll forgive.

And maybe you're dreaming when you feel the blood trickling from your forehead.

There's no pain so it must be a dream, at least for these few seconds before you open your eyes to behold the arm of that chair in which you're slumped, also wet with blood. You reach up, feel the crease in your dome, above your left eye.

Cue the pain . . .

"*Piedade!*" you howl, knocking over the lamp. No answer and you've now kicked that the empty bassinet and realize there's not a single mewl or screech or babble.

She's gone, with her son, a backpack, and nothing more.

No use screaming her name again. You grope for the burn, recharged and readable. Never mind the blood, the double vision, the noise in your dented skull like the bell in the Founders Library at ole Howard U.

The last thing you see before your knees buckle is the green icon moving up Georgia Avenue, crossing rapidly into Maryland. The app delivers a screen message with a loud tone: the subject on U.S. Route 29 North . . . Colesville Road will move out of range in thirteen minutes . . .

"*Piety,*" you mumble with a queer grin as you skitter, crablike, to the bathroom.

She got you good. Face and scalp bleeds like a milk calf's neck slit for slaughter, son, you know that. But it can't kill you. And there, in the sink, lay the implement. An iron. Lucky for you it wasn't hot, and she didn't decide to finish you with the cord.

Piedade's cleaned out any prescription meds with a name or address but at least you find some peroxide, damn if it doesn't still have a bite. With the cut washed, you seal it with the scavenger's poultice of toothpaste and baking soda. No bandages in there. Walking your hands along the hallway wall, you move to the kitchen.

That rusty fridge has an ice tray and you load one of Piedade's tee shirts with the cubes and hold it to your head.

Her ass is long gone, and yeah, with Esme whom she alternatively lauded and pissed all damn night, that holy night, because who else does the little trollop have. Can't go to Bracht, right?

On the burn's spider-web fractured screen it seems Piedade's backpack has halted. Somewhere in Silver Spring from the looks of it. You're not even sure what neighborhood this is because it's pulsing right on the Beltway, 495. Lord, if she chucked it over the side onto an embankment, you're fucked. Esme would have found the device. But Esme would have plinked it on another car, right? Because both these bitches are devious.

They're playing each other, son. You can't see that, even with head throbbing?

And as for Mr. Sugars, your Christmas wake-up call arrives . . .

"What's your sit-ref Cornish? I'm counting on your lead as the payoff for your disappearing act tonight."

"Not gonna salt your game, Mr. Sugars. I got 'em both penned in."

"*What do you mean 'both?' You have a hunnert percent make on this witchdoctor hooker, whatever . . . and the other, with the kid?*"

You labor not to slur or pass out.

"Both. Period."

"*Any idea if the target has gotten this girl high, hooked her on dope . . . the baby okay? Just asking because we don't need more loose ends . . .* "

"Girl's . . . okay. Baby . . . looks healthy. A boy. And your target . . . all three of them are at a house . . . no number I can see. Just brick rowhouse . . . red. Ft. Stevens Drive and Sixteenth. I'm in the shrubs across the street from the house."

"*Outstanding! Stay right there . . .* "

"But . . . it's going be tough . . . I need another hit . . . not the Narcan shit . . . just the stuff. Can you, maybe warehouse it so I can get it afterward. I mean, if you're really going to snatch her, turn her over to the cops, ICE, maybe take to this chick and baby to Family & Child Service . . . I shouldn't be there . . . "

"*We still need to ten-twenty but look, call me a softie. Mr. Bracht was still nervous you'd relapse but we found that black girl—Verna? Sort of pudgy but attractive . . . runs your shelter?*"

The hair on your neck is tingling and whatever vomit was rising now halts, dries up, flakes into the stomach. Make sure she's okay, son. Then parry. You know how . . .

"Franciscan Brothers run my place, s-sir . . . "

"*Aw, not where the nuns are,*" he cracks in a bizarre, chatty tone, as if he's yukking it up with another smug buzz-cut white suit in the car. "*Next door, in the So Families Might Eat place. When she checks her mail room at home . . .* "

"You have . . . her home address?"

"It's what I do. Anyhow, she'll see a Christmas package. For you, in care of her. Final payment of your fee, let's call it. But listen . . . try to hold it together. So—the address?"

Why send it to her home address? *Lord* . . . just stay cool as a fan in Alaska, son . . . you can do it . . . string him along, send him farther . . .

"Sir . . . um . . . I get the sense you aren't alone. In a bigger car. A four by four, big SUV?"

There's a pause and then, *"Just back-up. Good call. How'd you know?"*

"When you're called a crow, hyena, maggot, buzzard, you tend to notice things. And Mr. Bracht, he says 'scavengers' have to understand the predators' habits just much as preys', right?"

Whoever's his navigator now checks in. Mr. Sugars is suspicious and not biting on this delay and dodge anymore.

"That corner . . . that's not a house or apartment building. It's a school for rich hymies. Gimme an actual address."

"Across the street. Can't miss it. We wrap this up today. Mr. Bracht will be happy" You click off. *"Fuck you . . . "*

And now you're grinning only because Fort Stevens had popped into your head. Another one of your essays, back when school was as important as football. 1864, and the Confederates decided to get slick, sneak into Washington from the rear, kill a bunch of niggas, snatch ole Abe. But a few Union soldiers stopped them cold, at Fort Stevens, along with government clerks and black folks . . . like the ones Trump's spilled from paychecks in this shutdown. Abe himself went up to buck them up. Only President under direct fire. Even Madison ran like the midget slavemaster he was when the Limeys and niggas rolled in from Bladensburg in 1814. But

Abe, he got his hands dirty. Good to see useless cocktail party trivia history turned into a practical tool. Lure the overconfident monster into a backwater defile. Let him charge. Impale him, hold him until he bleeds out.

Or you could run. This time it's not a bad solution. You'd want your troops evacuated, safe. You access your brain's bottomless pit of names and numbers. Then you think about Esme, that baby. No rescue for them. Or that little broken child, Piedade . . .

CHAPTER 20

Pittance

THE COLD AIR OUTSIDE THAT FLOP house apartment slams your wound like a sledgehammer. The beanie cap barely covers your ersatz dressing, so even with the props you've just now borrowed from Piedade, anyone other than the Three Wise men on the street this wee hour of Christmas morning is going to run from you rather than help.

You choose another option, right there on the steps of the Fourth District station. Whatever you must do, boy—clad some brass on your nutsack to do . . .

. . . and those brass balls swing as you just walk yourself right into the brightly lit lobby. The white boy cop at the desk pops up, fingering his holster.

"The hell?" he says with a grimace, and another cop, a Latin, appears . . . ironically sporting a Santa Claus cap.

You face her and she's not even fingering the holster . . . because she's already got her piece out and aimed.

"I'm . . . in difficulty . . . please!" and you're waving an unopened box of Maximiliano's diapers, a blue rabbit made of yarn . . . a dented suitcase is in your other hand and you pretend it has heft. "I just g-g-got in town for Christmas. See my s-s-son. Baby mamma says she lived here but it was a lie . . . got jumped, robbed . . . my boy Fitzroy Cockburn . . . he's down on his luck . . . lives in the St. Jude's Shelter I hear—you can call . . . he gave me directions here but now I got no money to get back . . . but . . . I just need someone to call a taxi, take me northeast to where my c-cousin lives. His crib's past the old bus station? My cousin'll pay for the fare. Help me find my s-s-son. I swear . . . I swear I ain't lyin' . . . please . . . "

The tears are real.

The female cop holsters her weapon, pats you down while another officer arrives to cover her. She finds the burn, inspects the cracked screen.

"S-See, ma'am . . . it's busted."

A shrink once said that because of your many brain afflictions, it was impossible for you to understand the nuance and art of bullshitting. They're wrong again, aren't they?

The desk officer is about to call you a cab when the female cop, clearly rattled she almost blew a down-on-this-luck dad like you out of his socks on Christmas, announces, "I can run him down there. Gotta drop some paperwork by Four-oh-Five before they go off-shift anyway." She and her cohorts feign debating the rules until she snaps in your direction, "C'mon dude, let's go before I change my mind!"

She's not going to hit the siren and lights for you, nor is she big on small talk. So? This con worked. One for the legend books, for sure. And she only knows your name is Richard and you're lost, upset, and pray a lot in Latin.

The cop speeds you to another quadrant of the city . . . and you arrive quicker than you thought, owing to the utter lack of traffic on the darkened streets at this hour. The icon on your app remains near the Beltway and you're swallowing bile because yeah, Piedade probably chucked it in Esme's direction. And by now Mr. Sugars knows he's been scammed. You could end up in the morgue by Christmas dinner, Junior. You better pray this shit works, this evac. And that Verna will even come close to believing you . . .

. . . so, when you finally cross under the railroad tracks at L and Third Street you spot a landmark to get a bearing. Verna's place must be very close. It's the ancient, concrete Washington Arena, looking like someone sliced a beer keg down the middle and sank it half into the pavement. As a last bit of piss on the grave of Chocolate City, as highlighted in that *Washingtonian* issue: it's been re-tasked as an REI store . . . *yeah*, feeding gourmet MREs to yuppy hikers and skiers, peddling gear to white nutcases who spend their weekends climbing cliff-faces like Spiderman. You swallow your bewilderment as the cop starts to pry as to your true destination.

"No . . . this looks familiar ma'am . . . you can dump me here."

"Huh? You serious?" At a stop sign she turns to the reinforced glass and looks you up and down, "Pretty deserted here. No shelters, halfway houses . . . even a flop hotel . . . down this way."

She's laconic, flat. A female you. Note the trap laid with the flop hotel quip?

"Long time ago," you deflect, "my mom came here with her friend, a white girl she knew from the YWCA after it integrated. Came to see The Beatles . . . she was heavy-pregnant with my sister. My dad had just come back from his first adviser tour in Vietnam. Boy was he pissed. Week after that my sister was born and he accepted a transfer to Okinawa, Japan."

You are dying to tell her how Alma and your mother got all bruised, huh?

"I mean, The Beatles. This was historic. First appearance in America. Not Ed Sullivan."

"Who the hell's Ed Sullivan?" she asks. And it works. Sufficiently bored and not wishing to break any more regulations, she drops you on Fourth and guns the unit away.

You break into the shadows and dump the suitcase, the diapers. In few minutes you are on H Street, freshly scrubbed of the '68 riots, and yet even that imitation of the West Village and Lower Broadway in Manhattan, with its gourmet vegan spots and performance art and trolley to nowhere, is deserted. As a teenager, or big man on campus at Howard, you could get fried fish down here and watch fist-fights every night till the sun came up or the cops busted up the crowd. Now, it's yet another urban theme park, and there's Verna's building, per your video camera mind's eye . . . a block from where fried chicken wings with mumbo sauce has long given way to *poké*, whatever that shit is . . .

. . . and a soulless smoky glass window pill box, small terraces. A cramped lobby, not a damn soul behind the desk. This isn't New York, where doormen and supers abound . . .

. . . there looks to be a door around the corner on Seventh, next to the garage entrance. From your camping around these newer spots you know that the garage is the second-most secure entry other than the lobby.

This side door, however, abuts where the garbage chute empties into a huge green Dumpster. No cameras discernable. Lots of bikes racked there. Lots of snack wrappers and they ain't Hot Cheetos or Funions . . . healthy shit. Yet lots of crushed coals. This is the smokers' retreat, yeah. A good predator, an observant scavenger, always follows the grazing and spoor.

Yeah, Lil' Roach once boasted there's always a chink in the armor . . . though he thought that meant a mini-Chinaman, showing the way. Young ofays with no street sense—now where would they emerge and return, like prairie dogs yet with none of the prairie dog's caution? Easy—where the smokers come in and out without the hassle of the lobby. The door pops right open. And there's no one on the street to scout your entry.

If there was an alarm or sensor struck, a management employee or even officer friendly who shuttled you would have responded. And thus, with kismet smiling on you, you head for the mail room. Cameras will spot you; Mr. Sugars may have played you. Still, you step lively, like you live there.

There's nothing shoved in or taped to 2B's box. Yet before you vomit in panic, you see a stack of packages on the ledge on the opposite wall, and, as promised, there is a large yellow envelope marked hand delivery for Verna Leggett, no return address . . . and you tear it open anyway, praying it's not a late present from an auntie. The sight of gold and silver foil gift wrap and a red bow on the parcel prods a gasp and now you are looking back toward the exit, just in case. You slide to the cold carpeted floor with the twinkling box. Safe for a time in the shadows. You open it. Dawn's coming, and it will bring Mr. Sugars.

Nimchuk's business card's affixed to a box not unlike what you fished out of a wall and what started this whole mess. Just his name, a number. On the card's reverse side is a set of black blotches called a QR scan symbol. You pocket the card and slide open the box to see a document, and an old-school note. Rag paper, yet typed.

"Dear Ms. Leggett. Should Richard Cornish contact you, please share the contents of the gift box with your organization before you scan the QR on my counsel's card, which will give you details on his contact information etc. I wish to provide direct and legal aid for any potential liability you or the St. Jude's facility might face in the aftermath of his rampages, which have now come to my attention. In

the event he has not been arrested, I include a sample of the drugs he was taking when I met him to discuss employment in lieu of a direct reward for finding my grandfather's coins. Perhaps a police lab could get it analyzed. I feel responsible in that my cupidity for the man who convinced me to donate to you and St. Jude's has clouded years of experience and instinct. Please contact me through the scan info on the card ASAP, J. Bracht."

There's a check for SFME, ten grand. One for St. Jude's and the Franciscan Brothers. Another ten. A third made out to cash: fifteen thousand. Liquidated damages for any shit you've caused. Oh, you are a prime plucked pigeon, son . . .

In a plastic clip are five one hundred-dollar bills, sporting an ordinary handwritten Post-it note. "For your trouble, Ms. Leggett, and discretion."

Five bills? That's it. No, these rich ofays are not like you, Junior. To them you all are rubes, idiots, black and brown dumb fucking animals. A pittance—less than a hundred grand—providing cover, insulation, for murder, human trafficking, fraud, impersonating feds? Millions to see his son's little face, you'd bet. Why'd you think it'd be different? This elementary sort of artifice has served generations of Mr. Charlies well in this elementary sort of town, among these elementary potentates, before. Buying them off with even pettier indulgences, with paper trails one can see from outer space. Yep, he must think this is still that Chocolate City. Yet you still make that sort of a patsy. So yeah . . . *dead-up Goddammit!* You were right to come here first.

You take a breath, squeeze the gelcaps out of the box. Swallow one, yeah . . . if it's poisoned that's on you but hey, you pocket the other along with that last precious squirt of the Narcan Plus. That dose must've been the right stuff, for your head's instantly clear and you're dreading what you must do next. Indeed, there goes the burn, humming and rattling as if it's going to explode.

You eschew the elevator, take the stairs to the second floor, smash Verna's door buzzer twice. You make sure you're seen in the peephole and hit it a third time. Now you see light under the door . . . and hear whispers. Plural? And one's not a woman's . . .

. . . louder now: a man's cursing. Verna's pleading, and you can't tell if it's for keeping the door locked or letting you in. You take the gamble her neighbors on this floor are whitefolks who've fled for the holiday when you call out, "It's Dickie, Verna. *You are in danger.* Tell this man to open up so you can pack, get out. Come on!"

The loud whisper through the door is a male's alright, and it warns you that she's going to call the police, and that you're a sick motherfucker. That is, until you wave the checks, the money by the peephole.

"This was to be your bribe . . . they set me up. Mr. Bracht, Verna. Mr. Bracht and his coins. The coins were bullshit. They were after Esme because Esme kidnapped his breeder. Kidnapped his son. Do not call the cops!"

The pause is only a few seconds, but to you it's an hour. The lock trips, the door parts only the length of a chain, and there's a dark-skinned brother there eyeballing you back. He lacks your height and wingspan. Broad nose, close-set eyes, skinny goatee. Still, he must be some gym-rat as he's bare-chested . . . swole and rippled. A quick look down shows pajama bottoms tight to his meaty thighs like he's the Hulk in those bursting purple pants . . .

"Let me in, man," you say, keeping your voice low, your hands high where he can see them. All you brandish is the opened gift box and contents. You search beyond him and see

Verna in the ambient light . . . hair wrapped in green silk, hands clutching a short *kimono*-style bathrobe closed. "*Verna* . . . this isn't me being tripping, fiending. I-I found her thanks to your print-out . . . but you gotta listen . . . I'm being rational . . . *rational* . . . I'm not who I was when I ran away after you brought me to those Mexicans and they gave that bullshit story about the coins . . . "

You hear loverboy scoff, "She was never out with you alone."

"Verna, the coins were a diversion. This woman, *my woman*, Esmeralda Rubio . . . stole them from Bracht to bait him. Then they were pretty much bait for me, too, or a test. And now he's after her, he'll hurt her . . . he's already killed people . . . look . . . he's sent this stuff to you . . . it's got checks, cash. Think—why would he deliver it here? How would he even know where you live?"

Man-candy unlatches the door and instantly you see homeboy's got a fireplace poker and he's gripping it like Tiger Woods ready to lay it down on you. You present the note, the checks, cash, the card, all of it as if you're a supplicant and Verna's the Queen of Sheba.

"See? Bracht wanted me to comb the streets . . . to find Esmeralda. Because of a baby, not gold. His legacy. She was getting high with him, supplying girls for him, for the gangs. The girls supplied babies for *gringo* couples. He had the perfect cover, like priests who run altar boys. It was his job to keep the illegals and drugs from coming in. Now it's real estate, money . . . yeah, *perfect* hustle . . . hell that's prolly why he left Trump. It was getting too hot. Best cover is being rich, right? Not a government title . . . "

Her man's puffing, "Verna he's high, he's a loon . . . this is fucked up so call, finish this."

"They hooked me from jump, Verna. Got me wriggling on the line . . . only question is, how they gonna gut me. Please, get dressed, send loverboy home, fast because it is *not* safe."

She twists away from you as her man keeps you at bay with the poker.

"This . . . this is all insane, Dickie," she mutters. "And . . . this stuff in this note . . . what drug are you taking, this 'di-methyl-fee-what? . . . I swear to God—"

"*Verna!*" you cut her off, and that makes the man-candy's face contort. "I take it so I won't relapse. I take it because Bracht's man hooked me, okay. Listen, do I sound the same? Do I look . . . the same? No. I'm not that old piece of shit."

The muscled-up lover growls. "I'm gonna knock him out and I'm getting the cops . . . "

"Tim, *no!*" she finally shouts. "He . . . he would have knocked in that door if he was lying, stalking me . . . "

"Bullshit!" And he's winding up, this time like a major leaguer at the plate.

"*No!*"

She's pulling at his big arms and you wisely back up. A sane person would have had the cops there, hauling you away. Yet, *shit* . . . she believes you?

"The guy . . . works for Bracht and his lawyer, must be ex-military, ex-feds . . . he delivered this shit. He's coming back for you, loose ends . . . that's why I need your help. I got to gather Kate, Princess . . . "

Yes, it's a wild tale and you are wide-eyed and sweaty . . . yet her eyes are on you in a way you've never seen. As if you are indeed lucid and rational no matter the details.

" . . . and we have to swing by the jont . . . SFME . . . scoop up Black Santa . . . "

"'Black Santa?'" the man candy huffs with a wince. "That's a name? You tripping on *loveboat*, nigga? Verna, I'm done."

Her bare feet seem frozen into the oriental rug. And it's too late to try to knock her man out. He's younger, stronger.

Verna, instead, levies the blow with words.

"Tim, I'm getting dressed. Do not answer the buzzer. *Wait for me . . .* "

"Are you nuts?"

"My mother is the only person who calls on the landline so if I'm not back by nine you tell her I am still picking her up for Christmas dinner at Cece's . . . "

"What about me? My flight leaves Reagan at noon and . . . *shit* . . . this Twilight Zone shit!"

She loses it.

"Then pack and get on the damn plane!"

She storms into the bedroom. He won't lower the poker but his jaw's sure enough down.

"No one gets to be innocent, bruv," you counsel. "No matter how reverent. Faithful."

"Oh *hell* no . . . "

She pulls on random yoga pants and a sweatshirt, shoves a Nationals cap over her pinned-up hair and you two are out the door without another word to this Tim. God help her for what you've done . . .

"*Shut up,*" you hiss at the air.

"Tim's a good man . . . *shit* . . . this is a nightmare. What am I doing?"

"Where's your car parked?"

CHAPTER 21

No Escape

IT ONLY TAKES A FEW MINUTES to rush from H, swing around the empty Capitol to give the Cap Cops a wide berth, then shoot onto Pennsylvania Avenue.

The flashing traffic lights on a deserted boulevard fronted by empty granite edifices are not what greet you. Rather, it's the pulse and glow of magenta, blue, and almost phosphorescent search lights when Trump's hotel, once the old Post Office Pavilion comes into view. The jont has become a gilded bunker for cronies and favor seekers; at first you figure it's the usual security buffer from protesters, but they must be those crazy Antifa mugs to be out on a frigid Christmas-damn-Moring. Yet as Verna guns the Mini closer to Constitution, you see more cop cars, more shadows dancing off the bright lights . . . two ambulances and hook 'n ladder . . .

"Something crazy, between the hotel and museum," Verna indeed gasps.

"Pull over, away from the cops!"

The fright in your voice is palpable and she shudders, hesitates before she calms enough to find a safe spot, in the cut, near Seventh Street and the Archives.

You tell her to wait, turn off the lights and motor . . . and you are struggling to be unobtrusive, normal—as much as a lug like you, alone, can be in the pre-dawn blackness of Christmas Morning. Don't lope or jog, just walk steady. That's right, son. You got it . . .

. . . but then you see Kate, bathed in the garish light of a Park Police unit parked sideways across two lanes of Constitution; she's hunched over her cart, toes almost purple from the cold. There're two men and a black woman in civilian overcoats talking at her but she's not responding . . . so you walk a lot faster, breaths heavy . . .

. . . it's a female MPD cop and a burly Park Police officer with a walrus-like mustache who stop you. Play it cool. Tell them you know that woman, tell them she's Kathleen McCarthy and she's your friend, she's homeless. Stay composed. They flank you, walk you to the scene.

Before the po-po start clamoring for your name you sprint free of them; Kate rises to embrace you in her stubby arms. She's convulsing, such is the force of her tears.

It's just a few seconds and you see one of the men in coats holding a plastic evidence bag; enclosed is Princess's wig, sopping with blood.

Your howl outmatches Kate's bawling.

"Dickie . . . you know how lil' and delicate her heart was . . . lil' like her. Satan tore it out!"

"*Why* . . . " you cry. "There were shelter beds, dammit!"

She's buried her face in your chest and all you hear is a muffled, "You know we don't belong in those places. We're free, out here with you . . . "

Now Princess is free. All the way.

You pull her loose, and she can now see the rage in your eyes.

"An old white man in a suit, looks like these cops! He touch her, he do it? *Answer me!*"

Two detectives, at first standing off, immediately close in around you. One barks, "If you have info you need to come clean. Give me your name!"

A gurney, this one topped by a body bag, heads away from the second ambulance toward the medical examiner's black "meat wagon."

Kate mutters, "No . . . no she was trying to help . . . him . . . someone bashed his head in. And she said something strange . . . "

"What . . . ?"

She gets close now and whispers, "She said, 'They got Dickie's shit with them.'"

You pull away and your fan club follows. The coroner's aides are about to lift the gurney when you yell for them stop. A detective unzips the bag and the smell is familiar, as is the face, and that single cheap clipped-on braid. This child wasn't long for the world. But you weep that he met his end in such bloody horror . . .

"Kid's a what, trans-whatever," says one of the detectives coldly. "Blow jobs, small time trapping like pills. Head trauma, see . . . " And you clench your wet eyes shut as he reveals, "Bunch of junk in his hands, his pockets . . . from old pictures, to buttons, pens, a damn Purple Heart medal . . . key chains. Like shit someone's scavenged . . . you know how these lowlifes are."

The woman types something on her phone screen, then looks at you and presses, "Hey you—you know this vick as well?"

Saint Peter had the right idea when the centurions were out closing loose ends.

"No." The ambulance holding Princess's body pulls away, lights flared and rotating, siren silent. "But that woman, Kathleen. I wanna to take her to the shelter."

"If you work at a shelter you got ID?"

You aren't going to leave Kate. But what now?

"Yes, hello?" comes your savior's voice. "I'm Verna Leggett, director at So Families May Eat . . . here's my ID . . . this is my assistant Mr. Richard. We can take Mrs. McCarthy . . . "

"She's a witness. Not to the original assault, but, when this other vick . . . "

"*Princess*," you snap. Her name's Princess . . . "

"Uh-huh . . . when *Princess* went to the aide of the primary vick. We'd just need a permanent address or contact for Mrs. McCarthy if there's follow-up."

When they match all that mess to you, Junior, there'll be follow-up like a motherfucker. Follow Verna's lead . . .

"In care of me at SFME. Ok . . . let's all go, put her to bed . . . understand that Christmas is not this. This is not who we are."

The cops all chuckle, as if Verna is a social justice rube or nun, and they are the final arbiters of who isn't human enough. You both grab Kate and she whines about her cart, but you can't take it now. You let her grab some clothes, one doll and a small CVS bag and the three of you beat it for Verna's car.

So you do your inventory of who's still alive: Marta and Pashmina are dug in almost as deep with Otis Place having their back. LaKeisha? Good luck sneaking up on her. James and that bunch, likewise, scattered. But there's Black Santa . . .

. . . so it's time to get back-up. Not perfect, but back-up nonetheless or else there's no escape for any of you. You ask

Verna for her phone. Stop shaking. Get some bass in your voice. Pray you recall the number since your last high . . .

"*New phone, muvfukka, who dis?*"

"Dickie. You'll *want* to help . . . for that shit K2, as heinous as Ghenghis Kann's . . . "

"*Dickie . . . shit. You callin' . . . on a phone? Wait, dis a burner, moe? Make sure it's a burner.*"

"I need a gatt."

"*Heav'ns ta besty . . . y'all hate firearms, correct? Ha! Besides, St. Nick's already been here an' gone wiff shit from the Commonwealth of Virginia's gun-show finest.*"

"Gimme what ya got, cuz. Hundred percent discount."

"*Got some jhi-good Twenny-fives and three-eighties. Mouse guns. Y'al can't handle anything nastier. Comin' fo' Christmas Dinner then?*"

"No time, moe. Devil's already got a head start this morning."

. . . and you watch the taillights of that Mini disappear into the cold murk. Nothing but trusting your grim and grimy ass stopping Verna from cocking back her pretty round head and screaming *what the fuck have I done* . . . then dime you to the cops. Nothing . . . but checks, one made out to cash. You housed the five bills.

Scary thought, huh, her turning on you, Bracht's payoff on her or not? Not as scary as stepping up to the ramshackle half of the duplex, babbling practice lines like some hapless boyfriend a hair's breadth from being kicked to the curb.

"They will pin the rap on me . . . but I will say . . . 'I'm Richard E. Cornish, Junior . . . may I speak on the phone to the *Washington Post* . . . and CNN, please . . . and that Mueller motherfucker—does he still have staff?' Oh, and April Ryan and Joy Reid, please and Soledad and yeah,

NBC? Is Lester Holt available? Yeah, please because I have a story for you.'"

Not once do you mention Maximiliano. You might want to think about him . . .

. . . yet maybe not at this second, because the door flies open and here's Croc in all his busted glory aiming a .45 Colt—nickel gleaming in the streetlight's pallor—right at your face.

"Nigga I got neighbors. Thought it was some hostage shit out here," he chortles, thumbing down the Colt's hammer.

"It's cool . . . stand down, moe."

"So that was no joke when you said you had no time and Lucifer was running wild." He looks you up and down. "Plus I check my peep hole I'm like damn, that Dickie Cornish? Nah."

He's leaning on his cane; the only thing reptilian on him this time is that scaly slouch hat. Otherwise, his bare flesh and draws are bursting out of a nasty terrycloth bathrobe—with *yes*, a pair of dirty Crocs shod on his swollen feet.

"You lookin' ta be a OG like pops, son. Git'n here!"

He checks the empty street before shutting the door. One floor lamp's on, illuminating a beat-up and garish artificial Christmas tree . . . purple, with white ornaments. Acrid smell of cigarettes . . . and burnt *chiba* down to the stems . . . and something like bean dip from the stove is hanging in the air. He cautions you about noise. His infant nephew and other house guests and family are slumbering upstairs.

You sit opposite him this time rather than next to him on the sagging sofa. And despite his warning about noise, he grabs his mobile and swipes to a tune. His wall speakers come alive and stir with an oldie.

The song calms your beating heart, sweetens your sour mind . . . because it's Donny Hathaway's *This Christmas*—yes, the coloredfolk staple—yet sung and rendered by your damn Go-Go all-stars like the Junkyard Band, Rare Essence and ole Chuck Brown. Hell, it's Christmas, 1995 and you got your first set of Air Force dress blues on after basic, and y'all are young and bouncing and laughing, and Esme's dress and hair's making all the Jack and Jill alumnae tense and jelly . . . until there's the *pop-pop-pop-pop* of gunfire, and shell casings pinging . . . and yet again, some fool Croc's angered ruins yet another house party . . .

"Yo, Dick . . . stop lunchin'," you hear Croc call, snapping you from your fugue. "Got something for that ding in your crown." He points to some sterile wipes and a bunch of wide adhesive bandages under a scattering of *Essence* magazines spread on the coffee table along with food-crusted bowls and silverware. "For a minute wiff yo' dang mouth open you looked like y' ole whiteman Benedetto in one his fits." He does the battlefield medic dressings perfectly.

"I'm in trouble, man."

"Then I'm yo' trouble-man," he says, discarding the spent wipes and bandage backings. "Check it." He presents a Dunkin Donuts box.

You lift the pink and orange lid. Inside are two pistols. One's larger, a Smitty 99. The one looking like a black and silver water pistol is the .380. Thought he only had the .380s? Well . . .

"Merry Christmas, boo . . . from your boy Croc. Only real OG that's 'O,' as in alive."

You tap your fist to your chest, then inspect the gatts.

"Wish I had a betty fo' ya. Had a nice one and shells but had to give it to my boys down Tappahannock, Virginia."

"Country bammas or rednecks cooking that ice?"

"Nah, man. Quails and vols and mourning doves. Besides I ain't fittin' ta cut a prime shootin' iron like that into a shortie. Anyhow . . . that three-eighty's the Seecamp, pretty much new. Muvfukkas swear by it, but Hell, I'm still carryin' my ole cheap-ass Lorcin from back in the day . . . an' hand ta Gawd . . . it ain't failed me yet in the pinch. It rid me of my dear departed second wife when she givin' me head on this very sofa twelve years ago, New Year's Eve . . . and she had them Baltimore niggas coming by to bust in the moment I was bustin'. My lil' wonder took them out and put one right in her temple before her brain could tell the bitch ta bite down."

You're handling the Smitty. Croc tosses you a clip and you pop it in like an expert, keeping the safety engaged. You're glad you didn't have this down by the Trump Hotel or else there'd be some dead asshole cops before you'd probably kirk yourself in a rage. Still, Croc knows you haven't pulled a trigger since George H.W. Bush was President . . . and never, ever in anger. But the snout of this mug would look so good in Mr. Sugars' mouth.

"I'll take this Seecamp. You keep the Smith and Wesson."

"Suit y'self. But the Smitty's gonna get you out of the jam in a blaze. The Seecamp's for finer details."

"A *jhi*-pickle, my nickel," you recite, from a funny retort you all practiced as teens, among the white boys in blazers and khakis and white girls in plaid skirts and saddle shoes. "Best . . . *best* you stay low, too, despite whatever you hear about me."

The burn rattles again. This time you motion to Croc to hit the lights, in case the caller's across the street. Given the number of times his various homes have been riddled with bullets during a phone call, Croc's way ahead of you . . .

"*One opportunity, Killer. One, to make things right, restore some semblance of equilibrium, and keep those you care about safe—you copy?*"

"Mr. Bracht want a refund?" You put the phone on speaker and Croc's tripping—jaw slack, head shaking . . .

"*Cracking wise . . . and showing creative initiative, savvy, disruption, misdirection—you've certainly grown into a prodigy, Cornish. Unlike the stinking, mumbling derelict I first met . . .* "

"You sound like someone I know, Mr. Sugars."

"*And you better thank your lucky stars he's a Marine, served his nation . . . and he's gorked-out . . . otherwise I'd take your punishment out on him.*"

Lucky stars . . . *phew* . . .

"You fucked up. You killed my friends and you shouldn't have involved Verna . . . and now Esme's aired out with the girl and the prize."

"*Mr. Bracht's idiosyncrasies demand that me and Mr. Nimchuk be nimble, creative, resilient. Money trail is another loose end, and I disagreed with laying with this Verna person until we made your location. Good luck depositing those checks now. But see, unlike you, I follow orders.*"

Croc's getting antsy. "Nigga they trace calls, ya know," he whispers.

Yeah, but you want this cracker to understand the scope of how much you want to kirk his ass.

"You thought you'd put blood in the air, cause a frenzy, see what shook out, right?"

His voice is gruffer than usual, hurried. Bracht is plucking his last nerve, no doubt. "*Just how do you see this playing out, Cornish?*"

Croc's up off his fat ass and tossing about old papers and tchotchkes inside a beat-up chifforobe in the corner until he fishes out something resembling a submachine gun of 1990's SWAT vintage, feeds it with a thin banana clip . . .

"Playing out? Well, I may let Bracht stay alive. The world finding out what he is will be worse than dying. I've eaten garbage out of a bin. I know what that's like."

"*Given that you are garbage, you think anyone will care?*"

"Yes. ICE and DHS aren't gonna be happy your boy's dragged them into his personal perversions and ego. They got enough of that to handle now." When you hear him chuckle you suck in a breath, release it, slowly, so he hears you. "I'm waiting, Mr. Sugars."

So's Croc, who's locked and loaded and leaning close to hear the rest.

"*Okay Cornish . . . let's dicker.*" You watch Croc grin, but your stomach is roiling. "*The baby. He wants his son.*"

"What about Piedade? Esme?"

"*Mr. Bracht says to hell with that crazy little cooze. And Esmeralda Rubio. The three of you can become a darling little family for all I care.*"

You're shaking your head at Croc. Something's not right.

"And then all's forgotten, we all go home? *Nah*, y'all will come at me and mine regardless. So kiss my ass. If you make a move, I'll end you."

His molars scrape as he hisses back, "*You and what army?*"

Croc's grinning a platinum-toothed grin back at you.

"I have an army, Mr. Sugars. One you all step over and on and hold your nose at every day . . . isn't that why Bracht wanted me?"

You hear him bark to someone else before he returns, repeats, icy and monotone, "*The baby. You keep the whores.*"

You click off before he says anything else; your pupils have shrunk to pinpoints. You motion to Croc.

"Text this number right away. Tell Verna who you are. Ask her to have St. Jude's do a bed check and if . . . Black Santa . . . Fitzroy Cockburn, isn't there, tell her to get back to me, fast."

"Why don't you just call this place yourself an' say yo put this Santa nigga on the phone or else it's his ass?"

"Because the Devil doesn't like loose ends."

Croc thumbs out a text. You hear a ping tone. Incoming. Croc holds it at your eye level and you read.

no need 4 bed check. security says fitzroy eloped after midnite.
ru ok?

It's the like the air was sucked out of Croc's living room, popping at your eardrums, caving-in your ribs and diaphragm.

"I-I need a car."

"This ain't back in the day when I had a new whip each Saturday, nigga! My sister's is in Maryland and my older nephew needs his for—"

"*Car, motherfucker!* This cracker on the phone, he's right. No escape unless we deal!"

He winces at the palpable pain and horror carried in your voice. "Come on. I keep Pop's ole ride," he motions you toward the kitchen, away from the room where you lay zooted, then bolted from not a few days prior. "But fuckin' mouse guns, nigga! I should give back the Smitty and you take this H n' K. You watch him piss his draws when you come out wid this mug, ra-ta-tat-tat!"

"No," you whisper. "Just the car."

You both pop in the alley behind the rows of duplexes and vacant lots, and a hint of pink appears in the eastern sky, tinging roiling gray clouds out there above. On the ground, you are followed by the glowing eyes of staring feral cats.

"My babies," Croc gushes. "Feed 'em each week. Spayed and neutered, real live . . . "

You trail Croc's thick limping form to the row of small, obsolete garages some white people have turned into rental units. He unlocks the door on his, lifts it, and some paint, already peeling, floats off like the snowflakes the sky portends.

Inside, *Lord have mercy that thing screams Croc's dad alright!* Oldsmobile Cutlass Supreme, red top color, silver vinyl underwrap, whitewalls. Bizarre spoiler in the back . . .

"Two hundred-twenty-one horsepower," you blurt, as your affliction's intact, "V-six DOHC . . . "

Croc pats your shoulder and says, "Here're the keys. Treat it right. I'm lookin' at you and thinking we can make it. Time don't have to glass us, right?"

"I'll bring back Oscar's whip, not a scratch."

"Nah, fuck the car. Take care of *yourself.*" You embrace and as you break he grunts, "Now it's hurt. Who can make more hurt. What'd Father Salazar say when them mugs expelled me from tenth grade? . . . *tuque, prínceps milítiae coeléstis, Sátanam aliósque spíritus malígnos, qui ad perditiónem animárum pervagántur in múndo, divína virtúte, in inférnum detrúde.*"

This big ole mug recited that dead tongue like the Pope's an amateur! So you whisper "Amen. You might just be joining them in Hell, but tonight you're Prince of the Heavenly Host."

"Nah. That'd be that lil' Three-Eighty, full clip . . . "

CHAPTER 22

Light and Frost

YOUR MOUTH IS OPEN AND SWALLOWING shallow breaths.

All you see is the street in front of you; not even the Capitol glowing like a great big cake in the de-frosted windshield.

All you think about is the tracker on Piedade's baby bag. That is, until the pain shifts from your forehead to the top of your skull, as if the Devil himself is prying back the bone, inserting something thrashing, wriggling, into your brain. And chews on you, feel it? Yes, it's saying you will see her again . . . and if you embrace, will you nuzzle her neck, cry a heartful of remembrances and remorse? Or will you choke her ass dead, for Eva and Fred, for Princess, for that kid, for Sabine . . . and that baby, born into sickness . . .

. . . and at a stoplight you lift the phone and see the tracker on that baby bag is still transmitting. Was on the move when last you looked. Then it halted . . . now, on the move again. You see an icon for a Walgreens 24-Hour not far from the ping. There, above the Beltway in Wheaton. A honked horn rouses you as the light turns green. Stay on course, boy—how's that for encouragement? And snow flurries are invading again, in bursts, so be careful.

You are now skirting Takoma Park, along rows of ancient frame bungalows occupied by folks slowly waking to a lean, cold Christmas morning, leaner still, now that Trump cut off even stormwater and sewage funds because they declared themselves a sanctuary, and put up wanted posters of him for the crimes listed . . . and there're too many green lights so you say fuck-it and hold the phone up and look and yes, the ping has moved yet again—two miles, *fast.*

It then dies, valiantly—fruitlessly? Yeah, just for you. There . . . over the icon and silvery roof of Holy Cross Hospital . . .

. . . just as you look up and see the ruby brake lights, the white hatch and mudguards of a small truck, yes, square in front your wide eyes . . .

. . . and you're stomping the Cutlass's brake pedal . . . and it's your tightened ass that thanks Croc for preserving the pads and calipers on the first performance car with front-wheel drive, eh?

That reflection lasts less time than the skid and screech on the wet pavement.

"The kid's ill again," you croak to yourself as you whip out from around the truck on the green, as if you didn't almost grow a truck axel for a brow. "The RSV came back? Yeah . . . they were packing up to make a break for it and he got sick again!"

Look, it's been awhile since you've been behind the wheel, Junior. That muscle car's no joke, and you are fishtailing on ever-wetter curves . . . sun's up . . . snow's transformed to a misty drizzle . . .

. . . do you even know how to get to that damn hospital?

Okay, then bust a right here and merge onto Piney Branch . . . pedal to the metal, boy . . . hit Sligo, bust a left. Take that under the Beltway, turn right into the parking lot by the ER. See?

The clouds part to release a pulse of light from the sun, and for an instant the rays coat the tiny, frigid raindrops with gold and freeze on impact with pavement and steel, swathing everything, only for a second, boy, with light. Remember when Alma told you what it meant: the Devil beating his wife? Yeah, back when thunder made you cry and so did that notion.

"It's the west wind, a cold front . . . blowing the rain, snow-flakes ahead of it. Meteorological."

Whatever you say, boy. Devil's real . . .

"No demons . . . they're just men. Mr. Sugars, Bracht. Just like me . . . "

Nuff said. Because you better get clever, Junior. The parking lot toy cop let you in the lot but to motor up to the ER you see some beefy niggas through the glass in guard uniforms . . . and a metal detector. ID check. Quick left turn, cruise the main entrance at the soaring glass edifice refacing the old building. Same deal. In your addled state you'd never really peeped to what was going down out in the provinces. This is truly MS-13 country, and they don't take holiday breaks. Their vics and casualties end up here, or up at Shady Grove, eh? Couple that with the usual Christmas cheer of irate ex's, revenge-minded noncustodial parents, trippin' tweekers—get clever, fast, or you aren't getting in.

Your heart's about to burst your sternum . . . but then, *hmmm* . . .

. . . demo'd debris, all sorts of construction shit . . . there, in and among two ginormous orange Dumpsters and another smaller blue one shaped like a big turtle shell with the words "Medical Waste: Hazard" stenciled in white. And not a soul around, unlike the area near the ER. You pull the Cutlass between them, as a siren's song tugs at you. *Yeah*! Hyena, maggot, crow.

When you cut that big-ass motor you see the last wing to be renovated. No guard but there're staffers moving around beyond the glass and that one sliding door with all the beware-this, and notice-that signs festooning it.

You flip one of the orange Dumpster's lids. So much for sorting and hazardous waste!

Lots of syringes, right—never any needles! Busted wheelchairs, walkers, canes. Baby diaper packages. Surgical staplers, packs upon packs of catheters. Saline IV flushes, a pulse oximeter, dozens of boxes of sutures . . . more catheters. Whole Hill-Rom beds and chairs, lots of chairs, dozens of empty three-ring binders and a bunch of blood sugar monitors that looked like McNugget dipping sauce containers from Mickey Dees . . .

"Come on . . . come on . . . " as you indulge your nature.

Wait . . . an old computerized whole pill dispensing machine? Touchpad terminal attached? They'd toss *this*?

You monster the machine upright with a grunt . . . there are servos in that thing, a hard drive, that touchpad . . . you could get serious money! The true gem of that carcass catches your eye, there in the cold rain refracting and reflecting the inapt sun beams. Underneath, see it? Boxes of surgical steel forceps, hemostats. Good shit to poke and pry with . . . uterine dilators—they're metal so they must be of some use. You pocket them and they are clinking around in there with the little .380, toss the rest into the car. Gloves, yes you stash a few. And on the bottom layer, dry thanks to clear plastic wrap: dozens of old white lab coats . . . names stitched on them.

Idiots'll bury anything in a landfill, cheap, and thanks to Agent Orange jacking budgets, no one's inspecting. Near that, more personal crap from offices. Forgotten street shoes for the commute home, misplaced clothing . . . lost briefcases and old purses and bags . . .

. . . and you leave the Cutlass in the one coat that fits, the name "Kav Hosseini, M.D." and "Pediatric Neurology" embroidered over the pocket. You clip a piece of a name tag with a photo ID and "Hamilcar Gonzales" to the opposite lapel. Someone's green striped necktie on your black collared shirt. Anything to distract. Leather portfolio tucked under one arm; the innards and chassis of a discarded BiPAP machine under the other.

You look like someone who indeed slid down a hospital rubbish chute . . . but *damn* . . . time this right, boy . . . wait for a lull . . . *go*!

The glass door slides open and you are in, pushing this junk in your white coat, following the signs away from the old building wing into the crystalline and steel new one. And you aren't making eye contact, just keeping that old prosaic face of yours, remember that one? Not too deadpan, just convey busy, for you are walking right into Pediatric Emergency and the guard, wearing a Santa Claus cap . . . oh, he's jockin' you for a second but lets you move right by. You, hulking you, with the crease Piedade put on your bean still evident and a Seecamp .380 stuffed near your balls. You must be doing God's work on the day of his son's birth or this dude is an idiot.

Right away you note one thing, and it's why they trashed the lab coats. With some exceptions, most of the staff and docs are wearing purple or mint-green scrubs, a few have some fly neoprene vests on to look all space-age warm. They bristle with ID badges and bar-coded things . . . of which you have half . . . with someone else's pic on it.

Yet yeah it is either kismet or God because this jont is mad bustling, and any folk checking you out are doing so plainly because you're a big man, Junior, not your coat.

"Hit the door release . . . *thanks!*" you hear behind you.

"Um . . . yeah . . . " With your butt you hit a steel disk and a door swings wide. Two purple scrub-clad nurses push-pull a gurney carrying a little girl with short blonde hair. Though connected to a dangling IV bag, she's awake and waves at you.

"Merry Christmas . . . Happy Hanukah . . . Happy Kwanza," she chirps.

No way you can keep this going. Plan B's just to bum-rush and ask for anyone answering Esme's and Piedade's description, with or without the baby. Yeah, not viable. Still, you scan the waiting room. Nothing. Maybe you should hit the adult ER waiting area but a quick look in that direction yields just clumps of tired, terrified or dejected folk. Before you collect stares in return, you duck into the men's room, hit a stall.

The prop's going to be bullshit, soon. You slough the coat and tie. Stack the BiPAP and stuff around the toilet, uncrumple your own coat and leave.

If Mr. Sugars was there, he'd have jumped you in the shitter, so calm down. Try to act like a visitor or something and thank goodness you kept Hamilcar's clip-on ID. Just don't put that big black coat on. You'll look like the angel of death in a damn pediatric unit . . .

Hard to focus on faces when you spent so long avoiding folk in shame. Good thing you only need to see a face once. Thank your affliction for that.

Hold up. That one, right there. *No?* Move to the water fountain, get a drink, be cool.

There? No. Along the huge windows, on those uncomfortable damn chairs? No, just stacks of magazines and folk watching game shows and CNN . . . and . . . *wait* . . . walking along the row of chairs, looking for magazines . . . picking one up, inspecting it, keeping or discarding . . .

. . . and now your pulse is a bass drum in your ear when she finds an open seat, reclines, crosses her legs in that way only she does—with a stretch, a pointed toe. And the light and ice both illuminate and shade her and in that weird tableau she's a caricature of what you imagined from that picture James stole—yes that was her, another facsimile yet still her essence.

But now? It's her . . . but it isn't her. The cheeks, the flesh. All succulence and color and juice are gone. And yet there's so much extra flesh . . . held at bay by the black leggings covering her thighs and upper calves; extra veins pulse along her bare pale ankles and tops of her feet shown from the simple black ballet flat shoes she wears. She never wore such shoes, always heals or extravagantly beaded sandals, and her ankles and toes were painted and perfect and bronze. A simple gray hoody covers that paunch and heavier breasts, and the headband corralling that hair you called "stygian" and "black opal" well, it's something someone would wear at the gym and this one looked like it had been worn in too many workouts.

You duck back to the safety of the bathroom alcove but just fucking stand there, staring . . . and patients and visitors and staff alike brush past you, obscuring their frowns like you're one of those dormant Jewish *golems.*

Eating garbage . . . shooting that fennie. Mere consequences, huh? There's the cause.

Up the broad steps into the open plaza you roam, hardly a torpedo boring toward a target and more as a nervous teenager moving on a girl at a gym dance, back when a teenage Croc could get you all the skeezer ass you wanted, but you aimed higher, eh?

You take an adjacent chair as she thumbs through an *InStyle* with some female rapper dolled up on the cover.

"*Tu 'sapo' esta aqui . . .* " you whisper.

Of course, you could be wrong. This might be someone else, after all these years.

At first her head's frozen and a mobile phone falls to the nubby carpet, bounces. A woman calls to her in Spanish and tries to pass it to her, but she won't reach, she won't speak. And the magazines on her lap fall to the floor as well, and all these poor souls stuck in a hospital on Christmas morning go back to their own pains, fretting, mourning rather than watch the pantomime of you, you star-crossed junkies, you flophouse paramours . . . together again.

Her full lips dry, unadorned, she whispers the sweet words you literally have almost died to hear . . .

"I-I have a knife. You touch me and I *cut* you."

"Esme. Come on."

"You won't hurt Piedade again . . . you won't hurt anyone, *ever . . .* "

Freakishly, your pulse is slowing as you speak to her. This ghost. "I'm your *sapo.* Right?"

"Stop . . . "

"So you know I won't hurt anyone unless they glass me first. She hit me and ran out with Maximiliano . . . and now all of us are in danger."

"*Puta madre . . .* I'll get security, Dickie, focking swear."

She leans down for the phone, leaves the magazines, then pauses to drink you in. Not the comatose homeless gorilla she recalled before she dumped you.

"How sick is Maximiliano?" you ask. "The RSV come back? Flu?"

"*Cuño . . . Ricardo . . .* " No "Dickie?" And she's trying to play off as much as she can. You, too, are a ghost.

She looks to a nurse collecting old school clipboards from the triaged walking wounded.

"Don't even try it," you warn with a camouflage smile. "Because you don't want to explain yourself, or me, when a scene's made." She won't look you in the eyes no matter how you track her head movements. "You can't look at me because you *know* me," you say, still with a pasted-on smile and low tones. "You know that girl is lying about me just as surely as Bracht has fucked her mind, messed her up forever."

That does it. She finally locks eyes with you. Those deep black pearls, those haven't changed and won't till the day she closes them forever.

"*Dios mio . . .* you don't get it, do you?"

You push your lips to her ear. You've won, boy. You've won because she does not swat you away, or recoil, or even register a cringe on that face you've dreamt of for years.

"I want for us to be free. Not even together. Free. With Marta, all of them. So what don't I *get*, Esme?"

"*Sapo . . .* go *. . . vete . . .* please." But this time, she reaches for your hand. Squeezes tight. Releases it, just like the last time you saw her.

"No."

She swallows hard then mutters, "The boy isn't breathing well, again."

Yeah you were right. Good. Means you can keep them here. Bad. Means Mr. Sugars can find you, here . . .

"You been creeping for months in bad weather. It's not your fault."

"She's in the exam room with him. Poor *niño*, Dickie . . . "

Ah, a hairline crack . . .

"So you don't believe her?"

"That's not important."

"*Shit* . . . " You lower you voice as the visitors and waiting afflicted indeed stare, "You gotta trust me. Look . . . walk with me. You can kick me in the nutsack later and run but just walk with me now, to the vending machines . . . *please*." And to your surprise, she complies, follows you to a bank of snack and soda machines.

"You want me to believe you . . . about Piedade, eh?" she pouts as you shove coins into a machine for a pack of Strawberry Pop-tarts likely a one-year-old. "Will you, *Ricardo* . . . believe me about *mi Donna* Eva, *Don* Frederico?"

"Don't call them by those pet names please." But it shows she remembers. Or remembers how to hook you. "Coffee," you mumble.

"I have too much in my blood, *sapo*. I can-no see straight . . . "

"No, for me."

You tear open the Pop Tart package, gobble one in an instant as the coffee cup drops. You watch it fill, summoning some spine. After a gulp the of the acrid computerized brew, you crouch to her eye level . . . and you better be prepped for that kick . . .

"Bracht's never gonna let us go. This merc, ex-DHS bald cracker . . . the one I figure killed our friends . . . he probably . . . probably is going to find out where Marta, Pashmina are

. . . so we gotta work fast. I'm going to call my friend LaKeisha. You remember her?

That iron *chica* bullshit just melts, palpably, as she hunches over, lets out a sound like you knuckled into her viscera.

"You led them . . . to Marta?" she wheezes.

"You led *him* to Eva and Fred. We both have some praying to do. And so does Black Santa. He'd been helping me find you. And he's . . . he's their mole, I'm certain now . . .

And he's split, no word. You know damn well what that means on the street. He's not stupid enough to hide, so either he's gone to Mr. Sugars to save his ass or Mr. Sugars found him, cut off a piece of him and showed it to him. Results are the damn same.

"Go back in, check on Maximiliano. If there's any damn way to get the boy discharged with meds, do it. I got cash here to pay them—hush money going to my friend Verna after they were going to set me up." You shove the five U.S. Grants in her hand. "Meet me in the red car I'm gonna pull around. We got twenty minutes, tops, here, Esme."

Her look softens, oddly.

"Dickie . . . you go to rehab? You . . . *clear*. Like when we were young . . . "

"I was never clear. There's always something wrong. Twenty minutes!"

But she's not moving. She's cupping her head in her hands. *Damn.* And you're whispering, prompting, and hell if she's frozen in place like she cannot take another step in her life. Ever. Luckily that's something a lot of people do in that place, as the guard and other staffers cease studying you two. You look up because the crystal lobby is darkening, as if a pall's descending from heaven . . . or ascending from a lower, nastier place. Guess the Devil beat enough tears from the missus, and the wind's picking up, portent of another storm shooting in from the west.

"It stops here," she moans, muffled by fingers now bare and boney, none of those joyous rings adorning them . . . yet she still features the blood red polish. "Jaime won't kill Marta or *mi sobrina*. He will threaten, as if Marta can suffer more . . . but never take their lives."

"Mr. Sugars is going to call any second if not come through those doors so—"

"*Pensar, Ricardo!* Jaime . . . he won't murder his own sister. Half-sister, truly . . . "

She reaches out with her eyes . . . as it seems you plain didn't hear what she just told you. *Oh, but you did.* You're just sinking inside yourself as the light deserts the frost on the picture window glass.

"Stop . . . you aren't making sense . . . Piedade said you were jealous . . . that Bracht's grandfather had a side family that Bracht's daddy carried financially, too . . . and—"

She cups her scented hand across your mouth and yes, folks are now watching.

"Dickie . . . *Don Maximiliano José* . . . was my father, too. Marta and I had a different mother." She winces as you suck a breath through her fingers and hold it. You got to exhale, take another, son. She drops her hand and you feel as if your head has fallen with it. "Jaime's mother gave birth to him in Texas when she was visiting relatives. Her husband was supposedly inspecting properties and building sites hundreds of miles from home. But that was a lie."

You melt onto one of the older, uncomfortable benches. You've been whored, son. And she stands over you. Violates you . . .

"Don Maximiliano José came back across the border with his son and wife. Jaime is—what do the *gringos* call such children to demean them? *Anchor baby*. This always feeds his hate." She pauses when she sees your stare, empty as when you score. "Dickie? Are you listening? *Mi amor?*"

"Don't call me that," you whisper, still staring into the ether. "*Finish* . . . "

She nods, tearing up, and tells you, "So Don Maximiliano José came back to Mexico with his new son, to tell my mother, Marta's mother, Marisol Rubio, whose husband worked for him and was a very proud and ignorant man . . . that he loved her but he could no longer have the affair. He wanted his only son, heir to all Don Porfirio Maximiliano Bracht-Hernandez, *el Patron*, built, to have new power, north of the border . . . "

"*No mas*," you mutter, aping the words Esme wrote on that card, the one you found in that stinking trash-out, seems like million years ago.

"Sí . . . '*no mas.*' *Familia enferma* . . . even Piedade couldn't take it anymore. *Los Solonzaronas* . . . my father made Jaime promise to that when he was old enough, had the means, that he, too would continue to provide for that other family . . . even get them green cards when he was here in Washington. He also made him promise not to hate me, or *mi madre*, or Marta. Jaime loaned me money for apartments, and you know what I did with it, don't you, *sapo*? Because for you and me, it is either medicine, or escape. It cannot be both. *Tu madre* dies to get away from your papa, *mi madre* takes drinks, drives into an electrical pole. Don Maximiliano José . . . he die, knowing his *gringo* son is a pervert and monster . . . who touched Marta, touched me when we were all young. He can't keep his hands from me when I return, four years ago, when I leave you. Because Jaime made me leave. And all Jaime says when he is inside of me, making young girls like Piedade watch, or me watch him, is that *I am the disgusting one* . . . from *las drogas, los negros* . . . "

She's grinning through the tears. Somehow you don't find that strange, as it happens to you all the damn time.

"Piedade said . . . you did drugs with him? Piedade said . . . "

"She's damaged, *mi amor*. Worse than the girls I try to save to spit in Jaime's face when your Land of the Free, Home of the Brave knew Jaime was raping girls, trafficking them with *mafiosi Mexicanos* . . . and the mara salvatrucha. Only Jaime could get a truce like that going . . . over flesh. And hundreds of children, turned over to perverts, or sent to *gringas*."

With her help, son. *With her help*. She's an addict. You all lie. Don't let her snow you.

"And I was not jealous of that brat *puta*. It was envy. That she was just a distant cousin, from a side family. A little plaything from El Estor. She could live with her shame. But me, oh *sapo* . . . I try to die many times in your arms, so I would not die in his . . . "

You rise from the bench; you can't even look at her. Everything you wanted to do to her when Bracht became your patron, you want to do now. You see your fingers at her throat.

"This motherfucker . . . he knew about me all this time, right? Blames me for you being all fucked up. Put me on to find you because he's twisted. But it wasn't me . . . it was you . . . just *you*, you fucking witch . . . "

She's the one who's now deadpan. Tone flat. Eyes drying as quickly as yours have moistened.

"He never knew about you by name at least, you, black men, were abstract. Dickie, I was drowning in myself and you were roaming the streets . . . I had to make a move. I had to condemn myself to *Xilbalba*, the Maya Hell, for him to take me back, keep Marta out of it, to keep others safe. And he keeps me close because no one—not Trump's people, the TV, the FBI, his rich fock-ing friends . . . *no one* . . . could know about me. Piedade could be some little side piece. But me, I was the liability along with *las Soloranzanas*."

You whisper, "*Familia maldito*."

She nods.

"I took his treasure: what Piedade carried inside, to punish him. Maybe I knew he'd come after you, okay? But you survive, *sapo*. It's what you do."

And she moves to you, to touch your face. She's trembling like she's outside in that bizarre shower of ice and sunlight. You told yourself in many a dream you'd recoil. You should now. You won't. You told yourself you'd reach for her throat. You don't.

"Listen, that little boy . . . your sister, your niece and her son, they deserve a clean slate no matter how messed up you and I are, have always been. Now go get her and the baby. Red car . . . "

She nods, saunters slowly to the examination bays after flashing a paper visitor ID clipped to a cheap string lanyard she'd been hiding all this time.

As if the Devil's been keeping tabs, that mobile to Perdition buzzes in your pocket.

"Killer, I will deactivate your burn . . . can't track it but I can leave you blind, deaf and dumb and I will swoop in before you go to ground in some nigger and spick cesspool, because it's what I do. I got you made somewhere in Silver Spring . . .

Bluff, dance. Just give her time to grab that little strumpet and the baby.

"I know why you call me that now. Children died because I couldn't tell the difference between a school and fuel dump. For that and my life since, it's the burning wheel for me. Only thing that'll ease my suffering is knowing I won't see you there. You'll be down in the place where they roast motherfuckers who shoot death up an already weak, helpless person's nose so they won't struggle . . . and tell themselves it was just a job, or duty, while rich bastards get richer."

"*Right. Well, here's a reminder of your sit-ref when I do catch you . . .* "

You hear . . . moans . . . *agony.*

"*Bred'rin . . .* " Black Santa whimpers. "*Mi deserve di Devil's wrat' . . .* "

And you hear a scream, almost in a woman's pitch. The next voice is Mr. Sugar's.

"*Street garbage who couldn't keep his story straight. Yeah, he found you, plugged you into us. Kept us abreast of your transformation into someone useful. But then he crapped out. We'll kept a little of him for you as a memento . . .* "

Stay cool even though you want to rip your own rotted teeth out by the root.

"Tell Bracht to come back home from Vermont and I'll deal. *Stamp.*"

There's a pause, some whispers, then, "*Roger that. Because the deal's different now. Mr. Bracht wants the baby—you already knew that. Now, he wants Esmeralda Rubio, too. Christ on a cracker, eh? New deal: your life, the lives of everyone you know, for them.*"

"And Piedade?"

"*Not my problem. Or yours.*"

The alternating wisps of ice, snow and cold rain slacken on the huge windows. Sunlight cuts into the lobby . . .

illuminating Esme like a spotlight on a stage . . . and she's bounding to you.

Suddenly there's another voice shouting something in your ear, and Mr. Sugars sounds like someone kneed him in his sack, when he hisses, "*God dammit! I got you made, Killer—stay where you are, stay on that burn and no one has to die!*" And he's gone.

It's only as Esme reaches you with eyes fluttering and voluptuous lips quivering, that you notice she's alone . . .

CHAPTER 23

La Brigada

"Esme get your coat! This phone's going to track her . . . "

"*Carajo*, Dickie . . . *es así como me encontraste?*"

"This bastard's not going to shut this phone down but the tracker battery's gonna go any second. See, that's her. Now come on."

You're pointing to the screen . . . she's got to be on foot with the baby and very little else in this cold; the signal's fading under the damn Beltway, on Sligo Creek Parkway, and you are pushing Esme out into the cold, toward Croc's Cutlass. It's then you see that first guard who let your through—the one in the Santa Claus cap—running out after you, along with some white woman. Guess little Maximiliano's run up quite a bill—no valid insurance once checked against Esme's bogus benefits card.

Knock him out, Junior . . . but *whoa* he's got a sidearm. Not likely to use it over a balance due but he's yelling and about to draw his radio to notify the other toy cop at the exit gate. The clinking in your coat pockets reminds you of your scavenged medical gear . . .

"Run that way!" you shout to Esme, then you turn, pull those damn things that go into the cooch and Lord, if they don't look like little missiles. That's exactly how you use them and they send the white woman screaming back toward the ER entrance. The big mug gets one in the cheek and blocks another with his forearm. Dumb move, as the sting knocks the radio from his hand. You're off to the cover of the Dumpsters.

You jump in and sure enough the signal's stationary, then moving, then stopping, moving again. With the whip's pistons purring you know this won't take long once you bust out, and sure enough the main gate's open, with more security guards buzzing about the parking lot in the Cutlass's wake like angry yet leaderless bees.

She must be in the area around the golf course on the other side of the Beltway, and all you must do is neutralize any hero who's watching you grab her and the baby. Still, her fleeing on foot, with a bundled sick child and in cold muck and snow has an ill *Uncle Tom's Cabin* or *Dr. Zhivago* taste to it and that taste is churning your gut. And Piedade's white enough and you're black enough so that any cop witnessing you chase her like a slavecatcher or Cossack will burn you down in nine-millimeter slugs.

"She must've seen you from the examining room," Esme opines, breathless.

"No . . . no way. And not enough time to get away. She glassed you, Esme, soon as you got there. Prolly some meds for the baby first. You don't know this bent girl like I do now, *trust*!"

"H-Her bag was still there. *Dios mio* . . . nurses say . . . she called an outside line . . . "

"It wasn't Mr. Sugars that's for damn sure. Bracht—does she have a straight number to him? Esme . . . *dime!*"

You gun the engine and swoosh under the eight lanes of Beltway into a neighborhood of pine trees and brick split-level homes. No sign of her. The signal's dead. You're cursing and slamming the wheel as you stop.

"She will stick close to the houses, ask for help, for the baby."

You swing the Cutlass onto a wooded suburban street; orgies of torn wrapping paper and new gadgets and slurping of mulled wine are likely going on inside.

"*Mira*, Dickie!" Esme shouts, pointing toward the huge golf course, blanketed in tranquil white.

A drab and dented gray Nissan with Maryland plates . . . one of those Pathfinder crossovers so not huge, is stopped at the entrance. Blinkers on. Like two, three dudes inside . . . and the rear right door is wide open . . .

"What?" you grunt with a sigh . . . before she's clawing at your arm. Something about Piedade's coat.

"*Ahi*! In the car!"

The right rear door slams, but the right front opens, slowly . . .

. . . Burton Sugars isn't a squat Latin in a bubble-jacket, hair carved like Stripe's . . .

You're frozen for a second and a second is all it takes for the *pop* . . . *pop* . . . *pop* of three shots to hornet by the Cutlass and whistle into the trees . . . maybe into someone's Christmas morning breakfast table. Two more rounds fire but you've already flipped the gear lever and punched the accelerator. The front-wheel drive muscle car fishtales in reverse.

Esme's screaming and you're groaning but the damn wild motion throws the shooter off in the Pathfinder. The thing spins a spray of water and slush as it peels onto Sligo Creek Parkway, then jumps the curb onto a field because you've recovered and put the cowboy spurs to that Detroit engine. This Pathfinder is no Jeep but it's cutting across a lawn and now a soccer field and onto Colesville Road, way above you.

"Who the *fuck* . . . the *fuck*! *Brigada*?"

"Why would they do this? She never talk to them. Only me, I was contact!"

"Then you better find your people and tell them what happened, eh!"

You rocket onto Colesville Road, north, and sway from Silver Spring but the Pathfinder's at least a traffic light ahead, and your recent drought of driving time is beginning to show as you struggle to maintain the chase, almost ding a few folk on their way to grandma's as you pass. Won't be but a matter of time before Mr. Sugars gathers his quick intel on shots fired and a car chase . . . barely a mile from the hospital.

Quickly you figure, and what you figure isn't good . . .

"Esme . . . who'd you mess with, when you got those girls into the Soloranzano safe house . . . and the cops pinched a bunch of MS-Thirteen muv-fuckers right? I know what happened to the girls . . . what happened to the gangsters?"

"*Que*? Arrested . . . "

"But it wasn't the feds, it was MPD. And your girl Piedade told me Bracht knew about the trafficking . . . that you snitched to spite him."

"*No*! I am *Tía* to all . . . I did it to . . . to—" She pauses, and yeah, she either had forced it from her brain, or was blind to lil' brother's side businesses. "No federal charges . . . the girls deported . . . he works with all the gangs . . . yes . . . "

"You're to call the *Brigada* dudes *now*! Find out as much as you can. Then damn it you pull the trigger and you tell them scoop your sister, your niece and great-nephew up I don't care how fucking sick Marta is!"

Speaking of pulling the trigger, you could have used that gatt, Junior. A stubby .380 but that Pathfinder was plastic. You showed restraint. Mr. Sugar's is wrong about you. You're the man, they are the devils . . .

"Not that simple."

"Dickie, what?" Esme calls to you as she fingers numbers on her simple old flip-phone. When you don't answer she's on with someone who sounds like she's twelve, and the rapid Spanish begins. The Pathfinder is just in view as fewer lights and a straightway gives the Cutlass room to do what Cutlasses do.

"They say be careful . . . " Esme tells you.

"No shit!"

"No . . . they are going away from where . . . they must be leading us away. Something is wrong . . . his base is in Gaithersburg, Maryland and in the city, not out this way."

"Who's base? You know who took her—already?"

She nods, sheepishly. "It was Blinky. Blinky Guzman . . . 'Corto' his boys call him. For *El Chulo Corto* . . . little pimp. He ran little girls, come up from the border or on planes from El Salvador, Guatemala, Honduras. He is a bug . . . he is afraid of me, and the *hechizos, la magia* . . . "

Sure enough, you see the Pathfinder swerve left at the next crossover, just before Colesville Road changes back to U.S. 29 and pretends to be a highway, with on and off ramps. The vehicle skids across the turn, against the light and suddenly is now southbound. Yet rather than swing into the right lane, it's in the far left as if positioning for a broadside.

You reach into your crotch and pull out the .380, hand it to Esme.

"I know you know how to use this mug so chamber a round . . . *now!*"

She pulls the slide hurriedly, mumbles a prayer and plea not to hurt the baby as she hands you back the pistol.

You notice the Pathfinder's brake lights pulse. You lower the window, slow up as well . . .

. . . *son, you're stone crazy!*

"Get down!" you holler.

First time driving in years. First time firing a weapon . . . in anger . . . at a living thing. You're on the trigger before the greazy little fuck in the Pathfinder's back seat. Or rather, low—at the engine, the tires, anything to mark the vehicle.

Pop . . . pop . . . pop . . . pop! The ejected shells ping around the interior, and Esme is shrieking, thinking they are Blinky Guzman's rounds.

But the return fire's inaccurate again; Croc's machine is a tough moving target.

Still . . . did you hit the baby? Piedade? The mugs inside . . . this Guzman bastard? You aimed for the tires, engine block . . . will they cross the median, hit holiday revelers? Well, in the rearview mirror you watch the Pathfinder swerve . . . the driver maintains control . . . yet you swear you see smoke from the hood but it's all in quick glances before you can pull over onto the shoulder. By then, the Pathfinder's gone.

There are a few seconds when all you hear are each other's breaths. You grab for the burn. It's still powered up. You finger that infernal number. This time it takes a couple of rings for the piece of shit to answer.

"Looks like we were both bandjacked, Killer. Happens in our business when we're risking our asses for clowns and the intel's sketchy, the locals untrustworthy. At least I can get a bead on the baby, likely within a couple of hours, assuage some hurt feeling, close those loose ends."

"I still have Esmeralda—your boss is obsessed so don't lie anymore and say that hasn't messed you up."

"You and the rest are so over your heads, you just can't fathom. You're like babies fighting men."

"When this is over, I'm going to beat you to death."

"Not today. You've been a real prodigy, Cornish. I'd be grieving after I put a blade in your carotid artery. So long . . . "

The phone's dead . . . now what? You put the Cutlass in gear and surge onto Colesville, then execute the same turn as the wounded Pathfinder likely took. South now. Back to ole once-Chocolate City. Home.

"Call this number I'm about to give you. Tell Verna Leggett you are Esmeralda Rubio. Call the police. MPD. Tell her to tell them that Black Santa's missing, picked up by drug dealers who assaulted him for snitching. Tell her to make it good. Lie."

"Why can't you do it?"

You don't answer. You must *figure* . . . and even when Verna insists on speaking you decline. Your big brain's got to simmer, then cool, eh?

"Is there a speaker on that little thing?"

Quickly you hear Verna's voice, troubled.

"Dickie . . . take me off speaker . . . Dickie? Alright then. Was that her . . . that was her, so she's real and the shit's gotten real. Park Police came by St Jude's with a warrant and Father Phil told them he'd pray for them. They'll come to this side eventually and then someone will ID me as being with you last night, by the Trump hotel."

"That's why you call MPD, make it a big deal. One set of blues will smoke screen the other. And if it's on the news, then the man who took Black Santa will know there will be heat. Is Katie okay?"

"She's here, only on twenty-four-hour hold. There's no room."

"For me, either. The pills these . . . *people* . . . gave me. I'll start falling apart when they run out, then fiending and then I'll be shit again . . . " You see Esme staring as you say this, and for the first time in years you feel her hand on top of yours as you grip the steering wheel tighter. "If you have any spare staff, and that homeless van . . . can you hit the Peets Coffee at Metro Center. Woman named LaKeisha. Can't miss her. A little jumpy, but . . . look if they tossed her out for Christmas then go to the Kabob House on K. They are open, feeding people. She'd be there. Bring her to SFME and—"

"The center is already over-exposed thanks to me trusting you, Dickie. I can't do that."

"These people . . . Bracht . . . is serious. You think you're going to live to see that hush money feed kids? No. The Parkies are there as part of the set-up but they are blind . . . but when they see the MPD cars there, and someone crying for Black Santa on camera, not only will they back off, it'll be a force field Mr. Sugars'll avoid. He's got enough trouble now anyway."

"And you?"

"Verna, please! I need LaKeisha, I need you to call the police . . . set her up somewhere with wifi and ask her to put the word out for Jenn. Queen Jenn. Then shut the door."

Esme takes the phone, makes another call as the District border on Sixteenth Street comes in view.

"La Brigada, they say they can find were Guzman is taking Piedade and the baby. Someone who says he knows you might

have an idea . . . name is Stripe? I think . . . I read his *cartas* maybe . . . *los drogas* . . . he lies a lot."

You nod, pressing the gas. "He might be our only hope."

"An' your friend, who look like Santa?"

Your mind plays a rapid reel of his laughing. There's nothing more to say.

"I have an army to raise and no time to do it. Guzman's going to get hooked up with Mr. Sugars dude to turn over Piedade and the child, likely for cash."

Esme says, "Will he will Corto . . . his boys . . . and Piedade?"

You are bone weary, and while the pangs of chemicals fighting over which bonds to what's left of your brain have yet to rack you up, the pangs ripping up your stomach are no better. You haven't eaten an actual meal in two days. Not a thing in your former state as a forager, but your body's now artificially re-set to a more normal drive.

Esme's on her phone with her contacts, who are likely a mere tick less vicious than Guzman's MS thugs. The latter's favorite hobby is cutting up other teens and leaving pieces out in Spotsylvania County. Your destination's another safe house on Meridian Place NW, between Fourteenth and Sixteenth down in the bosom of Spickland and supposedly insulated from the MS rudeboys. So she cuts off her call when you peel away for a McDonald's drive-thru, open even on Christmas.

"You can't stop . . . Dickie, *no puedo creer esto!*"

"Just like old times, huh?"

"No—then we'd be scoring. Four a.m. Egg McMuffins, after . . . "

And you both laugh. Inapt, but necessary otherwise you'd both explode. You order everything bad and heavy you can think of and motor back out, and you eat fast as you drive, because if you wolf it down you won't linger on Black Santa's screams . . . or something you promised yourself in the hospital you wouldn't ask Esme.

And yet you're about to before she cuts you off, still smiling.

"*Chinga* . . . what were those things you threw at them in the hospital. Looked familiar . . . "

"Cervical dilators," you say straight-faced.

She's cracking up now, eating your fries . . . and yet the mirth ceases when you kill it with, in the tenderest of tones, "What was it like . . . when they murdered Eva and Fred? I dreamt it, all of it. They dosed them with the shit in the nose, then beat them, right? Strangled Fred? Piedade said you were there. So why they need me? Mercs, ex-feds like Sugars . . . they hold you down to watch? Please don't say you led them to their place. *Please* say they found you first, made you go in, as a decoy . . . then you escaped."

She swallows hard, then whispers, "I swear *mi amor, mi sapo* . . . they thought they knew where I was hiding. They knew nothing. They killed them. It's what they do. Stoli, he keep me in the projects and then I go back to *La Brigada* to hide . . . those men could find me no more. So they found you."

Suddenly no one's talking until you turn the Cutlass onto Meridian from Sixteenth, pull into the alley behind a rowhouse topped by a spired cupola. All the windows are taped with newspaper and despite the chill outdoors it's hot as their native lands indoors, thanks to space heaters and some abuelas barely four and half feet tall boiling shit over portable electric burners. You wonder if this place would take out the whole block if there's a fire.

There's a lot of hugging and rapid Spanish when they see her, dirty looks for your big black ass. Indeed, aside from the midget grandmas no one in there seems to be over thirty-five. You fully expect to see those kids from the botanica on Georgia Avenue in there, and yeah, a few teenagers sporting high school swag and gear are milling about. One asks Esme about Piedade and sighs when she gets an answer . . . then fires back in Spanish that Piedade was a bitch anyway, but the baby is innocent. She and another girl pull Esme away before there's any more debriefing.

Besides, the apparent honcho, some young dude in a reflective construction vest and muddy work boots, yes because the Yankees don't want to work on Christmas, is pushing a finger into your chest.

"Yo, Big Man . . . you fucked this up, you did this, moe," he says and swear to God he sounds like he's from right off the block, across in Anacostia. "We had it under control. Even when they set up my cousin for killing them old folks up in the apartment!"

"Hold up, youngster."

"*Sho*! *Cállate*!" a younger woman behind you hisses. "Give me your gun . . . "

"I'm not going to fight y'all. I just need a new phone." She's taking the gatt anyway. "Extra clip in *la Carrucha* out back. I expect this returned and the car not messed with. The owner's a crocodile . . . "

"We're aren't a gang, eh?" the woman corrects you.

"You had everything under control?" you shit-talk. "Like letting *Tía* run with Piedade and the baby to the hospital . . . with no backup?"

The girl's chuckling.

"We gonna bring Ernesto for you . . . *Stripe*," she announces. "You stay here. Many things happened this morning."

"You right about that, but no, I go."

That pushy *hombre*'s sneering, shaking his head. "Stripe and the others tell us about the ole man . . . he around here the other night runnin' his mouth about *Tía* Carolina. Said he had money for info. Said anyone who helped wouldn't be deported and shit . . . now who says stupid shit like that?"

"*Black Santa*," you whisper, dipping your head and fighting any inclination to weep.

The woman shows you her phone's screen. TV station's website. Verna worked damn fast, but Mr. Sugars is faster.

It's an old mugshot of Black Santa . . . says he's wanted in the Christmas Eve murder of Victor Lee Stansfield, age twenty-nine, a.k.a. "Stoli," known to be a drug dealer "*in the rapidly gentrified Petworth and Park View neighborhoods, now besieged by street crime of twenty years ago, which some city officials say is the result of the Trump Administration's draconian elimination of many healthcare and housing programs, and aide cuts to community policing. Fitzroy Cockburn was last seen at the St. Jude's Mission-So Families Might Eat complex today; police will not confirm that he was assaulted or kidnapped in reprisal.*"

Loose ends. And the set-up continues. How long before they re-instate your "rampages?"

You hear cries upstairs and are startled. The others register barely a ripple and you quickly hear, "*Ricardo!*"

They let you break away and bound up the stairs and you soon see the cries are of happiness. Marta lays in a bed, oxygen tubes in her nostril and an IV swaying but she's in tearful laughter as her sister plays with a pale yet nappy-headed baby. Pashmina's sitting next to her mother, calm, no glower. Esme's gushing, babbling in Spanish.

"Thank you," Marta calls to you. Her sister nods.

But you know all of this is gone as gizzards and gravy in the morning unless Bracht is stopped. Dead ass. Mr. Sugars is pissed but he follows orders.

"I've got to go while my head's still straight, get some stuff moving." You call downstairs. "Now will somebody get me a damn phone?"

CHAPTER 24

Requiem for Blinky Guzman

THE HONCHO CALLS BACK UP TO you, "*Calmate, culero!* Here ole man!" He tosses up a red iPhone thing and luckily you catch it before it bounces on the railing. Then again, looks like your old burn except much dodgier, refurbished. "Unbricked. Don't lose it."

Esme passes the child back to Pashmina and reminds you, "By now, Corto is getting in touch with Sugars for a meet."

"Corto—you mean Blinky?" Pashmina sneers. "He a toy gangster, auntie. Otis Place's got your back and'll mess him up."

"He's no toy," you press her. "These mugs are bad enough on their own, but they got cover from someone who used to be DHS. High on the mountain. The only advantage we have is that Blinky still thinks he's got the dap, a bulletproof hall pass from Bracht's people."

"How can we win, Dickie?" Marta wheezes from the bed, now infused with some fight.

Well, you figured, didn't you? Ah, that trove among the jigsaw pieces in your skull's still deep. How does any colored people, factionalized, beat up on Mr. Charlie? "By combining my army with you all's. And splitting theirs."

Verna answers your call with a fretful, "*I-I think Mr. Cockburn's been murdered.*"

"Yes."

"Dickie . . . "

"Let me speak to LaKeisha."

"*Jon Snow! A Red Wedding we're planning?*"

"Can you crack a phone, or another laptop, if I can get it?"

"*Had the chieftains and Taliban callin' buttfuck sex lines, Jon Snow. Why-ya gotta ask!*"

"Standby, stay safe, do what Verna tells you to do. Now, where's the Queen? She at Cavalry Clinic, sleeping for Christmas? New Endeavors?"

"Jenn? Jon Snow you know she won't go where they won't take Thunder. She's outdoors. She's okay . . . she's watched and safe."

"She's got to okay all the folks, off the street and on, to help."

"*She won't let you down, Dickie.*"

You're off the phone. You've got to go.

"Is Verna good to you, *sapo?*"

"She trusted me when she had no cause, she's risking everything."

"Not like me, then."

"I promised I'd fix this. I will do it, okay . . . "

And with that you hear a familiar voice from the stairwell.

"*Oye*, Rain Man. Lemme see you all swole and shit, bro'!"

Stripe's sweaty and grinning those cheap rotted fronts. He smells. Not that it bothered you before because you smelled worse. He holds out his hand. Yeah and you take it, shake.

"Damn bro' that's hard, you hurt my hand, eh? Looka you." His weasel eyes point upward and suddenly he's whispering. "*La bruja* . . . she up there, eh? She no hurt me, eh?"

"*Escúchame con atención*, okay? Past is past, for all of us, okay? Where do you think Guzman is now with the baby. The baby of the rich *blanco* who'd been protecting him?"

"I-I try to warn you, bro' abou' that fat *maricon* . . . he talkin' shit . . . "

Past is past, remember! The look you give him shuts him up, pulls him back on track. "Um . . . Corto? Um . . . he no bock up Gait-ersburg wid him *carnals*. He no more than two mile from here, bro'. Use him *tio*'s when hide in city. Mt. Pleasant, too many peoples know him . . . too close to these *Brigada* peoples so he down closer downtown."

The young woman who took the Seecamp chimes in. "Thirteenth and Harvard. Under control, like we say. No *policia*, no ICE around. Very quiet."

"The kid's still a little sick. Respiratory issues."

Stripe shrugs and says, "Corto, him, no go nowhere, bro' wid a sick baby."

"Why are you out of the woodwork like a cockroach—to help? Them, I can see. But why me? You afraid of the *hechizos*?"

He's dipping his head, much the way you used to.

"Get clean like you . . . have place to eat an' sleep like you." He looks to the people sitting, watching TV, playing on their phones. All hiding from something. "Have them respec' me bro' . . . *serio*."

"*Serio*? Then you're coming with me, to Blinky's. You're gonna stake it out." You hand him the phone the honcho tossed to you. "Guess you'll have to unbrick another for me," you quip to the honcho, who's now furrowing his face to the point it even makes you wince. "And my weapon, please?"

The honcho relents and motions his head to some teenagers in another room to raid a plastic chest full of what look like stolen mobile phones, then looks to you. "I can't spare back-up. Call if there's movement once you check it out. But don't stay away too long."

You get the gatt back. This time there's one in the spout . . .

. . . and you're easing that engine down Thirteenth, as any cop would drool over the sight of that Cutlass, you at the wheel, and a Latin miscreant, head out the side like some dog, chortling his delight.

"*Chivo*, Rain Man! *Le carra es arrecho!*"

Hey, if Blinky had posted lookouts then y'all have already been made. But the name of the game is keep them contained till Mr. Sugars makes a move.

You park across Sherman on Harvard, and the sight of you and Esme's *alma mater* up the hill grows some hair on your nuts, as maybe you are about something, fighting for something. It's daylight and so you stick to the alleys, slower, more deliberate and boy when this kid's given a task, told he's no homeless shit, he gets serious fast. He's creeping up ahead, checking the usual spot where these thugs would have a lookout posted—even someone's girlfriend on a bike, or an auntie with a kid. Yet it's also Christmas, hardly a soul out and about . . .

. . . and there's the damn Pathfinder. Bullet holes in the chassis. A doughnut spare on the rear left wheel. You mean to do that, Wild Bill Hickok? Not bad!

The rowhouse is almost a mirror image of the Otis Place boys' little hotel and clubhouse uptown right down to the spired cupola, rotting porch roof, paint peeling from the bricks. Only more gentrifying Charlies Juniors and Beckies down this way to complain. Guess they don't complain too loud. Plus Stripe reveals that Blinky's uncle is a revered custodian at the charter school on the corner. Yeah, a school . . . a hundred feet from an MS-13 larder and flophouse.

Stripe volunteers to part a rip in a chain-link fence along the alley, hit the rear of the place and scope it. From there he'll perch until it gets too cold or he's relieved, or at least he pledges so, and you believe him. You'll slide along the small path separating one bank of rowhouses with this *tio's*; there are a few windows and you have just the height to peep in and scurry off. Just pray no one's in the corresponding windows of the other house across that path.

Maybe it's time to pull the .380. If those yuppies back on Georgia Avenue two nights ago thought you were undercover po-po, maybe that will work again if some random chick taking a pre-Christmas dinner jog spots you.

You move, slowly, along the wall, and lucky for you no living soul's present. And this house has blinds rather than a taped-up sports or metro section. You peer up and don't see any moving shadows. Those Dumbo ears only catch a soccer game color commentary. Nothing else. Not even a baby's cry.

The shade isn't fully lowered, so you gulp air and then dart up. Someone's asleep on a sofa. Black jeans, Air Jordans, a black turtleneck. No one and nothing else . . .

. . . there's a tap on your arm and in silence you almost put a round in Stripe's eye.

"*Ven por aquí . . .* " he whispers. And he leads you to the rear steps that usually stop at a door to the basement. Except these are piled with three bodies. All with bullet holes to the chest or head. All quiet . . .

You tell him to stay, amble back to the side window and raise your head slowly. That dude's chest hasn't moved. In his nostril . . . there . . . a little trickle of blood.

"Fuck it! Stripe get over here!"

He's frozen in place but you run over to grab him. Oh, he thinks you are beyond crazy now, beyond reckless. But something in your big brain says yes, all is indeed quiet . . .

. . . and you're opening both doors because they are unlocked as if in a horror movie, squeaking wide to welcome you both.

The TV in the front parlor's blaring in Spanish; before you hit that you pull on the surgical gloves you lifted from Holy Cross, shout to Stripe to put on a pair.

With the house silent you check the one on the sofa.

He's got a gatt in his dead hand. A hole in his neck.

You check the kitchen. Some ejected shells, blood, some drag marks off some toppled chairs, but no bodies.

He's going up the stairs without you and you call him back. When he doesn't comply, well son, you're up the steps in three bounds and there you find him, pointing down at an open closet.

"*Corto . . . aqui.*"

Blinky Guzman's sitting crosslegged on what looks like a pile of bedlinens. His dead eyes are frozen open, upturned, and a filmy yellow. His skin's pale as if a dozen vampires sucked his neck. His black hair is coiffed to look unruly, like he was in one of those boy bands on TV the girls Piedade's age like.

"Piedade . . . Maximiliano?" you gasp. "If they don't pop up in two seconds we go."

"*S-Sótano?*"

"Fuck the cellar. Check in there then we are audi!"

The door to the smaller bedroom's open and he enters, trembling. You're no braver, even with the little gun. The master bedroom's down the hall, past Blinky. You kick the door in and all you see is an empty baby bag. Empty box of disposable diapers. The rest of the stuff, even clothes strewn across the floor. But no Maximiliano. Not even that plush blanket Piedade swaddled him in.

"*N-No* . . . " you whimper, and it's not any dirge for Blinky Guzman. His *carnals* maybe found out about his cupidity for rich *gringos* and cutting deals with old Homeland Security black baggers.

Something on the unmade bed catches your eye before tears form for a dead baby. A ripped box, taped with a prescription label. "Rx Dimetapp pediatric drops" and another for albuterol. An inhalant. But no nebulizer around. You smile. Maybe the boy's alive, just taken....

. . . and you smack yourself in the face, hard. No *carnals*. This was Mr. Sugars, had to be. Yeah . . . way above your head.

"*Stripe, come on!*"

He's on his knees, poking at Blinky's body.

"The fuck, Stripe—you wanna wait for the cops?"

But you look down to see a plush baby blanket with the linens. You tug it. A lithe arm is slides out, and the delicate hand still gripping the blanket is painted with smudged glittery nail polish.

She must have been dolling herself up, for Bracht. Poor little girl. Piety . . .

The acid geysers up and you run to a toilet to spit it out, followed by a mournful bellow.

"*Bébé* . . . where?" Stripe calls.

"Kid, let's go . . . " you wheeze. You don't want to see her dead face again. A face twisted by men, not devils . . .

. . . so you are pulling Stripe down the stairs and you make for the front door, only to see the inside tainted with red spray paint that you missed when you crept in.

"VIVA LA BRIGADA OTIS PLACE!"

"*Qué?*" Stripe intones to you, frowning.

You aren't frowning. For now, the terror finally slams you broadside. Another set-up.

And your new phone's screaming at you, because *he* was right. You are a child in comparison.

"Get to the car! *Run!*"

You two reach Eleventh Street, out of breath, when the first MPD units shriek around the corner from Girard Street. You push the kid through a bare hedgerow, and it tears at you like concertina wire; still, it's cover, as two SUVs pass, another halts for a radio check.

"*Be advised six-one-seven alpha we have shots fired, repeat shots fired, fourteen hundred block Meridian Place Northwest . . . disengage from Girard address to the scene . . . expedite!*"

CHAPTER 25

HIC

STRIPE'S SHRIEKING LIKE A GIRL AS you jam the Cutlass up Eleventh—a maple-lined street quiet compared to Georgia, Thirteenth or Fourteenth . . . running stop signs, the occasional red light . . . dodging languid parallel-parking holiday visitors . . .

"They no give me any number bro'—this fokkin' phone no work!" He swallows tears and snot then cries, "This mon . . . him a *soldado*? Him kill us?"

"I dunno, kid," you answer grimly, breathlessly. "But he's schooled us . . . hell yes."

You look to Stripe and he winces, as your face is back to that deadpan, that distant sick calm like you are off a special education junket.

"We can-no win?" he whispers.

"We can make them stop . . . " And that depends on Jenn; no way you can find her in time. Your *figurin'* is shattered, Junior.

Yet on the broader avenues on either side of you, there's one promising sign: more MPD units and DCFD fire trucks converging where you are headed.

"Means something's still popping," you mutter. "Means Mr. Sugars isn't as smart as he thinks he is." He needed you, didn't he, to plumb the streets? Well, these same streets can Stalingrad any arrogant ofay who thinks they can get in and get out once the alarm's raised . . .

. . . yet still you warn Stripe, "He's prolly monitoring the police scanners or hacked their calls. These black baggers can do that . . . so we stash this bitch a couple blocks away and—"

"*Oye!*" he cuts you off "I got a way. I sleeps sometime, get food from Santa Esteban . . . Saint Stephen . . . Newton Street. I know way in an' out when they try preach to me, eh? Tunnel . . . *y carbon* . . . very old . . . "

"Coal?" And you're recalling something that kid Paco said. That Stripe was a caveman? "There's another way—right . . . can we get close to Meridian Street?"

He mumbles something, shakes his head. There's an old tunnel, yes, he babbles, and you dissect from the limited Spanglish terms that it served a Prohibition speakeasy gracing the spot the Woodner high-rise displaced over seventy years ago.

"Goddammit think Stripe!" Shooting around a lumbering Metrobus containing a few glum holiday workers rattles the kid enough to do so.

"Okay . . . *mierda* . . . another . . . uh . . . *tolva* . . . chute . . . they long-time ago bring in coal for heat church, priest house, big rooms . . . *tolva*, come to tunnel . . . liquor tunnel."

"Where?" you shout, jerking the wheel to the right onto Monroe, tires screaming on the cold pavement.

"Opening, crawl in, up Hertford Street, we come in behind Meridian Place, okay?"

"*My boy!*"

For an instant you smile, but that's evaporating fast as you think of your last side-kick's fate; likely dumped in a culvert pipe, portly body beset by other scavengers.

Push that crap out your mind, boy! He was a Quisling, right? You got business to do . . .

. . . and sure enough there's a ring of blue playing the devil with folks' Christmas, just above the ant hill: east to Holmead, west to Sixteenth and the Park. North, no way to tell. Yes, if there's a siege it means people are alive, and Mr. Sugars didn't get what he came for: Esme.

You dump the Cutlass on the bare-limbed edge of the park and hike north, then east toward the flashing blue and magenta. As you near Sixteenth you grab Stripe's arm.

"No shit, *sin retroceder ahora,* okay? Be responsible for someone, when no one else gives a fuck, *comprende?*"

He swallows hard, nods, whispers, "This way . . . "

Double-handle trap doors like those on tornado shelters the hillbillies and bammas got in Oklahoma are dug into a 1920s-vintage garage in a side alley off Hertford. The padlock looks like it was busted back in the fat days of Obama and is there for show.

Inside's black and smells of piss and sewage. The rusted ladder down is lousy with Department of Public Works and power company warning placards. Guess they gave up on it, too. There is a little light, though. From upward, shared with storm water grates. It's oddly warmer there in that fetid tunnel, and that's the only thing that bothers you, aside from electrical cables twisting out of the brick lining like writhing pythons, every couple of feet. The rest tastes like home.

"*Orale* . . . coal chute . . . *mira* . . . "

He seems to have bat or mole in him because you can barely make out a metal lid some feet ahead. He says from here on, you all are on your bellies all the way to Meridian Street. Again, for you, it's familiar.

The lid gives away with a grunt and you follow him atop a brick riser that was a coal receptacle seventy or more years past, and there's even a collectable prize—for someone with your affliction, at least—on the tunnel floor, an old coal scuttle, rusted almost bright orange in the meager light and looking like a World War II Nazi helmet.

The chute's worse than the tunnel. The rust is like a rasp on your skin and clothes; at least you don't have to crawl on your bellies, but are your hands and knees much better? Then, more unnerving than the darkness is the exhausting incline, up . . . and the rumble of tires on the pavement above, the vibrations peppering your heads with debris.

And voices. Cop radios, cries of frightened or wounded folk, mostly in Spanish.

At another iron lid that was a central dump for the coal your phone finally stirs . . . and you both gasp because you can hear someone official and officious ask whose damn phone is on ring! You see it's a text . . . glowing with words that make you shudder . . .

Come soon Jesus they took them.

One thing, though. Who's is this? You never got a survey of anyone's new number.

"*Come on,*" you groan, twisting around on yourself in the defile until your feet are on that lid, and with every bit of once-dormant sinew in your thighs you leg-press that bastard open. Slowly and with as little a squeak and creak as earthly possible.

Once you both of shimmied out, you realize you are barely in the cover of a plank fence right next to backyard of the

Brigada house on Meridian. You want to say well done, Stripe, but the kid's hyperventilating he's so scared. You are, too—from the exertion. The fear's already been swallowed up by a resolve to break Mr. Sugars' neck. But, oh, it'd good to school him once before he dies . . .

. . . you go first through the basement door. Gun tucked. Yeah, big risk, but there's no way to tell who's ready to dead who in that house. The broken glass and cracked plaster don't make for hushed home invasion. Don't need to be Little and Big Roach to understand that. But the sirens, alternating threats and pleas on a bullhorn, and a hovering chopper above surely help.

You two aren't finished wriggling off the filthy, fractured concrete floor when you hear the distinctive click of a pistol hammer. And staring at you is very old, very fat woman in lime green satin pants, dingy white bedroom slippers and a cardigan, a very large caliber revolver in her shaky little mitt, long barrel swaying.

Before you can hiccup Stripe shows some nuts and maturity; hands up he whispers, "*No policia, no mafiosi . . . no mara salvatrucha. Este es Ricardo, quien rescató a Tía Carolina. Este es Ricardo . . . el Gran Hombre Negro . . .* "

She's terrified . . . as shown on the faces of the children now popping from the shadows one by one, and an old man, wielding a mophandle like he's a fucking samurai. It's old homey who speaks first, still waving that mop handle as grandma levels the cannon.

Stripe tries hard to give you the instant, pertinent translation. The codger says the lookouts on the roof fell like icicles but nobody heard gunshots. Then everyone's ears popped; eyes went blind from explosions and bright flashes, and men—*blancos*—crashed through the upper patio door and one of the front windows. But they spoke Spanish . . . badly, so everyone knew they were Yankees anyway. They said, "Fuck you Otis Place, we are MS-Thirteen and will hack your children to feed big fish in the Potomac waterfalls," like they've done to many others. And they wanted *Tía.*

"Pero los hombres pensaban que las personas eran solo refugiados, niños . . . " the old dude recounts, rapid-fire. "No! We have guns. Many guns."

And many *blancos* died or were wounded, trapped. They took *Tía's* niece and baby and screamed for the people to let them leave. But the police started coming and everyone was shooting at one another. Now the police won't let anyone leave. The old man and his wife volunteered to watch the babies, guard against the cops busting in from the rear . . .

"Why would the police help MS-Thirteen?" you ask the old man, in English.

"Becau' gang and *federales,* one no live wid-ou' de odder, like *hormiga* . . . piss ants . . . an' acacia tree . . . "

Abruptly you all hear another burst of intelligible bullhorn banter, some shout . . . and, faintly, a baby's cries. An older fuss than Maximiliano's, almost verbal. And that's enough to fire what little juice you have left as you to rush past all of them including Stripe, and they won't yell out so they're hissing, grabbing, mumbling for you to stop!

Up the steps, out of the basement door there're faces of fear and shock, blood, bodies. Sounds of moans and prayers . . . and the baby's crying. Smell of burnt powder and emptied bowels. The living have barricaded themselves behind overturned sofas and chairs or huddled in corners. From the bullet holes in the walls, the wrecked windowpanes, splintered door frames it's clear the po-po had filled this place with rounds right after the *Brigada* and Mr. Sugars' mercs did their thing. You pray aloud that Marta and Pashmina aren't among the bodies . . . relief washes over you just for an instant when you spy Marta, behind you and in a corner of a small room, barefoot and resting against a wall as a young woman cups her hand in hers. There's still an IV-line wriggling from her arm so some bastard must have torn her from it and shoved her to the ground floor. Thus explaining . . . *Lord have mercy* . . . the baby . . .

"Don't loose it," you mumble and for the first time, in a long time, you're exhorting yourself rather than answering to the air. Hard to do in the face of all that hurt. Unmedicated.

You finally notice what might have been a heap of laundry but is, rather, a white dude's body there on the floor, perpendicular to your waist. He's wearing a pair of very whitey khaki trousers, cheap kicks and a flannel shirt under ski jacket; he's staring at you, mute, but there's nothing behind those upturned eyes. And he's fingering the trigger guard of an AR-15.

You are old. You are five-eighths still a bun, a Scooby smoker. There's no Hollywood action flick tumble over and grab the gun before someone takes a shot at you. You've only used a rifle like this once in Air Force basic anyway . . .

. . . *and where's Esme?*

You summon the balls to move your head slightly to the left, to scan the hallway. Above you spot two Otis Place young men, nines aiming down from the stairway landing. Below, crouched on the floor and bleeding is another merc, but he's very much alive and leveling another AR-15 at a figure down the hall, almost parallel with you but obscured by an open closet door and overturned chair . . .

. . . on the floor below the foyer to the front door, resplendent in a tweedy topcoat, daddy corduroys, those Maine duck shoes like he was going to some horse-jumping bullshit out in Virginia, is Mr. Sugars himself . . .

. . . and he's resting the spout and silencer of a big, black pistol on Pashmina's trembling neck, as she struggles to keep her wriggling son quiet, still, as if he's oblivious to the horror.

"I want a panel van . . . white, unmarked, delivered on Fourteenth," he says, calm and frosty, into some mic trailing off an ear bud. "Clear way to the Beltway, Beltway to Baltimore-Washington Parkway, not Ninety-Five . . . " He then screams toward the shattered glass of the front door. "Did you get that, too?"

Whoever's in his ear acquiesces; the bullhorn reverb hits before another reply "*Everyone withdraw to Fourteenth.*"

Do your thing, you man with the plan!

"This is pretty damn Tango Umbrella, clusterfuck, SNAFU, Mr. Sugars!"

"That hurts, Killer . . . "

"The MS thugs and Otis Place set-up—that was textbook. But murdering Piedade . . . and this—"

There's noise from across the hall, from the person obscured by the door, so deep it's palpable, like that ugly sound you make if you fall on your back and the wind and piss leave you . . .

"No way out. All because Bracht's screwed us all, Mr. Sugars!"

"*Sapo* . . . "

Oh shit, boy. Think fast.

"D-Donchew friggin' move, bitch!" Mr. Sugar's wounded henchman shouts through the pain. "Got her dead . . . dead in my sights, asshole!" Then to his boss, "Should I drop her, Burt?"

Now you pull the .380, cock it . . . yet there's no order from Mr. Sugars.

"Where's Maximiliano?" you engage.

"Out of my hair. Didn't think my mission-life, my career, would end on that note, though."

You hear Esme's throaty voice next. "Dickie, please stop! I will go with him to end this! The police will let us leave . . . "

"Esme, I know want you're trying to do!" you holler. "*Don't*! He's going to kill Pashmina and the baby . . . just like he murdered Piedade and ripped her child from his blanket . . . like he murdered my friend Black Santa . . . and my Princess, and that kid . . . and Sabine, and even that motherfucker Stoli . . . and like he murdered Eva, Fred . . . *because he has no honor*!"

You hear the other goon call, "Shut the fuck up!" then "Burt . . . hang-fire? What're your orders?"

Still nothing.

Is it the miracle pills? Or something newly born inside you, boy. Onaccount you call to the henchmen, "Hey whiteboy, Burt Sugars is a now HIC . . . *head in the clouds*, as you army boys say, eh? No better than shit thugs like Blinky Guzman. Garbage who's become a garbageman. Like I was. So welcome to the fam, Mr. Sugars, of we niggas and spick animals, right? And you are gonna get shot by cop snipers . . . because our mutual employer's mania is getting to be a liability."

Finally, Mr. Sugars replies with, "Nice psy-ops, Cornish, but save it. And I didn't kill . . . I pay others for the work."

"Then I didn't kill, either. Just sat in a room with intel and pictures. You, Mr. Sugars, you deaded folk face to face. Folk we all loved or knew."

This time, no shrieks, no all up in the crazy plea. Just a calm, soft, "*Sapo* if you love me let me go with him and Jaime will make it stop."

Stay icy . . . put one of those dilator things up your ass if need be but just hold on!

"That true, Mr. Sugars? Will he make it stop? Because if you think you're leave here with Esme, out that door with this *Dog Day Afternoon* shit, you're more zooted then I've ever been. You're the loose end, Mr. Sugars. Trying to save yourself and deliver Esme in this ham-fisted way, to a fucking lunatic and now . . . *oh hell yes*, it's gonna be on every phone and TV set and I don't even do that social media stuff. Trump himself might be catching big feelings if he sees this, and someone says, 'we got word from a credible source that this is Jaime Bracht's personal mess.' Hope the wife's got a nice insurance policy on you."

"S-Start crawling toward me, bitch. *Muévete!*" shouts the merc on the floor.

Gamble, son . . .

"Mr. Sugars, there's another way . . . "

It's just a "*thooomp*" sound. Then a hiccup or gasp . . .

. . . Pashmina emits a horrid open-mouthed yell. But Esme, well . . .

. . . she's silent as the merc with the rifle slumps over.

"You had me at 'HIC,' Killer," Mr. Sugars announces. You tilt your head to see him unscrewing his silencer. "I'm all ears."

"In the basement there's a coal chute that leads to a tunnel that will put us out off Sixteenth. It's how I got back in here, so you know it's no lie. That I'm offering it, means you know it's no lie. That I'm offering it to *you*, who should die by my fingers, means it's no lie!"

"So I leave, and what? Tell Bracht happy Father's Day, it's over?"

"Yes. Tell him to stop. Bet there's FBI out there now, DHS . . . even ICE. I'm sure none of them have read Fitzgerald . . . how the rich, they ain't like us . . . how they use us up . . . "

You see something you thought was a stress and fatigue and withdrawal-induced mirage. Mr. Sugars—sweating, talking to himself.

"Call off these spicks, Killer, so I can get to the basement."

By now Stripe is at your heels. Even he's not convinced Mr. Sugars won't blast on you all before the MPD Tac officers come busting in to finish off the rest.

You shout at the armed *Brigada* boys but they aren't having it. Stripe does his best and did you really expect them to heed his slimy ass? You plead and it's not working . . .

"Esme, tell them to let him go!"

"*Sapo* . . . "

To sweeten the pot, he loosens his grip on Pashmina. Now Marta has crawled up to the end of hall, weeping, pleading. Still, these knuckleheads won't budge.

The bullhorn sounds and Mr. Sugars claws at Pashmina, holds her close.

"Negative on the van, the unencumbered lanes. My name is Special Agent Szabo, I am taking over negotiation from the Washington Metropolitan Police Department."

His phone beeps simultaneously.

"See, Mr. Sugars. Like us, you don't matter."

You rise, hands up . . . mostly conspicuously in the *Brigada*'s line of fire.

"*El Gran Hombre Negro* get down! *Ultima oportunidad*!"

There's a pop sound . . . not like a gunshot, more hollow, like a balloon exploding. Then another. Mr. Sugars howls in disgust and raises his pistol, firing wildly . . . out the window. Esme screams and bolts toward him as Pashmina yanks herself and her baby from him to run toward her . . .

. . . just as the first tear gas bombs crash through and instantly veil and assault your eyes, bite into your nostrils.

You lunge for Esme but lose her in the damn fog and now volleys of something stinging, like nuclear-charged, are bursting through as well, and best you shield your eyes doubly because they are hard rubber. In the chaos, you hear "Dickie!" from Esme's lips . . . and then a figure hits you as if he's a human bowling ball. Flattens you until you roll over, low to the floor, where the gas hasn't reached.

That's Mr. Sugars, yanking Esme, who looks to be dazed and bleeding from her forehead, into the stairs toward that cellar.

You aim the .380, fire . . .

. . . the round glances off his thigh but puts a good rip into the corduroys and his meat. He cries out like a woman would and you laugh, even as he pulls her down.

Stripe's voice hit you. "Over here! *La Policia*! They come . . . "

"No!" you holler, coughing, "Get to the basement. There're kids, old folks down there!"

You swing to where Marta and Pashmina cower, grope in the cloud and find Marta's frail arm.

"Get this way to fresh air, away from the cops! I'll bring her back, I swear!"

In the basement, no other lives have been taken. Just huddling children and the old woman minus her piece, helping the old man off the cold concrete floor. She points to the blood trail, leading to the iron lid . . .

"Stripe do not let the cops, anyone, find that hole."

"But wha' now?" And he's about to say "Rain Man," but changes his lip's shape at the last minute and utters, *"el Gran Hombre Negro . . . jefe?"*

"What I was gonna do from the beginning. Raise an army."

He can't be moving too fast and Esme's putting up a ruckus because you can hear it. Maybe he'd taken your prodding too much to heart and put a round in her head so he could bust out with minimal claw marks on his face. Or yeah, you could easily catch up them . . . and then what, shoot it out in a crawl-space's height of darkness, then a dank tunnel?

No. You disappear into the chute, the gasps and clangs and thuds of Mr. Sugars dragging Esme, just ahead . . .

CHAPTER 26

Deadest Reckoning

THE CUTLASS IS WHERE YOU LEFT it and you are gunning it toward the Park, then down into Adams-Morgan. Whatever the best route is from your memory, avoiding the scene on Meridian Place, heading south to the shelter as the street lights buzz on and the melt of the day refreezes.

Hell no, it wasn't a mistake *not* to track the blood trail coming out of the tunnel. Mr. Sugar's is glassed, he just doesn't know it yet. If Esme can keep him from panicking like he did, she will be fine. You will find her. Just keep telling yourself that, Junior.

You pull into the parking lot and jump in the St. Jude's entrance. Immediately Father Phil, Sister Maria-Karl beset and besiege you as you storm toward the bridging hallway to SFME.

"What is going on? Why do you look like that, Richard?" the priest presses.

"Where is Fitzroy Cockburn?" the nun adds as they scurry behind you. "He was supposed to do Santa again this morning, but he disappeared before curfew . . . "

You halt and turn, and this time you give Black Santa the honor of a sniffle, a tear. And your chest is billowing when you look them dead in the eye and ask, "You see or hear the news? What happened . . . Columbia Heights?"

One nods, the other shrugs.

"The men who did *that* killed *him*. Then tried to . . . t-t-to . . . " *Oh no.* It's back? Swallow it or be it, Junior, "tried to . . . say . . . he was a bad man. He was . . . my friend."

Dry your fucking eyes!

You twist away from them, dare the SFME guard not to buzz you through.

A staffer escorts you—or rather, scurries after you—to Verna's office, and there are sleeping bags, cots shoved up against the walls, in every alcove . . . children sit in them, stare, as do single young women, old women, a man cradling a sleeping baby in arms.

Verna's up from behind her desk, dressed in leggings and a sweater and she rushes to you, hugs you like you are home from a battle. She peels herself from your chest before your eyes can plead for a kiss.

"What happened here . . . the people?"

"Worse than I feared," she says with a sigh as she grabs away your coat. "What'd Tupac say, long time ago, about recession hitting the street . . . misery before the mainstream notices."

"Please . . . I need to see LaKeisha . . . and I need some food. Lots of coffee. A place to wash my face. I can't be over at St. Jude's." You are about to fall over, pass out; she pushes you to the sofa. "Cops been around?" you finally ask.

"No. Listen. I will get you food, I will bring her in. You can use my washroom right there if you need to. Just do not leave. Understand?"

"Don't let me sleep," you beg her from the plush sofa. "They have Esme. I got her . . . then I lost her. I always lose her, Verna. Over and over again."

As you sit there like a stomped toad you realize it's still Christmas Day. Very soon, blessed people will sit down to a holiday meal. Yet uptown, bodies are being zipped into bags, kids are being questioned as to the birthplace of their parents—indeed, some of the very folk cocooned in those bags. Marta is in the hospital, next to Pashmina and her child. Marta is cursing you . . .

. . . and LaKeisha trundles into the office, and her head's wrapped in purple and orange scarves, looking like a whole rummage sale ended up on her back. But all three of her remaining children are open, lit, logged-in and under her arms, ready.

"The Wall always falls in George R.R.'s books. But the undead aren't the worry. It's the people who fail." She types on one of the laptops. "Lightning-fast connections here."

"Just wanted to see if you can monitor anything, MPD, DCFD too. I don't want . . . those people on Meridian Place put in cages for my mistake."

"They will be. So you better work hard."

Verna returns, carrying a tray with a hamburger on a toasted bun, fruit cup, lemonade and coffee. Tucked under her arm is a clean collared shirt.

LaKeisha rubs her hands, bites her lip and says, sheepishly, "He has to go. He has to work."

"Not before he eats. Dickie whatever it is you are trying to do, you'll faint before you do it. Now eat, slowly. And here's another shirt. That's torn . . . blood all over it thank the Lord it's not yours . . . "

Now you got what, three women checking you now? Yeah, chew your food then handle your business.

With a mouthful of burger you look to LaKeisha, who's typing away on all three machines and request, "Don't tell Verna what you've cracked into. I don't want her getting in trouble."

"Cracked?" Verna complains, mouth agape. "Hold up . . . when you told me she was at Peets or the Kabob spot you didn't say a damn thing about her being a damn hacker, Dickie."

"Righty-oh," LaKeisha mocks. "I'm not that good, Sansa Stark, okay? Look at me. Kinda hard to do this shit on the street, keep current. I'm just lucky. And don't worry they won't trace it through your wifi router." LaKeisha grabs a spoonful of your fruitcup and advises, "Now . . . looks like MPD's holding off arrests on weapons charges . . . see here, United States magistrate activity . . . that's about as far as I can get without the FBI and NSA coming to the ghetto, right? They are being good guys because if they file charges, some of those people might go over to ICE juris-diction. Good thing you got Anglo bodies carrying unregistered military grade firearms that they have to explain or else all of those people would be on a bus, shackled. Even the citizens . . . "

Shaking her head, Verna pours herself then you more coffee. She's looking at you intently, and this time your eyes are stapled right to hers as she sits.

"We may have to move Kate," she tells you. "Detoxing, bad. Family wants nothing to do with her. I don't understand—her own sons? One's a damn Senate staffer"

"Disgust, shame. You all don't even know . . . "

You're still staring at one another. Letting what's unsaid stay that way and it's she who punks out first. Not her fault.

Being drawn to someone like you has got to be more surreal than what she's seen in the last twelve hours.

"So maybe—Bracht's scared," Verna surmises, trying to sound like a detective. "Calling in chits from his boys? Must be getting the White House nervous . . . if they even know yet."

In her flat effect LaKeisha taps away and calls over, "Nothing but the official line. 'More violence among immigrants and idle poor besmirches the holiday for all Christians. What happened to peace on earth, goodwill to men?' Bastards. People are mean. That's gotta stop."

You clean your plate and Verna beams like a housefrau from back in the day, like your mother, back when she cared.

"Thank you," you whisper.

Verna now switches up on you, as she passes you your coat, yeah like your mother who had to disapprove of at least something to show she wasn't mush and mollycoddle, right?

"Dickie, Frank brushed off your coat a bit. There's . . . things . . . stuffed in the pockets."

"I took some shit from a hospital."

"No . . . you know what I mean. I'm not gonna say a damn thing . . . but . . . "

You whip out the Seecamp and eject a round, catch it. "Just a mouse gun, Verna. See? I'm no goon, ya hear?" You slip on your coat. "My plan all along was to negotiate a cease-fire when Bracht realizes he's got more loose ends than a frayed carpet, and he knows his future depends on letting things lay. Cause we in this town know how to shut up and let things lay. Mr. Sugars has fucked himself and bringing Esme to Bracht ain't going to mollify a monster. We got them all off balance . . . "

LaKeisha yanks herself from her digital trance and says to you, "That's when the monster's most dangerous, Jon Snow. When it realizes the humans aren't afraid of it anymore."

She's right.

"Keesh . . . custom limo . . . Hyundai Equus, Virginia plates DP-425. Prolly registered to StoneTower Capital. See if you can find out where it might be . . . "

"Photographic memory. Glad I don't have that."

"I suspect Monday will be the bullshit high tide here," Verna warns. "If not from the law, now the Feds looking for you, then HHS inspectors and they will lean heavy on us and Father Phil. Something will pop off, and I can't handle it if I know you're not coming back."

You smile at Verna. The smile grows one on her face, answered by an eye-roll from LaKeisha.

She can't know the smiles camouflage the twitches in your cheek, the twinge in your scalp. The old wooly vacant babbling Dickie's coming back. Crow. Maggot. Hyena. Then none of this will matter. But at least you'll be able to waterproof your next canvas cocoon with little kids' white glue . . .

. . . and you're glad you ate, slurped that coffee, because you feel almost as decent as when you popped the happy pills and snorted the Narcan plus. Croc's likely thinking you've expired and his daddy's whip lay banged-up in a river gorge in West Virginia, but you don't have time to let him know. Not yet, because you're back on Georgia Avenue in that head-turning car, pulling into the yet another hospital.

This one's not as glittery as Holy Cross, but it's yours. As in blackfolks'. Alma, born at Old Freedmen's like your mother. You were the outlier, birthed in Okinawa, but it was where you'd go for your tonsillectomy and gridiron bumps and scrapes . . . and then with Esme when candy took it's toll on the ole kidneys or liver or you couldn't shit for four days.

Good ole jont. Yeah, sort of a dull pallor, second-hand feel from serving people like, well, Jenn. Or you. So much so that the students have their own entrance, own waiting room. Still, no one stares as you lope down the hall toward a double room packed with familiar faces. You think you see Black Santa on the ward, carrying a balloon. Waving. Probably is him, in some form. Waiting for you . . .

. . . they pack the room around the Queen's bed but crowd you like a celebrity warrior as you enter, reverently. There's a muffled yelp in a tattered Trader Joe's bag and you see two eyes and a snout peeking from it. At least Thunder's okay.

"See dat ole bitch in de udder bed, my Dickie?" Jenn says.

There's an old woman, reading glasses perched on a cherry-like nose, scanning a month's old *Essence* magazine. Trying to ignore the maybe dozen bums plus you in the small room.

"Dat bitch loss her foots to da suga, an' her footless ass still tryna clibe out dat bed an' stump my ass ta deab onaccount de Queen snore . . . g'head and roll dem eyes. I sees ya an' so do T'under." She motions you closer.

"I want the word out. I need eyes on the jont, place called StoneTower in Old Town Alexandria. Night and day. Maybe rollin' and pizzin' folk who work there, coming out." She takes your hand as you speak. "And on a lawyer's office on K Street. I really need this one pizzed. Name is Alexander Nimchuk. Blond, siddity. I know Marcus, that white girl Billie—friends of Jabreezy who hang on K. Marcus can do right if he's clean. The girl, too. I need a phone, not a laptop, not a wallet, Amex, Master Card, fuck it. *A phone.* Y'all know how . . . "

Jenn releases a cackle besting any Halloween witch's. "Git dese mub-fuckahs, Dickie."

Platoons of you bums, with a single purpose, a single eye, ear . . . better than that Facebook or Twitter or that email or instant-whatever. And at your command.

Your first hit comes from LaKeisha, on the unbricked *Brigada* phone.

"That limo . . . I can track it from the contractor StoneTower uses to do maintenance on their fleet, and I can see some of their routing notes. It's at Reagan National, picking up on a private flight from Burlington, Vermont. Mean anything?"

You nod and affirm, "Now that I have permission, yes. He's back, early. Now we move." You click off and whisper, "I'm coming Esme. Piedade . . . I'll get your lil' boy back."

. . . and it's funny how Alexander Nimchuk is suddenly summoned to work the day after Christmas, when typically only the younger attorneys are camped out eating their suburban mothers' bland dressing and cold turkey or ham as they're closing deals or wrapping up litigation before the new year.

Funny how the elevator from the garage is jacked-up from White Boy Bob sleeping and farting in there, and thus the Somali dude must summon the repair person and security.

Funny, too, Nimchuk's reaction when he sees Marcus ambling toward him on the sidewalk as he must leave the building to get to the garage like regular people do. Marcus is a gentle brute like yourself, supposedly. He looks nothing like you, of course, but to these ofays in their office suites all nigga bums look alike . . .

"Scuse . . . scuse me sar . . . I got ta get farecard to Minnesota Avenue station, see my lil' girl for Christmas . . . "

Ha! He's only relieved a split second when he realizes it isn't you and tells Marcus to fuck off and Marcus is all bump and grab and Nimchuk's in a damn panic, swiveling right into this hillbilly girl who says her name is Mollie sometimes because she uses it, says Jabreezy. From the neck up she's scary. But from the unbuttoned men's collared shirt under her frayed hooded sweater, and the strategically ripped sweatpants, have mercy, Nimchuk's getting a decent show. And she doesn't smell half bad.

Good thing Marcus trashed the printed pic of Sandy's from the firm website. LaKeisha's been blowing up Verna's office printer all night; and, no, Verna'd rather hit Walgreens in the morning than go back home for fresh undies. Her new roommate's not so picky. Blowback's coming . . . but at least she says she's bringing Father Phil along, calmed her own staff down. Had to. The shelters have become your damn command post . . .

. . . and poor Sandy's being accused of eyeballing Marcus's white woman. Of grabbing titties and a slice of panty through the sweatpants rip. Sandy's cursing in Ukrainian and to the average bystander he sounds like Dracula and it brings quiet to the crowd even in these sparse days of shutdowns and occasional redneck tourists. A bike cop swings to the ruckus but Marcus has already motored his big ass down toward L Street with Sandy's watch, yanked right off his wrist; Mollie's disappeared into what's left of the old food court at International Square. She dumps Sandy's tricked out iPhone to Berniece in the ladies' room.

And Berniece is handing it to you.

"And y'all tell that man who give that money at the McDonald's he was rude, and I gave him all his change back."

There's a twinge in your left foot, a spasm in your jaw as you hug her goodbye to hop on the Metro and get back to SFME. How long you going to soldier through it? The flavor that you savor, the hair of that damn dog, well, a puff of Scooby might hold it at bay, or might just crash and burn you. Not good to have heavy on your mind when you're doing battle with these people . . .

. . . and the ride to L'Enfant Plaza's bumpy and delayed, and God knows if Mr. Sugars doesn't have operatives following you, watching the church and shelter . . . or ghosting Marta and Pashmina at Washington Hospital Center, masquerading as a security while the cops, ICE and the FBI go cage-match over what to do about the all of those folks they pinched on Meridian Place. Stripe's prolly the safest mug out there because no one knows where the hell he is.

Your only relief comes when LaKeisha sees the phone, chuckles.

"*Phew* . . . I was afraid it was going to be Android, working Google's op system. iOS is a menstrual cramp, Jon Snow, but doable."

"Then do."

She'd made some foraging requests to others in your army to help with the endeavor and you've always tried to stay away from the line between scavenging and retail thievery. Best to let the experts work.

"Nothing going on at StoneTower," you report. "At least nothing noticeable. And I didn't bother with his house. He'd be dumb as well as crazy to pull shit there, either. So the limo dumped his wife, daughters at home. Hasn't moved?"

"Uh-huh," LaKeisha replies. "Now don't bother me. We're all making this up as we go along. Could take an hour, could take a couple days and yeah, yeah I know we don't have a couple days . . . "

Verna returns and joins you, hunched over as LaKeisha pops the phone cover and works, first disabling the "locate" feature. You can feel Verna's hand on your shoulder.

"Twenty-four hours now," she says, sighing. "Only thing for sure is this Sugars guy needs medical attention. You sure Esmeralda wasn't wounded?"

"Not physically. But she's a lot safer than Mr. Sugars."

"You think he'll try to pull what the MS-Thirteen stooges tried?"

"No. His type doesn't think that way . . . despite what he did to people I love. What he might have done to you if you let your guard down and tried to spend that hush money."

"Thank you."

You just don't know what to say next . . .

. . . so a call relieves you of that.

"*Dis Isaiah. I need someone.*"

"Huh . . . ?" His accent places his origin somewhere on the African continent, south of the desert.

"*This Isaiah, friend . . . I friend of Esteban . . . Stevie . . . I live near Metro, on Duke Street. Many months and de cold is killing me. I hear word, from Jenn, Washington D.C.*"

"Yeah . . . *yes* . . . and I know Stevie. Are you near the place, where the white people are, the office?"

"Yes, only coin phone, CVS. Somet'ing happen. Very strange. Ambulance come, take sick woman from office . . . but it day after Lord's birt' . . . no many lights on in office. I ask woman dere and she say maybe some cleaner fell and was sick. Den another woman say no cleaner in dere, place closed. No refuse in bin, bin have not'ing because of Lord's birt' . . .

Ambulance men, no Alexandria, no Arlington. I be in bot' when sleep too much in cold. They very nice people.

Dese white men . . . I dunno . . . "

"Thank you, Isaiah . . . "

Think, boy. Either nothing . . . and this man sounded about as addled and clueless as you on a good day . . . or everything.

"Keesh . . . you sure that limo's stationary?"

"I'm bizzzzzzzeee," she complains. But then she checks her third laptops, perched on her knees while the other two teeter on Verna's desk. "Unh-unh, nothing but I can't vouch for the app . . . ."

So much for permission, given by the Queen. An army of misfits, miscreants, maladroits, malingerers . . . it isn't a unit, Junior! It's what it is—homeless basket cases bothering folk, mis-interpreting, misremembering. And here you are, cising and champing yourself into believing you can be a commander . . . just like you play at being a detective . . .

. . . and yet, after some whispered words signaling the end of her manic phase, LaKeisha slowly, stoicly proclaims, "Uncle Sam'll regret training me so well. Fuck GrayKey and Cellebrite. Always looking for the tiger, and never the mouse, coming in . . . through the *neighbor's* house . . . "

"*Hold up.* It's done? It was that easy?"

"Still fracturing but yeah. Uploading in a minute. Law firm stuff . . . financial stuff on StoneTower . . . it'd take me all night to break the encryption . . . but anything with Bracht directly, once my little helpers busted iOS: naked. You said they were ace boons . . . you and me against the world, so fuck the world . . . " She turns in her chair and looks at you, not Verna. "Arrogance."

"He's Ukrainian and an orphan. You think like your target, right?"

"Nope. It's just arrogance. That's the weakness. Ignorance helps. I used something the Army, FBI, and such should never ever share with private security companies but this Yam in the White House, he says everyone gets a taste at putting down people who are already just hanging on. Spying on their phones, their kids . . . so I use their tools."

"The data, Keesh . . . okay? You are a queen, the dragon-lady, but eyes on the prize."

Damn, someone's smiling on you, boy. Gabbing about "data" when a couple of days ago you were ass-deep in debtors' garbage.

"I'll store it on Viserion. Emails . . . here . . . texts . . . incoming and outgoing calls . . . here."

There's a knock on the door; a staffer wants to talk about someone trying to break into Ft. Knox and a fight in the single women's wing, and here's Verna waving her off, content being party to a felony.

"Look at that text . . . yesterday," she gasps. "*Tsukor* . . . English alphabet spelling Ukrainian and Russian for sugar. Blame my liberal arts education for that . . . " It's a text, in Ukrainian . . . to Bracht, who responds in Spanish, you finally confirm. *Come back. Everything's fucked. Mr. Sugars screwed up. Cornish responsible. Woman's not where the child is. Child safe.*

"What's the latest call?" you ask.

"Looks like right before he was pizzed," LaKeisha replies.

"Anything to StoneTower . . . or a private ambulance company?"

"Huh? I dunno . . . still uploading . . . but of these, that's got to be Bracht's mobile he's blowing up but no one answers. Then there's a call to . . . okay, an eight-one-four area code.

Quick reply then another from Bracht's mobile . . . then here it sits connected to my machines."

"You mean your dragons . . . " you quip as you check your adopted phone's Google. Something else you had very little practice with before you ceased being a basic sleeping-eating-shitting animal.

"Dragons?" Yeah, she's in the trough. Just where you don't want her now that your blood's quickened.

"Central Pennsylvania . . . " Verna declares, faster on her phone screen. "Can you comb the emails, texts?" she suggests.

"Can I? Yes. 'Can' relates to ability . . . "

You pull away from the table, revving that big brain, praying the jigsaw pieces stay fused.

"Don't crowd me!" LaKeisha protests. You're praying she keeps it together, but she can go into a spell any second, remain dark and brooding for an hour, for a week, listless . . . obsessed. "Wait," she calls abruptly. "Vid on his Photo app . . . first thing labelled . . . "

She plays it, there on the laptop screen and everyone's looking very tidy-white and rustic, Lands End, Filson, and Ralph Lauren catalog-ish in wool and jodhpurs and leather cowboy dusters, on a redwood deck, firepit ablaze. In the distance are high yet knob-like hills stippled with Fall's reds, oranges, and yellows.

And here's Bracht himself with a beer in one hand, stroking his daughter's flaxen hair with the other.

"It's just going to be s'mores because all that's running are forkie bucks, doe yearlings." To which Sandy replies, camera phone a bit shaky from his Eastern European chortling, *"Central Pennsylvania's only other pastimes when there're no whitetail is*

cooking crystal meth, popping Oxy with your cousin-wife, collecting disability in a MAGA cap . . . "

"They mean deer?" Verna observes, sighing.

Yes, you note that, but the video's winding down with Bracht shooting him a look, as if he said "pussy" in front of the girl. If she was a *vaca*, plucked from migrant trains or held in a detention cage, stamp . . . well that's funny. But not *my* little white blossom.

The next video is of that same daughter, posing like a model in her twelve-year old's version of a bikini and dripping wet after getting out of a steamy indoor pool, same Fall mountains in the backdrop.

"*Chudovyy!*" Uncle Sandy beams. "Is that purple nail polish on your toes?"

Verna makes a face and says, "God-damn . . . what do you figure? Your cool points aren't out the window, yet, Junior.

"Help me find a map on your screen or this phone," you whisper. "Breezewood, Pennsylvania. That's where he's gone. That's where Esme and Maximiliano are."

Verna slaps you on the back, smiling.

"We need something more precise than Breezewood," LaKeisha huffs, grimly.

"Nah, Keesh. Dead reckoning is fine for me. A scavenger improvises." You draw a deep sigh, knowing how stupid that must sound, then say, "Find anything that can give me something closer."

As LaKeisha grumbles computer shit, "geotags" and "Google Earth." Verna's demeanor is deteriorating fast, with the smile first to evaporate. Yet she keeps her hand your back, steadying herself from the dread washing over her.

"I thought . . . we're going to the news, social media...some people in Congress with what you have . . . maybe get D.C. police to confront him? I mean, you're not . . . going?"

You ask LaKeisha to print a copy of some of the texts, emails, then load the rest of the phone's innards on this nugget she calls a "flashdrive."

You then turn to Verna.

"Please don't hate me for this. But I'd rather you hate me then look at me the way you did . . . when I was the way I was."

She's tearing up, boy. She excuses herself for a likely non-existent administrative shit.

"Bravo-Yankee-Echo," you hear LaKeisha faintly mock, "Bravo-India-Tango-Charlie-Hotel . . . head in the clouds . . . "

CHAPTER 27

Country . . . Dark

A SPLINTER OF SHUT-EYE, CLEAN DRAWS and socks, more black coffee, a banana. That's what you allowed yourself before returning the Malibu to Croc. And that's supposed to be the easy part . . .

. . . but Croc's working you.

"You need a shotgun, cuz."

"Just needed the whip, moe. Creampuff's reliable."

"Man, let me come with. What the fuck you know about monsterin'? This ain't the football field. This be crackin' skulls and gunplay and y'all need backup for that. I'm in good shape—see?"

His belly conquers the zipper of his Nineties-vintage leather jacket; he's wearing a frayed bedroom slipper on his diabetic left foot.

"Nah, I'll be ok."

"Tote more ammo at least. Two more clips, here—for a fuckin' mouse gun. You sure you don't favor a shotgun?" You shove the extra clips in a flap of the proper holster he gave you, fastened to your belt at the small of your back. "I'm just not feelin' this. *Jhi*-yeah it's a lion's den, white

321

men with thirty-oughts like Trump's sons in Africa . . . plus bodyguards."

Why don't you tell him how you've been preparing. Watching that Youtube thing on the phone again: "Elementary Surveillance Techniques," by some old ofay in a cowboy hat, bigger gut than Croc's. "Disarming Electronic Monitoring Devices and Remote Cameras," and of course, some "ex-Green Beret" talking out his neck about "Neutralizing Armed Sentries and Security Personnel with Stealth." Impressive . . .

"I'm already gonna stick out like a peppercorn in a rice bowl up there in crackerland, so the last thing I need is . . . " A sick sensation like a full-body hunger pang tears through you. You'll be dropping to your knees soon, in full sick fits or full fiends. Either one's a showstopper.

"You alright, moe?"

Shake it off, damn you!

"Last thing I n-need is . . . state troopers, sheriffs, nosey white broads on their cell phones, bothering me, dig?"

He shrugs at your rookie naivete, leads you around to a Hyundai—one of the little SUVs—Maryland plates, boring-ass faded blue.

"Registration's in the glove box. Not that you have a driver's license so you may get shot just over that, but hey, you be you."

"Thanks."

"Last chance for the shotgun . . . easy thing to learn."

Time's wasting. Sunrise is a couple of cold hours away. He tosses you the keys . . . then looks down at a man prone on the wet, moist pavement opposite the abandoned Giant super-market . . . wrists and ankles lashed with a zip-tie, mouth swaddled in duct tape. Beyond him, the brightly lit sign reading "Iverson Mall" winks-out for the night.

"My boy goin' borrow your ride—really your auntie's ride, for that matter—awhile. Any last-minute details—sticky brake pedal, treble levels you don't want him to fuck with? No? We cool?" He looks to you. "We cool. Bon voyage. Left a little grub, little Gatorade, flashlight and shit . . . and a pee pot . . . in the backseat."

You climb in, punch general directions into the map function. The rest is going to have to be by your nose, as Bracht's jont is off a private road and the approach is sketchy. You aren't going up there to commando him anyway. You're going to, well . . . cajole?

Already you don't like the chosen route—around the damn Beltway in Virginia, back into Maryland, up 270. There's a grin despite the quickening pangs and pains and you resolve to plunge in through the anus of your hometown, punch your way out the other side, bust north to the Mason-Dixon.

"Stay in touch with Verna at that number. If there's a double cross and any of those folks taken in the shit on Meridian Place get put in an ICE camp or herded down to jail, you relay that to me. Might need that backup. You know any hard spooks living up there?"

"Yeah," he snorts through a chuckle. "Three hard niggas in Pittsburgh . . . but they'd have ta Uber there . . . "

You're grateful he's made you laugh . . .

. . . because the dark is suffocating you, feeding off you. No light but the highbeams on the white lines. Must be like those bathyscaphes on the ocean floor you read about as a kid . . . it's the dark, not the cold or depth, that's the monster. Obscuring abyssal canyons below you, giant seamounts above you . . . freakish big-jawed minions just ahead of you, right?

You, Mr. Sixteen Minutes of Youtube-certified Expert Detective. Of no fixed address! *Ha*!

But buck-up—you've had unnerving dark drives before. This is nothing, son. Remember coming back home in that taxi, late, to tell your mother you'd been kicked off the team, lost your money . . . sold the car to pay for the scores of the bitch you are on your way to rescue, again, and oh, the fucking irony and allegory there? Sitting in the ambulance as she hemorrhaged out her woman parts just before she died, rather, forced herself to die. Or in the back of Croc's whip, teen peach fuzz on your chin, heading down past the ole Mickey Dee's parking lot off I Street Southeast . . . to point out which of those smug, nasty Mr. Charlies in training, and lil' Missy Annes slumming in their pastel outfits and BMW coupes—re-upping their powdered blow, pills, herb—had hurt your sister. Croc and the boys did their thing. Drove you back to the Eight and E Barracks. Ample street lights there, but for you, it was dark, bleak, endless . . .

. . . and you will yourself awake after two eighteen wheelers driven by snickering peckerwoods up in the cabs box you out and sound their horns in triumph over the colored interloper. Damn, you must be getting closer to Breezewood . . .

. . . no moon tonight. Only thing in your favor before sun-up, Mr. Amateur. Your only landmark now is the forest of interstate signs as you near the only glow on the horizon you've caught since the Maryland border. I-76, Pennsylvania Turnpike junction with I-70, West to Pittsburgh, East to Harrisburg and Philadelphia, I-99 North to State College . . . U.S. 30, Lincoln Highway. That's the one. You can feel the pressure in your abdomen when you see that sign, yet the urge subsides abruptly. *Uh-huh* . . . the man-up hormones are kicking in.

The town itself is as Bracht described: motels, gas stations, repair shops, every fast food logo imaginable . . . truck stops humming with big rigs like the ones that fucked with you. It's like you imagine Las Vegas, eh? Yeah, lights and more lights but nothing really behind them. And then a vast empty dark, all around.

You follow the auntie-like voice on the navigation system, careful to obey the law, to smile even if not many living souls are on the road. *Shit*! Pennsylvania trooper unit in that parking lot over there; township cop pulling out of the Pizza Hut over here. Thank goodness . . . headed in the other direction. Probably biting what local talent the truckers are entertaining in their cabs. Though . . . a man like Bracht might have the yokels in check, right?

To the east, five a.m . . . .not even a hint of pink tinging that dark, frosty sky.

Make a left turn on Mountain Chapel Road, says the auntie navigator. And there she concludes. *Can't help your big ass no more . . .*

. . . the image LaKeisha printed shows a small outbuilding near the entrance to the half mile of private road. That's what you're peeping now, silhouetted against the glow of what might be the only streetlamp for miles. Might have meant something when he was a Homeland Security muckety-muck. Down the road, a hundred feet maybe, a dirt road to what looks like a dirt lot and small garage . . . "Penn State University Forestry Management." The road ends at the lodge—from the air, a weird H-shaped house with a wrap-around deck hugging one wing, that barn or whatever turned into an indoor pool adjacent to the other. Main entrance appears to be at the middle connecting section, fronting a circular driveway.

You decide to stake out the opposite side of the middle section. Bright tactics, son. A defile everyone's got to squeeze through, like a bridge. You open the Hyundai's rear hatch for your gloves, a wool cap, that long black coat of yours that has been through more in the last four days than the years in some asshole's closet before he donated it. There's a quilt back there, rolled up; Croc said it's in case you need to pull over. Did you?

Nah, he didn't. *Yeah,* he did. You see the stunted barrel out one end . . . unroll the quilt reveals a shotgun, 12-gauge. Notebook paper a child would use says, "*Teehee, motherfucker. I told you. Stock is pistol grip so hold it waist high, front. It's a Mossberg (previous owner collateral). Thank me later. -C*" On the next sheet are little drawings and stick figures showing you how to load and shoot. Six shells rolled up in there with the weapon. Time to put some pine boughs all over this Hyundai like the man in the video advised. Then hike . . .

You stick as close to the edge of the road as possible, keeping the small flashlight beam low and close. With your eyes directed downward forty seconds out of a minute, yeah you might not twist an ankle, but you surely could run face first into a bear's ass. But you trudge on, there in the forest . . . in the notch between two mountains . . . in the dark's endless quiet gullet.

Yet the pace, the cold biting at your skin . . . the loneliness . . . is something known.

You twitch a smile.

As you pass the gravel access road to the university's hut there's a flash of light on the naked birches and oaks to your right. You douse yours, leap into the brush. Crouch.

Sure enough, your ears catch the grind of tires on that ill-tended road, echoed through the bare trees. Pray you camouflaged that SUV well but it would seem whoever's tear-assing through the blackness plain didn't notice, or else they would have called the cavalry from the main road.

It's a Benz SUV, matter of fact, churning up the cold dust and pebbles as it whooshes by you. Couldn't get a good look but there weren't but one or two people in there. Once the dark sucks up the red brake lights, you rise, pick up the pace. It's hard to breathe, eh? Not from the icy air . . . it's your pulse, slamming your throat so hard it's fluttering your larynx.

Smile's gone, however. You ain't catching no one asleep now!

It's at least twenty minutes before you can make out lights ahead. Into the woods proper you go, moving around the lodge in tighter circles. Your eyes are more accustomed to the dark, and creatures all around you, the odd shapes crunching underfoot, are just props to you. Nothing to fear.

In your final arc you come to the tree line. Phone's still got service but there's nothing incoming noted. You check in with a text that you are at the house, keeping the phone in the leaf clutter to dim the glow. You get a thumbs-up emoji in return.

Who has late-model Mercedes Benz SUV Virginia plates? You type.

"Beyond capability." Guess LaKeisha's not the queen her manic self claimed. Shit. You're too close to the house. You turn off the phone . . .

. . . and with a little wind to creak branches, and the night creatures either resting in warm winter burrows or high in the trees silently peeping you, the noise from the house is the first thing you sense . . .

Shouting, loud and violent. Yeah, glass breaking . . . reproach flying.

The hearth fire's almost living glow, it sucks the inhabitants away from the stern, stationary room lamps likely in the rest of the house. And though the noise, the light, emanate from one wing, there are shadows moving back and forth between the other.

No baby's cry, yet.

This isn't any fantasy movie villain, son. Trip wires, infrared cameras? Henchmen with headphones and mics, spike-collared German Shepherds? *Nah.* You count to three, unsling the shotgun, sprint lively onto the open grass to boxwood and holly hedges screening a brightly lit bank of windows in the corridor connecting the two wings. If you're going to kneel to your mother's gilded idols, best do it now . . .

" . . . *Sancta Maria, Mater Dei, ora pro nobis peccatoribus, nunc, et in hora mortis nostrae. Amen.*"

And damned if she doesn't intercede, just as a tiny kiss of pink appears on the mountain at your right, almost insignificant in the entire tar-like empty sky but there it is. And you hear the muffled wail of an infant . . .

. . . and the cries grow louder, and you're looking up at the dark even the stars and planets struggle to pierce, and you think of Piedade, you think of Black Santa, too. They died because someone was inconvenienced . . .

"Thank you," you mouth to the sky . . . as now a shadow moves beyond the curtains. The shadow bobs and sways as it walks, halts, turns to backtrack, moves forward again. Like someone struggling to calm the baby.

There are harsh, horrid voices to your right, in the wing of the house with the hearth, the roaring all-night fire challenging the all-mighty dark. Yet above you, coming into the space between curtains . . . is a lullaby . . .

"*Mistress turtle cannot dance so it just sings along. As the monkey on the flute plays a slow and happy song.*"

In the *K'iche* you once tried to master, to impress *her.*

And Esme emerges in the light. Swaddled in a long blue satin bathrobe, white lapels. Her hair is pinned up yet looks frayed and frazzled, her eyes are hooded. And she sings to Maximiliano, a cousin born to her cousin, fathered by her brother.

You are just about to pop up when another shadow arrives. Limping.

It avoids the part in the curtain, reaches for her but she's resolute. You hear Mr. Sugars do something you'd never expect before he killed his own man on Meridian Place: plead.

"Christ . . . *please* . . . just come to the den, talk to this fucking clown so we can resolve this once and for all. He thinks he can keep you socked on the side like it's Green Acres and you're his new cursed family. He's got to fly you out of here now . . . "

"Fuck you," she hisses.

Attagirl.

You grit your teeth, sneer, as he claws her close to him.

"If it were up to me," you barely register. "I'd put a bullet in your head . . . Bracht's, this faggot lawyer's . . . and drop this kid at a firehouse, get my ticket to Belfast and send for my family. Now let's go . . . "

"T-Tell him I'm getting dressed. Maximiliano must take albuterol for his lungs. Then I'll come."

Mr. Sugars releases her.

"Ten minutes, whore. Ten damn minutes!"

He limps away. When the shadow hits the other wing, you rise under Esme's tearful gaze.

At first, she doesn't seem to note the tapping with your finger, such is her lament and the baby's fussing. Or maybe she thinks it's just boxwood scratching from a breeze? You risk a clink with the shotgun's short barrel . . . and she looks down. She's shaking the baby, squinting . . . then cannot contain a gasp, as if you were killed back in the city and haunt her here in this isolated place. As she spins, cowers, you wave, put your face to the pane's lower part, touch your finger to your lips . . .

She searches down the corridor. Looks to the pane again. Nods, gushes tears. Smiles. Get her back to where she was going, boy. This is the opening. No second chance . . .

. . . the window to her room is high from the ground, cut small into the lodge's logs. You get a Tim into the rocks that are the facing on the lower portion of the home's outer wall . . . but she waves you off quickly. She points to something on the glass . . . the size of a quarter. You don't have to have telepathy to know it's a sensor. She points toward another window along the wall . . . even smaller, gives a thumbs up.

She hits the light; she raises the blinds and you see it's a bathroom. She opens the window, takes the shotgun first. She pads the toilet with towels then pulls your big self through . . . you are about waist-in when there's a knock on the outer door.

She's a pro, yeah. She quickly rushes out, flips the nebulizer attached to the child's bassinet and the tube immediately puffs vapor.

"I'm on the toilet and the boy is getting his treatment!" she yells, rushing back to the gently close the bathroom door. If it was Mr. Sugars, there'd be no knock.

The bedroom door opens, and the next voice you hear is Nimchuk's. That must've been him tearing up here.

"Ms. Rubio, Jaime wants you as soon as you are dressed and the child is stable," he calls in that slight accent, and like that bastard Mr. Sugars, the ofay sounds stressed. "There are items, realities, we must discuss . . . "

"I'm coming. Please tell him my . . . *mi ciclo* . . . *la menstruación* came. I'm just trying to clean myself for him . . . "

"Eh . . . alright. And keep the windows secure. The dog was nervous in the den. Likely black bears again, looking for food . . . "

He leaves and you realize your ass is wriggling out the window, free for any black bear to take. She pulls you through and you slither to the tile floor. You kiss each other's lips for the first time in years. Now maybe the last.

"Up that road, then to the county road on the right, is a Hyundai SUV. It's in a clearing right off the shoulder beyond a deer sign, I-I shoved . . . shoved . . . " Hold on, son. " . . . some pine branches and shit all over it. Take him, get the fuck out. You can reverse the navigator and just drive . . . forty bucks in the glove box."

"No . . . no."

"If you just can't go anymore or you get stopped . . . then find any state trooper, Penn or Maryland, okay? Not local cops, not here."

Yep. A pro. Maybe like you . . . good at surviving. She says she already pushed some medicine into the kid's tiny mouth so he's at least calm—even though she's wrapping him up, then rigging a sling with the scarves and other women's clothing that's oddly available in the rustic chest of drawers by the bed. Never mind that shit. Just get them out . . .

. . . you leave the nebulizer on and gently push her out the window with a coat, hat, crocheted scarf. Then you pass the treasure, the cargo. He's squirming but thank both black and white Jesus he's quiet. No room for anything but a spare disposable diaper. His meds, a bottle of formula. You give her the flashlight.

"Make for the woods," you whisper, "by the indoor pool, then turn right along tree line to the road. Don't stop, move fast. You'll hit the SUV in about a mile. Take the Three-Eighty."

"No. Not being caught with that. You need it. There's an extra man in with Jaime."

"If you have to turn yourself in, tell them to do a DNA test on you, the kid . . . demand Bracht take one." You smile. "I learned that on a video."

"*Sapo*," she calls, her voice disembodied by dark. "You could have stopped. He was going to stop. He promised me. He would clean the mess and stop."

"You really believe that? Mess is too big to clean without wiping us all out." Just tell her the rest. Might be the last thing you do on earth, Junior. "Besides . . . I'm not going to back to what I was."

"I loved . . . what you once were." And with that she turns to the forest. And you remember something about a dog . . .

CHAPTER 28

El Balam Chi

YOU SUFFER ANOTHER PANG AS YOU rack the shotgun. The pain's so bad you're driven to your knees and need the weapon as a crutch to get you back up. That's a good carrot . . . and stick . . . for Bracht to use on you, Junior. If someone doesn't blow you out your Goodwill surplus socks first. Just live long enough to parlay. You ready?

Face to the floor, you peek under the heavy oaken door to see if anyone's loitering in the hall. Nothing, so you open the door, slowly, poke the murder stick's gun-gray snout out for the first sniff. Again, nothing.

Now, your original situational awareness shows its flaw, boy. Only one way at Bracht, and that's that narrow corridor connecting the wings. If you don't want to the end up like 54th Massachusetts Colored going at Ft. Wagner, you must be quick and you will have to kirk some white men, ugly. Nothing uglier than a shotgun; you-know-who blew the face meat off many a future nail shop owner's cousin down in them spider-holes in Bao Loc, 1970. You got the nutsack to do that? Remember what Croc said, son—don't hold it like a rifle . . .

. . . be better if you could run up on someone but the hall's clear, and all you catch is more shouting. That dog you heard about barks to punctuate each phrase of disagreement this time, and he sounds like a big motherfucker. You don't want to murder a dog. Kicking off those Tims gives you a little extra soundproofing. You shove them in your coat pockets and shuffle down the corridor, past paintings of hunted and hunter—from the American frontier to Roman mastiffs taking down giant stags and boar . . . to the last, a replica of Maya warriors dropping turkeys and tapirs with arrows and sling stones . . . and naked humans are part of the kill as well. A jaguar aids them as if a loyal hunting dog, and a buzzard—the scavenger—hangs back to peck at the leavings. It's that one you fix on . . . glom on, halt on. God help you son . . .

. . . and you peek through the space in the double doors; you only see Bracht, standing behind a bar, mixing a dawn cocktail and looking toward two heads, facing away from you, seated on the leather sofa facing the fire. The dog's a Rottie. Square head and squarer shoulders. Resting on a woven mat on the tiled floor. But now he raises his head, whines . . .

. . . as you burst through those doors, such a supple carved cherrywood, and Mr. Sugars turns to look over the lip of the sofa . . .

"Sonuvabitch!" he hollers, and you answer with a shell to the sofa's back. He dies in a snowstorm of feathered lining, pulsing from a hole. Sorry Mr. Sugars. Couldn't count on your merc ass for a coup d'état.

Now the dog's rushing forward as Nimchuk, once seated in a leather lounger to the right of the hearth dives over Mr. Sugars' twitching body onto the floor . . . and you are down the steps, firing at the goon directly across the room from Bracht. You know he's there because he's shouting for Bracht to get down or get hit in his crossfire. The blast spins the man like an ole school top and you see the pink spray from what's left of his shoulder steal the orange from the flames for an instant.

And that poor dog. You give it a blast just as it lunges. The lead pellets blow the tile into the Rottie's path. A few small shards are like razors into the paws and chest, and the animal immediately slides to a halt, rolls into the shadow cast by Bracht's billiards table against the firelight.

Bracht screams to match the volume of the goon's shrieks, the dog's cries. You're ready for him to draw down on you but you aren't here to blast him.

"Get over here muvfucker!" you command. "Ten fingers in the air . . . now!"

He raises his arms but won't budge.

"Fuck . . . *you*. Why can't you just be—"

"A piece . . . of shit . . . a dirty addled animal?" you pant. "A maggot, a hyena, a crow, huh?"

You wave him to the center of the room, but he's still glued to that spot. "Damn you, I'll take your arm off with this thing if you pull a gatt from behind that bar." You hear Nimchuk's cowering. "Or maybe do it to your attorney. Be interesting to see him write lies with just one arm . . . "

"C-Cornish . . . whatever you thought you could accomplish . . . " Bracht growls, face wet with tears, snot, " . . . oh, it's already deep dish baked." He then looks to the sofa. "Did he hurt you? Please tell me you're alright . . . *querida*? All's forgiven, as before. Now you see both of us in a new light, huh?"

Over the sofa's lip comes a shaking hand, still wearing a wool glove, and a head pops up, still wearing the cap and crocheted scarf donned . . . after wriggling through the bathroom window.

"*Lo siento . . . sapo . . . dios mio . . .* pl-please . . . "

And you lower the murder stick, praying the bile will stay down, praying you won't heed the fiending call, boiling in that stomach as well, to use the damn thing on yourself.

"Why?" you cry. *"Again?"*

"I'm weak," Esme sniffles, coughs. "It was so cold, the forest. Then what? Where would I really go? What would happen to you if you kill Jaime?"

"It's almost like the tag we used to play, my big sister and me," Bracht snorts. "It's a dance . . . oh yes, not to everyone's taste or understanding, Cornish. But a dance. I pull, she pushes. She cuts, I bleed. But in the end . . . *el jaguar . . . el Balam Chi . . . no puede cambiar sus manchas.*"

"Where's the baby?" you grunt, raising the shotgun and knowing you only have two shells left. "It was Piedade who was loyal to you because she was a fucking child, warped by . . . both of you . . . and she's gone. Now where's the baby?"

"On the sofa," Bracht sneers. "You almost killed him when you came in here blindly pumping away, like the savage you fucking are! But he's a good boy. He's got his sleepy meds. He's a good boy. Now what's the endgame here, Cornish? More money? Or you want to end your life by killing me? Because Esmeralda is mine. Always will be mine, because I do not judge her, hurt her, berate her as long as she acknowledges she is mine. All you've done is indulged her weakness. Like her stepfather, her mother . . . my mother. For almost thirty years, starting with her escape to a nigger college, my God. I can write a check tonight to the ol' alma mater . . . get some Hip-Hop child a scholarship so they don't affirmative action out a smart kid at a real university."

You can't even hear him. Your pulse is in your ear and what other sound gets through that is smothered by the bellows that are your breaths. He could be cocking a revolver that's aimed at your nutsack.

"Esme . . . I got a pocketful of document copies . . . emails, texts. He calls you a fuckpig, and a junkie who'd be dead were it not for your perfect tits and ass . . . even as a trussed up middle aged tart. That part of the dance? Murder part of the dance? Not just Eva and Fred."

She's crying. That's it. Saying nothing.

Bracht sneers, "Sandy, you can change your underwear and stand up now. I suppose you want clean slates for all the cockroaches and *vacas* in the District of Columbia? Ha! My old colleagues on the West Wing of Ringling Brothers Barnum and Bailey were getting a tad nervous, right Sandy? Again, they don't understand. You'd think these ferrets who work for the Weasel-in-Chief'd understand that it's cash that opens and closes doors, makes things run, not insane rants and Mussolini proclamations. Sandy? You hear me—how dare those morons judge me! Pry into *my* business!"

Nimchuk indeed rises. "Jaime, yes, we have big problems, but fixable. Everything is fixable."

Really?

"Mr. Nimchuk," you whisper, coarsely. "You can f-fix any-anything?"

He nods in the firelight, points to Mr. Sugars' corpse, the newly minted corpse of the gunsel across the room . . . even the dog. "It can be done, paper it over. I have . . . a meeting Tuesday, in secret, with the associate attorney general, ICE. Fixable."

"You can help me stay . . . clean. The drugs Mr. Sugars gave me?

He nods again. The jigsaw pieces in that brain are brittle again. So what are they telling you to do?

"Okay," you mutter. "Fix this . . . "

You swivel the Mossberg and send a shell into Bracht's head. What was Bracht's head . . .

Once the sound leaves your ears you see Nimchuk, flash-frozen . . . and Esme running to the bloody pulp that was her lover and half-brother.

"This ends tonight, Mr. Nimchuk," you declare over her wailing, and the baby's new cries. "Suffices to say . . . we . . . we have your phone and sucked out the data before you bricked it. I want anyone picked up at Meridian Place for that fake war—amnesty. I want the cash released for St. Jude's and SFME. As Bracht's memorial. There are grandchildren of a man named Fitzroy Cockburn—ten grand to share. Treatment for Kathleen McCarthy, a new hip for a woman named Jenn. Gift to seed a mental health center at a place to be determined, on Georgia Avenue, in the name of Fred Cross and Eva Boudreaux. Cancer treatments for Marta. Her sister. The good sister. And yeah, you better press like fuck on all those turds-on-high about that amnesty part. Can't stop the kids being in cages. Can stop the one's being auctioned off, right, motherfucker?"

"Mr. Cornish, I . . . "

"*Unh-unh.*"

"I . . . *can* do it. It will take some time but . . . but what do *you* want?"

"Already told her. I'm not going back to what I was. I just want to do right and do right by people. But that bank check for me will do nicely after you dose me that stuff. Looks like you have a new client, *miy tovarysh* . . . "

Still aiming the shotgun with one hand, you sit on the stone steps.

"And . . . Miss Rubio?"

"She's an undocumented alien. Call ICE."

"*Dickie . . .* " she sobs. "I-I want to stay with you. And the baby . . . "

"She has delusions of being a witch, a shaman. She might need medical attention in Mexico."

"What . . . what about the baby?"

"He's mine . . . until he's yours. Like your ride is mine, until it's yours again. Don't fuck around . . . *Sandy.* You're free of all this. Thank me later. Now empty you pockets of cash . . . the car keys. Give it here."

Esme curses you in *K'iche,* spits at you, gnashes her teeth, tugs at that once beautiful black hair as you move to the sofa, scoop up Maximiliano.

"Reach into my inside coat pocket, Mr. Nimchuk." He does so and you smile. "A sample of what we accessed . . . on your ph-phone. I'll be seeing you on K Street, real soon."

"*Fuerza negra! Puta madre!*" she hisses at you as you walk by, ignoring her.

"A loose end, here, Mr. Nimchuk. Deal with it as you see fit. But hey, we did wrap it up by New Years."

As the sun chases the cold mist out of this little notch in the mountains, you're fastening the child's carry-all into the seatbelt. He looks at you the same way he did when his mother plopped him on your lap. With curiosity, not fear. He squirms, coughs, and seems to be relieved, even amused, as a gob of phlegm from his little troubled lungs hits your face.

"My name is Richard E. Cornish, Junior, little boy. And I'll take care of you until someone else can. And then you will never hear my voice again. I swear."

CHAPTER 29

Equilibrium

"*Diligis Dominum Deum tuum ex toto corde tuo, et ex tota anima tua, et ex tota mente tua, et proximum tuum sicut teipsum, Amen,*" Father Phil recites, all pimpish in his violet stole and white surplice.

"Do you believe in Jesus Christ, His only Son our Lord, Who was born and Who suffered?"

"I do . . . " you whisper. You look to Verna, who smiles, tries to hold Maximiliano still for the water, the oil, the salt . . .

Once anointed, you take him back to the pew and one of the novice nuns holds him. You look across the aisle at Marta, still on oxygen, Pashmina clutching her. They came but they don't speak to you, don't look back at you. You know you'll be in a church soon, grieving over Marta. Just not today. Father Phil asks Brother Karl-Maria to ring a hand-bell. One ring for each man or woman touched by this child and sent to the afterlife for it. Most in the cramped nave of St. Jude's chapel have no clue why he asked that. Most don't know why you refuse to rise and take Communion, the main floor show of this vaudeville, or why Father Phil is nervous about inviting you up.

But Lord, doesn't Verna look good in that skirt, that blouse and slouched hat, and doing you a favor to act as god-mother up there, so this little boy can be right and proper before the Lord, when no one else in his short life thus far truly had been. With some of this extra money it shouldn't be too hard to find him a permanent home; some of the candidates sit in the pews, and not as bidders. The only stipulation is he keeps his name. And no one has a problem with it.

After a song by Sister Maria-Karl, the service ends and you shake hands and kiss Verna and hug some of the troubled men in there. You wave to Croc who trundled in on his cane. You look for Stripe yet you know you will see him up on the street soon enough, in trouble then not. And some folks ask if the Scooby-Doo and Xanny and booze still call you, but you have weapon against it, tenuous, eh? Temporary?

And no one asks about Esme, as the Uber picks up Marta and Pashmina, and the gentle snow falls. They whoosh off and you swear Marta waves, but, well . . .

. . . Verna's called you a car, then promises to find LaKeisha an apartment as all new SFME employees must have a permanent address now that this last shutdown is over and Congress timidly peeks into corruption in the Department of Homeland Security in slow motion.

Someone tells you there's footage on the news of Agent Orange bawling over the closed casket of Jaime Bracht as Pence brays on about the parable of the prodigal son, and the sin of suicide, and the duplicity's so thick you could dollop it on a slice of shit pie as the bigshots and bankers look on and his widow's presented with a folded flag there at the Texas megachurch. Those ofay sumbitches should thank you. Yet they will never know your name, son. That's how it works in Rome . . . Sodom . . . Berlin-on-the-Potomac . . .

. . . and so the driver's complaining about traction on the streets and short-budgeting on salt trucks and plows, as he like so many others in his side hustle are from balmier climes.

"Soldier's Home should be okay, man," you counsel. "Just watch the hill on Upshur."

You're rolling up Georgia Avenue, and through the beat of the wipers you see the same people, shivering in the cold. Peach doing doughnuts in her wheelchair. James hitting up folk for ones and fives. Little black girls in little pink parkas tossing snowballs. White people clowning on cross-country skis.

At the next intersection there's a man, hunched over a steel mesh garbage bin. Snows making his stilted 'fro look like a plug of white cotton, and it's sticking to the blanket he wears on his shoulder. You order the driver to stop and he does, as you are sill a big, big man.

You get out and see he's not hungry, at least not right now, as he's drinking from a thick paper cup of steaming hot soup. He's just wet, cold.

You dig around in the bin, find an umbrella skeleton, just as you found for James it seems a million years ago, wrecked from the high gusts earlier before the Baptism. A temporary vinyl sign touting new apartments converted to easy rental when no one could pay $300,000 for a one-bedroom condo flaps loose off an abandoned storefront. You shake off the wet snow, show him how to bind the vinyl to the frame, shiny side up.

"This'll keep you dry until you get to the shelter."

"Fuck da shelter."

"Nah, bruv. Head over to the CVS on New Hampshire. I'll be there after dark. I'll find a spot for you. If not, you can grab some floor in my jont."

"Y'all ain't no faggot, right, tryna fuck me are ya?"

"Stamp, bruv . . . I'm Dickie Cornish. Jont's right across from my ole college, one room and a bathroom, a hot-air oven and a hotplate and a laptop my friend hooked up so I can watch my movies and my dad's Redskins . . . up the stairs from a barbershop and Mexican snack jont."

The Uber driver honks.

"Remember, the CVS, bruv. Here's my card. Just got 'em today. City program grant." Uh-huh, to shut you up. "Helped me with my rent. My first gig . . . I help do truancy stuff. For now. I mean, I wanna—"

The man's in a coughing fit. He waves you off. And the card flutters down, moistens in the dirty slush.

Richard E. Cornish, Jr. Investigations and Security

Maybe you will find him again, get him dry, fend off pneumonia for an extra day.

The driver's had enough.

"You getting in, sir, or what?"

"I'll walk. Don't worry."

"Soldiers Home . . . it's up several blocks. You sure?"

You nod, shoving your hands in the pockets of your Goodwill topcoat. Nice stuff in there, cast-off. Might have belonged to a K Street lawyer.

"Why the Soldier's Home. You don't look that old."

"Visiting my father."

He says something in an exotic language, maybe from the Pacific Rim, then praises, "You are a good son."

"No," you say after a sigh. "I'm a bad son. He was a bad father. I just want to be near him . . . so I can think on my own. And call it even."

"Oh, he will be happy to see you."

"He's catatonic. Won't even know I'm there."

Don't count on that, boy. Don't even . . .

Acknowledgements

GRATITUDE TO MY LITERARY FAMILY, WITHOUT which there'd be no Dickie Cornish: my aunt and former Associated Press Arts Editor Dolores Barclay, Peter Carlaftes and Kat Georges at Three Rooms Press, the galaxy of talent and heart at Crime Writers of Color, my colleagues in Mystery Writers of America (member since my first novel in 2001, *Sympathy for the Devil: an Angela Bivens Thriller*, Random House). Cannot forget George Pelecanos, Gary Phillips, Gar Anthony Haywood, and crew. Grace Edwards and Eleanor Taylor Bland. Walter Mosley. Chester Himes. Hammett, Chandler, Kaminsky. We paint with verisimilitude.

Love to my tribe and circles of family, pals, students, entrepreneurs, provocateurs. Best love, however, to my wife Dianne, for keeping me on track whenever I thought the train would derail. You know best, you always have.

Finally, thank you for speaking to me, you visible invisibles. On the streets, in the train stations, on cots in the shelters. *Scavenger* is neither nonfiction crusade, nor feelgood whitewash. It's a novel. It just is. I guess that is a fitting motto for this year . . .

—*Christopher Chambers*
Washington D.C.
Summer 2020

About the Author

CHRISTOPHER CHAMBERS IS A PROFESSOR OF Media Studies and a novelist published through Random House, MacMillan, and Three Rooms Press. His previous works include the novels *A Prayer for Deliverance* and *Sympathy for the Devil* (NAACP Image Award nominee); the graphic anthology (with Gary Phillips) *The Darker Mask*; and the PEN/Malamud honorable mention story "Leviathan." He was also a contributor to the Anthony Award-winning anthology *The Obama Inheritance* and *Black Pulp 2*, as well as *The Faking of the President*. Professor Chambers is a regular commentator/contributor on media and culture issues on SiriusXM Radio, *ABC News*, and *HuffPost*. He resides in his hometown of Washington, D.C. with his family and German shepherd, Max.

RECENT AND FORTHCOMING BOOKS FROM THREE ROOMS PRESS

FICTION

Rishab Borah
The Door to Inferna

Meagan Brothers
Weird Girl and What's His Name

Christopher Chambers
Scavenger

Ron Dakron
Hello Devilfish!

Robert Duncan
Loudmouth

Michael T. Fournier
Hidden Wheel
Swing State

William Least Heat-Moon
Celestial Mechanics

Aimee Herman
Everything Grows

Eamon Loingsigh
Light of the Diddicoy
Exile on Bridge Street

John Marshall
The Greenfather

Aram Saroyan
Still Night in L.A.

Richard Vetere
The Writers Afterlife
Champagne and Cocaine

Julia Watts
Quiver

Gina Yates
Narcissus Nobody

MEMOIR & BIOGRAPHY

Nassrine Azimi and Michel Wasserman
Last Boat to Yokohama: The Life and Legacy of Beate Sirota Gordon

William S. Burroughs & Allen Ginsberg
Don't Hide the Madness:
William S. Burroughs in Conversation with Allen Ginsberg
edited by Steven Taylor

James Carr
BAD: The Autobiography of James Carr

Richard Katrovas
Raising Girls in Bohemia:
Meditations of an American Father

Judith Malina
Full Moon Stages:
Personal Notes from 50 Years of The Living Theatre

Phil Marcade
Punk Avenue: Inside the New York City Underground, 1972–1982

Alvin Orloff
Disasterama! Adventures in the Queer Underground 1977–1997

Nicca Ray
Ray by Ray: A Daughter's Take on the Legend of Nicholas Ray

Stephen Spotte
My Watery Self:
Memoirs of a Marine Scientist

PHOTOGRAPHY-MEMOIR

Mike Watt
On & Off Bass

SHORT STORY ANTHOLOGIES

SINGLE AUTHOR
The Alien Archives: Stories
by Robert Silverberg

First-Person Singularities: Stories
by Robert Silverberg
with an introduction by John Scalzi

Tales from the Eternal Café: Stories
by Janet Hamill, with an introduction
by Patti Smith

Time and Time Again:
Sixteen Trips in Time
by Robert Silverberg

Voyages:
Twelve Points of Departure
by Robert Silverberg

MULTI-AUTHOR
Crime + Music: Twenty Stories of Music-Themed Noir
edited by Jim Fusilli

Dark City Lights: New York Stories
edited by Lawrence Block

The Faking of the President: Twenty Stories of White House Noir
edited by Peter Carlaftes

Florida Happens:
Bouchercon 2018 Anthology
edited by Greg Herren

Have a NYC I, II & III:
New York Short Stories;
edited by Peter Carlaftes
& Kat Georges

Songs of My Selfie:
An Anthology of Millennial Stories
edited by Constance Renfrow

The Obama Inheritance:
15 Stories of Conspiracy Noir
edited by Gary Phillips

This Way to the End Times:
Classic and New Stories of the Apocalypse
edited by Robert Silverberg

MIXED MEDIA

John S. Paul
Sign Language: A Painter's Notebook
(photography, poetry and prose)

FILM & PLAYS

Israel Horovitz
My Old Lady: Complete Stage Play and Screenplay with an Essay on Adaptation

Peter Carlaftes
Triumph For Rent (3 Plays)
Teatrophy (3 More Plays)

Kat Georges
Three Somebodies: Plays about Notorious Dissidents

DADA

Maintenant: A Journal of Contemporary Dada Writing & Art
(Annual, since 2008)

TRANSLATIONS

Thomas Bernhard
On Earth and in Hell
(poems of Thomas Bernhard with English translations by Peter Waugh)

Patrizia Gattaceca
Isula d'Anima / Soul Island
(poems by the author in Corsican with English translations)

César Vallejo | Gerard Malanga
Malanga Chasing Vallejo
(selected poems of César Vallejo with English translations and additional notes by Gerard Malanga)

George Wallace
EOS: Abductor of Men
(selected poems in Greek & English)

ESSAYS

Home Is the Mouth of a Shark
Vanessa Baden

Womentality: Thirteen Empowering Stories by Everyday Women Who Said Goodbye to the Workplace and Hello to Their Lives
edited by Erin Wildermuth

HUMOR

Peter Carlaftes
A Year on Facebook

POETRY COLLECTIONS

Hala Alyan
Atrium

Peter Carlaftes
DrunkYard Dog
I Fold with the Hand I Was Dealt

Thomas Fucaloro
It Starts from the Belly and Blooms

Kat Georges
Our Lady of the Hunger

Robert Gibbons
Close to the Tree

Israel Horovitz
Heaven and Other Poems

David Lawton
Sharp Blue Stream

Jane LeCroy
Signature Play

Philip Meersman
This Is Belgian Chocolate

Jane Ormerod
Recreational Vehicles on Fire
Welcome to the Museum of Cattle

Lisa Panepinto
On This Borrowed Bike

George Wallace
Poppin' Johnny

 Three Rooms Press | New York, NY | Current Catalog: www.threeroomspress.com
Three Rooms Press books are distributed by PGW/Ingram: www.pgw.com